AN ENCHANTED KISS

Melissa stared into Cody's beautiful brown eyes for the longest time. When she realized she was staring, she tried to look away and couldn't. Cody seemed to be having the same trouble. After a moment, he slowly walked back to the table and put a hand on Melissa's shoulder. It burned like fire through her simple calico shirtwaist and apron. Melissa fought the impulse to put her hand on top of his.

He blushed. Melissa was enchanted. A second before he kissed her, Melissa realized he was leaning toward her, and she met him halfway. As soon as she felt his lips on hers, she uttered a tiny mew of longing.

His lips were soft and warm and wonderful. Melissa wished she could melt into his embrace. She wanted to give herself up to Cody O'Fannin, to become part of him, to shift her burdens to his broad shoulders and never have to worry again. She knew she was being fanciful. Worse, she was being a fool. Again.

But Cody was gentle and strong, and even though she knew kissing Cody was wrong, it didn't feel wrong. Her arms went around his broad shoulders and she kissed him back.

Other *Leisure* and *Love Spell* books by
Emma Craig:
ENCHANTED CHRISTMAS
CHRISTMAS PIE
ROSAMUNDA'S REVENGE

A Gentle Magic

EMMA CRAIG

LOVE SPELL BOOKS   NEW YORK CITY

Leisure Entertainment Service Co., Inc. (LESCO Distribution Group)

A LESCO Edition

Published by special arrangement with Dorchester Publishing Co., Inc.

Printed in the United States of America.

A Gentle Magic

Chapter One

Once upon a time, on a crisp November day in 1870, Cody O'Fannin and Arnold Carver set out to ride back to their ranch. They'd been visiting the tiny settlement of Rio Hondo, which squatted between the banks of the Spring and Hondo rivers in the heart of New Mexico Territory's Pecos Valley.

Bachelor cowboys and cousins, Cody and Arnold had settled in the Territory after the Great War, intent upon establishing themselves as ranchers in the rough land that was becoming known as cattle country. Their enterprise had prospered, and Arnold planned to return to Georgetown, Texas, soon and bring back his intended bride. He'd already written to her, and expected an answer to his letter any week now.

Cody figured he could stand having a female in the house. At least females could cook, which is more than he or Arnold could do. Brides aside, he was happy today because during their sojourn in Rio Hondo, he and Arnold had contracted to sell two prime bulls to John Chisum, owner of the largest ranching operation in the area.

His mind was at peace, the fall weather was fine, and Cody, who harbored a poetic streak in his soul and appreciated such things, pointed out a flock of migrating sandhill cranes to Arnold. Their feathered bellies flashing white in the sun, the birds formed a ragged, honking checkmark against a cloud-smeared blue sky. Cody was fond of those birds. He didn't bother to speak, since he knew Arnold could see them as well as he. Neither man wasted breath on trivialities.

A brisk wind blew, and Cody gazed about with satisfaction. The Territory was a hard place; uncompromising. It was as apt to chew a man up and spit out the pieces as not, and Cody loved it more than he'd ever loved anything, except for Arnold and his family back home in Georgetown. The Territory, unlike his family, didn't try to constrain him. There weren't any rules out here, save those a man made for himself, and as Cody didn't much care for other people's rules, he appreciated it.

The plains had already endured the first frosts of the season. Indeed, it had even snowed one day in October, although the weather, never predictable in these parts, had turned warmish again. Today the land glittered like acres of rippling gold under the sun's hard rays. Cody observed a distant herd of antelope that warily watched him back, prepared to bound away if he looked as though he was taking too keen an interest in them. He grinned in sympathy. He knew just how they felt.

He and Arnold were riding in companionable silence about three miles southeast of Rio Hondo, and

Cody was contemplating his ranch and his future with pleasure, when a shrill scream shattered the peace of the morning. Startled, he looked at Arnold, who looked back, every bit as shocked as Cody.

"Cougar," murmured Cody, his heart pumping wildly.

"Comanch," countered Arnold.

Ever ripe for adventure, neither cousin shrank from either possibility. Instead, they exchanged a grin, then spurred their horses in the direction from which the scream had come.

Accustomed as they were to the difficult land they'd moved from Texas to conquer, both men were prepared for any number of perils, from wild cats to wild men. Discovering a woman in the back of a rickety wagon and in the final throes of a hard labor was a possibility that wouldn't have entered either of their heads if they'd been given a year to think about it.

Arnold's mouth dropped open.

Cody, the more loquacious of the two, uttered in an awed voice, "Holy God."

The woman screamed again, an anguished sound that tore through the fall morning air and galvanized Cody into action. Tossing his horse's reins to Arnold, he bounded from his saddle.

He unhooked a bundle from his pack and sprang onto the wagon bed. "Boil up some water, Arnold," he commanded, recollecting tales his granddaddy had told him about his trip to Texas with a wagon train during the spring of '43.

If Arnold had asked, Cody wouldn't have been able to tell him what he planned to use the boiling water for, but Arnold didn't ask, so Cody was spared thinking up an answer. A docile, accommodating fellow, Arnold dismounted, wrapped his horse's reins around

9

a straggling mesquite bush, unhooked a dented iron pot from his own saddle, and ran toward the river to obey his more forceful cousin.

Cody's heart quailed when he knelt beside the woman. Since he and Arnold settled here, Cody had earned a reputation as a lark-loving, wild fellow, ripe for adventure, and one who feared nothing the Territory had to offer. As it was man's land, it had not offered him much experience with females. He'd never been within hollering distance of one in this extremity. His few encounters with ladies of easy virtue in Rio Hondo had been carried out in darkened rooms, and had been brief and to the point.

Nevertheless, Cody had never shrunk from danger in his life. He didn't shrink now, although this situation seemed likely to involve him in more danger than even the Pecos Saloon on a trail drive Saturday night.

"Ma'am?" He had a hard time getting his throat to work.

The woman panted hard. Her eyes had been squinched up tight. They flew open now, and she looked at him but didn't seem to be able to answer. She'd knotted a handkerchief, upon which her teeth bit down. She was sweating like a pig, and her face was as pallid as a virgin snowbank except for two hectic red splotches on her cheeks that looked almost feverish. Tears trickled from her eyes. Cody didn't know if they were from fear or pain, but he begrudged her neither. A zinc bucket filled with water stood beside her.

"Ma'am, don't try to talk. I've delivered lots of beeves. I expect I can help you here."

He thought she nodded but wasn't sure. Another spasm wracked her, and he winced in empathy. Quickly he tore off his jacket and thrust it aside, rolled up his shirt sleeves, and untied his bundle. From it he extracted a hunk of hard lye soap, and used some of the water in the bucket to wash his hands and arms up to the elbow.

The next part was tricky. He sucked in a deep breath. "Ma'am, I'm going to have to see what's going on here. Please don't take this personal."

She didn't seem to be in any condition to make objections. She certainly offered him none, so Cody gingerly lifted her skirt up over her bent knees. She'd removed her drawers already, for which he could only be thankful. Her swollen abdomen looked like a mountain and quivered with the strain of what was going on inside of it. Taking another deep breath and feeling horribly uncomfortable—Cody had suffered a rather strict upbringing, during which he'd been taught that proper females were to be viewed only fully clothed—he looked between her legs.

"Lord Almighty," he breathed, "I think I see a head."

He hadn't meant to sound quite so astonished. After all, seeing a head was probably a good thing. He gulped hard and looked at the woman's face again.

She'd opened her eyes, although she still looked awfully frazzled. The weather was cool, but sweat dripped from her face.

"Listen, ma'am, I'm going to try to make up a better pad so's the baby won't fall out onto the dirty wagon bed. All right?"

Her head jerked up and down. Cody took it for an affirmative, and jumped down from the wagon again. He snatched the blanket off the back of his saddle, unrolled it, and flapped it hard to get the dust out. Then, with a tiny itch of regret, he reached into his saddlebag and grabbed his one good shirt and two clean bandannas. He expected other men before him had been forced into greater sacrifices. At least these would go for a good cause. Deciding not to think about it, he returned to the wagon bed.

Using the greatest of care, he lifted the woman's legs and positioned the blanket and shirt, trying to make her as comfortable as possible, while at the same time forcing himself to overcome his own embarrassment. He'd never been so intimate with a female in his life, barring those few times in Rio Hondo. This seemed even more intimate than that, for some reason. He soon had his emotions in hand once more.

"That any better, ma'am?" Immediately, he felt contrite. "Don't try to answer, ma'am. You've got enough to do."

She accepted his suggestion literally and undertook no reply. Cody took up his vigil once more, and peered between her legs. Feeling uneasy about it but striving to do his duty, he splayed a hand on her abdomen and tried to feel out what was going on in there.

"Can you push again, ma'am? I think we might have something here."

She gave another jerky nod, shut her eyes tight, and Cody saw her face turn a blotchy red as she pushed with all her might. Turning back to the task at hand, he saw her efforts were bearing fruit, so to speak. A slimy head inched farther out from between her legs. Although small, that head looked awfully big for the space through which it had to pass. Cody tried to quell his own terror by telling himself that women did this sort of thing all the time. He was only marginally successful.

"It's coming, ma'am. It won't be long now." Cody peeked at her face again, and his heart stumbled. "You just rest a minute, ma'am. Here." He yanked the bandanna from around his neck, wet it in the bucket, wrung out most of the water, dripped some into her mouth, and then mopped her face with it.

His chest burned with fear for her. She looked so young and frail. And she was definitely alone. Where the hell was her man?

Another pain struck her, and Cody commanded his mind to cease its unprofitable wanderings and concentrate on the job in front of him. "Okay, ma'am, push now. We'll see if we can't get this over with."

Only later did he think that probably wasn't the most delicate way to phrase the matter.

"Everything all right up there?"

Cody had forgotten all about Arnold. Casting a swift glance out of the wagon, he discovered his cousin hunched over a fire, his back to the action. The pose was so typical of Arnold, whose feelings were so tender that he often cried at calvings, that Cody grinned in spite of the perilous circumstances.

"I think so." Cody watched Arnold's shoulders heave with his big sigh and felt a squeeze of affection for his big, tender-hearted cousin. "Got that water ready yet?"

"Almost."

"Soon as it's ready, boil up a cup of that sassafras tea we got at McMurdo's. This lady'll need some pretty quick. I think the baby's almost here."

A deep, shuddering groan from his patient jerked Cody's attention back to her. She screamed again, and everything inside of him clenched. Sweet Lord have mercy, he'd rather be in the middle of a shoot-out with a herd of cow-thieving bandits than right here, right now.

"Set the pan of hot water beside me, Arnold," he said, his voice absolutely calm. As if by magic, the pot appeared at his side. Cody reached for one of the two clean bandannas he'd set aside and dropped it in the water.

Then, in a rush of fluid, the job was done. Trying to pretend this was nothing more nor less than another calving, Cody carefully picked up the slippery infant, cleaned the mucus out of its mouth, tied off the cord with thread from his bundle, scalded his hand wringing out his bandanna, cooled it, and carefully wiped the baby clean. As soon as he lifted it, it began to squall. A gust of breath he'd been holding left him in a whoosh, and that was the first time he realized how scared he'd been about this child's fate.

He forced his hands not to tremble as he wrapped the infant in his last clean bandanna. It wasn't much of a baby blanket, but then, it didn't seem to be much of a baby. The thing was tiny, and it fit into the bandanna just fine.

"All right, ma'am, it looks like you have yourself a nice, healthy little girl here."

Holding the baby in his two hands, he looked at the mother for the first time since the birthing. Tears flooded eyes as blue as Texas bluebonnets and flowed rivers down her pale cheeks. Yet the woman smiled a smile as big as the sky, and Cody felt something inside his chest give, as though a sealed door had just blown open.

"Thank you," she whispered through her tears, and her gaze locked with his for a heartbeat.

Cody swallowed and handed the baby to her. Then he sat back on his haunches and watched as the new mother investigated her daughter. Strange emotions swelled in his breast.

An hour or so later, Cody and Arnold found themselves making an unscheduled trek back to Rio

Hondo, Arnold driving Mrs. Wilmeth's wagon—the woman's name, they'd learned, was Melissa Wilmeth—Cody trying his best to keep her from being too uncomfortable as they rattled along in the wagon's hard, rocking bed. Their horses walked placidly behind, tied to the wagon.

Cody's nerves, generally as steady as Cody himself, jumped like frogs' legs in a hot skillet. He chalked it up to circumstances—he was worried about Mrs. Wilmeth's state of health—and spoke to her gently in order to calm himself down. "We'll settle you at McMurdo's, Mrs. Wilmeth. He's a kindly fellow, and he'll be glad to look after you for a while until we find your husband."

"Thank you."

Mrs. Wilmeth's voice was breathy and soft. Cody's brain registered an impression of shredded cotton, as if it had been ripped somehow during her ordeal. For the merest second, he harbored the scandalous wish that her husband would never show up. He brushed her cheek with his hand and then wondered what had possessed him.

Yanking his hand back, he said, "You going to be all right, ma'am?"

She didn't look all right. He knew she was weak as a kitten and had lost a lot of blood. He got the impression she hadn't been very well cared for during her pregnancy, and was suffering for it now. She looked more haggard than a female should ever look.

She drifted in and out of an unconsciousness that might be sleep or might be fainting spells, and her state of exhaustion made Cody sad. He expected she'd be a pretty little thing if she was spruced up. She sure loved that baby girl of hers. Her love seemed almost odd to him, now that he knew how much effort had gone into the birthing of it.

15

"Thank you," she whispered, giving him another shy glance. "I think I'll be all right." She paused, and Cody saw her swallow. "I can't begin to thank you, Mr. O'Fannin. I just can't even begin to thank you for your help."

Ill at ease, Cody bowed his head and tried not to look at her. Hell, a man just did what he had to do. He told her as much, sparing her the profanity.

"No," she said, her voice surprisingly firm, considering her state of weariness. "You went out of your way to help me, and I thank you for it. You must have been almost as scared as I was."

He had been. Probably even more scared, if it came to that. He didn't say so, since he didn't think his fear did him any credit. "Shucks, ma'am, it was nothing."

She shook her head, but seemed too fatigued to argue the point. Instead, she shut her eyes, held her baby close, and dozed some more.

Cody wanted to stroke her hair and face. He'd never known such tender urges before, and as he was a fellow who prided himself on his stalwart independence, he held himself in check. He did try to steady her by bracing himself against her shoulders, although he tried to keep any physical contact at a minimum. It wouldn't do to be getting familiar with another man's wife, after all, even if he had just delivered their baby. And where the hell *was* her husband? he asked himself for at least the hundredth time.

Cody was frowning hard by the time Arnold mumbled, "We're here."

His head snapped up, and he saw Alexander McMurdo, his black pipe clenched in his teeth, standing at the wide double gates of his wagon yard, almost as though he'd expected this. Which was, of course, impossible, unless Mr. Wilmeth had showed up seeking help. But then, people would have come out looking for them. Glancing down at Mrs. Wilmeth, Cody saw that her eyes had opened. She was as white as a newly laundered sheet, and looked about as wrung-out as one, too. His heart pained him for a moment.

"You just rest here, ma'am. I'll make arrangements with McMurdo."

He thought she might have murmured her thanks again, but he didn't stick around to make sure. Her continued gratitude made him edgy. He bundled up the shirts and bandannas he'd used earlier and edged to the wagon's tailgate.

As near as Cody could figure, nobody in Rio Hondo knew Alexander McMurdo's age. The old man merely was, and always had been, and he never seemed to change. He'd arrived in Rio Hondo several years before. He claimed to have come from Scotland originally, but nobody knew when or if he'd traveled out west immediately or languished somewhere else in the eastern part of the United States before he'd made his way to the Territory and established his wagon yard. McMurdo's soft burr always gave Cody a happy feeling in his middle.

The wizened old fellow strolled up to the wagon as Arnold maneuvered the mules through the gate. "Whatcha got there, Cody?" he asked, ignoring Arnold, as most wise folks did. Arnold invariably deferred answers to Cody anyway.

"Woman had a baby out there alone on the prairie, Mac." Cody's voice ably conveyed his bewilderment over this state of affairs.

McMurdo clucked his tongue. His face was heavily whiskered, but Cody was sure he saw the old man grin. "A baby, is it?"

He didn't sound nearly as surprised as the occasion warranted. Every now and then Cody got a shivery feeling about McMurdo—not unpleasant, but uncanny. It was as if the old fellow knew things before anybody had a chance to tell him about them. Cody got that feeling now and tried to ignore it.

"A little girl." He bounded down from the wagon and wiped the sweat of nervousness from his forehead. "Say, Mac, do you suppose this lady and her baby can stay here while Arnie and I go out and look for her husband? She says he took off when she went into labor, going to head to town for help. He never came back." So as to spare Mrs. Wilmeth's sensibilities, Cody didn't share with McMurdo his opinion of a fellow who would abandon his wife under similar circumstances.

He got the feeling McMurdo understood without having to be told.

"I expect we can work something out," the old Scotsman said. As limber as a lad, he hopped onto the wagon's bed and squatted beside the woman. Cody followed him, feeling unaccountably protective toward Melissa Wilmeth.

"How're ye feeling, Mrs. Wilmeth?" McMurdo asked softly.

Cody frowned and tried to recall when he'd told McMurdo the woman's name. Then McMurdo put one gnarled hand on the woman's fair head, and Cody blinked and rubbed his eyes. The strain of helping Mrs. Wilmeth must have robbed him of more sense than he'd thought. He would have sworn he saw sparkles shimmer in the air where McMurdo's hands touched Mrs. Wilmeth's hair.

It must have been a trick of the light, he decided at once. That was it. The brilliant autumn sunshine was merely picking out dust particles and making them shine in that strange glowing way. It was kind of pretty, actually, once you got over the surprise of it.

Then McMurdo gently bared Mrs. Wilmeth's baby's face, pressed a hand to the tiny head, and the same thing happened. Cody shook his own head hard, trying to rid himself of the eerie impression.

Shoot, he must be in bad shape. Maybe he could talk Arnold into having a shot of something stiff before they headed back out to search for the missing Mr. Wilmeth. Neither cousin was a big drinker as a rule, but occasionally life called for something stronger than water.

McMurdo looked over his shoulder at Cody, and Cody read concern on his ancient face. His heart squeezed painfully, which surprised him. After all, Melissa Wilmeth was nothing to him. Cody had always eschewed associations with proper females, because he didn't want entanglements in his life. He had goals; he didn't need distractions. He couldn't stop his heart from hurting in this instance, though, goals or no goals.

"She can stay in my back room until she's recovered, Cody. I expect a big, strong lad like you can lift her down and carry her inside." The old man's smile broadened, showing a set of remarkably white teeth in his beard and easing Cody's aching heart somewhat. "The bed's all made up."

It occurred to Cody to ask why the bed was all made up, but he didn't. Hell, for all he knew, McMurdo always had a spare bed ready for emergencies. He was sure glad of it today.

"I'll carry the baby inside," McMurdo added, following his words with the action.

"Right," Cody said, his mouth suddenly dry.

He realized his hands were sweating at the prospect of lifting Mrs. Wilmeth, and he wiped them on his trousers. Then he bent down next to her and murmured, "I'll try to be careful, ma'am."

"I know you will," she said, and her soft, warm breath brushed his cheek as she put her arms around his neck.

Cody's heart thundered when he lifted her, which made no sense to him. Shoot, a body'd think he cared about her, the way his insides were tumbling and skipping. Not only was he a fellow whose head wasn't apt to be turned by a female, but this one weighed remarkably little, considering she'd just had a baby and all. She sure didn't weigh as much as the cows he wrestled on a regular basis. There was no reason for him to be straining in this odd manner. Still, his heart fluttered and he grunted as he stood with her in his arms. His breath was coming in little gasps by the time he bore her out of the wagon and onto the dirt yard beside it.

He stopped for a moment to gather himself together and looked down to find her head resting on his shoulder, her fair hair spilling down his shirtfront. His arms tightened around her unconsciously, and he told himself it was to steady her.

His throat was as dry as the desert around them, and he was out of breath by the time he'd carried her into McMurdo's tidy little mercantile establishment and deposited her on the bed in the back room. She looked up at him and smiled, and Cody felt as though she'd punched him in the guts. While McMurdo handed Mrs. Wilmeth her baby again, Cody silently swore at himself to get a handle on his nerves. This would never do.

"You going to be all right, ma'am?" Cody tried to pitch his voice to sound impersonal and didn't quite make it.

"Yes. Thank you."

"She'll be fine, Cody, m'lad." McMurdo winked at him, taking Cody slightly aback. He didn't understand that wink. "You and your cousin just go on along now, and I'll have a pot of stew made up by the time you get back."

McMurdo's stew was about as famous as anything could get in Rio Hondo and vicinity. He generally had a pot of it bubbling on the stove, and a man could buy a bowl of stew, a slab of cornbread, and a beer or a cup of coffee for five cents. McMurdo's stew made camping at McMurdo's Wagon Yard a more pleasant experience than one might expect if one was used to other wagon yards in other settlements. Or even if one wasn't.

"Thanks, Mac. We'd appreciate that."

Firmly taking himself to task for allowing his nerves to get the better of him, Cody clapped his hat onto his head and turned to leave. His nerves had the running of him today, however, and made him turn around one last time to see the patient. Her big blue eyes stared at him. She looked as fragile as a china doll and as pretty as a flower on McMurdo's spare bed, her baby clutched to her bosom.

Unable to find appropriate words, Cody nodded to her. She gave him a wavery smile and mouthed the words, "Thank you." Her sweet expression branded itself onto his brain and stayed with him all the way out of doors and onto his horse. It still haunted him as he and Arnold downed the twin shots of whiskey McMurdo pressed upon them and then walked their mounts out through McMurdo's huge wooden gates.

"Don't be too late, boys," McMurdo advised in a friendly voice. "I'll wait supper for you, but I expect Mrs. Wilmeth needs her nourishment."

Rattled, more than a little irritated, wondering how in hell they were expected to time their search,

Cody snapped, "Well, it all depends on when we find her man, don't it, Mac?"

McMurdo chuckled. "Ye ain't goin' to find her a man out there, Cody."

A man? Hell, they didn't want *a* man. They wanted this woman's husband. Or, at least, Cody expected she did. He wasn't sure what he wanted, although he had a fair notion that it wasn't Mr. Howard Wilmeth. He jerked his head around and glared at the old man. "How do you know that?"

McMurdo shrugged and turned away. Cody stared after him for a minute until he decided he had better things to do with his time than gawk at an enigmatic Scotsman's back. Muttering, "Well, hell," he dug his heels into his horse's flank and trotted after Arnold, who hadn't paused. Which was characteristic of Arnold. A slave to duty, Arnold was. Cody admired him for his singlemindedness.

"Hold on, Arnold," he muttered, "I'm comin'."

Arnold gave him a bland smile and didn't bother to speak.

Chapter Two

McMurdo's words proved to be right. Cody and Arnold followed the fairly clear trail Mr. Howard Wilmeth's horse had made away from where they'd found the wagon. From time to time they lost the trail, but they always managed to find it again. Even so, they searched for hours and didn't see hide nor hair of the man himself. Or any other man.

Along about four in the afternoon, his stomach grumbling from hunger, his head aching, and his mind in a turmoil, Cody looked up from where he'd been squatting on the desert floor, pushed his hat back, and scratched his head.

"Well, hell, Arnold, I don't know where the hell this man went, but he sure as hell ain't here."

Arnold nodded, then shook his head, which was typical of him. "Wonder where he's got hisself off to."

Cody wondered, too. "Beats me. Criminy, now why

in God's name do you suppose he headed away from Rio Hondo?"

Arnold shrugged.

"I mean, if my wife was having a baby, I sure as hell would head for the nearest settlement, wouldn't you?" If he left her at all; Cody didn't think he'd leave his wife under similar circumstances. If he had a wife. Which he didn't. Not that he wanted one. He cursed silently and commanded himself to stop thinking about it.

Arnold shrugged again.

"It looks to me as though he hightailed it away from her and Rio Hondo and everything." Cody looked to his cousin for confirmation, but this time Arnold didn't respond at all, which was also typical.

"He ran into somebody here." Cody pointed at the earth, which had been churned up some hours earlier. "Might've been Indians," he added, as if Arnold had asked, which he hadn't.

Arnold, in fact, sat as motionless and stoic as a wooden Indian himself, watching Cody think. Arnold generally let Cody do the thinking, which was all right with Cody, as his thought processes traveled more quickly and along clearer paths than did Arnold's.

Frowning, Cody remounted. "Well, I reckon we can't do much more searching today. It'll be dark soon, and we won't be able to find anything. I can't see which way they rode off to. He can't be too far away, but damned if I can figure out where he went."

Neither, evidently, could Arnold, who shrugged again.

Cody didn't say what he was thinking: that he feared Indians had found Mr. Wilmeth wandering around, lost, and killed him for his horse and belongings. Most of the horses that had stirred the dirt back there had been shod, but that didn't mean anything. Indians were as apt to ride shod horses these days as white men. Hell, most white men didn't waste shoes on a horse's back hooves, anyway.

Fool man. Served him right if he did get himself slaughtered by Indians.

Immediately, Cody's conscience pricked him. Although his conscience was an occasionally unreliable instrument, he knew very well that, while such a fate might have served Mr. Wilmeth right, it wouldn't help his wife any. Or his widow, if his suspicion proved correct. Yet they hadn't found a body. Maybe the man was still alive. Cody wasn't sure how he felt about that.

"Well, we'd better get back to McMurdo's and tell him what we found."

"Didn't find nothin'."

Irked with his cousin for being so literal, Cody said, "I know that. That's what we have to tell him."

"And her."

After a moment, Cody muttered, "Yeah. And her, too."

They didn't speak again until after dark, when they steered their weary horses into McMurdo's Wagon Yard for the third time that day.

Melissa Wilmeth stared at her baby, and wonder consumed her. She'd been sure neither of them would survive their ordeal on the desert. Even after that wonderful man stopped to help them, she'd felt too weak, too sick at heart, to presume she'd survive. It wasn't, in fact, until that odd little elderly gentleman laid his hand on her head that she'd begun to believe again.

How could Howard have left her? In her weakness and her pain, Melissa couldn't stop her tears from leaking out, even though she hadn't cried over Howard for ages. She used to cry over him all the time. She'd known for months that he no longer loved her—if he ever had—but how could he have left her there in her extremity? Having his baby, for heaven's sake! She didn't even care about Howard any longer; she certainly never wanted to see him again.

Still . . . He'd just abandoned her there. He'd shouted at her to shut up, said he was going for help, and left her. She'd shrieked after him not to leave her alone in the wagon on a hostile desert having his baby, but he hadn't even turned around. He'd hunched his shoulders over in that way he had, and he'd left her.

"How are we going to live now, baby?" she asked her daughter. It seemed a bleak question to ask an infant, but Melissa sure needed an answer.

"How're you doing, ma'am?"

The soft question came to her from the darkened doorway, and it startled her. Looking up quickly, she saw her hero—the man who'd saved her baby and her life—standing there, twisting his hat in his hands, looking uncomfortable. A lamp had been set out in the room behind him, and his body made a dark silhouette against the soft, bright halo of light. He looked mysterious and magical that way, and the impression appealed to Melissa.

There was no sign of Howard with him, and Melissa's heart gave a leap of joy, which seemed unaccountable to her. After all, she was a woman alone with a baby and no means of support. Not that Howard had been of much support, either financially or morally, but at least he'd been there. Until he wasn't.

"We're much better, thank you," she answered softly, feeling quite shy herself.

"We—uh—we didn't find your husband yet, ma'am."

She let her glance fall so he wouldn't be able to discern her satisfaction at his words. Such satisfaction was shockingly wicked; she knew it, and she couldn't help herself.

"Oh."

"I think we found where somebody might have found him, though."

"Oh?"

He shuffled his feet and moved his shoulders, his edginess obvious. Melissa wished he'd come into the room and sit beside her on the bed. She wished he'd cup her cheek as he'd done earlier in the day, when she'd felt so weak. She understood the futility of idle wishes, though, since she'd been wishing all her life, so she didn't expect anything of the sort to happen.

"Yeah. We—my cousin Arnold and me—we'll go out again tomorrow morning and look some more. We can get some men together and search for him. McMurdo says the county sheriff has gone to Carlsbad, but that won't make no difference. We'll keep looking till we find him, ma'am."

Melissa bowed her head, her smile deserting her. If they looked hard enough, they probably would find him, and then he'd come back. She guessed there was no hope for it. She'd married him; she was stuck with him. She whispered, "Thank you."

"It's no trouble, ma'am."

She heard him take a step into the room and looked up, hoping again in spite of herself. He stopped after that one step, though, and made a small, uncertain gesture with the hand holding his hat.

"I'm glad you're all right, ma'am. And I'm sorry you had to go through—well, what you went through—

without your man. Reckon I'm no great substitute for your husband."

Oh, he was a wonderful substitute for her husband. A magnificent one, in fact. She didn't say so.

Melissa watched the face that spoke those words in fascination. It was a forceful face, and a good-looking one, and it was attached to a body that inspired trust. Cody O'Fannin stood a solid six feet. He had big hands, Cody did, and Melissa knew for a fact they were both capable and gentle. They were attached to strong arms and broad shoulders, and the entire package was carried about on a perfectly male torso and supported by thick, muscular legs encased now in worn denim trousers and heavy, dusty boots. Cody O'Fannin seemed to be a man accustomed to working hard and succeeding at it, two attributes Melissa had never encountered in a man before. They made her heart ache almost as much as his face did.

It was a tanned face; not classically handsome, she supposed, because it consisted of too many hard planes and angles to appeal to some women, although it certainly appealed to her. His hair looked blond, but she had reason to know, because she'd seen that head bent closely over her, that it was actually dark brown and only bleached to blond by the harsh territorial sunshine.

His mustache was blond, though, and it drooped rather rakishly around his soft, almost pretty mouth. Melissa had a suspicion he'd grown the mustache to make himself look older. It worked to a degree, although nothing could quite disguise the vigor and youthfulness in his dark brown eyes. Unless it was kindness she saw reflected there. Unfamiliar with kindness, Melissa didn't consider herself a judge of such things.

Since she didn't know what else to say, she said, "Thank you" again.

She went to sleep once more shortly after Cody left her. McMurdo woke her to eat and drink. His stew was delicious, and with every bite she took she felt stronger. Then she slept again, waking only to feed her daughter. Once during the night she thought her hero was in the room with her, but it might have been a dream.

When she awoke in the morning, Cody O'Fannin and his cousin Arnold were gone. Melissa felt horribly disappointed not to have had the opportunity to see him again before they resumed their search. She prayed alternately that they would and that they wouldn't be able to find Howard.

Cody knew he and Arnold had to get back to their ranch pretty soon. He didn't feel comfortable abandoning Mrs. Wilmeth without making a strong push to find her husband, however, even though his own feelings on the subject of Howard Wilmeth remained ambivalent. He knew a woman needed a man to support her; that went without saying. And he supposed it was unjust of him to dislike Howard Wilmeth to the degree he did. After all, he hadn't even met the man.

Out here, though, a body judged a man by his actions. Cody judged Howard Wilmeth's actions to have been foolish, if not downright cowardly and despicable. Still, he was Melissa Wilmeth's husband, and she needed him.

Nevertheless, and although he knew it didn't help Melissa, Cody was more pleased than not when he and Arnold returned to McMurdo's again that night without having found Mr. Wilmeth. His unsettled feelings about Howard and Melissa Wilmeth's marriage troubled him, as did his feelings about Melissa herself.

It didn't help him sort them out when McMurdo gave him a conspiratorial grin and told him to go in and pay a visit to the patient. He bridled a little at the old man's attitude but knew he couldn't complain without looking like a fool.

Feeling abused by circumstances in general and by McMurdo in particular, Cody pushed the door to McMurdo's back room open and peeked in. He didn't want to disturb Melissa if she was sleeping, but felt an almost ungovernable desire to see her again.

He stopped short in the doorway, startled to find her propped up against some pillows and nursing her daughter. Her shoulders were naked, her breast plainly visible, and her head was bowed over the baby, to whom she was cooing gently. She had braided her hair, and the coils gleamed like gold as they fell over her white bosom and the dark head of the infant suckling at her nipple. Cody's throat tightened, and some emotion with which he was unfamiliar nestled in his chest. She looked up quickly, and he saw her blush right before she pulled up a sheet and covered her baby's head and her breast.

Cody suppressed his initial impulse to turn tail and run away, slamming the door behind him. He'd never been a coward in his life. He sure as the devil wasn't going to run away from a woman and a baby. No matter how naked and beautiful one of them was.

"Sorry, ma'am. I just wanted to see how you and your baby were doing." His own cheeks felt warm, and he had an awful suspicion that his blush was as fiery as hers.

She offered him a shy smile. One of Melissa Wilmeth's smiles could last a man a week or more, Cody decided on the spot.

"That's all right, Mr. O'Fannin. Katie was just taking a little supper."

Cody took a step into the room, unsure what to do now, but feeling a powerful pull toward Melissa. "Um—you named the baby Katie, did you?"

He watched, fascinated, while she gently pulled her daughter up from under the covers, placed her against her shoulder, and patted her on the back. Recalling what his sister had told him after her first child was born, Cody realized she was burping the baby.

"Yes. I had a sister named Katherine, and I've always loved the name."

Cody noticed her use of the past tense and a pang of sorrow pricked him. His heart was too blasted soft; he knew it. And no matter how many high jinks he kicked up in an effort to harden it, he hadn't succeeded yet. He took another step toward the bed.

"You, um, named her after your sister, then?"

"Yes."

She glanced up from her child, her tender expression still in place. Cody felt that look clear down to his toes. He felt, in fact, as though his insides were melting as he stood there.

"Katherine died of the cholera when she was only fourteen," Melissa continued. "She was three years older than I, and she was more like a mother to me than a sister."

As soon as the words were out of her mouth, Melissa looked down again, as if she was embarrassed about having told him this much of her life's story. Cody found himself wanting to know more. In fact, he wanted to know everything. Since he was horrified by the weakness in himself—indeed, he wasn't even sure he had a right to the knowledge—he didn't ask.

Instead, he said, "That's nice. I mean, it's nice you named your baby after her. Cholera's a tough one."

She didn't answer, although she did peek at him again. Cody thought he detected a question in her glance and felt silly and oafish, as if he should have begun this conversation with what little news he had, instead of stumbling around and wasting time with names and so forth.

"Um, we didn't find your husband, ma'am."

"No?"

In the dim atmosphere of the small back room, he couldn't make out the expression on her face but knew it must be one of disappointment. "No. But Arnold and me—well, we'll keep going out and searching, ma'am, until we find him or find out what happened to him. I know how important it is to you."

Cody could have kicked himself as soon as he heard what he'd said. *Find out what happened to him.* Good Lord, how could he have said anything so guaranteed to frighten the woman?

Melissa Wilmeth didn't flinch or take him to task. "Thank you," she murmured, her soft voice feathering over Cody like silk.

A burst of light startled both of them and made Cody jump as the door suddenly opened at his back. Turning quickly, he saw McMurdo, a big grin on his face and a steaming bowl of his famous stew in his gnarled hands.

"Here, Cody boy," the old man said with a wink. "Make yourself useful and help Mrs. Wilmeth eat her supper." He thrust the bowl of stew into the hand not occupied with Cody's hat.

Cody looked stupidly at the bowl of stew, then at McMurdo. "Huh?" he said. Then he said, "Oh, sure. Yeah, I can do that."

The old man chuckled. "I'll bring you a bowl, too,

and you can keep our Mellie here company. And when you're both through eatin', if she isn't too tired, I think you ought to sit with her for awhile, lad. The poor lass needs company. I haven't been any to her today, because I've had a wagon axle to repair, so she's been in here alone all day with her daughter." He wagged a crooked finger under Cody's nose, making him blink. "But don't wear her out, y'hear? She needs her rest, too."

A soft giggle from the bed kissed Cody's ears as effectively as lips. His heart went all over slushy, even though McMurdo's commandment brought all of his conversational insufficiencies stampeding into his brain.

"Well, I reckon I'm happy to help, Mac. Don't know how much company I'll be." Hell, he was used to hanging around with Arnold, who didn't speak for days on end if he could avoid it, and then usually only opened his mouth to agree or disagree with something Cody said. The only females he'd talked to since he and Arnold left Texas three years ago were whores. He knew what to say to a whore. New mothers were a mystery to him.

McMurdo winked. "Ye'll do fine, lad."

And with that, the old Scot departed to fetch another bowl of stew. Left alone with Melissa Wilmeth and with a bowl of stew in his hands, Cody guessed he was stuck. The best thing to do was feed her the food. He turned toward the bed and saw that she'd pulled her nightgown up to cover her bare shoulder and lowered the sheet. The baby slept in the crook of her arm, and Melissa was looking at Cody, her big eyes shining. He hoped it wasn't from fever. The thought that it might be made him swallow his anxiety and finish his trek to her bedside.

He sat on the chair next to her and set the bowl on

the bedside table. "You comfortable, ma'am? You need anything?"

"I'm fine, thank you."

Cody looked doubtfully from her to the bowl of stew. "Er, can you eat all right, ma'am, or do you need some help?"

A faint flush stained her cheeks. "I'm a little sore, Mr. O'Fannin. If you wouldn't mind propping up the pillows at my back, I could sit straighter and it will be easier for me to eat Mr. McMurdo's lovely stew. This noontime, he propped that board across my lap, and I managed not to spill anything."

Cody saw the board to which she referred, and got up to fetch it. He then did as she suggested and plumped the pillows at her back. In order to get her settled, he had to touch her shoulder, and he realized that what he'd taken for a nightgown was actually a man's old worn-out work shirt. Hell, where were her own clothes? They must have been in the wagon. Hadn't Mac brought 'em inside yet?

She was too thin, too, he decided with a sharp twinge in the region of his heart. Delicate. That's what she was. Melissa Wilmeth wasn't meaty and robust like the whores at the Pecos Saloon. It amazed him that she should have endured the agony of childbirth with as little apparent damage as she'd sustained. She probably could stand some medical attention. Too bad there wasn't any to be found in these parts.

"I—er—don't reckon Rio Hondo has any doctors, ma'am, else McMurdo would have sent for one. Mac's a good man in a pinch, though. We all generally go to him if we have any problems. When my cousin Arnie busted his arm, Mac fixed him right up."

Not, of course, that a broken arm could in any way

34

compare with the ordeal of giving birth, Cody thought, wondering where his brains had gone begging. Without half trying, he could say the stupidest damn things. It was because this woman rattled him, is what it was. He didn't understand the effect she had on him, so he clamped his lips shut and finished positioning the pillows at her back, only stopping to look at her when he was through fussing.

Long lashes fluttered over blue eyes, and Cody felt another strong pain in his chest. He slapped a hand over it, and wondered if he had a touch of heartburn. Probably not, since he hadn't eaten anything yet.

"Mr. McMurdo has been as good as any doctor I've ever met, Mr. O'Fannin." She peered up at him and gave him a look he'd never even dreamed of receiving from a female. She looked so sincere, he had to turn his head away from her.

"And you, too, Mr. O'Fannin. I—I guess I've already thanked you, but I want you to know how much I appreciate your stopping to help me, a stranger." She glanced away, too, obviously embarrassed. "I—well, it must have been awful for you."

It had been. It had also been wonderful. Cody, who had no experience in speaking the secrets of his soul, unstuck his tongue from the roof of his mouth and said, "It was nothing, ma'am. I was glad to help." He hurried to fetch the board she needed, hoping like thunder she wouldn't thank him anymore.

As soon as he had settled the board and set the stew on it, McMurdo returned with Cody's own supper.

"I'm going to get you a glass of milk now, Mellie," McMurdo said with a broad smile and another wink.

"Thank you, Mac." Melissa smiled up at the old man.

McMurdo winked again and departed.

"He told me to call him Mac," Melissa said to Cody, as if she owed him an explanation for having used the familiar name.

"He tells everybody to call him Mac. Won't let anybody call him 'mister.'" Cody took a bite of his stew as he scrambled to recall how to carry on a conversation with a virtuous woman. He used to know, back before he started living with the huge, silent Arnold on the huge, silent plains. "He's a good cook."

"Yes. This stew is delicious."

The baby, Cody thought suddenly. He ought to say something nice about the baby. He stole a quick peek at the infant and realized with horror that it looked like Benjamin Franklin, only uglier. So much for that. He took another bite of stew.

Fortunately, before he felt compelled to speak again, McMurdo returned with the glass of milk for Melissa and a cup of coffee for Cody. "Drink up now, Mellie m'dear," he said. "Got to get strong for little Katie there."

Melissa smiled warmly at the old Scot, and Cody's heart fluttered. He'd almost recovered by the time McMurdo left the room again.

Cody watched her carefully to make sure she didn't need him to adjust her table or anything. He got the impression Melissa Wilmeth wasn't one to pester folks to help her, and he didn't want her to be any more uncomfortable than she had to be.

She seemed to be faring well, so he went back to worrying about what to say now that he'd ruled out telling lies about the baby. He wanted to know all about her but didn't feel right in asking. At last he decided she deserved some information about the search he and Arnold were undertaking on her behalf, even though he hated even thinking about Howard Wilmeth, much less talking about him.

"Er, Arnie and I scoured the area southeast of Rio Hondo yesterday, looking for your husband, and we went sort of northeasterly today, ma'am. I expect tomorrow we'll head a little westerly, although I don't know how he could have got that far. Unless somebody took him that way. But then, he'd have told 'em to bring him here, I reckon."

Oh, hell. Cody wished Arnold were here to hit him for being such a bumbling idiot. Maybe Arnold wasn't so dumb after all. At least keeping mum all the time, he didn't stumble around with his words like Cody was doing now.

Melissa lifted her head. Cody got the impression she wanted to say something, then changed her mind. After a moment, she said, "Thank you."

He was really sick of her thanking him all the time. Especially for looking for her husband. Hell, what did she expect, anyway? That Cody would abandon her to her fate like Howard Wilmeth had done?

Because he was so nettled by Mr. Wilmeth's behavior and understood it so poorly, he said, "You and your husband—did—er—do you plan to settle in this area, ma'am?"

"I guess so."

She guessed so? What the hell did that mean? He glanced up from his stew to find her toying with her own meal. Because he didn't trust himself not to blurt out his feelings about people who traveled into perilous country without a specific plan as to what they aimed to do there, he pointed at her with his spoon. "Better eat up, ma'am. Mac isn't a doctor or anything, but he generally knows what folks need. If he says you should eat, you should eat."

"Thank you." She took a hasty bite. Cody got the impression she did so to avoid a scolding. He felt his eyes narrow as his puzzlement grew.

"You from around here, ma'am?"

"Oh, no. We're from Boston."

Boston? Hmmm. That might account for some of the foolishness Cody had perceived in Howard Wilmeth's actions. After all, he didn't expect a man from Boston, Massachusetts, would be conversant with the perils out in the Territory—although he sure as blazes should have read up about them before he set out to cross it with a female in his care. "You travel all the way from Boston by yourselves?"

"No."

She didn't seem to want to look at him any longer. She took another bite of stew and then made a show of checking on her baby, even though Cody could tell from where he sat that the kid was sleeping soundly. He recalled his own dislike of people who pestered him when he didn't want to be pestered, even as curiosity drove him to persevere in this instance.

"You mean you started out part of a wagon train or something?"

"Yes."

"What happened? You get separated from the rest of them?" And how, he wanted to ask, was such a thing possible? Unless the whole train took sick and died of camp fever. He'd heard of such things happening, although it still wouldn't explain why the Wilmeths had persisted alone.

"Um, yes."

Melissa took another bite of her stew. Cody got the feeling she did so to stall for time, as if she needed to think of a good story to tell him. Not that there was any story good enough to excuse her husband's infamous conduct.

Irritation bloomed in Cody's chest, and he wanted to shout at her to just spit it out. He knew his reaction to be irrational, so he took another bite of stew, too, and chewed on that to keep from chewing out Mrs. Wilmeth.

"We, uh, that is, Mr. Wilmeth and the leader of the train had a disagreement. The rest of the train pushed on toward Amarillo, and we headed south."

A disagreement, huh? Must have been a pretty hard one, to have sent the Wilmeths venturing out on their own. Cody pondered this development for a moment, then volunteered cautiously, "It's mighty rough country to travel through alone, ma'am."

"I know."

"Comanches and Apaches both live out here, you know. They generally leave folks alone, but they're kind of provoked about white folks settling on their land. They've been known to attack 'em once or twice."

She swallowed hard and stared at her stew. "Yes. I know."

Now Cody felt bad. She was clearly embarrassed about admitting how stupid her husband had been. He hardly blamed her. Howard Wilmeth's behavior wasn't her fault, though. Still, Cody knew full well that women had a hard row to hoe in this life. They were at the mercy of their men, and if their men turned out to be stupid or worse, the women suffered for it. He spared her his opinions on the subject.

"Well, I'm sure glad Arnie and me found you."

"So am I." She gave him one of those smiles that went through him and lit him up inside. "I don't know how to thank you."

He wished to God she'd quit trying. Her thanks embarrassed the hell out of him. "Just eat your food and get strong, ma'am. That's the best thanks Arnie and me can have." He added, "And your baby, too," because he knew how important babies were to their mothers.

Obediently, she spooned more food into her mouth.

"We'll find your husband, too, ma'am," he said in order to make her feel better.

She glanced up quickly, and looked down again just as fast. "Thank you," she whispered.

Cody got the faintest impression she didn't mean it that time.

Chapter Three

Melissa knew she was a wicked woman. She was wicked to have forsaken her mother and run away from home with Howard. She was wicked to have hated the poverty into which she'd been born. After all, she knew it was one's duty to accept one's fate or to improve oneself by oneself. She hadn't done either one of those things. Instead, she'd put her life into the keeping of Howard, as leaky a vessel as God ever put on earth. Now look what had happened to her.

She was wicked to have been embarrassed by her mother who, in spite of her ragged appearance and ill humor, did her best to support the family she'd been saddled with. Melissa was, in fact, so wicked that her own father hadn't wanted her. He'd abandoned Melissa, Katherine, their brothers, and their mother before Melissa's first birthday.

She was certainly wicked to harbor fond feelings for a man who had been a complete stranger to her until he'd stopped to help her. She was doubly damned for hoping he'd fail to find Howard, the father of her own child—or that he'd find Howard dead.

Her heart hurt as she gazed at her daughter and realized she hoped her own baby's father had perished out there on that desolate desert. What kind of mother was she, anyway?

What a fool she'd been to think she could escape her origins by marrying Howard Wilmeth, a man who epitomized everything she hated in a world she longed to escape. She should have been stronger than to have capitulated to her own desperation and his cajolery. She'd known he was offering her false coin even as he offered it. She should have searched for other options. How in heaven's name had she expected to find an escape with Howard, who had been born and bred on the same mean streets as Melissa herself?

As the old litany of blame chorused in her brain, Melissa experienced a feeling of utter hopelessness.

"You can't find something if you don't know where to look, darling Katie," she murmured to her child.

But what would she do if Cody O'Fannin didn't find Howard—or if he found him dead? What could she do to support herself and her daughter out here in this hard, clean land? She, who knew nothing about life outside the filthy city streets upon which she'd been born and bred.

At least she seemed to have acquired a friend in the strange Scotsman, Alexander McMurdo. He was such a benevolent old soul, and appeared so little inclined toward harsh judgments. Maybe Melissa could swallow the remains of her pride and ask him for suggestions about how a widowed woman could get on in life out here in the Territory.

If she was a widow. . . . She hoped she was, even as her hopes spun her thoughts miserably back into a vortex of guilt for being so wicked as to hope for Howard's death.

As if he'd heard her mind's tumultuous longings, Alexander McMurdo pushed the door to his little back room open and peered in.

"You awake?" he asked softly.

She couldn't help but smile at the dear old man. He reminded her of a softhearted troll, the way he peeped 'round the door frame. This territory was truly an astonishing place. As mean in its own way as the Boston slums she'd left behind her, Melissa had yet met two good men in as many days—three, if one counted Cody O'Fannin's cousin, Arnold. Arnold was so taciturn, it was difficult to determine whether he harbored the same kindness Cody possessed in such abundance, although Melissa felt sure he did.

"Yes, thank you, Mac. We're both awake, and Katie's already had her breakfast."

He strode to the side of the bed, smiling broadly. "Good. Then I'll help with your pillows and bring ye in some good hot porridge."

Melissa loved the way McMurdo's lilting burr handled his *r*'s. They rolled off his tongue like a waterfall. "We always called it oatmeal back home."

McMurdo whacked the pillows and propped them up behind Melissa's back. "Pisht. What do Americans know about porridge?"

"Not much, I guess. Your porridge is better than any oatmeal I ever ate at home." She didn't mention that oatmeal had often used to serve as breakfast, lunch, and dinner when she was little, and that she'd grown to hate it as an emblem of the grinding indigence in which she'd lived. In fact, she was giggling by the time McMurdo had finished manhandling her pillows.

"Aye, 'tis the truth, Mellie, and don't you be forgettin' it." He gave her a broad wink. "Now, I found something else for your breakfast this morning, too."

"Mmmmm. A treat?" To the best of her recollection, Melissa had never indulged in good-natured banter of this sort. It made her heart feel light and airy.

"Aye, as near a treat as a body can come by in these parts. I discovered an orange rollin' around in me very own pantry."

Melissa's eyes opened wide in astonishment. "An orange?" She spoke the word with the reverence it deserved, lowering her voice to a whisper.

"Aye. As orange an orange as an orange can be."

Melissa had eaten an orange twice before in her life. Her mouth watered as she recalled those other two times. Her taste buds remembered the delicious, juicy sweetness of the fruit, even if her imagination wasn't quite so talented. "Oh, my."

McMurdo left her with another wink. Melissa stared after him, unable to think of a single other thing to say. An orange. An *orange*. Good heavens.

Her wizened benefactor returned a few moments later bearing a tray upon which sat a steaming bowl of oatmeal that he'd doctored with brown sugar and thick cream, and a plate crowned with an orange cut into eight small sections. As if to remind her where she was, he'd placed a yucca pod in the center of the sections. It sat among the orange spokes like an exotic desert crown and looked strangely beautiful to Melissa.

"Thank you." Her respect for such abundance led her to maintain her voice at a whisper.

"Ye're quite welcome, lass."

Melissa looked up quickly, something in McMurdo's own voice having caught her attention. He was peering down at her with such a sweet, sympathetic expression on his face that her breath caught. He patted her shoulder. As his hand moved through the air, it seemed to stir errant dust particles and make them glimmer like tiny diamondlike dots. Melissa closed her eyes for a second to clear her mind of the odd impression.

"You eat up now, Mellie m'dear. After you finish all that, maybe we can think about what to do wi' ye after Cody and Arnold come back this evenin'."

His suggestion, which a moment earlier Melissa had herself been contemplating with dread, now struck her only as immensely practical. She nodded, picked up her spoon, and said, "All right. Thank you," surprising herself.

He left her with another wink, and Melissa ate her breakfast. She'd never tasted anything as sweet as the orange McMurdo had found "rolling around" in his pantry. She decided to ask him about it, worrying that he must have paid a fortune for the rare fruit. She'd pay him back someday, somehow.

A lifetime of watching people cheat each other in order to provide themselves with the common necessities of life hadn't yet vanquished Melissa's finer urges. She wanted to do good. She wanted to *be* good. And she would be. Somehow, some way, she'd overcome the obstacles her past had heaped in the road to her future and become a good, useful woman and a good mother to Katie; she swore it silently to herself.

She'd prove to everybody that she could be a decent person in spite of her less-than-savory beginnings. In spite of her ill-advised marriage to Howard Wilmeth. She'd show them all.

Whoever "they" were.

*   *   *

Cody was mad as a wet hornet when he and Arnold made their way back to McMurdo's at four that same evening. His temper had been smoldering all day long, ever since he'd discovered the whereabouts of Mr. Howard Wilmeth.

"I never expected him to be such a lousy, stinking coward," he muttered to Arnold. It was not the first time since the cousins had left Hugh Blackworth's ranch that he'd done so.

"Never expected him to be alive," Arnold murmured back.

Cody shot him a hot look. "I wish he wasn't," he declared, and then felt guilty about having spoken such a mean-hearted truth aloud.

Arnold, evidently neither surprised nor outraged by Cody's outburst, merely shrugged.

"If Mrs. Wilmeth has the sense God gave a pea, she won't go back to the bastard."

His heart and brain in a turmoil, Cody wondered how he could go about convincing the pretty little brand-new mother to abandon her marriage to a man who had abandoned her. Even if a woman did need a man in order to survive out here, she'd be better off alone than with a snake like Wilmeth. Some men didn't deserve to call themselves men. As far as Cody was concerned, Howard Wilmeth was one of them.

His brow beetling, he pondered ways in which a respectable woman, on her own and with a child to support, could earn a living in New Mexico Territory. There must be a way, if he could only think of one. Then he spared a moment to wonder why he was trying.

Hell, she was nothing to him. He'd come out here to the Territory in order to avoid entanglements, and to create something by and for himself. He didn't need to be worrying about Melissa Wilmeth.

He couldn't seem to stop worrying about her, though. Like a dog with a bone, he worried her problem, and worried it and worried it. By the time the cousins returned to Rio Hondo, Cody would have been hard-pressed to decide whether he was more angry with Howard Wilmeth or with himself.

He left Arnold to tend the horses while he entered McMurdo's little shack and made his way to the back room. Every time he approached that room, his heart began to speed up like a roadrunner on loco weed. It did so now, and it annoyed him.

When he opened the door and poked his head around the frame, that same heart recoiled in horror when he beheld Melissa Wilmeth clutching a tiny swaddled bundle—which must be, Cody reasoned, the baby—to her bosom, her face awash with tears. Alexander McMurdo sat beside her bed. The old Scot was gently patting her hand, but Cody didn't notice that part; he had eyes only for Melissa's patent unhappiness.

Cody had only harbored soft emotions for a female once before in his life, and the attachment had ended badly. He didn't have any desire to go through *that* again. It was also true that he possessed undying loyalty to his cousin and his family. Anybody in the Rio Hondo area knew he could be counted on to back up a friend in a fight or give a hand to a person who needed it. There wasn't a cowboy in the area who would have pegged him as a fool for a woman. He proved them all wrong that day, though, and could only be glad afterwards that nobody besides McMurdo was there to witness his folly.

"Hey!" he cried, forgetting for the moment to remember that he was nothing to Melissa and she was nothing to him. "Hey, what the hell are you doing to Mrs. Wilmeth, Mac?" He took three giant steps toward the bed before he remembered who was what to whom.

McMurdo turned around and smiled his knowing smile. "Don't shoot me, Cody boy. I'm only trying to help our little lady here straighten out her circumstances."

Melissa had jerked violently at Cody's bellow, and now stared at him, wild-eyed, a hand sheltering her baby's head, as if to protect the child from him. From *him*, a fellow who wouldn't hurt a fly unless it hurt him first. At once Cody felt silly. He swallowed, unclenched his fists, took a deep breath, and tried to calm down.

"Sorry," he muttered. "Didn't mean to scare you."

He was glad when Melissa seemed to relax. She didn't offer him a welcoming smile, but pressed a hand over the sheet at her breast, as if trying to settle her own thundering heart. Tears stained her cheeks, and Cody had a job of it to stop himself from rushing to her side and using his own bandanna to wipe them away. What in name of glory was the matter with him?

McMurdo clucked his tongue. "Pisht, Cody boy, ye'd think we was in here plottin' to overthrow the government or somethin'."

Cody didn't care about governments, and he didn't look at McMurdo. His whole concentration was on Melissa Wilmeth, who still seemed frightened. He was proud of himself when he forced his lips into a smile. With a valiant effort, he also eased his rigid stance and murmured, "I beg your pardon, Mrs. Wilmeth. I didn't mean to barge in here and scare you. I—er—I thought something had happened to upset you, is all."

It was, perhaps, the silliest excuse he'd ever made for poor behavior in his life, but it was pretty close to the truth. He'd been ready to kill Mac for hurting her, is what he'd been, but he couldn't make himself confess to that much lunacy. Mac wouldn't hurt anything. In his sane moments, Cody knew that as well as he knew the sun would set this evening.

Melissa passed the back of her hand across her cheeks and gave a tremulous smile.

"It's—it's all right, Mr. O'Fannin," she said in a tiny voice that fluttered over Cody's overwrought senses and did much to assuage them.

"We're just figurin' out how Mrs. Wilmeth and little Katie here can get by out here in Rio Hondo, Cody boy. Maybe you can give us a hand."

Cody stared blankly at McMurdo, who winked back. McMurdo said volumes with those winks of his. Cody noticed how eloquent they were for the first time today.

"Er—sure," he said, positive now that his brain had taken to visiting elsewhere. Who the hell was he to help this woman figure out what to do with her life?

Nevertheless, he traveled the rest of the way to Melissa's bedside, sat in the chair Mac patted invitingly, removed his hat, and settled it onto his lap. He was too nervous to cross his hands over its crown, as his mother had taught him was proper, courteous behavior, but he did manage not to blurt out anything else stupid. Instead, he waited for somebody to say something to which he could respond in a rational manner.

Alexander McMurdo picked up the conversational gauntlet as if it was the most natural thing in the world to do; as if Cody hadn't just made an ass of himself. Good old Mac. He never seemed to be at a loss for anything. Thank God. That made one of them.

"So, as I was sayin', Mellie and me were ponderin' what she should do now, Cody m'boy. I was thinkin' she'd probably be better off without that man o' hers, as he's a little too shaky in his upper works to entrust with the care of a female and a baby. What do you think, lad?"

Shocked to the toes of his well-worn boots, Cody felt his mouth fall open as he gawked at Mac. Then he felt his eyes squint up. Mac was talking as if he knew what had happened to Wilmeth, and that wasn't possible. Was it?

"Wait a minute, Mac," he said, struggling to regain his sense of order in the universe. "What do you mean, she'd be better off without him? What do you know about him?"

McMurdo adopted the innocent look of an angel merely visiting these earthly cesspits on a holiday and shook his head. Cody wouldn't have been much surprised to discover a halo lurking somewhere in the vicinity. "Not a thing more than what Mellie here's told me, lad. Why? Did you find out something?"

Cody peered at the old man narrowly. Damned if Mac didn't look like he already knew everything. More than once since he'd met the wily old Scot, Cody had gotten the same impression, although today he found it more irritating than usual.

As if he understood and wanted to help, McMurdo murmured, "So tell us all about it, Cody. Did you discover anything about Mr. Wilmeth's whereabouts?" He folded his hands and settled them demurely in his lap.

Cody gave the old man one more good long look, then glanced at Melissa and cleared his throat. He wanted to fling her husband's lousy behavior into the room like a dead skunk so that nobody could avoid it, pretend it was something else, or argue with him about it. But years of training in conventional manners prevented him from doing anything so ungenteel.

"We found your husband, ma'am."

Her eyes opened so wide, Cody saw white circles surrounding the deep blue irises. Damn, she had beautiful eyes.

"You did?" Her voice sounded breathy and not altogether delighted. Cody took heart.

"Yes, ma'am."

"Do tell," McMurdo muttered.

Cody's gaze shot to him and thinned again. The old man looked as innocent as the new dawn, and Cody didn't believe it for a second.

Nevertheless, he said, "Yes, ma'am. Apparently some of the cowhands who work for Hugh Blackworth found him wandering on the desert. I guess he was lost and disoriented." He didn't believe *that*, either. "Blackworth's foreman, Grant Davis, said he seemed dazed and delirious. They took him to Blackworth's place and doctored him up."

Then Cody clamped his mouth shut, pinching his tongue between his teeth to keep from blurting out his feelings about a man who'd been discovered by a whole throng of helpful men and yet hadn't bothered to tell a single one of them that his own wife lay helpless in the back of a wagon giving birth to his own child. The effort of suppressing his anger on the matter made him stiffen in his chair and crimp his hat brim between his fingers.

"Ah," said McMurdo mildly. "Sunstroke, unquestionably."

Cody gave him another exceedingly sharp look and

grumbled, "Yeah." Right. In the middle of November. Sure, it was sunstroke.

"My goodness," Melissa whispered.

Cody couldn't tell what her feelings were on the matter. "Yes, ma'am." He cleared his throat. "Er, your husband said he was too sick to come here with me. He said he'd be along when he's feeling better." His stomach turned over and cramped up after he reported Howard Wilmeth's offensive words.

"Hmm." Mac studied him thoughtfully. "Well, Cody m'lad, Mellie here and me have had a real heart-to-heart chat today. Of course, she'll need to ponder long and hard what to do, but we've discussed it. I've told her what I think she needs to do."

After a pause, during which he looked from the old man to the young woman and back again, Cody said, "And what's that?"

Mac chuckled. "I already told you. I think she ought to refuse to take the bastard back. Of course, that means she'll be havin' to support her baby and herself without the help of her husband. Frankly," he added with a sly wink, "I don't see that Mr. Howard Wilmeth's been of much use to her so far anyway, so I don't expect her bein' without him will make much difference, except to make her life more pleasant."

Cody was profoundly shocked. The cheek of Alexander McMurdo, daring to voice aloud the secrets lurking in his own heart, struck him dumb for a moment. He could do no more than stare from the audacious old man to Melissa Wilmeth, who suddenly seemed even more fragile and helpless than she had before. Cody worked his mouth several times, but nothing emerged.

Melissa, he noticed with horror, had begun to weep again, silently, terribly, miserably. His hands gripped his hat brim so tightly, his hat was likely to bear the marks for the rest of its days.

As if he'd not just shattered every single one of Cody's notions about the rightness of things, Mac began speaking again in a bland voice. "So I have me an idea or two on the matter but thought you might like to have a say in things, too, Cody, m'boy, since you're pretty closely involved."

That brought Cody's mouth clanking shut. "I am?" His voice, he noticed, was as hoarse as if he'd had the croup for a week.

Melissa whispered, "Oh, no, you've done enough—"

"I'd say so," Mac cut in. "After all, ye're the one who found her, lad. I expect ye'd like to see her established somewhere."

"Well, of course—"

"Oh, but he's already—"

"I want her to be—"

"—so much that—"

"—happy, and her kid—"

"And besides, it's my—"

"But she's married—"

"—life and my daughter and—"

"—to that bastard, and—"

"—I think I should have—"

Mac held up his hands, and both Cody and Melissa stopped speaking instantly. Cody blinked, sure he saw those damned sparkles glittering in the air around McMurdo's fingertips again. They vanished immediately, if they were ever there. Jehosephat. He shook his head hard, and wished he knew what in blazes was going on.

"Now," said Mac, smiling, "where were we?"

After a brief moment of silence, Melissa muttered,

"If I recall correctly, the two of you were busy managing my life."

Cody stared at her, amazed by the bitterness he heard in her voice. She wouldn't look at him, but plucked at the blanket covering her lap. Her cheeks had flushed pink and her lips were pinched together tightly. She still looked sick and weak, but his heart registered a moment's elation that she could show such spirit. He'd always admired spirit in a filly.

Mac laughed heartily. "Pisht, Mellie m'dear, I don't want to manage your life. No more does our poor Cody here. But you must admit ye have some hard decisions to make."

Another second or so passed in silence. Then Melissa swallowed and said, "Yes. Yes, I know I do."

"And old Cody here"—Mac whacked Cody on the shoulder, surprising him so much he nearly toppled out of his chair—"is just the lad to discuss the matter with."

Melissa looked up at that, directly into Cody's eyes. Cody, who hadn't yet recovered from the wallop Mac had administered, found himself trapped by her serious, sky-blue gaze.

"He is?" she asked.

"I am?" he asked, breaking the hold of her eyes with difficulty.

"I think so," Mac said jovially. "After all, it's your ranch that's going to be left shorthanded once Arnold heads back to Georgetown."

Cody's heart skipped a beat, and he sat up straight. *"What?* What did you say?"

Mac rolled his eyes and looked chagrined. "Tut, tut, I wonder if I'll ever learn to guard me old tongue."

Frowning furiously, Cody growled, "I doubt it. Now, what the hell did you just say?" He jerked his

54

head toward Melissa. "Sorry, ma'am. Didn't mean to swear."

She shook her head as if to give him leave.

Mac looked honestly contrite. Cody didn't know whether to believe his expression or not.

"I am sorry, lad," the old fellow said. "I should have let Arnold tell you himself. He got a wire this afternoon whilst the two of you were out searchin' for Mellie's husband."

"He did?"

"Aye, a telegraph wire." Mac nodded solemnly, as the occasion warranted. Nothing but bad news ever came by the telegraph. The telegraph was too expensive a medium by which to relate good news.

Cody's heart fell. "Who died?" he asked, dreading the answer.

Mac grinned, his aspect so alien to the depressing occasion that Cody didn't believe it for a minute. Then he resented it.

"Nobody died," the old man said, relieving Cody of his most pressing worry.

He squinted at Mac. "Then what did the wire say?"

The door opened at that very moment. Cody, Melissa, and Mac all glanced at it. Mac murmured, "Mebbe ye'd better let poor Arnold tell you himself, Cody lad."

The expression on Arnold's face made Cody's soft heart lurch and propelled him out of his chair and halfway across the room. "Arnie! What is it, Arnie?" Cody hadn't seen his cousin look so distraught since Arnold's eighteen-year-old spaniel died.

Arnold looked up from the paper he held in his hand and didn't answer. His big brown eyes were as soft and sad as a milch cow's. His gaze sought Cody's and his miserable sniffle struck Cody's senses like a blow to the jaw.

Rushing the rest of the way to Arnold's side, Cody put an arm around his shoulder and began patting him on the back as he led him to Melissa's bedside. "Here, Arnie, you sit down here, and tell me what's wrong."

Lord, if it wasn't one thing it was six others. Cody settled Arnold on the chair he'd lately deserted, and kept his hands on his cousin's shoulders to give him courage. Poor Arnold. Whatever was in that wire had knocked him cockeyed with a vengeance.

Melissa and McMurdo also watched Arnold apprehensively. Cody noticed that Melissa seemed to have suspended her own misery in favor of offering sympathy to Arnold, and he appreciated her more in that moment than he could say.

With a trembling hand, Arnold lifted the wire. "It's—it's Loretta." His voice trembled as much as his hand.

"What's the matter with Loretta?" Cody asked sharply. Oh, sweet glory, he hoped to heaven Arnold's intended hadn't died. He didn't much care for Loretta himself, but he knew Arnold worshipped her—from afar, which was probably the safest way to deal with a female of Loretta's stamp. But Cody would never say so to Arnold.

Arnold looked up into Cody's eyes, and Cody swallowed a lump in his throat. Poor old Arnold. If Loretta wasn't dead already, Cody might be tempted to do away with her for putting that expression on his cousin's face.

"She ain't comin'," Arnold whispered in the voice of doom.

Cody stood up straight again. "What?"

Two tears spilled out of Arnold's eyes and trailed down his cheeks. Cody felt awful for him.

"She ain't comin'. This here wire says so." Arnold

held up the paper in his hand a little higher.

Three weeks before, Arnold had sent a letter to his girl, Loretta Pine, who awaited his summons in Georgetown, Texas, advising her that he'd be coming to fetch her soon. At least, Arnold had felt sure she still awaited it. Every now and then a pang of worry about Loretta smote him. Invariably Cody had assuaged it by assuring Arnold that Loretta was a prime girl, and not one to welsh on a promise.

In truth, Cody figured Loretta was lucky to have snared Arnold. He couldn't feature her having found another fool within the limited confines of Georgetown willing to marry her. He'd die an agonizing death before he'd tell Arnold so. Cody was nothing if not true blue to his cousin.

Now he snatched the wire out of Arnold's slack grip and read it for himself. Well, hell. Arnold was right and Cody was wrong. The damned woman *would* welsh on a promise. Her wire said that, after giving the situation careful thought, she didn't feel up to venturing out into the hostile Territory with Arnold. Cody mumbled, "Well, hell."

"I got to go to Georgetown, Cody," Arnold said suddenly, as if he feared Cody's displeasure but was willing to risk it for Loretta's sake and wanted to get it over with.

Mac didn't say a thing, but Cody was ever so conscious of the old man sitting there, peering at the ceiling, and looking as virtuous as a babe unborn. Or as little Katie—barely born. He gave him a scowl to let him know he wasn't forgiven for being both right and too blasted smart, then gentled his attitude for Arnold.

"You're going to Georgetown, Arnie?" he asked quietly.

Arnold passed his big hand over his cheek, taking

57

his tears with it, and nodded. He peered at Cody, his visage intense. "I got to go there, Cody, don't you see? I got to see her; to talk to her. She can't mean it, Cody."

She could, too. Cody refused to say so to Arnold, even though Arnold's trip to Georgetown would mean chaos on their little homestead.

Unless . . . His glance shot to McMurdo again.

The old man looked like a cherub. He still gazed at the ceiling, as if occupied in counting angels in heaven. Cody's glance slid to Melissa. She looked back at him, her heart in her eyes. That heart said it ached for poor Arnold.

Well, hell.

"I know it'll be hard on you if I go back, Cody," Arnold said, making Cody's attention swivel back to him. "But I got to go. I got to."

Cody knew it. He said so. "I know it, Arnie." Then he tapped Mac on the shoulder to capture his attention. It was all for form's sake. Cody knew Mac knew exactly what was happening; hell, he knew what was going to happen even before it happened. The old man's odd ways were close to driving Cody to distraction today.

Nevertheless, he said, "I expect this is what you meant, Mac?"

The old man smiled at him. Cody sighed. His chin drooped for a moment; then he lifted his head and surrendered to superior forces.

He turned toward Melissa Wilmeth. "Ma'am? Mrs. Wilmeth?"

"Yes?"

Her big blue eyes were so guileless that no matter how hard he tried, Cody couldn't convict her of connivance. This was all Mac's doing; he knew it.

"Er, ma'am, when you're feeling up to it, do you

suppose you'd be able to work for me at my place whilst my cousin Arnold travels to Georgetown? I can't keep the place up alone, and I only got me the one hired hand who works with the cows."

She blinked, clearly astonished. "You—you want me? To work for you?"

Cody cleared his throat, feeling both beleaguered and flustered. "Well—I mean, if you really mean you won't be getting back together with your husband— and I don't blame you if you don't," he hastened to assure her. "Well, then, I could sure use the help." He sighed deeply. "You see, ma'am, I can't handle the house and the cows both. Arnie and me, we used to share chores along with Luis, our hired man. With Arnie gone, I—well, I'll need help," he ended simply. Then he shrugged, feeling inadequate to express his situation any better than that.

He discovered Melissa's expression had changed from one of wonder to one of rapture. He felt even more flustered. Hell, he'd only offered her a job; she didn't need to look at him as if he was her savior.

"You mean it?" she whispered, sounding very much as though she didn't quite dare to believe him.

He didn't take exception because he recognized the wonder behind her words and knew she didn't really mean to imply that she doubted his word. If she'd been a man, he wouldn't have been so easy on her. "Yes, ma'am."

"Oh, my."

Cody waited for her to expound upon her breathless exclamation. She'd just opened her mouth, he presumed to do so, when a sharp sound came from the other room. Melissa's mouth shut. Mac looked up and frowned. Cody whirled around to face the door. Even Arnold lifted his unhappy gaze from the wire in Cody's hand and directed it at the door,

59

which burst open to reveal Howard Wilmeth standing just on the other side, glaring for all he was worth.

Melissa seemed to shrink back in her bed.

Arnold blinked.

Mac sighed.

Cody muttered, "Aw, hell."

Chapter Four

Cody hadn't liked Howard Wilmeth the first time he set eyes on him at Hugh Blackworth's ranch. He liked him even less the second time, in the back room of the mercantile in Alexander McMurdo's Wagon Yard. In fact, if he and Wilmeth had been alone, Cody might have been inclined to administer a lesson he believed the man deserved. A hard lesson. By hand.

Although Cody's fists bunched at his sides, he didn't allow them to get away from him. If he treated Wilmeth the way he wanted to, Cody was sure Wilmeth's wife would be appalled, and Cody didn't want to hurt her feelings. He suspected his own scruples were not shared by Melissa's husband.

After he'd sucked in a deep breath and figured he could hold onto his temper, Cody lifted his head and frowned at Wilmeth, who hadn't moved from the doorway. Cody's mood didn't brighten when he saw

Grant Davis standing behind Wilmeth. Davis, a swaggering, bragging, blowhard of a man, supposedly worked as Hugh Blackworth's chief wrangler. Cody doubted if Davis knew one end of a horse from the other. From all Cody had seen, Davis was one of Blackworth's hired bullies, and Cody didn't like him any more than he liked Howard Wilmeth. Well, maybe a little more. At least Cody didn't have any personal grudges against Davis.

Hugh Blackworth, a cattle man, ran the second-largest operation in the Seven Rivers country. His methods were even less honorable than those of John Chisum, and Chisum could be powerfully unscrupulous when he chose to be. And he chose to be quite often when smaller ranchers got in his way. Although Chisum generally began negotiations with offers of money, he had no qualms about resorting to more vigorous methods if money didn't work.

Blackworth, however, never tried to work out disputes amicably. He aimed for the jugular immediately: poisoning water, stealing cattle, cutting fences. He'd gone so far as to shoot a rival more than once. This particular solution to a problem was not unknown in the Territory, but people resented Blackworth for applying it because nobody liked him. They were more tolerant of others.

Cody and Arnold had discussed the matter, and Cody decided Arnold had been right when he'd said, "The feller's jist such a blamed cocklebur."

It was true; nobody trusted Blackworth. It was one thing to be at odds with a fellow; after all, disputes arose even among the finest of men. It was another thing to know there wasn't another rancher or cowboy in the entire Seven Rivers country who trusted a man. Not a single soul would turn his back on Hugh Blackworth for fear of getting a hole plugged in it. Cody suspected even Grant Davis would leave Blackworth's employ if another easy job was offered.

From what Cody had seen of Blackworth's men, most of them were just like their boss. All but a few of the good ones had moved on to greener—or, at any rate, more honorable—pastures by this time. Cody and Arnold had discussed Blackworth's hired help more than once, too. It was Arnold's contention that Blackworth had raided a prison to find them. Cody thought Arnold could be rather astute sometimes when he wasn't half trying. He wouldn't forget Grant Davis was around, at any rate, and he didn't want him anywhere near Melissa Wilmeth.

The curtains were drawn across the one small window in the room, and the atmosphere was dark. With Wilmeth's arrival, it began to feel ugly. It was a fanciful impression, but Cody couldn't help the crawling sensation in his guts. Arnold, Mac, and Melissa remained motionless, as if Wilmeth's sudden appearance had turned them to stone.

Cody fancied he could see Wilmeth's anger, too, and he recognized it. His was the kind of anger a weak man held for anything that dared point out his shortcomings. It was the kind of anger a feckless dream-spinner held against a practical man who worked hard and accomplished something. Cody had no patience with people like that, who blamed others for their own faults and didn't strive to better themselves—people who relied on luck.

In Cody's experience, luck favored the industrious. He wondered how Melissa had got herself saddled with such an item as Howard Wilmeth.

Since everyone else in the room seemed to have been stricken dumb, he handed the wire back to Arnold and took a step toward the door. He made a conscious effort to unclench his fists. "Wilmeth. I see you finally decided to see how your wife and baby are."

A soft intake of Melissa Wilmeth's breath behind him made him wish he'd done a better job of keeping his hostility to himself. He wished it even more when Howard's aspect became blacker and stormier, until he looked like one of the thunderheads that loomed overhead before a gully-buster hit.

Cody sighed, aggravated with himself. He glanced over his shoulder, hoping Wilmeth's wife or old Mac would say or do something; take the burden of orchestrating this scene from his own unwilling shoulders. He knew better than to expect anything from Arnold but silence.

Neither Mac nor Melissa said a word, although the expression of horror on Melissa's face decided Cody on one thing at least: Howard Wilmeth was not leaving Alexander McMurdo's Wagon Yard with his wife and daughter. Not today, he wasn't. Not unless he wanted to do it over Cody O'Fannin's dead body.

He hitched up his trousers. "She's too sick to move today, Wilmeth. She needs to get her strength back before she's fit to travel."

"Oh, yeah?" Wilmeth took an aggressive step toward Cody. His own hands clenched into fists. He reminded Cody of the banty cocks who used to strut around the farmyard back home in Georgetown.

Cody eyed Wilmeth's fists skeptically. He'd never harbored much respect for city slickers. If this fellow was from Boston, Cody figured he could best him in a fair fight. He didn't want to, though. Not in front of Melissa anyway. Besides, he didn't expect Wilmeth was the type who'd fight fair.

His glance slid past Wilmeth to Grant Davis, who lounged in the doorway with a toothpick in his mouth. Davis gave Cody a humorless grin and a shrug, as if to say he didn't know what was going on, didn't care, and had only come along for the ride. Cody expected he'd face no trouble from that quarter, and was moderately relieved.

He hooked his thumb over his shoulder. "Ask old Doc McMurdo there, if you don't believe me."

"I came here for my wife, damn it, not to talk to any doctor."

Grant Davis chuckled. Everybody who'd been in the area for longer than five minutes knew who Doc McMurdo was. Except, evidently, Howard Wilmeth.

He also appeared to resent a doctor seeing to his wife. He stalked the rest of the way up to Cody, stood toe-to-toe with him, and scowled up into his face. Now he reminded Cody of a squatty bulldog, showing off for a dog he was trying to impress. It wouldn't have surprised him much if Wilmeth had lifted a leg and peed on him. He sighed inside, and wondered what he was supposed to do now. Short of decking Wilmeth, he couldn't offhand see a way to keep him away from Melissa. He'd like to do that but didn't think he'd better. Wilmeth was, after all—and in spite of what Cody considered right—Melissa's husband.

"I'm not well enough to travel yet, Howard."

Melissa's soft voice startled Cody. It sounded out of place in the room, which had begun to bristle with barely leashed masculine violence. It apparently surprised her husband, too, because he blinked, as if only then remembering that it was Melissa, and not an argument with Cody, that had brought him here today. With a pointed sneer for Cody, he brushed past him and went to Melissa's bedside. Cody turned, prepared to watch him carefully. If he so much as looked as if he might hurt Melissa, they'd all be attending Howard Wilmeth's funeral tomorrow.

"So you had the kid," Wilmeth said.

Again, Cody experienced a fierce desire to bludgeon him.

"Yes." Melissa's voice sounded both frightened and conciliatory. Obviously, she feared either Wilmeth himself or that Wilmeth would make her travel before she was ready. "See? She's a beautiful little girl, Howard. Isn't she lovely?"

"It's a girl?" Wilmeth sounded disgusted. "Hell, Melissa, I wanted a boy."

"She's a beautiful little baby, Howard, and I'm glad she's a girl. I wanted a girl."

"You always were damned contrary, Melissa. I wanted a boy."

She frowned unhappily. "Well, you got a girl, and she's wonderful."

Wilmeth made a sound that clearly indicated his disagreement.

"And I named her Katie, after my sister Katherine, too." Melissa's voice was as soft as a dandelion puff. Cody loved it.

Wilmeth plainly did not. He snorted again. "Damn it, Melissa, don't I get any say in what the hell to name her?"

Melissa's lips set into a taut line. "You weren't even there when she was born, Howard. Why should you have any part in naming her?"

Cody, who had started to wonder if Melissa Wilmeth had a spark of spirit in her, was pleased to hear that she did. Her voice was quite tart, in fact.

Wilmeth took a step back, offended. He shot a glance around the room to see if anyone else had heard his wife's words. He most likely didn't appreciate having his iniquitous behavior spoken of aloud and in company. "Dammit, Melissa, I got sunstroke. I could have died."

"I could have died, too, Howard, when you left me there alone." She sounded staunch and steadfast to Cody, who wished he could applaud.

"Yeah, well, I was trying to find help."

"Were you? Or were you merely running out on your responsibilities? I understand you didn't bother to tell the men who found you that your wife was in the back of that stupid wagon, having your baby." Now she sounded angry, and Cody's urge to clap intensified.

"Oh, now, don't start in on me for that. I was sick, dammit!"

"And I was in labor!"

"Dammit, Melissa, don't you talk to me like that!"

"You deserted me, Howard. I know you didn't set out to seek help, and you didn't ask for it when you found it. You had the chance, and you didn't once mention me. You just wanted to leave your responsibilities behind you."

"Dammit all, it wasn't like that!"

"I know you, Howard. It *was* like that. I know it. You left me and the baby in that old wagon in the middle of the desert, and you weren't planning to come back."

"Now, you listen here—"

"You're probably sorry that nice Mr. O'Fannin ever found us, because now everybody knows what kind of man you are!"

"Dammit, Melissa—"

Cody couldn't stand it anymore. He started toward the bed, intending to grab Howard Wilmeth by the back of his jacket and throw him outside. With luck, the bastard would land in a prickly pear patch and stab himself. Sometimes prickly pear wounds got infected. If Melissa's luck was good, maybe her stinking husband would get gangrene and die.

A small gesture from Mac stopped him. The old man held up his hand, and those twinkly sprinkles made Cody blink and break his stride. He halted, confused.

Mac gave him a genial smile and rose from his chair to stand behind Melissa's husband. He put a hand on Wilmeth's shoulder, and Cody blinked again. There went those damned sparkles. He rubbed his eyes. The sparkles were gone when he opened them again. Thank God. Maybe he should get his eyes checked next time he was in Georgetown.

"Mellie will be stayin' here in the wagon yard for awhile, Mr. Wilmeth," Mac said, his voice mellow. "She's not well enough to go with you today."

Wilmeth, obviously unmoved by Mac's mellowness or his wife's frailty, frowned at him. "Who the hell are you?"

The old Scot's smile broadened under the influence of Wilmeth's antagonism, as if he found this whole situation wildly amusing. Cody didn't, and he couldn't figure out why Mac didn't seem to be the least bit worried. Wilmeth looked as mad as a peeled rattlesnake at the moment. And, since Cody pegged him for a coward and a bully, he'd go odds that Wilmeth would hit an old fellow like Mac before he'd try to hit Cody, who could fight back.

Oddly enough, Wilmeth didn't act on his anger. While Cody watched, fascinated, Mac gave a little tug on Wilmeth's coat sleeve, and Wilmeth turned around. He looked disconcerted when he eyed Mac's hand on his sleeve. Cody wondered what Mac had done to make him get that expression on his face. The old man must be stronger than he looked.

"What the hell do you want?" Wilmeth demanded belligerently. Again, he reminded Cody of some bandy-legged rooster, one who'd squawk a good fight, but who'd wait until a fellow was off guard to attack. Cody'd be sure always to sit with his back against the wall when in the same room with him.

"I want you to go away now, Mr. Wilmeth, and leave our Mellie to her rest and her baby." Mac's smile was as sweet as honey.

"But—"

"Come along now." Mac picked up Howard Wilmeth's hand as if he were a small child and turned to walk toward the door.

"Wait a damned minute here!" In spite of his hot words, Wilmeth stumbled after Mac.

Cody expected Wilmeth to resist harder, but he followed, as meekly as a kitten. He looked like he resented it, too; as though he didn't want to be doing what his feet were making him do. Cody got a funny feeling in his middle as Mac and Wilmeth passed him, the old man leading the younger one as if he was leading a steer into a feed lot.

"Shoot," murmured Arnold, and Cody realized he was surprised, too.

"Guess Mac's a lot stronger than he looks," Cody said. He knew that wasn't the right answer and still felt funny.

Arnold shook his head, staring at the door through which Mac, Wilmeth, and Grant Davis had just exited. "Shoot," he muttered again. The telegraph message he'd lately been weeping over lay, forgotten, on his knee.

"I'm glad he's gone."

Melissa's tiny, joyless voice made Cody whirl around. He saw her swipe the back of her hand under her eye, and realized she'd been crying. Not much, but she'd been crying. His heart crinkled up. She'd just had a baby, for the sweet Lord's sake. This should be a time of joy and wonder for her, not one of anguish and uncertainty.

He walked over and knelt beside her, since Arnie remained like a lump in his chair, and he expected Mac to come back in a second or two. He picked up her hand. "Don't worry, Mrs. Wilmeth. We'll take care of you. We won't let anything bad happen to you or your baby."

Cody didn't know who this "we" was of whom he spoke. He meant he'd do those things himself but didn't know how to say so, or, more to the point, if he had the right to.

A smile trembled on her lips. Cody felt as if a magnetic force was drawing him to her. He resisted it for all he was worth.

"Thank you, Mr. O'Fannin. Thank you so much. I don't know why you and your cousin and Mr. McMurdo are being so kind to me, but I can't thank you enough."

Because he feared he'd lose control and kiss her, Cody stood up. He continued to hold her hand because he couldn't make himself let it go. Her hand was small; too small. There wasn't enough flesh on her bones. However she'd made this trip out here, that damned husband of hers certainly hadn't taken proper care of her.

"Please, ma'am. It's really nothing." Because he felt almost desperate to lighten the mood between them, he forced a grin and added, "Shoot, you'll be sorry enough we helped you once you get to the ranch and have to work like a slave from dawn to dusk."

Her smile about broke his heart. "I won't mind, Mr. O'Fannin. I'm used to working hard." She glanced away from him, and gave a loving, wistful look to her daughter. "And it's so—so clean here. It's a good place to raise my baby. Not like what I'm used to."

Not like what she was used to. Cody felt the questions piling up in his heart and hammering to get out, but he didn't dare ask them. She was too fragile. She didn't need him hounding her for information, no matter how desperate he was to know every single thing there was to know about her.

When he heard the door open, he reluctantly released her hand and turned to find Mac reentering the room, a big smile on his face. He was brushing his hands together, as if to rid them of dirt. Some papers were stuffed into his breast pocket; Cody wondered what they were and where he'd picked them up.

"There. That's done with." Mac sounded intolerably cheerful; much too cheerful, to Cody's way of thinking and under the circumstances.

"Thank you," Melissa said.

" 'Twas nothing, Mellie m'dear."

"It wasn't nothing, Mac. I couldn't believe the way you just seemed to nudge Howard and he left with you. When he gets mad like that, he never gives up. He'll go on and on and on forever. He's like a barnacle on a rock."

Apt comparison, thought Cody. He'd thought much the same thing himself. "I think Mac's right," he said suddenly, surprising himself. "I don't think you should go back to your husband, ma'am. Not ever. Not even when you're feeling fit. I—er—well, I know it's not my place to say it or anything, but I think you can do better than him, ma'am."

He was sorry to see her bow her head, as if she was ashamed of herself. As if she had anything to be ashamed of! Cody wanted to hare out of the wagon yard, hunt Howard Wilmeth down, and shoot him dead.

"Of course Cody's right, Mellie," Mac said in a hearty voice. "You already knew that, don't you?"

"Yes, I suppose I did." She sounded totally defeated.

"Good, good." Mac reached into his pocket and took out the folded papers. Like a magician displaying a rabbit he'd just found in a hat, he snapped them and they unfolded. Cody stared, engrossed in the old man's art; he wondered if maybe Mac had worked in a magic show in the old country. "You're a smart lass, Mellie. My old granny used to say that it took a mighty good man to be better than no man at all."

Melissa stared at him, too. She apparently appreciated Mac's old granny's epigram, as well, because she laughed, and then seemed astonished that she'd done such a thing. "What are those, Mac?"

"Divorce papers," Mac said, as if divorce papers were of no more consequence than supper.

Melissa's eyes opened up until they were as round as the orange she'd consumed for her breakfast. "Divorce!" She sounded shocked.

"Divorce?" Cody not only sounded shocked; he *was* shocked. He'd never known a divorced person in his whole entire life. Not any that he knew about, at any rate. People didn't talk about such things. "You keep divorce papers here? In your wagon yard?"

Mac hitched his shoulders and grinned. "Why not? My old wagon yard serves abundant purposes in Rio Hondo, laddie. If ye'll take an old codger's advice, Mellie, m'dear, ye'll think hard on the subject."

"Divorce." Melissa's voice had dropped to a whisper.

"Divorce." Cody, on the other hand, had begun to see past the shock to the benefits divorce might afford Melissa. "Yeah. Think about it now, while the memory of his leavin' you on the desert all by yourself is still clear in your mind."

Melissa and Mac both looked at him, and Cody was embarrassed. "Well, it wasn't a very nice thing to do," he muttered.

"It was a wicked thing to do," agreed Mac.

Melissa was silent for a few seconds, then said, "Yes. Yes, it was. It was wicked. And it was just like Howard."

"Aye, I expect it was. If, after ye think on the matter, ye decide to file for divorce, it might be best if ye fill out the papers and and file 'em today, before you lose your nerve."

"File 'em today?" Cody felt an itch of irritation. "How the he—hoot's she going to file 'em today, Mac? This is Rio Hondo, not New York City. She's going to have to wait until the circuit judge comes back to town. 'Less the Indians get him first."

Mac's benign smile warned him that the old man had something else up his sleeve. Cody drew in a breath and held it, waiting for whatever revelation was forthcoming.

"The circuit judge, Henry Calloway, is in town right this very minute, you know."

"No," Melissa said. "I didn't know that."

Mac nodded gravely, but his eyes twinkled like diamonds. "Well, he is, and ye'll be doin' yourself a favor by filin' them things with him while he's here."

Cody's breath left him in a whoosh. "What's Calloway doing here? Hell, he was just in Rio Hondo a month ago. He's not supposed to be back until the spring." His eyes narrowed as he looked at Mac. This was all a shade too convenient in Cody's estimation, although he could think of no explanation other than coincidence to account for it. Cody didn't much believe in coincidence.

Mac shrugged again, and adopted the most innocent expression Cody had ever seen on a man's face. He squinted his eyes up tighter and tried to think. Unfortunately, nothing he thought of made any sense.

"But, Mr. McMurdo, won't people think worse of me if I divorce Howard? Divorce seems like such a— wrong thing to do."

Melissa's question was so soft and sounded so sad, Cody stopped squinting at the old Scotsman, and transferred his attention to her. He wished he dared hold her hand again, but he didn't.

"Ah, Mellie," said Mac in his gentlest, jolliest voice. "Nobody here will ever think ill of you, because you're you, dearie. We're all allowed to make a mistake or two in life, especially out here. Ye'd be surprised at what some of the folks in the neighborhood get themselves up to."

Melissa smiled at him. Cody wished she'd smile at him like that.

"Do you really mean it, Mac?"

"Of course, I do," Mac said.

"Folks won't hate me because I'm a divorcee?"

"Pshaw. Not at all."

"Well . . ."

Cody could see from the expression on her face that she was contemplating life without Howard Wilmeth with a certain degree of favor. He wished he dared butt in, but he didn't think it was his place to encourage her.

Mac said, "I don't want to hurt your feelings, Mellie, but Howard Wilmeth isn't a good man." Because she looked so miserable, he added gently, "You already knew that, didn't you, Mellie m'dear? You know it better than any of us, in fact."

Cody saw Melissa's lips tremble. She pinched them together hard to keep herself from crying and nodded. His heart gave a tremendous spasm. Lord on high, he wanted to help her more than he'd ever wanted anything in his life.

"All right. I'll do it." It looked to Cody as if it took all the strength in her body to say it.

Mac smiled tenderly down at her. "You're doin' the right thing, Mellie girl. It'll be the best for you and for your darlin' Katie. You know that, don't you?"

The old man touched Melissa's shoulder, and Cody saw those blasted sparkles puff up again like a cloud of glittering smoke, as his hand lay there. He shook his head. It must have something to do with the light in the room, and the dust. It was real dusty in Rio Hondo. Either that or his eyes were shot. He'd never had trouble with his eyes before. Maybe the harsh sunshine out here in the territory had burned them or something.

"I—I guess it is for the best," Melissa murmured. A little more strongly, she said, "Yes. You're right. Howard will never settle down and be a good provider and father to Katie. I've known it for a long time, I guess. Yes, I know it's for the best, even though the idea of divorce is so—so . . ." Her words trickled out and died.

"I know, Mellie. Most folks frown on divorce. But the law wouldn't have been enacted if people didn't need it."

"I suppose not. It's just so . . ." Again, she failed to find the right words and her voice faded.

"Most folks find divorce a shocking business," Mac said matter-of-factly. "I believe ye'll find that out here in the Territory, folks tend to be more practical than critical, however. There's many a fellow come out here to build a new life, leavin' the old one behind him in ashes. I don't see why a lady should be any different."

"So you think it would be practical for me to divorce Howard, then?" She looked up at the old man, and Cody showered Mac with silent blessings for making so scandalous a thing as divorce sound merely reasonable.

"Absolutely," Mac said with one of his innocent grins.

"And I wouldn't be"—she licked her lips—"bad for doing it?"

"Bad?" Mac chuckled. "Sweet Mellie, I don't think you could be bad if you tried for a hundred years."

She couldn't seem to look at him. Cody saw that she blushed, and thought it was endearing. "Thank you, Mac."

"You know you'll be better off without him, m'dear. And raisin' little Katie here with a nasty bit o' goods like your husband wouldn't be doin' her any favors. She's got to be your main concern from now on."

"Yes," she whispered. "I know you're right. Howard—well, I guess I was awfully foolish to marry Howard."

Her knuckles whitened as she gripped the blanket. Cody couldn't recall witnessing such pain and shame in a woman's demeanor before. Damn.

"You weren't bein' foolish, Mellie," Mac said, patting her shoulder. There were no sparkles this time. "You were tryin' to find a way out of a hard life. Sometimes folks have to do things they don't much want to do in order to escape."

Her head snapped up. "How did you . . ."

But Mac pressed a finger to her lips. "Ah, Mellie, I

know all sorts of things." He chuckled again. "Just ask our Cody here."

Cody frowned. How the hell *did* Mac know Melissa had been trying to escape from a hard life? Escape from what kind of hard life? He realized Melissa was looking at him, a question in her pretty blue eyes. He tried to stop frowning and didn't quite succeed. "Yeah," he said. "Mac knows all sorts of things, all right."

Mac's chuckle swelled to a laugh. "Right-o. And our Cody here is just the man to help you fill out them papers, too, Mellie." He winked at Cody, but continued talking to Melissa. "And if you want to know what a good man looks like, ye don't need to look any farther than Cody, either." He slapped Cody on the back so hard his shoulder blade stung. "He's the best one I know out here."

"Yes. Yes, he is." Melissa's delicate voice held conviction.

"He's my cousin."

Cody, whose face suddenly felt as hot as a live coal, had forgotten Arnold was even in the room with them. He looked down at him now, and found him smiling sadly up at him, utter conviction in his big brown cow's eyes. Arnold clutched Loretta's wire to his bosom, and Cody remembered why Melissa was going to be working for him.

That same afternoon, Arnold headed back to the ranch to pack for his trip and warn their hired hand, Luis, that a lady would be coming to keep house and cook in Arnold's absence. Cody decided Melissa could use Arnold's room. It was plenty big enough for a woman and a baby. He aimed to return to the ranch himself tomorrow and prepare the room for its new occupants.

When Arnold got back to Rio Hondo—with or without Loretta—they could think about adding rooms onto their house. Or building another one entirely. Cody didn't want to contemplate life so far in the future, but there was plenty of room for two houses on the property. He also didn't want to contemplate why, when he did give a thought to the future, his future always seemed to include Melissa Wilmeth. He chalked it up to a temporary aberration and let it go at that.

Although he'd been as nervous as a rabbit in a coyote's den at first, after he and Melissa had stumbled through the legal wording on the divorce papers for an hour or more, they had become almost easy with each other. There was nothing like trying to fathom legal jargon for taking the shy out of a man.

He still felt like ripping off his clothes and burrowing under the covers with her, but he knew he could suppress his desire. Hell, Cody O'Fannin was no damned Howard Wilmeth to take advantage of a woman's weakness. Melissa didn't seem so shy around him any longer, and that was a good thing.

"Do you suppose he has intuitive powers?"

Cody didn't need to ask who *he* was. "Intuitive powers?" He lifted an eyebrow and grinned at her.

She had been studying her baby's fingers, but his question brought her head up. "Well, you know. He always seems to know things before they happen."

Cody stopped grinning. "Yeah. He does that, all right."

"And he got Howard to leave without even shouting at him. I've never known Howard to do anything he didn't want to do before. Not without an argument, anyway."

"Yeah, he did that, too." Cody still couldn't figure it out, either.

"Maybe he's really strong?"

He looked down at her. She didn't appear to be any more convinced than she sounded. He shrugged. "Beats me."

Her sigh was huge, and it lifted the papers on her lap when she let it out. They fluttered back into place. Melissa's big sigh and those papers gave Cody a light hearted feeling he couldn't account for.

Baby Katie slept like a tiny, soft toy doll beside her mother. Now that Katie was a couple of days old, Cody was kind of getting used to her. He couldn't fathom why people always gushed over babies, though. Shoot, his ma and aunts and girl cousins and sisters used to about drive him and his brothers and boy cousins distracted going on and on about whatever lady's baby was the latest to be born in Georgetown. Cody couldn't understand it, although he guessed he could comprehend the attachment a mother must feel for one of the ugly little things. After all, if you had to go through that much pain for something, you'd sure as the devil better be attached to it, or the human race was done for.

"Do you think we did these right?" he asked, to divert his mind from its profitless wanderings.

"I hope so."

The smile she offered him hinted at humor and mischief, and made that catch in his chest start up again. Lordy, he wanted to help her; to undo the harm her husband had done. He hoped he could fatten her up some when she came to his place to work. There was lots of work to do on a ranch, true; but Cody knew there'd be enough food there, too, and people to help her with the hard chores. He'd take bets that Melissa Wilmeth hadn't eaten a square meal in much too long. And he'd also take bets that

Howard Wilmeth was about as helpful as a garden slug.

Damn that husband of hers. The man ought to be shot for bringing her out here when he didn't know what he was getting in to.

Cody deliberately relaxed his hands, which had tightened into fists. Every time he thought about Howard Wilmeth, he felt like punching something. Preferably Howard Wilmeth.

Henry Calloway visited Melissa Wilmeth that evening, and looked over the divorce papers she and Cody had prepared. For the first time since Katie's coming, Melissa got out of bed and dressed herself. Her clothes, which she'd worried would be too tight for her, hung loose. She seemed appalled by how skinny she'd become; Cody knew he was.

Most of the women Cody'd known in Georgetown who'd given birth had been chubby afterwards. Of course, those women had possessed husbands who cared about them. Melissa's past few months under the tender mercies of Howard Wilmeth must have been even rougher than Cody had guessed—and he'd guessed they'd been plenty rough. He steadied Melissa with a hand on her elbow, helped her out to a chair in front of Mac's potbellied stove, and tried not to show how her frail state of health worried him.

The circuit judge complimented Melissa and Cody on how well they'd done in filling out the papers. He didn't have to change hardly anything. He smiled as Melissa signed on the appropriate line. Cody was pretty sure nobody but he noticed the tears in Melissa's eyes when she handed pen and paper back to Judge Calloway. Maybe Mac noticed; Cody had a feeling not much escaped the jolly old Scotsman.

Cody slept that night on his bedroll, under the

stars, in one of the stalls Mac kept ready for visitors to his wagon yard. He felt good. He'd return to Mac's place in two weeks with a wagon, and carry Melissa and Katie back home with him. Mac had said she'd be ready by then; Cody trusted his medical skill.

The idea of establishing Melissa in his home sounded right to Cody. He stared up into the glittering heavens with lightness in his soul.

Chapter Five

Melissa didn't know where to look first. She wanted to take in everything at once but only had one set of eyes. For the most part, she kept her gaze glued to baby Katie and the adorable little puppy curled up between Melissa and Cody, but occasionally she turned on the wagon seat to stare at the cunningly carved cradle with which Mac had gifted Katie that morning, before Melissa and Cody set out.

"Must've been some family left it behind on their way west," Mac had said, twinkling at her like an elf.

Cody had stood there, scratching his head and staring at the pretty hardwood cradle, looking handsome and big and solid. To Melissa, Cody's solidity represented a glimpse of something for which she'd always longed, and with which she was unfamiliar: security.

"Some family just up and left it, huh?" Cody sounded skeptical.

"Sure," said Mac.

"You suppose they forget to take it with them, or what?"

The canny old Scot had only shrugged and twinkled some more.

Melissa, more weepy than she could ever remember being in her life—Mac told her it was because her body was adjusting to having given Katie life—had pressed her lips together and refused to cry. The cradle was the most beautiful piece of furniture she'd ever seen, however, and it was a hard task she'd set for herself. She must have run her fingers over the fine, smooth maple finish for fifteen solid minutes, trying not to blubber the whole time.

By the time Cody had pulled into Mac's yard with his wagon, drawn by two sturdy mules, to pick her up, Mac had managed to find the cradle, four flannel baby blankets, several pieces of yardage suitable for baby dresses, her dresses, and work shirts, a lilac bush in a washtub that he said she'd have to pamper until spring, when she could set it in the ground outside, some real gauze diapers, five oranges, some lanolin to keep her hands and Katie's bottom soft, two frocks that fit her, some yarn in various colors, and a puppy. Melissa wondered at the man's resourcefulness. Sometimes she was convinced that the man could truly work miracles.

Her situation in life, particularly now as she contemplated shedding her husband, confirmed her opinion of herself as unworthy. Mac and Cody behaved as though they disagreed with her selfassessment, and their behavior unsettled her, disrupted her notions of how the world worked and how the people in it thought and acted.

She was unused to receiving kindness. The kindness of these two men made her alternately ecstatic and uncomfortable. She wasn't accustomed to good things happening to her—unasked-for, free, and out of the blue—and waited nervously for the ax to fall.

From the small mercantile store Mac ran in conjunction with his wagon yard, Cody had picked up more supplies. Melissa felt guilty that he had to lay in such things as oatmeal and cans of condensed milk, but he said he'd need those items anyway.

"Don't worry about any of these things, ma'am," he told her. "I'd have to lay in a supply of 'em anyway." She tried unsuccessfully to take his advice.

Howard, of course, had not returned to visit her in the two weeks she'd recuperated at Mac's Wagon Yard; nor had he sent any money by which Melissa could repay Mac for his generosity and her keep. She was ashamed of Howard; she was ashamed of herself. She silently vowed that she'd pay these good men back someday, somehow.

Now, as the wagon crunched along over the dry, rutted road out of Rio Hondo, whenever she turned to cast another wondering look at the cradle or to steady the lilac tub, her eye caught a glimpse of the incredible landscape, and she wanted to stare at it, too. Or the sky.

The sky was bigger than anything Melissa had imagined before she'd come out to the Territory. Today it was the blue of Alexander McMurdo's eyes. Piles of clouds, pushed by a strong wind, scudded across it like ships under sail.

Until she'd headed west, she'd never thought about sky. She couldn't help but think about it now, because there was so much of it. It was as if the heavens were expanding. She fancied that they were growing and growing and would one day soon swallow up the paltry earth beneath them—and all the paltry beings who scurried around on it, trying to be important.

Compared to this impressive sky, nothing on this whole earth seemed important.

She felt tiny underneath the sky and surrounded by the vastness of the plains; like a speck of dust. Although it made no sense to her, the notion gave her comfort. Somehow her own problems shrank in significance when she compared their size to that of those incredible plains. She could imagine other people disliking the feeling.

She knew for a fact that Howard didn't like considering his own stature in comparison to the immense landscape; he'd said so. Said it made him feel puny. Melissa smiled grimly. Howard *was* puny; a small-minded man with a small, scabby heart.

As for herself, she loved the feeling of being out here, a tiny dot in the middle of all this extraordinary space. She wanted to stand on the flat earth, hold her hands straight out at her sides, close her eyes, and spin around and around until the cosmos picked her up and swept her away, or she disappeared into them.

"I've never seen anything like this country," she said, not for the first time.

Cody flicked his whip and grinned, and Melissa's heart fluttered up like autumn leaves in a gust.

"Don't expect you have. It's pretty big and flat out here, I reckon."

"Yes." She wasn't sure she should confess to the overwhelming sense of awe devouring her. He'd probably think she was foolish—and he'd probably be right.

The land was flat, all right, except where it swelled gently into small hills. Those swells were the only hint of gentleness she could detect anywhere. This wasn't a place for the faint of heart. Melissa couldn't account for why she liked it so well. She guessed it was because she was used to the suffocating, soot-covered walls, teeming streets, filthy gutters, and poverty of her home in Boston.

And the air! Melissa kept taking deep breaths, trying to get used to it. There had been days in Boston when the stench from the fish-processing plants and coal smoke was all Melissa thought she'd ever smell for the rest of her life. The air out here was so clean it almost hurt her lungs. She wondered if someday—if she was allowed to remain here long enough—she'd forget the rotten stink that still lingered in the back of her mind. Sometimes she thought it was that stink that marked her life and branded her for what she was.

Until now.

Melissa dared to wonder—only to herself, because the idea was new and tender enough to be blasted into oblivion by a harsh word—if she might become the woman she wanted to be here, in this grand, clean place.

There was plenty of dust and dirt here, too, but it was different from what she recalled of Boston. This wasn't the filth of too many people in too small a space, of too many gutted fish and too much blood, too little money, too little food, too little hope, and too much despair. Out here, the dust came from wind whipping across the hard, untamed frontier.

She noticed an odd, short, shelflike hill that appeared to stretch for miles and miles across the plains in the distance. "What's that?" she asked, pointing.

"Some folks out here call that the Mescalero Ridge. After the Indians. Other folks call it the cap-rock."

"Which do you call it?"

Cody shrugged. "I don't call it much of anything. I just like to look at it."

He smiled, and Melissa's heart turned over when she realized he loved this land as much as she did. And he'd lived on it for long enough to learn to hate it if it was hateful beneath its pitiless suggestion of promise. His appreciation made her feel closer to him and less foolish for harboring her own dreams.

In truth, she guessed many people might consider this an ugly place, with its barrenness and open space. To her it looked like an offering of hope. She might never be happy, but she had a feeling that if contentment lurked somewhere in her future, she'd find it here.

No matter where she looked, she didn't see a speck of green. There were a very few stumpy, straggly trees, but they'd lost their leaves, if they'd ever had any, and were as bare as old bones under the sun's cold, fierce rays. The first thing she needed to do, after she settled in at Cody's ranch, was sew her daughter a sunbonnet so her darling little baldish head wouldn't get burned. She bent and kissed Katie's cheek, which was as soft as new bread dough.

A thin flash of brown on the desert floor caught the edge of her attention, and she swiveled her head to stare at the ground. She squinted and searched in all directions but didn't see anything that might account for the impression of flying dirt she'd had. Then it happened again, again too quickly for her to focus on it.

"My goodness," she muttered aloud, puzzled and faintly peeved.

"Hmm?"

The deep grumble of Cody's voice sent a shock of awareness through her, as it always did. Melissa knew she was a wicked woman for harboring improper feelings for a man who wasn't her husband, but she wasn't surprised at herself. She'd known she was bad since she was old enough to know anything. For her daughter's sake, for her own sake, and for Cody's sake, she'd never let on that she was infatuated with him. Such an infatuation was just like her, though. The thought depressed her for an instant before she ruthlessly banished it. This was a new beginning for her; she wouldn't let her old life—or the woman she had been until now—spoil it.

"I keep thinking I see little puffs of dirt on the ground, but I can't find anything when I look."

"Oh."

When she glanced at him, he was grinning again. "Am I imagining things?"

"No, ma'am."

There was even a smile in Cody's voice, and Melissa sprouted gooseflesh in reaction. Good heavens, she was perfectly abandoned! Her mother had warned her how she was; Melissa, who hadn't gotten along well with her mother, wasn't happy to know her mother had been right.

She realized Cody was drawing the mules up. She thrust her shortcomings aside and looked at him in question.

"This is prairie-dog country, ma'am. I think what you're seeing are the little critters digging their homes."

"Oh." What in heaven's name was a prairie dog? Melissa imagined the kinds of dogs she used to see scrounging through garbage heaps back home and thought Cody must be wrong, because they were ever so much bigger than any animal that could have made that tiny spray of dirt. She'd never say so.

Unless . . . She cast a glimpse at the puppy McMurdo had gifted her with—for the baby, he'd said.

Was the pup a prairie dog? It looked kind of like a hound to her, although her knowledge about the various breeds of dog might conceivably fill a very small thimble.

"Yeah. That's what it is, all right. Look over there, Mrs. Wilmeth."

Melissa gave up on the puppy, followed the direction of Cody's leather-gloved finger, and saw another small shower of dirt. Now that she knew where to look, she realized the spray of earth landed on a little pile of freshly dug soil. As she watched, holding her breath in anticipation, she saw a very small rodent, the same dun color as the surrounding plains, emerge from the hole and look around, its movements sharp and quick. Then it dove back into its hole in the ground and flung out another spray of dirt.

"For heaven's sake, I've never seen anything like it." Hugging Katie, Melissa laughed out loud at the prairie dog.

"They can be a real nuisance," Cody told her, although he laughed, too. "They dig everywhere, and horses are apt to step in the holes and bust their legs."

"My goodness." She sobered. It seemed inconsistent of nature to have sent such a charming creature as a prairie dog out here to confound folks into thinking the land wasn't as perilous as it looked. It was the sort of inconsistency Howard would like, the kind that caught a person off guard and left him off balance. Melissa tried not to think about Howard. He didn't belong here. If God had decided to smile on her this once, she did.

"There's probably an owl hole or two around here, too."

"An owl hole?"

"Yeah. Burrowing owls live out here, too."

She lost her worries in surprise. "*Burrowing* owls? You mean, they dig holes in the ground and live in them? Good heavens, I thought owls lived in trees or—or in barns."

He chuckled. The sound of his uncomplicated amusement made Melissa tingle all over. She wasn't used to such lack of guile in people. Howard was as sly as a fox; he prided himself on the quality, in fact.

Not Cody O'Fannin. Cody O'Fannin was the way Melissa wished she could be: open, honest, trust-worthy, and not fettered by the legacy of a grinding, grasping, pinching, pitiful childhood.

"I expect there are plenty of owls in trees back east, ma'am, and in barns. Out here, there aren't any trees to speak of, and only a few of us have built barns. Out here the owls live in the ground."

"My goodness." When she'd first glimpsed this land, Melissa had been too sick at heart and of body to take any interest in it.

Now she felt a swell of love for the endless land-scape surrounding Cody's small, inconsequential wagon. The land looked altogether lifeless, yet there were prairie dogs on it. And owls. *Burrowing* owls. Melissa felt like laughing again but didn't want Cody to think she was demented.

He scanned the landscape. When he did that, his eyes narrowed, and Melissa saw lines at their edges. She figured the sun had leathered his skin to create those lines. Cody wasn't soft and cunning like How-ard. Cody was tough and honest, like this territory. His toughness wasn't akin to that of the blacklegs and hoodlums she'd known in Boston; his was the sort one associated with ambition, hard work, and achievement.

She sighed, wishing she deserved a man like Cody

O'Fannin. She didn't, of course. She deserved the Howard Wilmeths of the world, especially now that she was going to be a divorced woman.

Cody, fortunately, couldn't read her thoughts. He pointed in another direction. "Look over there, Mrs. Wilmeth. There's a herd of antelope."

She looked. Sure enough, after a moment of searching the endlessly beige landscape, she saw them. They looked as graceful and delicate as anything she'd ever seen. Another incongruity.

"How beautiful." Her exclamation nudged the puppy into wakefulness, and Melissa petted it absently. "How wonderful." She felt foolish when tears pooled in her eyes. She turned her head so Cody wouldn't see them.

"I love those animals," he said softly. "I love this country. Some folks don't like it, but I reckon I'm used to it. Or something."

Sucking in a deep breath and praying she wouldn't whimper and humiliate herself, Melissa said, "I'm not used to it, and I like it a lot, Mr. O'Fannin."

"You do?" She knew he'd turned to look at her, but she didn't dare meet his gaze since her emotions were so turbulent.

"Oh, yes. It's so big. It's a grand land. And it's—well, it's unspoiled, I guess is the word I'm looking for."

"Yeah," he said thoughtfully. "It's unspoiled, all right."

"And—and it's so—I don't know. Strange. It seems so hard, yet it's home to prairie dogs and those beautiful, graceful antelope."

Cody chuckled, and Melissa got the feeling he understood just fine.

A strange sound captured her attention, and she looked into the sky from whence it came. A flock of birds was passing overhead. They were big birds; geese, perhaps. They were beautiful, too, solid dark shadows against the puffy clouds. Their wings caught the sunlight and for a second they flashed like silver. The sight made her breath catch.

As she watched, fascinated, the lead bird dropped back from the point and another bird took its place, as if it were as natural a thing to do as flight itself, which it probably was. Melissa marveled at the nature of things and at the cooperation inherent in geese, or whatever those birds were, as opposed to people.

The people she'd known in her life weren't nearly so willing to trust or to help each other as those birds seemed to be. Of course, the people she'd known in Boston weren't like Cody O'Fannin or Alexander Mc-Murdo or Arnold Carver. The people she'd known there were like Howard Wilmeth.

Another ragged *V* of birds caught up to the first one, and the flocks melded together, until they had blended into one long, lopsided checkmark in the sky. A soft exclamation left Melissa's lips and surprised her.

"You like them?"

She turned quickly and found Cody watching the birds, too, a smile on his face. Her heart skipped. "Oh, yes. I love them. They're beautiful."

Cody gently slapped the reins and the mules began walking again. He kept eying the birds and smiling. "Sandhill cranes. They fly over to the bitter lake in the evening and nest there overnight. In the morning, they'll fly back the other way again. Reckon they find some kind of grain or seeds on the plains. You only see 'em in November and early December. By Christmas, they'll have headed south."

"Oh. I wonder how they know the way."

Cody shrugged and kept smiling. "I've often wondered that myself, ma'am."

Marveling at the sagacity of birds, who knew where to go and what to do even without words, Melissa whispered, "This is so different from what I'm used to." She and Howard hadn't known where to go—or what to do when they got there. Nature was an astonishing thing.

After a second, Cody said, "Reckon it is, ma'am. Hope you'll get used to it."

"Oh, I'm sure I shall," said Melissa. And she was.

The first clue Melissa had to the existence of a habitation on the spreading plains was the windmill. It stood stark and almost impossibly small, a shadowy skeleton, a dark-brown wooden toy against the hugeness of the emptiness surrounding it. Melissa blinked, unsure it was real—and promptly lost sight of it. She searched and searched before she spotted it again. Everything even remotely connected to humanity seemed so *tiny* compared to God's handiwork. She wasn't accustomed to it at all, but she found herself smiling.

Sensing a lightness in her traveling companion's mood, she slanted Cody a glance. Sure enough, his lips had curled into a very small grin, more of an expression of satisfaction than a full-fledged smile.

Melissa cleared her throat, which felt dry. They hadn't spoken for forty-five minutes or more. "Is that your place?"

"That's it."

He sounded well pleased about it. She didn't wonder at that. Cody and his cousin had made something out of nothing out here in this wilderness, and Melissa was impressed. She'd never known anyone who'd accomplished anything worthwhile before.

She licked her lips. "I'm looking forward to seeing it."

He turned his head her way quickly, and just as quickly looked away again. "It's not much, ma'am. It's just a bachelor establishment." As if he feared she might find fault with his home, he hurried on. "That is to say, it's not fancy or anything. Me and Arnold, well, we built ourselves a one-room cabin at first, but we've been adding onto it, you know, 'cause we were getting ready for Arnold to marry Loretta Pine and bring her out here."

"I see." Melissa pressed her lips together because she feared her smile would make Cody think she was laughing at him.

"I 'spect it might look pretty paltry to you, ma'am."

"Oh, I doubt that."

"Well, we don't have much wood out here, you know."

Melissa's gaze swept the plains again, and she nodded. "Yes." There wasn't a tree in sight, barring a couple of scrawny mesquites.

"The ground here is real thick. It's easy to make bricks out of it, if you add straw and water. The house is made of those bricks. Adobe, the Mexicans call it."

"I see."

"Our cabin sits by the river, ma'am, on a rise. Me and Arnold, we planted some willows and cotton-woods by the river. They're only a couple of years old yet, but they'll grow. Since the winds blow all the time, I planted some trees as a wind break. I expect it'll help one of these days. We brought us down some oaks and piñons, too, out of the mountains, but they're small yet. Don't know if the piñons will make it out here on the desert."

"I expect they'll grow, too," said Melissa, and the

words gave her a great sense of joy. They'd grow, and Katie would grow, and maybe, if Melissa and her daughter were very, very lucky, they'd set down roots, just like those trees were doing. Melissa thought it would be a fine thing to have roots in this incredible place.

"Yeah."

They rode along in silence for several minutes.

"Arnold and me, we planted us a garden."

"A garden?"

"Yeah. Don't grow much. You know, just onions and cabbages and carrots and such. For food, you know."

"Yes." Melissa cocked her head to one side. Her mother had tended a tiny patch of garden in Boston. They'd had onions, too, and cabbages.

"There's lots of minerals in the soil and it's not good for growing very many things," Cody went on. "But we have a ton of cow manure to mix in it."

"I expect you do."

He nodded and cleared his throat. "Yeah, that cow manure, it helps a lot."

"I'm sure it does."

"And Mac, he gets stuff in from back East sometimes. Peat moss and phosphate, or something like that."

"I see."

"Yes'm. I think Arnie planted some turnips, too."

"I'll be happy to tend a garden."

"Good. That's good. We put up a stake fence around it to try to keep the critters out."

Cody leaned over and feathered the reins over the mules' backs, which didn't seem to interest the mules much. Their pace didn't alter. Melissa judged the gesture to be one of nervousness rather than necessity.

Suddenly the job in front of her seemed daunting. Oh, she could sweep and scrub and cook, but what did she know about life on the frontier? Her heart pulsed painfully. She wanted so much to fit into Cody O'Fannin's life. If she had to work as his housekeeper for the rest of her life, it would be a far better fate than she'd any right to expect. Until a little over two weeks ago, she'd expected to have to be Howard Wilmeth's wife for however long her life lasted—and she hadn't expected it to last long, since Howard had the keeping of it. She suppressed a shudder at the thought.

"I'll do my very best to be a good housekeeper for you, Mr. O'Fannin." She licked her lips again. "I, ah, may not be used to the way you do things out here. I expect I'll have to learn."

His sudden grin took her by surprise and made her feel less frightened. "I expect so." He chirped to the mules. "Life's real different out here, ma'am, no matter where you're from. But the Mexicans and the Indians seem to have the hang of it. I expect Luis can show you the ropes. He's a good hand at the garden."

Mexicans and Indians. Those words, which Melissa suspected were meant to ease her worries, didn't. Scraps of information she'd gleaned from the newspapers Mrs. Bowlus, the woman for whom she used to cook and clean, had allowed her to read, caromed into her head like marauding beasts. She cleared her throat.

"Um, I—well, um, do you ever have any trouble with Indians out here, Mr. O'Fannin?" Melissa scanned the countryside. That windmill looked awfully small and incredibly isolated. As yet, she hadn't been able to discern another single structure that might in any way be connected with human habitation. Or a tame animal or another person, either.

If a band of warriors did decide to swoop down and scalp them all, Melissa couldn't perceive of any way she and Cody O'Fannin could stop them.

"Trouble?" Cody peeked at her from out of the corner of his eye. "Naw. Don't you worry about Indians, ma'am."

"No? Um, do you mean there aren't any Indians out here?" Melissa didn't believe it, and her heart ached when she thought Cody had lied to her.

"Oh, sure, there are Indians. Comanches and Apaches."

Comanches and Apaches? Melissa clutched little Katie more tightly and gripped the seat of the wagon so she wouldn't fall off in a swoon. *Comanches and Apaches?* Good heavens, from everything she'd read, Comanches and Apaches were the two most savage varieties of a savage race. She swallowed hard and tried to figure out a way to phrase her next question without sounding hysterical.

Cody seemed to understand. Before Melissa could unscramble her wits enough to formulate a coherent sentence, he said, "Most of the Apaches have been rounded up and sent to the Bosque Redondo, ma'am. That's near Fort Sumner, where Chisum sells his beef. Chisum's got the government contract, you see. We pretty much have to run our herds up to Santa Fe, except what we can sell to him or to stores and such."

She cleared her throat. "Oh?"

"Yeah. There are a few Apache bands still living in the area. And some Comanch. But they're having a pretty hard time of it, what with the war bein' over and the army bein' sent out here to wipe 'em out. Arnie and me, well, even before we came out here, we decided we didn't want any trouble with the Indians."

That was a relief. However, even if Cody and Arnold didn't choose trouble, how did they keep the Indians from causing it? Melissa'd heard they were a ferocious lot, Indians. Since she didn't quite know how to ask, she kept her mouth shut.

"A lot of the Indians' food has been wiped out by us whites, Mrs. Wilmeth. Arnie and me, well, we figured that if we set aside a certain number of beeves for the Indians, we'd save 'em the trouble of stealin' from us and make friends at the same time."

Melissa turned her head and stared at Cody's strong profile. "You let them have your cattle? For free?"

Cody cocked his head to one side. "I don't know as I think of it as bein' free, ma'am. It's kinda more like we're paying 'em rent."

He smiled at her, and Melissa felt her heart do that strange catching thing in her chest again. She stared into his beautiful brown eyes and managed to choke out, "I see."

Cody seemed to have trouble tearing his gaze away from hers. "In fact," he continued after a moment, "there's this Comanch we know called Running Standing who helped Arnie and me set up our smokehouse a couple of years back."

"Running Standing?" Merciful heavens, that was his name? Life was *so* different out here. Melissa thought she was glad of it, although the idea of fraternizing with a Comanche Indian named Running Standing gave her a funny pitching sensation in her stomach.

"Yeah. He showed us how to fix up the mesquite wood to smoke and preserve our meat."

"I see."

"Yes, ma'am. It's pretty good, too, the smoked meat. Lasts real well through the winter." He sliced her another look. "Reckon I'd better tell you what's in store for you, Mrs. Wilmeth. I expect our ranch won't be what you're used to."

"No," said she. "I expect not." She was sure she didn't mean that in the same way he did. For her, it would be an improvement.

"Well, we got us plenty of meat. Arnie and me—well, I reckon it'll be Luis and me while Arnie's away—we can pretty much get fresh meat whenever we want it. We always slaughter a cow and hang it, although we use our cattle for income mainly. But we have chickens and a couple of pigs. And there are generally plenty of rabbits and antelope around. The jackrabbits don't make awful good eating because they're so rangy, but they do in a pinch. There are prairie chickens, of course. Every now and then we'll even see a small herd of buffalo. They make pretty good eating, although there aren't near as many now as there used to be."

Buffalo! Melissa had read about buffalo, too—had even seen one at the zoological gardens in New York City once. She experienced a fierce, sudden longing to see a whole herd of them. She expected that if she could actually, really and truly, see a herd of free-roaming buffalo, she might believe she was living in the Wild West.

Joy filled her so unexpectedly that she almost laughed with it, and only caught herself in time. She couldn't imagine how she could explain her laughter to Cody O'Fannin, who had no way of knowing that until seven or eight months ago, Melissa had believed her fate lay in the grimy gutters of a squalid city slum.

"I put in supplies of canned goods from Mc-Murdo's. Running Standing showed us how to fix prickly pears to eat, too."

"Prickly pears? You mean the cactus?"

"Yup. They don't taste like much, but I reckon they're kinda like a green." Cody looked off into the distance. Melissa got the impression he felt uncomfortable. "My ma always made me eat my greens, ma'am. Said it was healthy. Reckon I try to do what she said, since she raised ten of us and we all made it."

"You have nine siblings, Mr. O'Fannin? And you all survived childhood?"

"Yes'm. Where we grew up isn't too much different than it is here, either. More trees, maybe. Well, a lot more trees, actually, because folks planted 'em years ago. But it's pretty much the same for all that."

"My goodness."

Melissa had never heard such a thing as a woman bearing ten children who lived through childhood and into adulthood. Children used to die of typhus and cholera and diphtheria and influenza and consumption all the time where she grew up. Dying had been as much a part of living as giving birth. There wasn't a mother she knew in her neighborhood who hadn't lost a child or a niece or a nephew to some ugly illness spawned by filth and want. Very few mothers expected to see their children live to adulthood; awareness of the perils made having babies a doubtful prospect. The married women Melissa'd known couldn't help it if they got pregnant, but most viewed the prospect as a precarious burden rather than a pleasure.

But *ten* children. All alive. She could hardly take it in.

She scanned the landscape again, a new respect for it growing in her bosom. The land was hard as rocks, but it was also clean and uncontaminated by civilization's waste and decay. "I'll try to remember your mother's advice, Mr. O'Fannin."

"Yes'm. I expect she knows what she's talkin' about when it comes to raisin' and feedin' folks."

"I'd say she does. Yes, indeed."

"Anyway, we got us lots of fresh meat and tinned fruit. We got us tinned peas, too, and a garden. We got lots and lots of dried beans, too, ma'am. I expect that's what most folks eat out here. Beans and salted meat or smoked meat. Lots of fish in the river, too."

"I see."

"The river runs close to the house, and Arnie and Luis set up a sort of irrigation system for the garden. We got us an inside pump next to the sink in the kitchen. It ain't fancy, ma'am, but it works."

"It sounds very nice, Mr. O'Fannin."

"Well, I expect it's not what you're used to, but it's pretty good for out here."

What she was used to was garbage, drunkenness, tribulation, suffering, and squalor. Melissa knew that anything she'd find at Cody O'Fannin's ranch would be far, far better than what she was used to. "I'm sure it will be fine," she said. "Just fine."

"What the hell do you mean she's not here?" Howard Wilmeth stood with his legs apart, his fists planted on his hips. He leaned toward Alexander McMurdo in a manner most folks would call aggressive, if not downright hostile.

Mac tilted his head to one side and contemplated how to explain his prior statement, which had been spoken in words simple enough for a child to understand. He decided not even to try. "She's gone to work on a fellow's ranch," he repeated in a voice as mild as a summer day.

"She's gone to work on a fellows *ranch?*" Wilmeth bellowed.

Mac nodded. He thought about smiling, but didn't suppose Howard Wilmeth would appreciate it.

"With the baby?"

Mac nodded again. He didn't bother to ask what Wilmeth thought Melissa had done with the baby, if he had to ask if she'd taken Katie with her. He noticed Wilmeth didn't refer to his child by her name; Mac wasn't surprised.

"Well, hell. I said I'd come back for her, dammit! How the hell could she just up and go to work on a fellow's ranch?"

"In a wagon, if I recall correctly." This time Mac smiled; he couldn't help it.

Wilmeth gave him a withering glare. "Don't try to be funny with me, old man. That woman's my wife, and she's got my daughter with her, and she's got no right to hare off with somebody else to work on his goddamned ranch!"

Mac's smile broadened and he shrugged. "Can't help you there, Mr. Wilmeth."

"When did she go?"

"Last week."

Wilmeth digested this information; it evidently gave him a stomachache, because his expression soured. "Who's ranch is she working on, dammit?"

"Cody O'Fannin and his cousin, Arnold Carver. They've got a spread out on the Hondo River, eight miles or so southeast of here."

"Damn. Are they the men who were with her the last time I came over here?"

"The same."

Wilmeth pointed a finger in Mac's face. "I don't like this, old man. I don't like it at all. She's got no right going off with other men. That woman is my wife, dammit."

Mac ignored Wilmeth's quivering finger. "So she said." *Poor thing.* He didn't say that part.

"I don't go along with people who help women run out on their husbands, old man, and I'm going to get her back."

"Mmmm."

Bored with Wilmeth's bluster, Mac walked past him and out through the door of his little house. He sucked in the tang of a crisp autumn morning and felt happy. It was good weather to begin in. He hoped Mellie and Cody would make the most of it, because they were both good people. Not like that fool in there. He squinted over his shoulder and discovered Howard Wilmeth stumping outside, too, looking furious enough to do violence.

Because it amused him, Mac flicked his finger. Wilmeth stumbled over his boots and fell on his face in the wagon yard. Dust puffed up around him, and he scrambled to his feet sputtering, spitting, and angrier than before. Mac chided himself for succumbing to the urge, but Wilmeth was such a deplorable example of the human male, he discovered he couldn't help himself. Another finger flick sent Wilmeth's hat flying off on a gust of wind.

"Goddamn son of a bitch!"

Mac grinned as Wilmeth chased his hat. He was wearing shiny new high-heeled boots, the old Scot noticed. Hmmm. The man hadn't bothered to send Melissa a cent with which to support herself or his daughter, but he'd managed to get himself a pair of new boots. "Cowboy" boots, the dudes called them.

That hat of his was new, too. It was a tinhorn's hat; the kind a fellow from back East would buy because he doesn't know any better. Mac figured Wilmeth'd had to go to El Paso or Albuquerque to buy a hat like that. Yet he hadn't found the time to visit his wife while she recuperated from having his baby. The old man shook his head, disgusted.

"Next time I see Melissa, I'll tell her you inquired after her."

Wilmeth snatched up his hat, which had come to rest, crown down, in a pile of fresh horse poop. He slapped the hat against the leg of his trousers. The trousers were new, too, Mac noticed.

"The hell you will. I'll tell her myself."

Mac shrugged. "As you wish."

Because Wilmeth was such a sorry excuse for a man, Mac made the wind blow dirt in his face. Before he'd wiped the grit out of his teeth and eyes, Mac made the wagon yard gate blow open and smack him in the butt. Wilmeth stumbled forward and fell down again.

Then Mac told himself to stop being childish, and he returned to his work.

Chapter Six

Melissa put the sweetly sleeping Katie into her beautiful new cradle, covered her with a pretty new flannel blanket, and pressed her fingers against the baby's tiny pink cheek. Katie had eaten, as greedily as any piglet, burped with absolute unconcern for polite manners, and fallen asleep with a bubble of milk on her lips.

Melissa hadn't believed it was possible for a person to love anything as much as she loved Katie. Mercy sakes, but her life had taken an amazing turn lately. As little as four weeks ago, she wouldn't have given a plug nickel for her chances of survival, much less enjoyment, out here on the huge buff-colored plains of the New Mexico Territory.

Not any longer. Now hope bubbled up inside of her, as irrepressible as soda mixed with vinegar.

She pressed a curved rocker with her foot, set the cradle to slowly rocking her baby, and took a moment to stare out the window and hug herself. She'd never, in her entire life up until now, ever, once, believed she'd be living in such luxury.

A whole house! She had a whole house, unattached to any other structure and unpopulated by any other family, in which to do all the things a woman did in her own home. Oh, Melissa knew this wasn't her house, but Cody O'Fannin was so amiable to her about it that he made her feel as though she actually belonged here.

"A week," she murmured to Katie, smiling. "We've been here a whole week, and he's been nice to me the whole time. He even compliments me on my cooking."

Cody's generosity of spirit astonished her almost more than this house of his, which consisted of four whole rooms. Luis lived in a tiny two-room adobe out by the corral, but he ate with Cody in the big kitchen in the main house. Melissa had been shy around Luis at first, but he was so amiable to her and so sweet to Katie that she no longer felt anything but friendship for him.

Luis liked to rock Katie in his arms after supper in the evenings while Melissa cleaned up. He sang soft songs in Spanish to her while Cody plucked out tunes on an old guitar. Melissa thought the music was a lovely accompaniment to her kitchen chores.

She'd never seen a man hold a baby on purpose before. The men she'd known in Boston had let the women take care of the children while they worked or drank. Until now, she would have thought there was something wrong with a man who actually seemed to *want* to hold a baby. But there was nothing wrong with Luis or Cody; Melissa knew it in her heart.

Melissa used to cook for Mrs. Bowlus. In fact,

she'd worked for the rich, disagreeable, tightfisted old lady for eleven years, from the time she was nine years old until she succumbed to Howard's sweet talk a year ago and married him.

Mrs. Bowlus had never trusted Melissa. Melissa knew she used to count the underwear in her bureau and the silverware in the pantry to make sure Melissa hadn't stolen anything. She used to resent it, but she also hardly blamed the hard-hearted old bat. People who came from where Melissa came from stole things; Melissa knew it, and she hated knowing it. She also swore to herself during her tenure with Mrs. Bowlus that she'd never sink to such abysmal behavior.

Her life with Mrs. Bowlus had taught her scads of recipes, though, and she appreciated them now. She knew them by heart, and every day in Cody O'Fannin's tidy little four-room adobe house in the middle of nowhere, she modified them, using the supplies available in her new home. It never occurred to her to deplore the absence of an ingredient. She adapted. Adapting had long ago become second nature to her.

With a big sigh, she turned away from the window, went into the kitchen, stirred her stew, and checked the oven to make sure her corn bread wasn't burning. It was almost noon. Any minute now, Cody and Luis would be returning to the house for dinner, and Melissa could hardly wait.

She knew this heaven couldn't last forever. Sooner or later, she'd have to deal with Howard. Right now, though, she didn't want to think about Howard or divorce or any of the ugliness she knew existed in her world. She wanted to enjoy this strange, new, comfortable life she was living, and pretend it could last.

The puppy whined at the kitchen door. Melissa had named him Perry because Luis said "dog" in Spanish was *perro.* Melissa adored that puppy. He was playful and charming and liked to sit at her feet while she sewed in the evenings. He also never messed on the floor, something Melissa appreciated more than she could say.

Laughing, she opened the door and pressed her hand to the wooden frame of the screen door Cody had rigged up to keep flies out. "Oh, Perry, you sweetheart. Have you been chasing prairie dogs?" She started to push the screen door open.

Perry looked up at her and wagged his tail.

Melissa blinked, sure she was hallucinating. As quick as a wink, she pulled the screen door shut with a slam, nicking poor Perry's foot. He leapt back with a yip of pain and peered up at her reproachfully.

"Perry! Oh, my goodness, *Perry!"*

Froth foamed from the puppy's mouth and dripped onto his front feet. He worked his mouth as if he was trying to spit out the foam, then shook his head, sending ribbons of froth flying.

Melissa latched the screen door and slammed the other door, a hand pressed to her hammering heart. *Oh, my God!*

Cody had warned her. He'd explained to her how it might be. Melissa wasn't scared of any illness but the one he'd so very carefully told her about. He said polecats carried it.

"Some folks call 'em skunks," he'd said in that slow, beautiful Texas drawl of his. "But they carry hydrophobia. If you ever seen one of 'em around the place, you just stay away from it and tell me, and I'll shoot it." He'd held up a hand as if to ward off a sympathetic outpouring from her on the hypothetical rabid skunk's behalf. Not that Melissa would ever question Cody O'Fannin about anything at all pertaining to life on the frontier. "I know it sounds cruel, ma'am, but there's no cure for hydrophobia, and it's mean on a body. Folks don't go easy when they get it. They go crazy and it's painful. It's best to shoot anything apt to be carryin' it."

Melissa had nodded, a little worried that some ferocious rabid skunk might swagger onto Cody's property and infect them all. She equated that mean, diseased skunk with Howard Wilmeth somehow. Then she'd gotten busy and forgotten all about Howard and skunks and hydrophobia. Until now.

For several seconds her heart felt like it was going to explode. When her initial panic settled into a more manageable terror, she wondered what to do. Although Cody had taken pains to explain how to use the rifle hanging over the fireplace in the front parlor, Melissa didn't quite dare get it down and shoot the dog. The very thought of murdering Perry brought tears to her eyes.

Deploring herself as a miserable coward and a weakling, she knew she'd have to let Cody or Luis do the awful deed. She couldn't shoot that dear little puppy.

She ran to the front door and almost fainted from relief when she saw Cody and Luis washing up at the wash trough next to the windmill tank. She ran outside.

"Mr. O'Fannin! Oh, please, come quickly! Something awful's happened!"

At her cry, Cody dropped the piece of soap he was holding, whirled around, and raced toward her, dripping wet. He'd taken his shirt off and didn't even pause to put it on again.

He ran up to her and grabbed her shoulders, looking scared to death. "What is it?" His voice was hard, desperate. "Oh, Lord, ma'am, is it Katie?"

Overwhelmed by the concern she read in his face, Melissa shook her head, her throat thick and aching. She forced herself to say, "No. Katie's fine. It's Perry. He's—" Suddenly the horror of the dog's plight hit Melissa hard. "Oh, Mr. O'Fannin, he's got hydrophobia!" She burst into tears of fright and sorrow.

Cody stared at her, dumbfounded. "Hydrophobia? But it's December."

He let go of her shoulders, and Melissa sagged in despair. She felt like a pure fool crying this way, but she couldn't help it. Perry was going to die.

December. She wiped her eyes on her apron and sniffled. "What—what does December have to do with it?"

Cody wiped his eyes, too—wet from water rather than tears—with his hands. "Well, ma'am, generally hydrophobia's more of a problem in the summer than in the fall."

"Oh." Wouldn't you know it? Her luck was so bad—or her influence so evil—that it had followed her all the way to the Territory and into December, and given that poor helpless animal a cruel, deadly disease out of season. "I'm sorry," she said, because she was, and she knew, somehow, that this was all her fault.

"Nothin' to be sorry about, Mrs. Wilmeth," said Cody, thus affirming him as the world's most wonderful, kind-hearted man. "Er, where's Perry now, ma'am?"

"Out back. I was going to let him in when I saw him foaming at the mouth."

Cody said, "Ahhh," and seemed to relax. Then he turned to look back over his shoulder. "Bring me my shirt, Luis."

"*Sí*, Cody."

Luis had stopped stock-still when Melissa burst out onto the porch. He'd stood like a statue, staring at Cody and Melissa in surprise, as they discussed hydrophobia. Now he shook himself out of his stupor, picked up Cody's shirt, and walked to the porch. His face registered his concern. Cody took the shirt and shrugged it on.

"I think this will be all right, Mrs. Wilmeth. Luis, will you go out back and check the garden? I think we might have us a dead toad."

A dead toad. Melissa didn't know what he was talking about. If toads carried hydrophobia, too, she thought Cody should have warned her, because she'd seen one or two in the garden after she'd been digging in it.

"Ah." Luis gave her a brilliant smile, as if what Cody had just said made all the sense in the world to him.

Melissa wiped her eyes again and wished she wasn't so ignorant about life in the Territory. December and dead toads? She feared she'd go distracted. Her heart still ached with the thought of poor Perry being shot. She swore she'd give him a proper funeral, no matter how silly it might seem to these men. She'd even pray over him. She wondered if that made her a sinner in God's eyes, and figured it wouldn't matter much. From all she'd gathered about God's grace up till now, she was already doomed to perdition.

"Um, I don't think I understand, Mr. O'Fannin." She went through the door Cody politely held open for her. "Do toads carry hydrophobia, too?"

He chuckled, and the sound of his amusement hit her awry. It seemed out of place; wrong in the face of what he apparently considered a minor tragedy. It wasn't minor to Melissa; it was a horrid, big, huge,

111

ugly tragedy. She'd never owned a dog before in her life. She loved Perry.

"No, ma'am. Toads don't carry hydrophobia. They're poison, though."

"Poison!" Good heavens. As much as she loved her new home, Melissa wondered if she'd ever learn to keep track of its multitude of dangers. Water hard enough to knock a body out, soil thick as bricks, rabid skunks, poison toads, Indians. What else? she wondered.

"Not bad poison. Not so's you could die from it, I reckon, but they've got some kind of stuff in their skin that makes them taste bad."

Melissa wrinkled her nose. Her life hadn't held many luxuries, but at least she'd never been driven to eat toads. She hoped she never would.

"You know how dogs are, ma'am," he continued.

No, actually, she didn't, never having met any dogs except the two lazy, overfed pugs owned by Mrs. Bowlus. She'd been fond of those pugs, though, and always wanted a dog of her own. She didn't honor Cody with this emptiness in her life. She gave forth with a wordless "Hmmm," and hoped it would suffice.

"They like to chase things," Cody elaborated.

"Yes. Yes, I've noticed that. Perry is always chasing jackrabbits and so forth."

"Yeah. Well, this time of year the toads hibernate, and they dig themselves holes in the ground."

"Oh." Melissa thought about it for a second. "I had to chase Perry out of the garden this morning because he was digging."

Cody chuckled again. "Figured that might be it. You probably disturbed a toad, and Perry was probably after it."

A glimmer of understanding began to flicker in

Melissa's brain. "Um, do you mean you think he might have caught a toad, Mr. O'Fannin?"

"Yup."

"And that the poison in the toad's skin might have made him foam at the mouth?"

"Exactly, ma'am. I reckon they taste real bad. Old Joe never did get over chasin' 'em. After the first one when he was a pup, he never chewed on 'em, though."

Cody had told her all about Old Joe, the dog he'd owned when he was a lad in Texas. Melissa had eaten up those tales, eager to hear about how normal children with real families carried on in the world. He hadn't mentioned the toads until now.

"My goodness."

They'd arrived at the kitchen door by this time. Cody opened it and Melissa peeked out, wondering if she'd find Perry in convulsions or dead on the ground. She found him sleeping on the horsehair mat outside the door. He looked up at her, dejection and accusation in his big brown eyes. The foam was gone from around his mouth. Cody pushed the door open and knelt beside the dog.

"Hey, Perry," he said softly. The puppy thumped its tail and ignored Melissa for this kinder human who didn't seem inclined to slam doors on his foot. "What you been doin', boy? You find an old toad in the garden?"

The dog whined a confirmation and butted his head against Cody's knee.

"Here it is."

Melissa looked up to find Luis striding toward them, a big fat toad cupped in his hands. "Don't look like it's hurt too bad." Luis held the toad out like an offering for them to inspect, a grin all but splitting his face. "This old toad will be all right. I think Perry

113

only chewed on him a little bit." Luis laughed a big, happy laugh. "He'll sleep for awhile and be back next year to eat up all them bugs."

Good grief. She'd made all that fuss about a toad? Pressing a hand to her burning cheek, Melissa mumbled, "I feel so foolish. I'm sorry for scaring you."

Luis laughed. "It's not your fault, Miz Wilmeth. You didn't know."

"No. I didn't know."

Cody grinned up at her, too. "It's all right, ma'am. It's kinda funny, actually."

Melissa didn't think it was funny. It felt like just another failure on her part; the latest in a lifelong line of them. She felt stupid and uneducated, and wished she didn't.

"I'm trying to learn."

"It takes a while, ma'am," Cody assured her. He let the dog in the house, and its nails clicked across the shiny wood floor in the kitchen. Melissa had already begun tying scraps together, intending to braid a rag rug to protect the floor. Now the click-click-click of Perry's toenails echoed in her head, reminding her of Mrs. Bowlus. The nasty old lady used to tick off Melissa's faults in that way, while Melissa stood, head bowed, hands clamped together beneath her apron, and wish she was a worthwhile person who didn't always do everything wrong.

Because she didn't want Cody to know how bad she felt about her mistake, she put on a serene face and folded a cloth and set it on the table. Then she put her pot of stew on the cloth. Both Cody and Luis sniffed appreciatively and complimented her on her stew.

At least she could cook up a decent meal. The knowledge didn't cheer her considerably.

* * *

A Gentle Magic

Alexander McMurdo clucked to the horse he'd just sent to rest a quarter-mile away from Cody O'Fannin's ranch. He carried a little pottery crock filled with yeast starter in his saddlebag. He aimed to tell Melissa he'd meant to give it to her last week, when she set out with Cody to work on his ranch. He knew good and well she didn't need it. Melissa Wilmeth had been making do her entire life; she could certainly make do without Mac's yeast starter.

The yeast gave him an excuse, however, and he took it. He'd left Rio Hondo for Cody's ranch as soon as he saw Howard Wilmeth head into the Pecos Saloon with Grant Davis. Wilmeth's penchant for nursing his grievances in alcohol and low company would give Mac plenty of time to warn Melissa that her husband would be paying her a call.

Mac wanted to make good and sure she didn't weaken in her resolve to leave the bastard. She had a chance to live a full and happy life with Cody O'Fannin, and Mac would do everything he could, short of weaving a spell with his magic, to make sure she took it. He'd learned centuries ago that people needed to work out their own problems more than they needed his magic. Every now and then, magic proved useful, but Mac used it sparingly.

He had a hunch Cody and Melissa wouldn't need it at all, once they got used to each other.

Howard Wilmeth sat in the Pecos Saloon, hunched over his beer. He'd been snarling a litany of bitter reflections on the state of his life and the perfidy of his wife for a half hour or more. The recipient of his complaints, Grant Davis, sat across from him, sipping beer and yawning from time to time. Davis, a phlegmatic individual at the most interesting of times, plainly didn't care.

"Goddamn son of a bitch," said Howard. "Bastard."

Grant Davis blew out a cloud of cigar smoke. He watched with evident interest as the blue of his smoke dissipated into the hazy atmosphere of the saloon.

"Dammit, she's my wife, and now she's gone to work for that bastard O'Fannin."

"Always heard O'Fannin was a pretty square fellow," Davis muttered, bored.

"Square fellow, my ass. He ran off with my wife."

"Hmmm."

"I aim to get him for it, too."

Davis cocked an eyebrow and appeared, for the first time in several minutes, almost interested. "How you aimin' to do that?"

Howard eyed Davis balefully, unhappy to have been asked to produce details. He was accustomed to being the brains behind a scheme, not carrying it out. He left the details to others—and they usually botched them. Fools.

He'd never personally carried one of his plans to fruition before. Nobody had ever asked him for particulars—well, except Melissa, and Howard had always found it easy to ignore her. After all, she was his wife. "I haven't decided on that yet."

Davis shrugged. "O'Fannin's been here for a few years now. Don't nobody not like him. His cousin and him, I hear they're good men in a pinch."

Howard shifted uncomfortably. He wasn't happy with this information being so matter-of-factly dumped into his ears. Hell, he wanted everybody to hate Cody O'Fannin as much as he did. These other fellows, hell, they'd hate him, too, if O'Fannin had run off with *their* wives. He frowned at his beer and didn't offer a comment.

Davis, unaffected by Howard's black mood, plodded on. "Don't think you'll get much help from Blackworth. He ain't got nothin' against O'Fannin that I ever heard about." He grinned sourly. "And O'Fannin's never come lookin' for his missing beeves, either." It was common knowledge that Hugh Blackworth augmented his own herd with cows stolen from other men. So far, nobody'd wanted to start a war over his unscrupulous business practices.

Wilmeth squinted through the thick cigar smoke. "You mean Blackworth would help if he didn't like O'Fannin?"

Another shrug greeted Wilmeth's question. Davis followed his shrug with, "I reckon. He won't, though. Blackworth's out to get Chisum. O'Fannin's small potatoes compared to Chisum. 'Sides, O'Fannin don't cause no trouble."

"Yeah. I reckon." Chisum caused Blackworth trouble. Howard Wilmeth had lived on Hugh Blackworth's ranch long enough to understand the politics of the area. John Chisum was rich and owned the most land and cattle. Blackworth wanted what Chisum had. Howard, who used to earn his keep working sporadically as a leg-breaker for an influential loan shark in Boston, was well versed in this kind of politics.

He figured he'd landed in the right place. Back-alley work was his specialty. If there were no back alleys in the Seven Rivers country, the principle remained the same. Blackworth needed stealth and brawn, and Howard could provide both. He'd carefully explained to Blackworth all the skills he'd acquired on the mean streets of Boston, and Blackworth had hired him on the spot. And if Howard had exaggerated a tiny bit, how could Blackworth ever find it out?

However, if Howard was going to be helping Hugh Blackworth secure his place in the world, he didn't suppose there was any law that said he couldn't do a little side work on his own. Not that Howard cared about laws as a rule, anyway.

He wasn't, on the other hand, overly fond of toil. Unlike his fool of a wife, who believed people were supposed to labor for a living, Howard had always tried to avoid exerting himself whenever possible. Thinking about Melissa brought another scowl to his face. Damned woman. He should have known better than to marry her the first time she refused to borrow from that damned old lady she used to work for. Hell.

She'd called it theft and said she was afraid she'd lose her job. As if the job mattered! Why in the name of God did she want that stinking job anyway? All she did was slave for a nasty-tempered rich witch for twelve hours a day. And the old lady didn't appreciate her for it, either. Old Mrs. Bowlus considered Melissa as much of an idiot as Howard did.

Howard had figured Melissa should grab what she could when she could, and never look back. Her argument that she'd surely be suspected for the theft hadn't moved him. Hell, if she was always going to be afraid of everything, she'd never get anywhere. When she'd told him she didn't think he'd get anywhere except into jail by doing things his way, he'd hit her. She hadn't spoken to him for a week, but he'd sweet-talked her back into his good graces. He was good at talking people around to his way of thinking.

He frowned as he took another swallow from his beer mug. Dammit, when had that woman gotten to be so stubborn? She never used to be stubborn like this. Howard used to be able to talk her into anything. Damned near anything, at any rate. He'd had to marry her before she'd let him touch her. That should have taught him a lesson, but it hadn't, and now she was his.

Well, Cody O'Fannin would learn the price Howard Wilmeth exacted on anybody who tried to take what was his. Howard planned to see to it. What would happen after he'd taken care of O'Fannin was another matter. After he'd dealt with O'Fannin, he'd deal with Melissa.

He drank down his beer and wiped the foam from his upper lip with the back of his hand. "They got any women in this place?" he asked gruffly.

Grant Davis gave him a wry smile. " 'Fraid you ain't gettin' your woman back from O'Fannin?"

"To hell with my woman," Howard spat. "I want me a woman now."

Apparently unaffected by Howard's bad mood, Davis looked over his shoulder. When he spied one of the Pecos Saloon's resident working girls, he crooked his finger.

"Hey there, Mac! C'mon in and have some dinner."

Cody had answered Mac's knock at the front door because Melissa was busy ladling pickled onions into a serving dish and cutting thick slabs of corn bread. He was delighted to see the old man again. Mac would be pleased by how well Melissa was looking since she'd come to live with him, Cody knew. He'd noticed from the first that Mac had a fatherly interest in Melissa's welfare.

Cody's interest in Melissa was far from fatherly, but he'd die before he let on. To anybody.

The old fellow's face wore the smile of a benevolent angel. Cody's own grin twisted when he saw it. As sly as a fox, is what Mac was, and Cody knew it.

"How's our sweet Mellie faring out here in the wilds, Cody m'boy?"

"She's doin' fine, Mac. And so's Katie. They both seem to like it here." Cody tried to hide the pride he took in saying so, but it leaked into his words in spite of his efforts. In truth, he was overjoyed by how well Melissa and her daughter were adjusting to life on his ranch. If he played his cards right, maybe he could convince her to stay. As his housekeeper, of course.

Mac flipped his hat and it landed on a peg on the hat rack Cody had brought from Georgetown. "Might get a touch crowded in here when Arnold brings his wife back."

Cody frowned. He'd been thinking about that, too. Land was plentiful out here, though, and he figured there'd be room enough for Loretta and Melissa both. And he'd sure as hell rather live with Melissa as his housekeeper than Lor—

"Hey," he said, confused.

How in the name of mercy had Mac known what he was thinking about? He squinted hard at the old wagon-yard owner and decided he'd better not ask. At the moment, Mac was twinkling at him like a happy little pixie. Cody frowned. Since he couldn't think of how to phrase his doubts without sounding like a pure fool, he decided he'd better not try.

"Well, come on in the kitchen, Mac. Mrs. Wilmeth's just serving up dinner, and it looks like there's plenty for all of us."

His heart stumbled and began to race when Melissa looked up, spotted Mac in the doorway, and broke into a brilliant smile. She'd just lifted the lid of the Dutch oven in order to dip out the stew, but she dropped the lid back into place with a clank, hurried to Mac, kissed him on both cheeks, and blushed.

Cody realized the quick stab of emotion in his chest was jealousy, and chided himself for it. Of course she'd kiss Mac. After all, the fellow was not only old enough to be her grandfather, but he'd pretty much appointed himself to the position.

"Oh, Mac, it's so *good* to see you!"

"It's good to see you, too, Mellie, lass. You're lookin' very well, m'dear." He held out the crock he'd brought. "Here, love, I brought you some yeast."

"Oh, thank you, Mac! I have some yeast proofing on the shelf behind the stove, but this will be wonderful. I can make real bread now."

Cody scratched his head, wondering why she hadn't asked about yeast before if she needed it. Hell, he could have got her some yeast, he guessed. At least, he thought he could. He was pretty sure of it, anyway.

Melissa took the old man's hand and led him to the table. "Here. You sit right here, and I'll set another place for myself. Oh, and you have to see Katie, too! She's growing like a weed!"

McMurdo nodded to Luis and chuckled. "A weed, is it? I'll have to see this."

Deciding he'd only look silly if he took offense at the way Melissa was fawning over Mac, Cody sat, too, and forced a smile. "A fat little weed."

Melissa's unaffected laugh was music to his ears, and he guessed he'd chosen the right course to follow. These two were friends. And Cody was glad of it. He thought he was, anyway.

"Yes, indeed, Mr. O'Fannin's right as rain. She's quite plump, my little Katie."

"That's as it should be," McMurdo said with satisfaction. "Smells delicious, Mellie m'dear. Are you sure there's enough?"

"Of course there's enough," said Cody, irked that Mac should think he'd begrudge a fellow New Mexican a meal. Out here, people took care of each other.

Mac gave him one of his sparkly grins, and Cody entertained the not-too-pleasant impression that the old man had been teasing him. "Mrs. Wilmeth's a real good cook," he added in order to be saying something.

"I knew she would be, Cody, m'lad."

"She's a real good cook," Luis confirmed. He smiled at Melissa, and she smiled back, rather shyly.

Cody sighed. He liked it that Melissa seemed a little unsure of herself. She certainly wasn't anything like Arnold's Loretta Pine. Loretta had no doubt whatever of her own worth—for good reason, Cody guessed, although he found her overbearing and hard to be around for extended periods. Of course, a competent female was exactly the right sort for Arnie; Cody couldn't deny it. Arnie'd be lost if he had to make decisions for himself and a wife, too. The mere thought made Cody wince inside.

Not Cody. Cody could make his own decisions, and he didn't favor a female who'd be forever second-guessing him or trying to boss him around. No, Cody favored a more delicately natured woman for himself. A woman like Melissa Wilmeth, for example.

Good God, what was he thinking? He cast a quick glance around the kitchen. Melissa seemed unaware of his thoughts; so did Luis.

Mac, on the other hand, was looking straight at him. He was apparently having trouble containing his amusement, too, as if Cody's thoughts were as transparent to him as glass. Not for the first time, Cody wished he'd stop having these prickly feelings about Mac. He frowned slightly as he held out his plate for Melissa to fill.

"Is everything all right, Mr. O'Fannin?"

Melissa's question sounded worried, and Cody looked up to find her pretty blue eyes bright with concern, as if she feared he didn't like the looks of her stew. His frown melted into a soft smile for her. He couldn't help it. "Everything's just fine, ma'am. Thank you. This looks to be the best stew I've ever seen."

Her smile sent little shivers up his spine. Her smile had a habit of doing that to him. Far too often, by Cody's way of thinking, her expression was solemn, as though she had burdens too heavy for her to bear. But her smile always seemed to send her burdens scampering. Lordy, he loved her smile. Sometimes he thought that if he made it his life's work to keep her smiling, his life would be worthwhile.

He caught himself thinking it again now and sighed, nettled. Hell, he didn't need any female, sweet-natured or not. He had goals and aspirations. Ambitions. Aims in life. He couldn't afford to have them slowed down or stopped by a woman. Especially not by a woman who was married to another man. He frowned, misliking the very idea of Howard Wilmeth. Especially in connection with Melissa Wilmeth.

"Delicious meal, Mellie m'dear."

Cody jerked his head up, having become lost in his own thoughts. Mac wore a big smile and looked as happy as a fly in syrup. He winked at Cody, scattering his thoughts.

"I have some news, though, m'dear, that I thought I'd better bring you along with my yeast."

Melissa laughed.

"Your husband came to see me. He wasn't happy to find you gone away."

Melissa's laugh broke off abruptly. Cody dropped his fork. Even Luis looked up, startled, and not gladdened by Mac's news.

Mac took another bite of Melissa's good stew and beamed at them all.

Chapter Seven

Melissa sat with a thump. "H-H-Howard?" The name came out of her mouth as though she'd never said it before. How could she have allowed herself to become so contented here, with Howard lurking around the corner, ready to spoil everything? She shook her head, dismayed.

How in the name of everything could she have forgotten Howard, the blight of her blighted life? The last time she'd seen him, he'd had a look on his face that had clearly told Melissa he'd get her for daring to defy him. She was, unfortunately, all too familiar with that look.

Mac patted her hand. Distracted, she smiled at him. She'd been so happy only a second earlier. She'd been living exactly as she'd always dreamed of living, serving up good meals to men who seemed like family, pretending that when she swept and dusted, she was doing it in her own home. Making believe that these were her own people. Forgetting the truth.

She brushed a hand across her forehead, wishing she could erase her past. "What did he want, Mac? Did he say?"

"Aye. He said he'd come to the wagon yard to take you back with him. I told him you'd made other plans and were workin' elsewhere."

Melissa swallowed and glanced at Cody; heaven alone knew why. Her life wasn't his concern, except that she now worked for him. "What did he say to that?"

McMurdo grinned like a mischievous child. "He didn't like it much."

"No, I expect he didn't." Her mouth had gone dry. She picked up her water cup and took a sip. All of the dinnerware in Cody's house was old and made of battered tin. The dishes weren't elegant, but they were serviceable. Melissa thought they were nicer than Mrs. Bowlus's fancy china, because they were Cody's. She noticed her hand shaking. "I don't suppose he liked it much at all."

"Did you tell him about the divorce?"

Cody snapped out the question brusquely and glared at Mac, as if this were all his fault. He seemed angry, a circumstance that Melissa didn't understand but hoped wouldn't continue. He wouldn't want her working here if Howard caused trouble; she knew it. Then, what in the world would she and Katie do? They might be forced to go back to Howard if she lost her job as Cody's housekeeper. The good Lord knew, she had nowhere else to go.

She fought the impulse to sink her head into her hands and moan. This was not the time, and definitely not the place, to fall into despair. She had a meal to serve. Recalling her duties, she rose from her chair on shaky legs.

"No," Mac said with apparent detachment. "I didn't bother him with the divorce. I figured Mellie should be the one to tell him about that, as it's her concern."

Melissa's knees almost gave out on her again. She kept them from buckling by sheer force of will. Oh, Lord! She knew Mac was right; it was her obligation to tell Howard that she was seeking a divorce from him—and to tell him why. But a lifetime of trying like the very devil to avoid conflict so as not to make her life any more complicated than it already was sat in her heart like lead, and made her dread confronting her husband.

How would he react to the news? Howard was not a good man; Melissa had known it even before she married him. She'd been an idiot to marry him in spite of what she'd known about him. Well, it was all rebounding upon her now, and she was going to have to pay for her idiocy.

"You did what you had to do, Mellie," Mac said gently, startling her. "Don't blame yourself for it now."

She'd managed to pick up the plate of corn bread and the crock of butter. She almost dropped them when Mac's mind-reading propensities struck her in such an unmistakable way. He didn't give her a chance to wallow in her shock.

"Blaming yourself for what in hindsight looks like it was a mistake is a fruitless occupation, m'dear. Everybody makes mistakes, Mellie. You're not the first woman to marry a worthless man, and you won't be the last. 'Tis a pity females have so few choices in this life, if you ask me. And you did get your beautiful Katie out of your union, so it wasn't all for naught."

"What the hell are you talkin' about, Mac?" Cody set his tin coffee cup down with a sharp clunk. He looked from Mac to Melissa in confusion.

Melissa swallowed again. "I—er—think Mac was reading my mind again, Mr. O'Fannin." She gave him a weak smile to let him know it was a joke. But it wasn't a joke, and the keen look Cody shifted between her and Mac told her he knew it, too.

"Yeah," Cody said, sounding grumpy. "He does that a lot."

Mac gave a good-hearted laugh. "Och, the two of you don't need a body to read your minds. Your thoughts are pasted on your faces as clear as day." He smiled at Luis. "Right, Luis?"

Luis, who had been watching everybody in the kitchen with keen interest as he gobbled his stew, nodded. "Sure, Mr. Mac. That's for sure."

Melissa carefully set the corn bread and butter down on the table, making sure her hand didn't shake this time. "Here's some honey for your corn bread, too."

"Ah, my favorite." Mac looked like he were peering upon the glories of heaven as he surveyed the bounty before him.

Melissa took a small serving of stew. She didn't want it, but she knew she had to keep her strength up for Katie's sake, if for no other reason. "Um, do you suppose Howard will come out here looking for me, Mac?" Oh, merciful heavens, she hoped he wouldn't!

"I expect so."

Melissa's hopes crashed and died before they'd had time to rise.

Cody's eyes narrowed. "Is he still staying at the Blackworth spread?"

"I expect he is."

"I guess that means he's working for Blackworth?" Cody posed his supposition as a question, although it sounded to Melissa as though he already knew the answer.

"I expect he is," Mac said again. He drizzled honey onto a piece of buttered corn bread, took a bite, and looked as though he'd been transported to some blissful, pleasant Eden unpopulated by people of Howard Wilmeth's stamp. When he'd chewed and swallowed, he said, "Ah, perfection," and smiled at Melissa.

She imagined her return smile looked anemic.

"Well, he'd better not try to cause any trouble for Mrs. Wilmeth, because I won't stand for it."

Cody sounded positively belligerent. Melissa turned and stared at him, confounded.

"Didn't expect you would, Cody m'lad." Mac took another bite of corn bread. The expression on his face exuded pure contentment.

"Dammit, I don't hold with men pestering women," Cody elaborated, his voice hard. "If he comes on my land to do it, I'll show him what I think, too."

Melissa blinked, unsure she understood what he meant. Her breath snagged in her chest and she felt a stab of something like wonder shoot through her. She pressed a hand to her heart to subdue it. She knew this good man couldn't possibly mean to be her champion. Not again. Good men like Cody O'Fannin didn't happen to the Melissa Wilmeths of the world. Not more than once they didn't, anyway, and he'd already saved her life once.

"Good idea," said Mac around another bite of corn

129

bread. "He needs to be taught a lesson, to my way of thinking."

"Damned right, he does." Cody stuffed a bite of stew into his mouth and chewed ferociously. "Makes me mad," he said as soon as he'd swallowed. "Pestering Mrs. Wilmeth this way. Hell, if he'd'a cared about her, he never would have left her there on the desert having his baby in the first place."

Mac grinned and nodded. Cody looked horrified. He swung his head around and goggled at Melissa. "Lordy, ma'am, I'm sorry. I didn't mean to say that out loud and all. Nor I didn't mean to swear."

Melissa's laugh bubbled up and burst from her lips, shocking her. "Please, Mr. O'Fannin," she gasped when she could catch her breath. "There's no need to apologize. You're absolutely right about Howard. You only told the truth."

Cody tucked in his chin and took another bite of his dinner. He still looked embarrassed, but Melissa thought he was the kindest, most wonderful man in the world. If she'd only met Cody O'Fannin before she'd met Howard—

Oh, how foolish she was being! As if she'd ever have had a chance to meet somebody like Cody O'Fannin in the area of Boston where she was born. Men like him didn't live there. If they were born good, they'd been warped by life and circumstances into crooked, unwholesome specimens long before they reached Cody's age.

She sighed and tucked into her dinner. She still wasn't hungry, but she knew she owed it to her baby and to Cody O'Fannin—and to Alexander McMurdo, too—to maintain her health. These men were the first people in her entire life who'd ever gone out of their way to offer her any kind of assistance. They'd done it of their own free will, and unasked, and because they were good, decent people. She'd be staked on a spike if she'd undo, for no better reason than rampaging emotions, all their wonderful good work.

"You got a brother, don't you, Luis?"

"Yeah. I gots lots of brothers. Carlos is about my age."

"He good with cows and horses?"

"Good as me."

Ever since Mac's visit earlier in the day, Cody had entertained a vague, unsettled feeling in his innards. He didn't like the idea of leaving Melissa all alone at the house for hours and hours every day while he was out on the range. "You think he'd be willing to come work for me for awhile?"

"I reckon." Luis shrugged. "You thinkin' of hirin' more men now? Before the spring drive?"

Cody shifted his shoulders, uncomfortable. He wanted to keep the real reason for this odd start of his—that he was worried about Melissa Wilmeth's safety—to himself. He didn't want to have to say, out loud, that he feared if Howard Wilmeth came for her one day while he was away, she might return to her husband out of guilt or some misguided feeling of obligation—or even leftover love for the bastard. "I reckon."

Luis shrugged again.

"You expect you could get him to come pretty soon?"

"How soon?"

"Soon." Cody wished like thunder Luis would quit pestering him. A yes-or-no answer would suit him down to the ground.

"I reckon."

Cody read the question in Luis's eyes and slouched his shoulders the other way. Then he hitched up his trousers, stared off into the distance, and tried to look thoughtful. In truth, thought had little to do with his actions in this case. Sentiment and a nagging feeling of worry propelled him. "There's some work I want to do around the house, and I don't want the fences to fall into disrepair or the cattle to run off while I do it. Don't want Blackworth to have an easier time of it rustling our cattle than he has to."

"Yeah? How come? You aim to set up housekeepin' or somethin'?"

Cody didn't appreciate Luis's knowing grin. He frowned. "Arnie's bringin' Loretta back here pretty blasted soon, Luis. She's not gonna like livin' in a four-room cabin. You don't know Loretta like I do."

Nodding, Luis murmured, "Right."

Cody tugged at the knot of his bandanna. The damned thing was strangling him. "Thought I'd get some lumber at Mac's and build me a porch."

"A porch?"

"Yeah. A porch. So's we can set out there after supper and watch the sunset and the birds flyin' south and so forth."

Luis considered this plan for a moment. "Sounds good to me."

"Honest?" Cody's surprise came through in his tone. Luis eyed him thoughtfully.

"Sure. Sunsets are pretty 'round here. Sounds good. Take the baby on the porch, me singin', you playin' your guitar, Miz Wilmeth knottin' them rags of hers. Sounds real good."

It sounded good to Cody, too. In fact, the picture Luis painted in his simple, uncomplicated words resonated way down deep in Cody's chest. He wanted it to happen.

Of course, that wasn't the reason Cody planned to build a porch—and to add as many rooms as he needed to add in order to remain in Melissa Wilmeth's vicinity during the coming days. Nor was it the reason he aimed to keep at it, too, as long as he remained worried about her safety. Until Cody knew exactly what, if any, plans Howard Wilmeth was hatching for his wife in that evil brain of his, Cody didn't want to let her out of his sight.

Since she wasn't, in reality, his responsibility—indeed, he had no right to feel any sense of obligation for her at all—he appreciated Luis tamely going along with his plans to renovate the cabin.

Anyhow, if Arnie ever did talk Loretta into moving to the Territory with him—a prospect Cody doubted, since he doubted Loretta—all of this work would serve a purpose.

The idea of Loretta Pine sitting in a rocking chair on Cody's new front porch didn't sit well with him. He tucked it away and decided he'd think about it later.

Chapter Eight

Melissa was more readily convinced than Luis that Cody's reason for working around the house was his desire to prepare a home for Arnold Carver's bride, Loretta. Cody was glad of it, because he'd have been really embarrassed if she guessed at his true motives

"I'm sure she'll love it here," she said—rather wistfully, to his mind. Then she sighed with what sounded to him like yearning. "It's a beautiful land you've chosen to build your future on, Mr. O'Fannin. This is a wonderful location."

"You really think so?" Cody was pleased.

"Oh, yes. Why, a person can see forever here."

"Yeah." Cody thought it was enchanting that Melissa seemed to have a turn for the poetical.

"And the river's lovely, too, the way it snakes along, winding its way through the plains."

"Yeah." He grinned.

"And those cottonwoods and willows you and your

cousin planted along the water's edge—why, I can just imagine how pretty they'll be in a few years."

"Yeah. Arnie and I thought so, too." Actually, Arnold hadn't thought at all. It had been Cody who'd planted those trees, because he had a touch of the poetical in his soul, just like Melissa.

She sighed again, heartily. "I'm so glad you built a window in the kitchen. I like to look out of it at the river while I wash up or cook, and pretend I belong here."

She blushed after her poignant confession, and Cody felt a clenching in his chest that traveled from his heart, down his chest, through his stomach, and right to his groin, which tightened in response. Damn! He had to get ahold of himself. This reaction to Howard Wilmeth's wife was not only wrong, it was frustrating as hell.

Cody, Melissa, and baby Katie paid a visit to McMurdo's Wagon Yard a few mornings after Mac's visit, Cody to pick up lumber for his proposed front porch, Melissa to replenish her kitchen supplies. Now that she'd been Cody's housekeeper for a couple of weeks, she had a fairly good notion of what she'd need. Besides, Christmas was coming, and she wanted to do something special for Cody.

Cody told her not to worry about the expense of her purchases. He might not be a rich man, but he could afford to stock his house. He didn't say that part, but only thought it. Then he wondered if there was something wrong with him that he was thinking defiant thoughts about money and homes and about whether he could afford to house a woman. What did he want a woman in his life for? Except as a housekeeper, of course.

It made his heart warm, though, to see how happy Melissa was to greet Mac, and how pleased Mac seemed with her renewed health under Cody's care. Because Cody did care for her. He cared for her the way that blasted husband of hers *should* have cared for her and didn't.

Cody's grudge against Howard Wilmeth seemed to be getting bigger and bigger as the days passed.

"Look what I found in the back room," Mac said before they left. Stepping aside, he revealed an old, scarred, but sound, cider press.

Cody gaped at it. He hadn't put his hand to a cider press since before he and Arnie left Georgetown. He used to love grinding the apples and screwing down the lid so that the juice was pressed out and trickled through the hole and into the bucket positioned below. He and Arnold always ended up with stomach-aches after a day of pressing apples because they drank so much juice, but he'd never minded. The juice tasted so good. Then his mother would bottle and process the cider, and they'd drink it all year long until it was gone, and then they'd pine for more.

Melissa said uncertainly, "Oh, what an interesting machine. What is it, Mac?"

Cody stared at her, staggered that anyone could live in the world as long as she had and not recognize a cider press when she saw one. What kind of life had this woman led until she came here, anyway? Surely they used cider presses in Boston. Didn't they?

Mac seemed unamazed. "It's a cider press, Mellie m'dear, and I'm sure our Cody here will be able to show you exactly how to use it."

"A cider press. Oh, my! I've heard of cider presses."

She'd *heard* of cider presses? "Didn't you used to drink apple juice when you were a little girl, Mrs. Wilmeth?"

She turned to look at him, and Cody got the impression she wished she'd kept her mouth shut. "Er, no. No, we, um, didn't have one at home when I was growing up."

"Shoot, ma'am, we had apple juice and cider all the time back home in Georgetown."

"Oh? That sounds very nice, Mr. O'Fannin."

Cody scratched his chin. "Reckon rich folks can buy apple juice if they want it." It was an experiment, to see if she'd confess to having come from money.

She didn't. She fussed with the baby and pretended she hadn't heard him.

"I 'spect maybe they didn't have as many apples in Boston as you had in Texas, Cody, m'boy," Mac said. But his eyes were sparkling like diamonds, and he looked like he was having trouble not laughing. Cody didn't understand any of it.

"I have some jars for the cider, too, if you can fit them into your wagon with all that lumber, Cody. And some apples. Bushels of 'em."

"Apples." Cody was busy pondering Melissa and how strange her childhood must have been without apples. When he realized Mac was chuckling at him and had just said something, he started. "Oh, yeah, apples." He squinted at McMurdo. "Where in Hades did you get apples, Mac?"

"Oh, they just turned up"

"Yeah," Cody said. "They just turned up." He repositioned a fifty-pound sack of flour to make room for the apples and the jars "There. I think they'll fit there."

"I expect they will."

Cody followed Mac into the back of his house and into the same room that had housed Melissa during her recuperation. He gazed wistfully at the bed, recalling how sweet and fragile she had looked holding her newborn baby. Lordy, he'd been worried about her. Cody had never seen such unalloyed love in a human being's eyes as he'd seen in Melissa's when she'd looked at her baby. It still gave him a lump, remembering.

."I keep 'em back here because it's the coolest room in the place," Mac said as he pointed out the apples. Cody and the old man carried them out to the yard and returned for the jars. Mac squatted in front of a wooden crate. Cody squatted on the other side, and the two men lifted the crate and toted it out to the wagon.

"Better pad it, lad, so's the jars won't break."

"Right." Cody packed the crate full of jars with the blanket he kept behind the wagon seat. Then he helped Melissa onto the seat, too.

Katie yawned at him from her mother's arms, and he laughed out loud. She was a cute little kid, Katie, and she was getting less and less ugly as the days passed. He'd never taken much note of kids until now; hadn't needed to. What did the carefree, wild-oat-sowing Cody O'Fannin have to do with kids? Or their mothers, either, for that matter? He took note of these two, though. They were quickly becoming a passion with him, and it worried him a lot.

Mac winked at him, taking Cody aback. Was the old man reading his mind again? Cody wished to goodness he wouldn't do that.

"Take care of each other, m'dears," Mac called as Cody clucked to the mules and the wagon lurched into motion.

Mac raised his hand. Cody got the feeling that a priest blessing his flock might have made the same gesture, although, not being of the Catholic persuasion, he had no idea what priests really did.

Then he blinked and stared hard at Mac's hands. Damn it, there went those blasted sparkles again, floating through the air, as if Mac was stirring them up from the atmosphere with his fingers. This sparkle-in-the-air nonsense was the oddest thing Cody'd ever seen in his entire life, and it only seemed to happen around Mac. Cody wished it would stop. He had enough things to worry about without fearing his mind was going, too. Sparkles, hell.

He was pleased as punch with the cider press, however. Mac was good for turning things up, whatever else he was. Sparkles. Cody could hardly stand it.

Melissa's happy sigh diverted his thoughts from their grouchy wanderings.

"I do like Mac so very much, don't you, Mr. O'Fannin?"

"Er, yeah. Yeah, he's a real nice guy."

"And so helpful." Melissa turned on the bench and gazed at the bounty piled in the wagon's bed. "My goodness, all those beautiful apples."

"Yeah." And that was another thing. Sparkles aside, where in the name of creation had Mac managed to get himself a cider press and six bushels of prime red apples? No answer occurred to him before they'd traveled the ten miles to his ranch.

In the next two days, Melissa almost forgot Howard Wilmeth existed. And to cap it all off, they'd just partaken of a delicious dinner of chicken and dumplings, augmented by fresh dinner rolls—the recipe for which Melissa remembered from her days with Mrs. Bowlus. They were very fancy—much more fancy, according to Cody, than anything he'd ever eaten before. Ridiculously pleased with his flattery, Melissa didn't bother to tell him that they were made out of regular old bread dough and twisted into bow-tie shapes. Cody and Luis's compliments were music to her ears.

The air was crisp. A late-autumn sun shone in a crystal blue sky made interesting by clouds floating across it in streaks and pillows. Capitan rose grandly in the distance, reminding her of pictures she'd seen of volcanoes. Capitan was such a majestic mountain, probably because it was all by itself, as if it ruled in this particular section of the universe.

There wasn't much wind to speak of, and when it did blow, it didn't blow a gale like it usually did. Sometimes Melissa wondered why the roof stayed on Cody's cabin, the wind blew so fiercely—and there was nothing to stop it, either, since there weren't any trees in the way. Cody had planted a row of Lombardy poplars to act as a break against the prevailing southwesterly winds, but they were shorter than Melissa at this point.

Melissa possessed a good imagination, though, and she often imagined how Cody's ranch would look ten years from now, when those poplars had grown up, and the cottonwoods and willows were thriving by the river. It would be a beautiful ranch one day. Gorgeous. Perfect. She wished she could be here to see it.

She decided not to think about that now because it made her sad. Cody had promised to take this Sunday morning off so that he could show her how to use the cider press, and she could hardly wait.

In truth, she'd already pretty much figured it out on her own, but she delighted in Cody's company. Luis joined them, and the morning seemed almost magical to Melissa, who'd never been part of this kind of group before. She had a feeling a Sunday gathering of this sort, around the cider press, was the type of behavior practiced by families, although she had no personal experience of families to guide her in the matter.

Katie slept in her cradle right beside the front door, in the shade of the house. Someday, one of those oak trees Cody had planted would grow up big and tall and shade the house right at that same spot.

Melissa looked forward to the porch Cody had begun building onto the house. When the weather got on toward spring, she could take Katie's cradle onto the porch and work outside, churning butter and doing her mending. She loved working outside on Cody's ranch, where everything was so uncluttered and clean and she could see forever and a day. There wasn't a sooty chimney pot or a grimy wall or a drunken neighbor or the stench of a fish market for miles and miles and miles.

If, of course, she was still here when springtime came. Again, she decided not to think about it.

Cody flapped out an oilskin, laid it on the ground, and set the press on it. "Just in case. Don't want to get dust in the cider."

"Good heavens, no." The very idea of dust polluting the sparkling fresh apple juice Cody had promised her gave Melissa a headache.

Luis filled a huge wooden tub with water, and they dumped a bushel basketful of apples into it. Luis scrubbed them with gusto, singing as he washed. After giving an apple a good once-over, he tossed it into another bucket.

"Rub-a-dub-dub, three apples in a tub—"

Melissa carried the bucket full of clean apples over to the cider press, which was awaiting the fruit on the oilskin. She giggled and joined Luis in his song.

Laughing, Cody asked, "How do you know that rhyme, Luis?"

Luis shrugged and kept scrubbing. "I dunno. Soldiers, I think."

"Soldiers? Soldiers taught you nursery rhymes?" Melissa laughed harder because Luis's answer seemed so incongruous. Soldiers? She didn't quite believe him.

"They don't spend all their time shootin' Indians, I reckon," Luis said. "They got families over to Fort Sumner, and some of 'em gots babies. Me and my brother Carlos used to work out there sometimes."

"Merciful heavens." Somehow Melissa couldn't reconcile in her mind the idea of a soldier at Fort Sumner kissing his wife and baby good-bye in the morning, and then heading out to kill another wife's husband and baby. She knew she was being soft-headed. The Indian problem worried her. She lived with a constant, nagging fear that one day a throng of wild Indians would burn Cody's house down and scalp them all in a frenzy of blood lust.

"Speaking of Fort Sumner," Cody murmured, dumping apples into the chute, "Chisum's agreed to run our cattle with his and sell 'em to the Indian agent there."

"Good deal," said Luis.

"Do you ever have trouble with Indians attacking a herd when you drive it to the fort?" Melissa turned the crank on the grinder and tried to sound casual because she didn't want these men to think she was a coward. Still, she used to read frightening stories about Indian outrages in Mrs. Bowlus's newspapers back in Boston.

"Oh, they'll steal beeves sometimes. Depends on if there's trouble brewing or if there's been peace for awhile. A lot of times it depends on the food supply, too. A few years ago, Goodnight and Loving were driving a herd and ran into a band of Comanch. Loving got shot up real bad."

Melissa swallowed a lump of horror. "Good heavens. What happened?"

"Oh, he died, I reckon. Bullet didn't kill him. It was the gangrene did him in, the way I heard it."

Gangrene. Oh, my. Although she vilified herself as a fainthearted weakling, she had to ask a question that had bedeviled her since she first came out here. "Um, do the Indians ever, um, attack ranches, Mr. O'Fannin? The bad Indians, I mean. Not like your friend Mr. Running Standing. I mean, it seems rather isolated out here."

Cody grinned at her. "You still worried about Indians attackin' and scalpin' us, ma'am?"

Melissa felt her cheeks begin to burn, but answered with the truth. "Well, yes. Yes, I guess I do still worry about Indians. A little bit."

"Shoot, Miz Wilmeth, *mi madre* always tol' me to don't borrow no trouble. She always say, 'You got enough to worry about, Luis. Don't go borrowin' trouble. You'll get plenty come your way all on its own.'"

Luis laughed. Melissa noticed that the morbid topic hadn't dampened his enthusiasm for washing apples appreciably. He gave up on nursery rhymes and started whistling, in fact.

"Luis is right, ma'am," Cody told her. "Anything might happen. But don't forget that Arnie and me, we have us an arrangements with the Apache and Comanch who live around here. We haven't had any problems so far because we keep our end of the bargain."

All well and good, thought Melissa, but what about the Indians? Did they plan to keep their end of the bargain? "Um, I read in the newspapers back home that Indians often don't do what they say they'll do, though."

Cody shrugged, a gesture Melissa considered extremely nonchalant considering the topic under discussion. She held her breath, waiting for him to elaborate. He didn't. Well, drat the man. Daunted but determined, she persisted. "Well, Mr. O'Fannin? After all, someone must have coined the phrase 'Indian giver' for a reason."

He shrugged again. "I reckon. But you know, ma'am, it's hard to talk to a fellow who doesn't speak the same language you do. Things get complicated. I know when I was trying to figure out how to deal with Running Standing so that neither of us got killed, it took a long time for both of us to sort out what the other one meant. I reckon sometimes people just get sick of it all and give up."

"Oh." That made sense. In a way.

"You know, folks grow up different. I mean, I grew up in Texas in a little town. You grew up in a big city. Running Standing grew up out here, and so did Luis. The way we see things probably has a lot to do with the way we all grew up."

"Yes. That makes sense."

Melissa felt subdued for a good five or ten minutes after she decided not to pursue the topic of Indians further. She didn't fail to notice, either, the rifle Cody had set out within an easy grab. Somehow, keeping a rifle at the ready like that didn't speak to her of an entirely peaceful existence. She endeavored not to dwell on it, although she did pull Katie's cradle closer to the cider press.

After awhile, though, she forgot about Indians and trouble and the what-might-happens in life, and succumbed to the beauty of the morning and the pleasure she took in the company of Cody O'Fannin and

Luis Morales, who had progressed from "Three Men in a Tub" and whistling to some Spanish songs he claimed his grandmother had sung to him when he was a baby. Perry, who obviously possessed no sense of proportion, was busy leaping at birds who dared fly overhead. Melissa felt just grand.

"You know, ma'am," Cody said after they'd been listening to Luis's fine tenor voice for awhile, "I was tryin' to come up with a way as to how you might set yourself up out here after your divorce comes through." He gave the screw another hard turn, pressing the wooden mallet down on the apple pulp and squeezing more juice out.

He sounded thoughtful, as if he'd been giving the matter a good deal of his attention. Melissa's heart, which had been light as a feather a second earlier, sank to her toes. "Oh?"

"Yeah."

He lifted his gaze to her. She noticed two little furrows in his brow, as if he was troubled about her, as if she presented a problem to him. She wished she could smooth out those furrows. Since she had no right to do that, she concentrated on the juice now pouring into the bucket Cody had placed under the press. Deftly, she switched buckets, since the one was getting full.

"Did you come up with anything?" She was proud that her voice didn't quaver with the aching in her heart. She didn't want to go anywhere else. She didn't want to do anything else. She wanted to stay here, on Cody O'Fannin's ranch, and be his housekeeper forever. At least, she wanted to stay here. She could think of other things she'd rather be to Cody O'Fannin than his housekeeper, even though she knew she was foolish even to consider them.

145

"Well, I thought a laundry would come in real handy in Rio Hondo, ma'am."

A laundry. Oh, my. "Yes," she said, endeavoring to keep any emotion at all out of her voice. A laundry. How—how—how perfectly hateful.

"Yeah," he said, his voice falling at the end. Melissa knew she'd failed to hide her feelings. "Reckon a laundry wouldn't be much fun."

She managed a laugh. "I don't suppose I should be thinking in terms of fun, Mr. O'Fannin. I have a baby to support."

"Right. Well, then, maybe you could set up as a seamstress, ma'am. I know there isn't much call for one yet, because most of the men buy their work shirts and work trousers at McMurdo's mercantile, but I reckon more families will move out here pretty soon. And there are a few ladies in the area. There's Blackworth's wife and—well, there's Blackworth's wife."

"Mrs. Partridge," Luis provided.

"Yeah. Her, too. Hear they went back East for a while so's he and the baby can meet her folks." He dumped apple pulp into a big wash basin and put more apples in the chute. "Well, reckon the place could use itself a seamstress."

A seamstress. Melissa liked that idea better, even if it did entail sewing for the woman for whose husband Howard worked. She nodded. "That's an interesting thought, Mr. O'Fannin. I must admit I like sewing a lot better than I like doing laundry."

"I expect Mac could get one of those fancy sewing machine things, too, ma'am."

Melissa considered the cradle and the cider press and the apples and nodded. "Yes. I expect he could."

They worked without speaking for awhile. Luis continued to sing pretty songs, but the beauty of Melissa's day had hidden itself behind a cloud. Cody O'Fannin wanted to get rid of her, and her heart ached with the knowledge. He evidently considered her a burden rather than a help. She'd begun to hope she was performing a useful service here. She should have known better.

"Mac said he might expand his mercantile. Maybe you could work there as a clerk," Cody spoke into her thoughts. She jerked her head up and looked at him. "That's what Mrs. Partridge used to do before she married her husband."

"Oh. Yes. That's a thought."

Actually, while her heart still hurt from knowing Cody didn't want her, Melissa found his last idea more appealing than any of his prior ones. At least she liked Mac a lot, and he was awfully kind to Katie. She wondered if she could keep Perry if she worked at McMurdo's. Perry was probably Cody's dog, really. She didn't own a thing. The knowledge made her sad.

"If anybody ever builds a hotel in Rio Hondo, they might could use a clerk there, too," said Cody in a considering sort of voice.

Melissa figured he was pulling nonsense out of the air now. A hotel in Rio Hondo? If her heart hadn't taken to aching so badly, she might have giggled. Rio Hondo was as big as a minute and catered to the ranching business. The only people who ever spent the night there were cowboys who stopped in McMurdo's Wagon Yard during trail drives, or ranchers coming to town for supplies. Every now and then, according to Mac, a family of settlers passed through and stayed at his place for awhile. She couldn't imagine anyone ever needing a hotel. She said, "Hmm," because she couldn't think of anything else to say.

"I don' think you oughta do none of that, Miz Wilmeth," Luis piped in suddenly, making both Melissa and Cody jump and turn to look at him. "I think you should oughta open a restaurant. You cook real good."

Cody resumed pressing apples and pursed his lips. "A restaurant. Yeah. That's not a bad idea, Luis."

It wasn't a bad idea at all, Melissa decided. If Cody O'Fannin insisted she leave his employ—and it looked very much as though he would, eventually—perhaps she could open a restaurant. The prospect of operating a restaurant appealed to her much more than any of Cody's other ideas had. A restaurant. Not bad. Not bad at all. Maybe she could go into business with Mac.

"I don' wan' you to leave Cody's ranch, though," Luis said, again speaking into her thoughts and startling her. She turned and eyed him, wondering when he was going to follow up on his thought. He didn't, so she decided to ask.

"Why not?"

" 'Cause you should oughta keep workin' here." Luis tossed another apple into the almost-full bucket at his side and squinted at Cody. "Why you wan' Miz Wilmeth to go work in Rio Hondo, Cody?"

Cody blushed scarlet. Melissa watched it happen, and could hardly believe her eyes.

"I don't want her to work in Rio Hondo," Cody muttered, sounding peeved. "But she's got to raise little Katie, and I was trying to help her come up with ideas to do it."

"Why can' she just stay here? She cooks better than you and Arnie, and with her sweepin' and cleanin', the house looks better than it ever did. I don' understand."

Cody gave the screw a vicious twist. "Hell, Luis,

I'm just thinkin' of when Arnie brings Loretta back, is all."

Luis grimaced gloriously, giving the impression of a man who's just heard a tremendous whopper. "You think Loretta's gonna come? You said she wouldn' last week."

Cody's blush deepened. Melissa watched curiously, wondering why he was so uncomfortable. He must *really* want her gone, if he was making up stories about Arnold Carver's affianced bride.

"Well, she might," Cody said in clipped accents. "And Loretta's not a female who'd take kindly to another female in her house."

Luis shrugged. "So build another house. From what you tol' me about Loretta, I don' 'spect I gonna like her much. And you won' neither."

Melissa blinked at Luis. She'd never heard Cody say a disparaging word about another human being—barring Howard, and Howard didn't count. Too curious to mind her tongue, she said, "You don't care for your cousin's fiancée, Mr. O'Fannin?"

Cody got up and went to fetch the bucket of apples at Luis's side. He stomped back to the cider press as if he wished people wouldn't persist in pestering him. "Oh, Loretta's all right."

"You said she's a powerful woman, gonna henpeck Arnold, Cody." Luis watched Cody in a puzzled fashion. For some reason, Melissa didn't quite believe his innocent expression and wondered if Luis was teasing his boss. She'd never have considered teasing Mrs. Bowlus and was amazed at Luis's audacity. Not that Cody was mean like Mrs. Bowlus, but still . . .

"Well, I don't remember every blasted thing I say," Cody barked. "How can a man recall every word comes out of his mouth?"

Luis chuckled. "You don' need to remember, 'cause I do. You said she was—"

"All right! All right, maybe I did say that, and maybe I don't like Loretta much, but whatever I said, Arnie might be bringing her back here, and she's not going to want Mrs. Wilmeth in her house. I can guarantee it. So we got to think of something else for her to do." He looked at Melissa, harassed. "I mean, we got to think of something else for you to do, ma'am."

Deciding to be sensible about this—because Cody was being sensible, and Melissa owed him—she said, "Yes. Yes, of course, you're right, Mr. O'Fannin. You're absolutely right."

Resolution. She needed resolution. A backbone. She had Katie to think about, and it was way past time to thrust her own wishes and desires aside. So what if she wanted to remain here with Cody O'Fannin? The reality of her situation was that Arnold Carver might return to this very ranch, with a bride in tow, any week now, and Melissa had to find a way to earn her keep.

With that unhappy thought in mind, she murmured, "I do like the notion of a restaurant, but I've never had anything to do with one. Do you have any idea how to go about establishing a restaurant, Mr. O'Fannin?"

Cody looked up from dumping apples into the press as though he didn't quite trust this new tone of hers. Melissa felt a stab of guilt for having given him so much as a moment of worry. "I don't know, ma'am, but I expect we can figure it out if we put our heads together."

Putting her head together with Cody O'Fannin's appealed to Melissa in a way she was sure Cody didn't mean. She would never say so. She wrenched her mind away from its base musings. "I'm sure Mac can help, too. He seems to have a hand in everything."

"Yeah," Cody muttered. "That's for sure."

The sound of horses' hooves pounding across the earth reached them, and they all turned to look. In the distance Melissa discerned a cloud of dust and what looked like thumbnail-sized horses galloping in the direction of Cody's ranch. She forgot all about how much Cody didn't want her around, and her chest squeezed with panic. Indians! It was Indians, and they were all going to die! Right here in Cody's front yard. And Melissa hadn't even had a chance to sample the apple juice yet!

Squinting into the distance, Cody grumbled, "Aw, hell." He looked up at Melissa from where he was squatting next to the apple press. "I think it's your husband, ma'am."

Melissa's panic abruptly changed to dread. She whispered, "Howard?" and wondered if she had time to hide Katie's cradle before those horsemen arrived.

"I think so, ma'am."

All things considered, Melissa would rather face Indians.

Chapter Nine

Perry entered into an ear-splitting frenzy of barking and danced around the gate until Cody hollered at him. Then he ran away, his tail between his legs, and huddled under the house. Stupid dog.

Cody had the presence of mind to have Luis take the apple juice into the house. He didn't want it to get polluted from those fools' horses churning up dirt in the yard. Melissa had been like a kid at Christmas about the cider press, and Cody didn't aim to have her treat spoiled. That is to say, he didn't aim to have it spoiled any more than her bastard of a husband was sure to spoil it now.

Howard dismounted and swaggered over to the cider press. Cody was pretty sure it was supposed to have been a swagger, at any rate. Howard Wilmeth obviously had little practice in riding a horse, and his butt and thighs hurt. Cody could tell. He would have mentioned the matter but was too mad.

The men who'd ridden out with Howard remained mounted. Grant Davis, who seemed to be Howard Wilmeth's bosom beau these days, crossed his arms over his saddle horn and nodded to Cody. Cody didn't want to, but he nodded back. He didn't really have anything against Grant Davis, except that he favored low company and worked for a son of a bitch.

"Where's my wife?" Wilmeth asked, his tone belligerent.

Cody was about to tell him to take himself back to hell and leave his wife alone, when he was startled to hear Melissa's soft voice at his back. He'd hustled her into the house with her daughter, figuring he'd handle Howard Wilmeth and spare her the bother.

"I'm right here, Howard. What do you want?"

Frowning, Cody turned and saw Melissa walking toward him, sans baby, her back straight, her expression stern. He admired her in that moment. He hadn't given her credit for possessing enough grit to stand up to her husband.

Of course, she hadn't stood up to him yet. Cody realized it, and his heart squinched.

"I want you and my baby, is what I want," Wilmeth shouted. "What the hell do you think I want?"

Cody took a step in Wilmeth's direction, intending to flatten him if he didn't stop cussing and shouting, but Melissa gave him a look, and he halted. Shoot, he hadn't known she could make her sweet face look so inflexible. He hoped her inflexibility concerned not going back to her husband, and wasn't only intended to keep Cody from punching Wilmeth's nose flat.

"Mind your tongue, Howard," Melissa snapped. "You're on Mr. O'Fannin's property now, and he doesn't care for bad language."

Cody felt his eyebrows lift. Well, glory be. Even if what she'd said was a prevarication—at least—he admired her for saying it. He felt the urge to applaud, in fact.

Wilmeth, obviously, did not. "Don't you start with me, Melissa. I want you and the kid, and I want you now. You're my wife, dammit, and you belong with me."

"No, Howard, I do not belong with you. Nor does Katie. You made that perfectly plain to me when you abandoned us out there on the desert."

"Now, just a blamed minute, Melissa. I didn't abandon anybody. I got sunstroke, for cripes' sake!"

"So you've said." Her tone clearly conveyed how little she believed him.

"It's the truth, dammit!"

"If you don't mind your tongue, Howard Wilmeth, I shall refuse to speak with you. If you don't promise, right here and now, not to swear, you can go away this minute and come back when you can control yourself. Or you can not come back at all, which would be even better."

Cody could hardly believe this new staunchness blazing forth in Melissa Wilmeth. She stood like an oak—a very small oak, to be sure, but an oak—with her little feet planted wide on the earth and her fists knotted up and planted on her hips. The expression on her face could match that of Mr. Pankhurst, the schoolmaster in Georgetown—an old-fashioned Presbyterian who'd never once spared the rod in all the years Cody'd endured his tutelage—and then some.

Howard ripped off his hat and swished it in a gesture of extreme aggravation. "All right, blast it. But I want this cleared up and I want it cleared up now. You're coming with me, Melissa. You're my wife."

"Not for much longer, I'm not."

As soon as the words left her lips, the world seemed to stop dead in its orbit. Even Grant Davis, who had been chewing on a toothpick and looking bored, jerked his head up and stared at her. His toothpick dropped onto his saddle and bounced to the ground, and he had to fumble in his shirt pocket for another one, all the while gawking at Melissa.

Howard, knocked speechless, gaped at her for several seconds. Then he gulped an audible breath. "What the hell do you mean, not for much longer?"

Melissa's expression turned stormy. "There you go again, Howard, swearing. I've never known a man worth anything who couldn't express himself without using foul language. Such dependence on blasphemy betokens a weak character and low standards, and I don't intend to put up with it."

She whirled around, aiming to leave her husband there in the dirt, but he hollered, "Wait! Wait a blamed minute, Melissa!"

Cody hoped she'd pay him no mind, but he wasn't surprised when she turned around again and scowled at him.

"What?"

"What do you mean you're not my wife for much longer, Melissa? Just what in hell—blazes do you mean by that? I got a right to know what you mean, blast it."

"I mean," she said with exquisite deliberation, "that I am divorcing you, Howard."

Again, time seemed to stand still while everyone digested Melissa's announcement. Grant Davis's head tilted to one side. It was the most emotion Cody'd ever seen him display, barring when he'd dropped his toothpick a couple seconds earlier.

Howard Wilmeth had to swallow several times before his words would come. After a moment, he said, "What—what do you mean, you're divorcing me? You can't divorce me."

"Oh yes I can. According to Judge Henry Calloway, who's the circuit judge for this part of the Territory, and whom I have consulted in detail, I have good cause, and I'm proceeding with the divorce. I've already filed the papers."

"Wait a blamed minute, Melissa! You got to have a reason before you can divorce a man. What reason do you have?"

He asked the question as if he honestly didn't understand. Cody experienced another fierce desire to knock him down, and to keep punching on him until that handsome face of his was pulp.

Melissa apparently felt the same. Cody saw her hands twitch as if she was trying to keep them in check. "Desertion, for one thing. And lack of financial support, for another." Her voice was as hard as a hailstone. "And then there's the little matter of those women of loose morals at the Pecos Saloon with whom you've been consorting."

Cody blinked, astonished. Shoot, he didn't even know Melissa knew there was such a place as the Pecos Saloon, much less that there were loose women inside it and that her husband had been consorting with them.

Howard stuttered something incomprehensible, but Melissa held up a hand to stop him before he managed to create a rebuttal. "Don't try to deny it, Howard. I've heard about your sordid associations from unimpeachable sources and know I spoke merely the truth. If you expect your wife to stand for the humiliation of her husband committing adultery with any vulgar female who comes along, you'd better find yourself another wife, because I won't tolerate such behavior."

"*Adultery?* Geeze, Melissa, watch your language."

"Ha!" The sharp syllable cut through the air straight to Howard Wilmeth and made him flinch. "Don't make me laugh, Howard! Watch my language, indeed. And this from a man who can't speak two words together without one of them being a crude profanity!"

It took him a second, but Howard finally found his footing. His brow beetled and he glowered at his wife. "Well, hell, what's a fellow supposed to do after his wife runs off with another man?" He aimed an accusatory finger at Melissa. "Don't you go getting yourself all up in arms about what I'm doing, Melissa. You're my wife, and you run off with this Cody O'Fannin character. I don't expect any judge anywhere will fault a fellow for finding comfort somewheres else in those circumstances."

Cody didn't like the turn this conversation was taking. For a few minutes there, he'd felt sure Melissa was going to win; that Howard Wilmeth would go away and never darken her life again. He wasn't so sure anymore.

"I didn't run off with another man!" Melissa's voice conveyed her extreme shock.

"That's what it looks like to me." Howard smirked.

"I'm working as Mr. O'Fannin's housekeeper, Howard Wilmeth, and you know it!"

"Oh, yeah? Don't look like it from here."

"How dare you? How *dare* you imply that there's anything untoward between Mr. O'Fannin and me!"

"What the hell else am I supposed to think? You're livin' here with him, aren't you?"

"As his *housekeeper*, Howard Wilmeth! As his *housekeeper!*"

Howard sneered. "So you say."

Melissa marched up to her husband, her hands clenched at her sides, an expression on her face the likes of which Cody hoped like hell she'd never aim at him. "You low, dishonest, vicious man," she said, her voice throbbing with rage. "You disgusting, despicable, venal *polecat!* Get out of here, Howard. Just go away. Don't ever come back. I'll see you in hell before I'll go back to you. And I'll never let you see Katie. I'll never tell her the kind of man her father is. She deserves better than you, Howard Wilmeth. *I* deserve better than you! You're despicable. You're corrupt, immoral, deceitful, and hateful. I never want to see you again as long as I live."

With that, she delivered what must have been a powerful slap to Howard Wilmeth's cheek, because it sounded like a clap of thunder, and he staggered backwards. Cody was impressed as hell.

Howard's hand reached up to cup his stinging cheek. Cody saw a vivid red handprint on that cheek, and his insides smiled. His outsides remained cautious. He'd picked up his shotgun as soon as he'd seen those horsemen approaching, and he was prepared to kill Howard Wilmeth if he so much as looked like he might strike back at Melissa.

"All right, Melissa," Howard said at last. "All right. I'll go away."

"Good." Melissa's expression didn't change—she looked like she was ready to continue fighting if it proved necessary—but Cody heard the triumph in her voice.

"But I'll be back." Howard turned on his heel, stalked back to his horse, and mounted. He wheeled the horse around, then yanked on the reins and wheeled it back again so that it was facing Melissa.

Cody winced in sympathy for the poor horse's mouth.

Pointing a quivering finger at his wife, Howard said, "You think you're smart, don't you? But you're not, dammit. There's no judge in the whole damned country will give my daughter to a whore and a slut and a no-good bitch who's living in sin with a man who's not her lawful husband. You'll see, dammit. You'll see. I don't want you anymore, but I'll take my daughter, damn you. I'll get her. You just wait and see if I don't."

With that, Howard turned the horse yet again and, with a gesture to his comrades, rode away from his wife. Grant Davis tugged his hat politely in Melissa's direction and then in Cody's before he nudged his horse and followed Howard.

Cody's blood ran cold when the implications of Howard's threat settled inside him.

Evidently feeling brave now that the possibility of danger had passed, Perry hurtled out from underneath the house and barreled after the departing horses. He chased their dust for a hundred yards or more, then turned and trotted back to the house, his tail proudly flying. He really was a dog. If Cody hadn't been so worried about Melissa, he'd have told him so.

Melissa stood as if rooted to the spot as her husband galloped away from her. Still holding his gun, Cody hurried over to her. He stopped short of putting his arm around her shoulder, squeezing her to his side, and kissing her, but not by much. He ached to do those things. Since he knew he had no right, he paused at her side and peered after the departing horsemen.

"You all right, ma'am?" he asked after a minute.

Melissa didn't reply. Cody got worried, so he

stopped staring into the distance and looked at her.

"Oh, Lord, ma'am!" He forgot caution so far as to put a hand on her shoulder. She'd turned white as a ghost and had her arms wrapped across her stomach, as if in that way she could keep herself from splintering apart. Cody's heart hurt for her. "Don't pay any attention to him, Mrs. Wilmeth. He can't do anything. He can't take Katie away from you."

It seemed to take every ounce of strength for her to stop staring after Howard Wilmeth and look up at Cody. Her blue eyes were huge in her pale cheeks. She started trembling like the ground will do when a herd of beeves is stampeding. Cody's worry shot up like a grouse out of the sagebrush.

"He's all talk, ma'am. He can't take your daughter. You know what Judge Calloway said. I was there, remember?"

"Yes," she whispered, and licked her lips. "Yes. Yes, I do remember."

"Anyway," he said, saying what was on his mind even though it seemed kind of mean, "he doesn't even want little Katie. He only said that to fret you."

The notion occurred to Cody that Wilmeth might benefit from spending some time with a baby—especially a couple of nights, during which his sleep was interrupted several times by its squalling. Learning what babies were like to live with might do the bastard a world of good and rid Melissa of him forever. He elected not to voice his opinion. He was pretty sure Melissa wouldn't greet it with favor, and it might hurt her feelings. Cody would do almost anything to prevent Melissa's feelings from hurting.

"Yes. Yes, I'm sure that's true, too."

"And you haven't done a thing that he can hold against you, either. You know it and I know it and Luis knows it. And we'll all say so."

"Yes," she said for the third time.

The truth and justice of Cody's speech didn't seem to ease her worries any, which indicated to Cody that she didn't know much about how life worked out here on the frontier. He decided, *to hell with it*, and put an arm around her shoulder to steady her. She looked like she was about to shatter into a million tiny, brittle pieces.

"It's true, ma'am. Nobody'll believe that you've done anything wrong. Leastways, nobody who knows me will." Damn Howard Wilmeth to perdition. Cody frowned, suddenly furious. "Blast it, ma'am, out here all a man's got is his word and his reputation. I've been here for going on five years now, and there's not a man in the Seven Rivers country don't know my word's as good as gold. Your husband—well, ma'am, I don't know what kind of name he's got for himself so far, but he hasn't been here long enough for folks to peg him. They know me, and they pegged me for a square fellow a long time ago."

He gently turned her around and steered her toward the house. Luis stood at the open doorway, obviously concerned. Cody nodded at him to let him know everything was all right. He wished it was. He did know that what he'd just told Melissa was the truth. Whether Cody's name as an honorable man would go far in a court of law if Howard Wilmeth pursued his threat was another matter. He didn't let Melissa in on his concern.

She looked up at him, hope blooming in her eyes. "Do you really think your reputation will help me, Mr. O'Fannin? By association? If Howard does try anything, I mean."

"Sure. I'm dead sure of it, Mrs. Wilmeth." If Cody'd had a spare arm, he'd have crossed his fingers so his fib wouldn't count. Since he had Melissa in one arm and was holding his shotgun in his other hand, he trusted his good intentions would negate his tiny stretcher in the eyes of God.

He guided her into the house and to a chair in the kitchen. "I'll make you up a nice cup of tea, Mrs. Wilmeth. That'll make you feel better."

"Oh, no!" She stood in a flurry, as if just then coming to her senses. "Please, Mr. O'Fannin, don't go to any trouble on my behalf. I'm sorry I fell apart." When she felt Luis's hands pressing down on her shoulders, she jumped and uttered a stifled shriek.

Cody chuckled. "You're nervous as a cat in a coyote's den, Mrs. Wilmeth, and I don't blame you. You just sit down there where Luis is pushin' you and I'll fix you up a cup of tea. There's no law says I can't make a cup of tea in my own kitchen if I want to, even if you are the cook."

She sat and looked up at Luis in chagrin. "Goodness, Mr. Morales, I'm so sorry. I didn't mean to yell at you."

Luis grinned. "No problem, Miz Wilmeth. Katie's still sleepin'. I just come in to tell you so."

"Thank you."

"Pour out three glasses of that apple juice, Luis. Mrs. Wilmeth's got to taste some of the good work we did this morning."

"Mercy, that's right. I need to process the rest of that juice, too."

Melissa's face started to look less pale, and Cody blessed her overdeveloped sense of responsibility. At least worrying about apple juice might get her mind off her bastard of a husband. And Cody'd help her with the juice, too, just to make sure her thoughts remained diverted.

* * *

The apple juice was every bit as delicious as Cody recollected from his days in Georgetown. He smacked his lips and glanced at Melissa, hoping she was enjoying it, too. She peered over at him.

"It's wonderful, Mr. O'Fannin. I'm so glad Mac found that apple press."

Cody snorted. "He finds the blamedest things around that place of his."

"He does, doesn't he?" She gave him a tiny smile. It looked like she had to reach way down deep for it.

All at once, something Cody'd been puzzling over surged into his mind. Before he had a chance to think himself out of it, he said, "How'd you know about your husband and the ladies at the Pecos Saloon, Mrs. Wilmeth?" He could feel his face get hot, and cursed himself as a blundering ass. Then, for the second time that day, he decided *to hell with it*. He wanted to know, dammit. "I mean, it's good you did find out about it, but—well, did Luis tell you or something?"

Melissa looked down at the table, clearly embarrassed. She murmured, "I—I don't know. It just occurred to me, actually." She looked up, her expression attesting to her state of confusion. "It just popped into my head. I honestly can't explain it." She shrugged helplessly and looked down again. "I only hope it's true."

Cody blinked at her, and her cheeks blazed with color.

"I mean, I don't hope it's true at all. I mean, how could I hope my husband has been consorting with—oh, dear."

Cody didn't know what to say, so he wisely kept his own counsel.

"What I mean is, I hope I didn't accuse Howard of something he didn't do."

Aha. Cody understood now. He said, "I, um, don't think you have to worry about it's not being true, ma'am."

She looked relieved. "Oh, thank goodness." She blushed again. "I mean—oh, goodness, you know what I mean."

"Yes, ma'am, I surely do."

"I still don't know what possessed me to say it, though. It just popped into my head out of the blue, and it was as if something beyond my control made me say it."

"Hmmm. Strange."

"Yes, it was very strange." She was silent for a moment, then suddenly burst out, "Mr. O'Fannin, are you sure I wasn't being dreadfully unkind to Howard? I didn't really malign him unjustly, did I? I'll be mortified if I did."

"No, ma'am," Cody said with conviction. "You didn't unjustly malign him one little bit. I've heard about him."

Her eyes went as round as pie plates. "You have?"

Cody sighed, and wished he were two people so he could make himself bend over and deliver a swift kick to the place where it would do him the most good. He felt like such a fool. But hell, it was the truth. "Well . . ." He looked at Melissa and decided she deserved to know. "Yes, ma'am. You hear things out on the range, you know, when you meet other men passing by and so forth. I'm afraid your husband's got himself quite a name as a frequenter of the Pecos Saloon."

He saw a flash of pain cross her face and doubly wished he could kick himself. But damn it all to hell and back again, Howard Wilmeth was a piece of cow manure, and Melissa deserved better. Cody'd do damned near anything at this point to keep her away from Howard—not for his sake, but for hers.

"Well," she said after another moment, during which the quiet hung over them like a mourning cloud, "I'm glad I was right, even though it hurts, knowing."

"I'm sure it does, ma'am. But it's probably better that you do know. It'll make what you have to do easier." At least, he hoped to glory it would.

"Yes." She let out a big sigh. "Yes, I'm sure you're right."

Back at McMurdo's Wagon Yard in the tiny village of Rio Hondo, Alexander McMurdo smiled with satisfaction and dusted his hands together as if he'd just finished a difficult job and was proud of the way he'd handled it. He'd lived long enough in the world to know not to take care of people's problems for them, but to let them do their own solving.

Several centuries ago he'd come to understand that a body appreciated life more if he—or she—figured things out on his own. Every now and then, however, especially when folks had to deal with frog spawn like Howard Wilmeth, Mac didn't mind implanting a suggestion or two.

Melissa looked as though her fears were hanging on around the edges of the good humor she'd adopted for his benefit. Cody wished he could wipe the haunted look from her eyes. He'd heard his aunt Luella tell him that it sometimes helped if a body just talked to another person. Not about their problems, particularly, Luella'd said, but just about anything at all. She used to say that nine times out of ten just making a body talk would be good for what ailed him.

Of course, Aunt Luella was the biggest gossip in

Georgetown, and Cody suspected she had ulterior motives when she drew people out. Still, Cody thought her philosophy made some kind of sense. Cody wondered if it would help Melissa if he drew her out a little bit—got her to talk about her life before she came out to the Territory.

He chided himself for using fancy talk as an excuse to satisfy his own curiosity. Hell, he was as bad as Aunt Luella. Then he noticed Melissa, her glass of apple juice forgotten in her hand, staring out the window in the direction in which her husband had headed, and he figured that even if his motives weren't a hundred percent pure, talk might help. He decided to begin with praise, and perhaps in that way keep the discussion from getting gloomy.

"You know, ma'am, the old place hasn't ever looked as good as it has since you came to work here."

She jerked her head around, his voice having startled her. "Thank you, Mr. O'Fannin. I truly enjoy working here. It's the sort of work I'm used to."

Interesting. Cody's ears perked right up. This was one of the first things he'd heard her say that referred to her life before the Territory. He refilled her apple juice glass and asked, as casually as he could, considering the avid state of his curiosity, "You worked as a housekeeper in Boston?"

She smiled her thanks and sipped her juice. "This is so delicious, Mr. O'Fannin. I've never tasted fresh apple juice before."

"Me and Arnie used to beg our folks to let us press apples back home in Georgetown." He chuckled. "Reckon it was the only chore they didn't have to hunt us down and badger us to do."

Melissa's faint smile wasn't terribly encouraging, but it was better than his feeble attempt at humor

166

deserved. Cody was modestly encouraged. He cleared his throat. "You were telling me about your job as a housekeeper in Boston, Mrs. Wilmeth?"

Melissa nodded and took another sip of her juice. "I wouldn't say I was Mrs. Bowlus's housekeeper, exactly, although I guess I did do pretty much everything for her. I used to clean and cook. She had a hired nanny to watch her children until they were old enough to go to boarding school."

"She sent her kids away to school?" Cody felt a great sense of shock. He'd heard of people shuffling their children off to boarding school but hadn't ever known anyone who'd actually done it. All of a sudden, Melissa took on an alien quality in his mind, like somebody from a different country or something. He didn't like the feeling. "Um, didn't she like her kids, ma'am? Or was she really rich?"

Melissa thought for a minute, watching the sediment settle in her glass. At last she said, "Both." Then she looked at Cody and giggled. Immediately, his idea that she was somehow different from him vanished. He was glad to see it go, and grinned back at her.

"She was real rich, huh?"

"Yes, and extremely stingy, too. I've never known a meaner woman." She shook her head. "I couldn't understand it. She had a beautiful two-story house surrounded by lovely grounds in Boston's best neighborhood, and yet she begrudged the tiniest expenditure."

Cody shook his head. "Don't reckon I've ever known anybody like that in my day, ma'am. Old man Martin was known as a tight screw in Georgetown, but at least he didn't send his kids off to boarding school."

"Well, Mrs. Bowlus hated spending the money, but

167

she hated having her children around even more, so I guess she was willing to pay the price."

"Shoot, I'm glad my ma wasn't like that."

Melissa laughed out loud. Cody wasn't sure what he'd said that was so funny, but he was pleased to have made her laugh.

"How long did you work for this Mrs. Bowlus character?"

Melissa's laugh cut off sharply. She took another sip of juice and looked at Cody over the rim of her glass, as if she weren't sure she should answer his question. He didn't understand that look.

Finally she said, "Eleven years, Mr. O'Fannin. Eleven long, not especially pleasant years."

"Eleven *years*. Lordy, ma'am, excuse me for saying it, but you must've started workin' there when you were a baby!"

Her cheeks got pink. "Not quite, Mr. O'Fannin."

Cody caught himself goggling and snapped out of it. "Pardon me for pryin', ma'am, but you don't look to be very old. It's hard to fathom you working anywhere for eleven years."

A big sigh leaked from Melissa's lips. She looked awfully sad for a second or two. "I was nine when I went to work at her house, Mr. O'Fannin."

"Nine? You were nine years old when you went to work for some lady as her housekeeper?"

"Oh, no. I wasn't her housekeeper then. I just did the cleaning and laundry until I was twelve or so."

Tilting his head to one side, Cody studied Melissa's face and tried to reconcile the daintiness of her features with a woman who'd been working for wages since she was nine years old. "Er, didn't you go to school, Mrs. Wilmeth? Don't they have schools in Boston?"

Her expression caught him off guard because it

turned hard and bitter and seemed out of place on her gentle face. "Oh, yes, Mr. O'Fannin, there were schools in Boston. There weren't any schools for people like me, however."

Cody stared at her, unable to figure out what to say now. After several uncomfortable moments, Melissa sighed again.

"I suppose I really should tell you about me, Mr. O'Fannin. It's not fair to keep the truth from you, since you've been so kind to me." She looked down at the tabletop. "You may not want me working for you any longer after you know, though, and I don't know what I'll do if you turn me out."

Turn her out? What the hell was the woman talking about?

"I won't turn you out, ma'am. Honest."

Immediately, he wondered if he'd just lied to her. What if she told him she'd been a thief or a jailbird—or, God save him, a whore?

No. Cody didn't know much about her, but he'd go bail that Melissa Wilmeth was a basically honest person, however wretched her background.

"Thank you, Mr. O'Fannin." She didn't sound convinced.

Chapter Ten

Melissa could hardly believe how well she'd stood up to Howard that morning. She'd never done such a thing in her life. She was alternately proud of herself and in mortal fear that Howard would carry out his threat to take Katie away from her.

Her mother used to tell her to mind her tongue or she'd end up in the same situation she herself was in. Melissa hoped to heaven her mother was wrong.

"If you talk to your employer like that, young lady," her mother used to say after delivering a stinging slap to Melissa's cheek, "you'll be out of a job and out on your rear end, and then what'll you do for money, hmm? If you think we live like trash now, try to imagine what you'll be living like if you can't earn any money. You'll not live with me if you get yourself fired from Mrs. Bowlus's establishment, Melissa."

Melissa had imagined it, it had terrified her, and she'd never spoken in anger to another human being since. Until today, when she'd yelled at Howard. And slapped him. Merciful heavens, she'd actually slapped his cheek. It had felt good, too, and Melissa was sure that meant something bad about herself.

And now Cody O'Fannin was demanding to know what her life had been like before she moved to the Territory. She guessed he deserved to know, although the mere thought of talking about it frightened her. What would he do when he realized he'd taken in the wretched refuse of a Boston dockside slum?

"Um, do you know anything about Boston, Mr. O'Fannin?" Melissa began after another fortifying sip of apple juice. She hadn't been lying when she'd told him it was delicious. Except for Mac's oranges, the last one of which Melissa had carefully divided up and shared with Cody and Luis only this morning, she didn't know when she'd tasted anything as wonderful as this freshly pressed apple juice.

"Not much," he admitted. "Not anything."

She gave him a tiny smile. "It's an interesting place. There are neighborhoods that would make you stare, they're so beautiful. The people living in them are so rich, you wonder how anyone could ever have earned so much money."

"I've heard that," Cody admitted. "Never quite derstood it, to tell you the truth, ma'am. I mea He shrugged. "I reckon a fellow gets used to he's used to, and it's hard to imagine anything Everybody lived pretty much the same in Ge town."

"Yes. I think I know what you mean, O'Fannin." She heaved a soft sigh. "Until I was years old, I thought the whole world looked and neighborhood. Then my mother cleaned me sent me off to work for Mrs. Bowlus."

She saw Cody's eyebrows lift, and she guessed that, while she'd told the literal truth, he probably wouldn't understand.

"We needed the money, you see."

"You needed to work when you were nine years old because your family needed the money?"

Melissa nodded. "Do you know what a slum is, Mr. O'Fannin?"

"A slum, ma'am?" He pondered for a moment. "Don't reckon so. Sorry."

"No, Mr. O'Fannin, I expect I'm the one who's sorry, because I *do* know. A slum is a neighborhood in the worst part of town. Back East, the slums spring up in old neighborhoods that have fallen on hard times, or around ports and docks. We lived near the harbor. Until I went to work for Mrs. Bowlus, I thought the entire world smelled like chimney smoke and rotting fish."

Cody said, "Oh." He opened his mouth, but closed it again. Melissa honored his discretion. *Oh* said quite enough.

"I lived in that Boston slum from the moment I was born until my sister Katherine died when I was twelve. Then I begged the housekeeper's job from Mrs. Bowlus because I couldn't bear being in the house where she died. Katherine"—Melissa had to stop and take a deep breath or break down. She didn't want this to be any worse than it was already.—"Katherine was my only companion, Mr. 'Fannin. The only person I could talk to." *The only* *'son I loved. The only one who loved me.* She re-
ed speaking those two truths aloud because they
ed pathetic. "After that I slept at Mrs. Bowlus's
o' and only went home to take my mother money
'ndays."

did you just have the one sister, Mrs. Wilmeth? I remember you telling me about your sister dying, and I was right sorry to hear about it."

"I had three older brothers, too. I was the youngest child."

Cody looked at her as if he wasn't quite sure what to say. Something acrid twisted inside her. She'd lay odds that his childhood had been the likes of which she used to read about in her few spare moments when Mrs. Bowlus condescended to allow her to read books from her own children's library—books containing mothers and fathers and happy, smiling brothers and sisters.

The next part was always the hardest. Melissa didn't like to think about it, and she hated like the very devil to say it out loud. The next part was what set her apart from other people; it was what stamped her as a worthless, undeserving slum brat.

"My father ran out on us when I was born, Mr. O'Fannin. My mother said he couldn't face having one more mouth to feed. She couldn't support us all without him, and two of my brothers were taken to an orphanage. I don't remember them at all. My other brother ran away from home when I was about fifteen."

Cody opened his mouth. Then he shut it. Then he cleared his throat. Before he could formulate some meaningless commonplace sympathy that would break Melissa's heart coming from him, she hurried on. "I think my mother blamed me, and I don't really fault her for it, but honestly, I don't know what I could have done to prevent being born."

"No," popped out of Cody's mouth. "No, it wasn't your fault, Mrs. Wilmeth."

"Thank you, Mr. O'Fannin." He was so sweet. Melissa had never known a man as kindhearted as Cody O'Fannin. She felt tears sting her eyes. "I know how hard my mother worked, though, and how difficult her life was." She studied her fingernails and spoke the most difficult thought of all. "I—I can't even imagine how awful it must have been for her to have had to give up her own children."

"Well, I should think it was! Pardon me for sayin' it, ma'am, but I think your pa oughta be hunted down and shot for leaving his wife and kids that way. I don't hold with a fellow running out on his responsibilities, ma'am. I surely don't."

Melissa blinked, surprised by his vehemence. His agitation was so great, it propelled him out of his chair, and he stomped around the kitchen twice before stopping at the sink and glaring out the window. "Pardon me again, ma'am, but I feel the same way about your husband." He whirled around and looked at her hard. "Ma'am, if you ever decide to go back to that man, I'll think less of you for it. I surely will."

Melissa opened her mouth, although she had no idea what to say in the face of Cody's declaration. He held up a hand to stop her before she could formulate a denial. She'd *never* consider going back to Howard. Not now, she wouldn't. Not after she'd lived with Cody O'Fannin for a couple of weeks.

"I know it isn't my place to say this, either, ma'am, but you're a good person, and you're a hard worker. You're worth ten of either of those men, ma'am— your father or that husband of yours. I don't know how you got hooked up with that man, ma'am, but if you'll pardon me for sayin' so, you can do better than him."

As much as Melissa appreciated Cody's kindness in saying those sweet things, still more did she appreciate how little he understood yet of her life in Boston and what it had made of her.

"Not in Boston, I couldn't," she said sharply, bringing Cody up short. His mouth shut with a snap, and he tilted his head again in what Melissa was beginning to recognize as his quizzical look. "Not in Boston, I couldn't," she repeated with less vehemence. "You still don't quite understand, Mr. O'Fannin."

He scratched his head and came back to sit across from her at the table. "I reckon I don't, ma'am. I can't see why a fine lady like you would have any trouble at all getting yourself a good man."

"That's very nice of you to say, Mr. O'Fannin." She meant it, too. "But, you see, Boston isn't like out here. There are, literally, millions of people there. I was born and reared in a slum near the harbor. Females who were born and raised where I was are *not* considered ladies. Except that my sister Katherine taught me my letters, I'd never even have learned to read and write. People who live where I'm from have an accent that's much different from the rich people who live on Beacon Hill, where Mrs. Bowlus lived. Even if one ignored my secondhand clothes and ill-fitting, holey shoes, I was marked, Mr. O'Fannin, labeled, branded. I couldn't open my mouth without people knowing where I'd come from."

"Shoot, no foolin'?" Cody seemed impressed, which surprised Melissa, who had been endeavoring like a Trojan since she was nine years old to rid herself of her dockside accent.

"Yes. No fooling. No decent man would have anything to do with a woman like me."

Cody scratched his head again and tilted it the other way. "That's stupid, ma'am. If you'll pardon me for sayin' so."

Melissa had allowed her shoulders to slump in dejection. She was so ashamed of her beginnings. She felt as though she was polluting the very air in Cody O'Fannin's kitchen by even talking about her dis-

175

graceful childhood. Cody's words jerked her upright. She stared at him. "Um, I certainly pardon you, Mr. O'Fannin—but I'm not sure I know what you mean. What's stupid about it?"

He surged out of his chair again. This time he headed for the stove, where he lifted the lid and lowered it again. Then he touched a flatiron, several of which were always set out on the stove, got his fingers burned, snatched them back, and stuck them in his mouth. He took them out again and flapped them in the air to cool the burn when he spoke.

"Mrs. Wilmeth, there isn't a single thing you've told me so far about your life that's your fault. Now, I understand that you come from mighty rough circumstances. Life must've been downright lousy for you in Boston, what with a father that run out on his family and a mother that blamed you for it, and your brothers havin' to go to a home, and your sister dyin' and all. But there's nothing there that's your fault. You weren't to blame for any damned one of those things—pardon me for swearin', ma'am, but it makes me mad, you tryin' to say that stuffs your fault, when it isn't."

"I—" Melissa didn't get to finish protesting, because Cody broke in.

"I know, I know. Folks get to thinkin' they're what the neighbors think they are. We had us a family in Georgetown that was plenty hard up. The man, Mr. Cutter he was, up and died of the flu one winter, and his widow was real troubled for a long time. Folks in Georgetown—well, they don't cotton much to accepting charity from their neighbors, even though we're always helping each other out. But Mrs. Cutter, she had to do sewing and take in other folks's wash and suchlike, and her kids didn't have the best clothes to wear and all that. Jimmy Cutter—

he and me were best pals—well, sometimes he got to talkin' about his ma and how hard she had to work and he'd get to feelin' bad about her. But I used to tell him, 'Jimmy, you can't help it that your pa died. All's you can do is help your ma the best way you can, and everybody in town will think the better of you for it.' And you know what, ma'am?"

It took Melissa a moment to realize he expected an answer. She shook her head. "No. What?"

"They did. Think the better of him for it, I mean. 'Cause they knew what had happened to him and his ma, and they admired his grit—and hers, too—for working hard to make a go of life even without them having a man around. That don't mean it was easy, because it wasn't, but there's not a man in Georgetown who wouldn't hire Jimmy Cutter before he'd hire most other men, because Jimmy's proved his worth." Cody nodded decisively. "Just like you've proved yours."

Melissa had no idea what to say, so she said only, "Thank you," and felt like crying. Nobody'd ever told her she was worth more than spit on the sidewalk. She didn't really believe Cody, but she loved him for saying such nice things. She even tried to make herself believe them, but she wasn't awfully successful.

"You're welcome."

Cody turned with a jerk and frowned out the window. He turned again, just as abruptly. "And that's not all, either, ma'am."

Melissa was almost afraid to ask, but she did anyway. "No?"

"No. You seem to think you're somehow bad for having a rotten father who couldn't face his responsibilities and deserted his family. Well, what about that Mrs. Bowling character you worked for?"

"Mrs. Bowlus?"

He waved a hand in the air. "Whatever. But what about her, ma'am? She didn't run out on her kids, but she did something just as bad. Worse, if you ask me. Hell, she sent 'em away! Now, how do you think *her* kids feel about themselves, when their own mother didn't even want them?"

She frowned, never having thought about the Bowlus children and herself as equal in any regard before this. "I don't think the circumstances are the same, Mr. O'Fannin."

"Of course, they're not the same!" Cody apparently realized he'd hollered, because he muttered, "Pardon me, ma'am. But it seems to me that the only difference between you and those kids is that they had money and you didn't."

Which is quite a difference, Melissa thought bitterly. She decided merely to nod.

She didn't fool Cody O'Fannin. "Yeah, yeah, I know. It's a big difference. And you don't have to tell me that their life was a hell of a lot easier than yours—pardon me, ma'am. But it don't look to me like their parents wanted them any more than yours wanted you. That doesn't mean those kids aren't worthwhile people."

"Of course it doesn't," Melissa said quickly. She realized the implication of her words a heartbeat before Cody's smile hit her.

He nodded. "There. You see? So why is it you're willing to cut those kids some slack and you aren't that nice to yourself?"

She stared at him, speechless, for a moment before she managed to stammer, "I—I'm not sure."

He nodded again, with more energy. "No. Me, neither. Hell, ma'am, you are who you are. From where I stand, I see a real nice lady with a lot of sand. I'd be willing to wager you're a whole lot more useful than either of those Bowlish kids, too, because you've had to make your own way in life, and you know how to get on. Hell, ma'am, their parents didn't even give 'em work to shape their natures by. I bet the two of them are like a rich New Yorker who come to Georgetown once. Expected the world to wait on him. When it didn't, he didn't know what to do with himself."

Cody grinned suddenly. He had a simply spectacular smile. "He learned, though," Cody said. "He learned real quick."

"My goodness," murmured Melissa, captured by the beauty of Cody O'Fannin. Beauty was an awfully soft word for such a potently male man, yet to Melissa, who couldn't think of another one, it fit. He was beautiful inside and out, and she wished she knew how he did it. If she was allowed to study him for several decades, perhaps she'd learn the secret of inner beauty, too, although she wasn't sure about that.

"Yes, ma'am," he said, less vehemently. "He learned." His gaze changed; turned from firm to pensive. He canted his head to one side and studied her.

She stared into his beautiful brown eyes for the longest time. When she realized she was staring, she tried to look away and couldn't. Cody seemed to be having the same trouble. After a moment, he slowly walked back to the table and put a hand on Melissa's shoulder. It burned like fire through her simple calico shirtwaist and apron. Melissa fought the impulse to put her hand on top of his.

He sank into the chair next to her. "I think you're a fine woman, Mrs. Wilmeth. A fine woman. You've got nothing to be ashamed of. You come from a hard beginning, but you've got yourself out of it now, and there's nobody can drag you back again unless you let 'em, because you've made something for yourself here."

"H-here?" Her voice quavered like an old lady's, and she was embarrassed.

"Here. For as long as you want to stay here, this job is yours. To hell with Loretta."

He blushed. Melissa was enchanted. She managed to whisper, "Thank you, Mr. O'Fannin."

"You're welcome, ma'am."

A second before he kissed her, Melissa realized he was leaning toward her, and she met him halfway. As soon as she felt his lips on hers, she uttered a tiny mew of longing.

His lips were soft and warm and wonderful. Melissa wished she could melt into his embrace. She wanted to give herself up to Cody O'Fannin, to become part of him, to shift her burdens to his broad shoulders and never have to worry again. She knew she was being fanciful. Worse, she was being a fool. Again.

She'd never felt this way with Howard. Before they were married, he'd always wanted more than she was willing to give him, and he'd managed to make her feel guilty for holding out. He'd pressed and pressured and cajoled and gotten mad, and Melissa had always been on edge and worried.

She didn't feel on edge with Cody. She knew, deep down in her soul, that whatever foul kind of person she was, Cody was different. He was an honorable man, of the sort she'd only read about until she'd met him. Cody was no Howard Wilmeth to take whatever he could get away with, and always want more than a woman could comfortably give.

Cody was gentle and strong. Howard was mean and weak. Kissing Howard—bedding with him—had always seemed improper somehow, even after they were married. Even though she knew kissing Cody was wrong, it didn't feel wrong like it had with Howard.

Her arms went around his broad shoulders, and she slanted her head and kissed him back. She heard him breathe a soft moan, and wished she could be a different kind of person for him. He deserved someone fresh and innocent and pure, not someone like her, who'd witnessed the basest side of life—and lived it, too.

"Lordy," leaked from Cody's lips and into her mouth. Melissa smiled. She loved his Texas talk and his Texas accent and his Texas ways. She loved *him*, God help her.

His work-roughened hands had been resting lightly on her shoulders. Now they slipped around her and he drew her more closely to his chest. He felt so solid, so strong, so *real* somehow. She never once got the feeling that he wasn't what he claimed to be, the way she did with Howard, who put on a different face for every occasion. She knew Cody was exactly what she saw.

Sensations skimmed through her body and lightened her heart. His hands now spanned her sides, pressing against her sensitive breasts. She had a shameless desire to feel those big hands cover her breasts. She knew there was no hope for her, that she was abandoned beyond redemption, but she couldn't stop what she felt. She wanted to make love with him.

Katie's loud screech from the other room separated them as if they'd both caught fire. Immediately, shame enveloped Melissa. Her hand shot to her cheek, and she whispered, "Oh, no!"

Cody, panting hard, stared at her as if he, too, had

181

been stunned by their torrid kiss. His mouth opened, but he didn't say a word.

Melissa jumped up from her chair so fast it banged against the table behind her. "Oh, Mr. O'Fannin! Good heavens, what have I done!"

She turned and ran out of the kitchen so fast she barely saw Cody's hand shoot out as if to stop her. She heard him say, "Wait, Melissa! Wait, Mrs. Wilmeth!"

She didn't wait. She grabbed Katie out of her lovely new cradle and rushed to the room the two of them shared. There she shut the door and leaned against it, shaking like a leaf.

"What have I done?" she whispered. "Oh, Katie, what have I done?"

She knew what she'd done even as she asked the question. She'd corrupted Cody O'Fannin, is what she'd done. Her base nature had overridden her feeble attempts at goodness, run roughshod over Cody's excellent qualities, and sent them both spinning out of control and straight to perdition. Oh, what a wicked woman she was! To have lured that good man into a vile and corrupt act was beyond bad. It was—it was—Melissa couldn't think of a word terrible enough to describe herself.

She gazed down into her daughter's innocent face and wondered if there was any hope on earth for the two of them.

Cody stared after Melissa, his body hard, his mind mush, and he wanted her back in his arms again. Lord God Almighty, he'd never even suspected a kiss could be that exciting. The few times he'd shared kisses with the girls at the Pecos Saloon hadn't felt like that. Not one little bit. Not even close.

He wanted Melissa Wilmeth so bad, he shook with

wanting. He wanted to bury himself in her, to lose himself, to make her forget all about that bastard husband of hers. Cody wanted her to think about *him*, Cody O'Fannin, and no other man on the face of the earth.

"Lordy," he whispered, shaken to his boots. He blinked several times, wishing his brain would get back to working again. It was whirring like a loose cog at the moment, at the mercy of his body, which was straining at his trouser buttons with wanting.

He shook his head. "Lordy," he said again, more loudly. The shake seemed to jar his thought processes cranking to a start.

What in the name of thunder would he have done if Katie hadn't started squalling? Would he have violated Melissa Wilmeth right here on the kitchen table? He blinked at the table, visions of a passionate embrace hazing his brain for a moment. Lord, he'd almost died when he'd felt the swell of her breasts with his hands. He hadn't dared cover those lush breasts and feel them as he'd wanted to, but he'd felt how soft they were, how full, how—

He shook his head again, hard, and said, "No."

He took a step toward Melissa and Katie's room, and stopped because he didn't know why he'd taken it. What in heaven's name could he say to her now? How could he ever adequately apologize to her? Hell, he was supposed to be helping her out by giving her a job. He wasn't supposed to be seducing her with kisses and embraces of a carnal nature, no matter how delightful they were. No matter how perfectly right their kiss had been.

No, no, no. That last thought just went to show how ill-fitted he was to this sort of thing. By rights, he should bite the bullet and own up to his actions. By everything he'd ever been taught was fitting and proper behavior in a man, he should now go up to that room, knock at the door, and demand that Melissa Wilmeth marry him. After all, folks didn't kiss like that unless they were promised. According to Aunt Luella, they didn't kiss like that even after they were married, but Cody didn't know as to whether he held with her opinion. Aunt Luella was a stodgy old biddy. Any wife of Cody O'Fannin's wouldn't be like her.

But that was the whole point. Cody O'Fannin didn't need a wife. He didn't *want* a wife. He had goals and ambitions. He had objectives to reach. He sure as the devil didn't need to be saddled with a wife—especially one who came equipped with another man's baby.

Which brought up another whole point entirely: Melissa Wilmeth was already married. And no matter how much of a son of a bitch her old man was, they weren't divorced yet. Hell, she probably wasn't ready for another husband and wouldn't be for years. Who could blame her, after going through what she'd gone through with Wilmeth? Cody sure didn't.

So why did it take every ounce of his strength to keep him from marching to Melissa's room, going down on his knees, and begging her to be his?

"Damn it to blazes," he muttered.

Cody snatched his hat off the rack by the kitchen door and stomped out to saddle his horse. He planned to ride until he was too tired to think.

Mac frowned and shook his head. Things had seemed to be going quite well there for awhile. What was wrong with those two that they insisted on fighting their attraction to each other every inch of the way? It was one of the strongest attractions Mac had ever seen in his career, and he'd been around for a thousand years and more. Cody O'Fannin and Melissa Wilmeth were perfect for each other. That's why Mac had brought them together in the first place.

"Hmmm. Perhaps you're moving a wee bit too fast for 'em, laddie. They *are* human, after all, and humans are an odd lot."

After considering the oddities inherent in human beings for a brief period, whilst enjoying the last of some whiskey he'd conjured, McMurdo decided further action on his part wouldn't hurt, and might even help.

"That apple press was a stroke of genius." He congratulated himself for that one.

"Christmas!" he cried. Christmas was right around the corner. Neither Cody nor Melissa would think it strange if Mac was to ride out to the ranch and take little Katie a Christmas gift. While he was at it, he could take Melissa a box of that Italian marzipan candy that Mac liked so well. There were one or two little things he missed about life as a wizard in Europe, but with a little extra effort, he managed. Or materialized, which was all that mattered, as long as he used proper discretion.

A piece of information telegraphed itself to his mind, and Mac frowned.

"The rotter," he muttered. "I'll tell 'em about *that*, too."

Howard Wilmeth wouldn't get away with it; Mac would see to it. Any man out here in the Territory who even thought about poisoning another man's water supply was worse than dirt.

Although Mac decided to leave more severe measures to Cody, he flicked his little finger.

Several miles to the southeast of Alexander McMurdo's Wagon Yard in Rio Hondo, New Mexico Territory, Howard Wilmeth fell off his horse.

* * *

Cody had never been in a state the likes of which he found himself in as he galloped. Alternately frustrated, furious, and befuddled, he rode and rode, until he had to slow down or hurt his horse.

"Sorry, horse," he muttered as the poor animal wheezed to a walk, its sides heaving. "Didn't mean to take out my troubles on you."

The horse, while offering Cody no reassurance, didn't seem to hold the hard ride against him. He began to mosey along at his usual pace, which was a sturdy clip.

Cody tried to take an interest in the scenery but wasn't very successful. He loved it, but there wasn't all that much of it to begin with, and he'd seen it all before anyway. Nevertheless, his gaze scanned his surroundings. It wasn't a terrific idea to venture out on these incredibly overwhelming, empty plains alone. No matter what he'd told Melissa to reassure her that no dangers lurked in the vicinity, Cody knew better than to believe it himself.

Anything could happen to a lone rider out here, from cougars to Indians to outlaws to so prosaic a commodity as a prairie dog hole. Folks who died out here seldom did so of natural causes, however, and prairie dog holes were easier to avoid than some of the other, less natural, phenomena. Cody figured danger was a part of the price one paid for daring to achieve one's dreams, and he was willing to pay it. On the other hand, he was no fool, and he kept both eyes open.

He'd been riding for about forty-five minutes and was almost to a sharp bend in the Hondo River when he drew up his horse and squinted into the distance. Since he wasn't sure what that was up ahead, he unsheathed his shotgun from its scabbard. Cradling the gun in one arm, he shaded his eyes with his hand and squinted some more. He nudged his horse on a few more paces, trying all the while to discern what he thought he saw.

"Shoot," he said to the horse. "Looks like somebody lost his seat."

The horse seemed unimpressed by this physiologically marvelous feat. Cody, of course, had meant that someone had fallen from his saddle.

Another horse stood grazing on some low scrub several yards away from the man Cody had spotted. Every time the man went anywhere near the horse, the animal backed up. From this distance, Cody thought he could hear cuss words. He shook his head. Whoever that was up there, he was a damned blockhead. He'd never get the horse back that way.

Recognition blindsided him. He sat up straight in his saddle and said, "Shit."

It couldn't be. Could it? He kneed his mount, sending it on a few more paces, then reined it in again. Succumbing to curiosity, Cody pulled out the looking glass he kept in a leather case in his saddlebag. It came in handy now and then, mostly for starting campfires, although Cody didn't like to admit it.

This time he put the looking glass to its proper use and leveled it at the man ahead. He twisted the lens until it was in focus, and then swore softly.

With a click, he folded up the glass, wrapped it tenderly in its leather case once more, stowed it in his saddlebag, and toed his horse into a walk. He didn't hurry. In fact, he planned to take a whole lot of time.

That was Howard Wilmeth up there who'd lost his seat. And Cody wasn't at all sure he aimed to help him find it again.

Chapter Eleven

Howard whirled around when he heard a horseman approach. He fumbled his gun out of its fancy tooled leather holster, but lowered it when he saw Cody already had a shotgun aimed at him.

Cody's lips tightened. The damned fool. Nobody but a greenhorn used a holster like that. Not tied low on his hip with the gun butt-backwards, he didn't. Out here a man required utilitarian equipment, and nobody cared if it was pretty. That damned fancy leather job had probably cost a fortune. This stinker hadn't bothered to send money for his wife and baby to live on, but he'd bought himself a fancy new—worse than new, inefficient—tooled leather holster. Cody could hardly stand it.

"Wilmeth," he said.

"O'Fannin," Howard said back.

"Lost your horse, I see." Cody didn't bother to keep the contempt out of his voice.

Howard grunted something wordless. Cody figured that if he thought it would do any good, he'd try to justify his mishap. He didn't, which led Cody to believe he'd at least learned enough in his short stay in the Territory to realize there was no good excuse for falling off your horse except under extremely unusual circumstances. There was nothing at all unusual about today that Cody could see.

Although he didn't much want to, he expected he'd have to help this fool fetch his horse. Nevertheless, he didn't want to turn his back on Howard Wilmeth. "Give me that gun of yours, and I'll get your horse for you."

"The hell I will." Howard clutched his gun to his chest like a little boy who's been threatened with having his favorite toy confiscated.

Cody shrugged. "Suit yourself." He clucked to his horse and began riding away from the stranded man. He listened as hard as he'd ever listened in his life. If he heard so much as the whish of Howard's gun through the air, he was ready to turn and blow him to kingdom come. He didn't have much faith in Howard's aim, but Cody didn't hold with men pointing guns at other men's backs.

"Hey!" shouted Howard, who evidently figured he'd have better luck with his voice than his bullets. "Hey, you can't just leave me here like this."

Since such a manifestly false declaration deserved no answer, Cody didn't bother explaining to Howard that leaving him there like that was exactly what he was doing.

"Hey!" Howard hollered again. "All right, I'll let you have my damned gun."

Cody drew up his horse and peered over his shoulder as if he was considering whether he thought Howard worth his trouble. He already knew he'd help him. Hell, a man of honor couldn't do anything else, even if the other man was less deserving of assistance than your average rattlesnake.

"Well . . ." He let Howard wonder for as long as he considered prudent, then turned his horse again and headed back to the man sweating on the desert.

He held out his hand, and Howard slapped the gun into it. "Shoot. Anybody'd think you didn't trust me, O'Fannin."

"I don't." It was the worst insult he'd ever spoken to another man, but Cody didn't care. He emptied the chambers and weighed the gun thoughtfully. "Nice weapon you got here, Mr. Wilmeth."

"It's a Colt .45," Howard muttered. "I got me it in Santa Fe."

Cody put a world of meanings into the look he leveled at Howard Wilmeth. He hoped he'd choke on it. Howard looked less repentant than Cody would have liked. On the other hand, his lack of remorse solidified Cody's opinion of the man as miles and miles beneath Melissa's touch.

"I'll get your horse."

Without waiting for Howard's thanks—which was just as well, since Howard didn't offer any—Cody nudged his horse over to the animal grazing on a clump of golden grass. Howard's horse looked up warily and whickered. Cody didn't blame it for being leery. He wouldn't want Howard Wilmeth on his back, either.

Because he disliked the man so much and felt like plaguing him, Cody clicked his tongue and flicked the end of his reins at Howard's horse to make it prance away.

Once it started trotting, Cody urged his own horse into a similar gait, and the two animals traveled along side by side like old chums for several yards.

Cody heard Howard bellowing behind him and grinned to himself. After he figured he'd tormented him long enough, he reached over, grabbed the dangling rein, and gently pulled the horse to a halt.

He dismounted and went to the horse's head and spoke soothingly. Horses were flighty creatures. Cody'd never harbored a whole lot of respect for them, being of a steady disposition himself and not inclined to find skittishness attractive, but he understood their value in the territory, and he honored their endurance. The old horse Cody rode today was about as matter-of-fact as a horse could get. Howard's horse, on the other hand, was more highly strung. After he'd cooed at it and cosseted it for several minutes, it calmed down.

"I know you'd rather not do this, horse, but I reckon I got no choice." His apology seemed to settle the animal.

Cody ran his hands along the animal's neck and peered at its saddle. He thought wryly that the saddle must belong to Blackworth because it was simple and useful—not at all in Howard Wilmeth's style. One of its saddlebags was open, too, and Cody noticed a blue-labeled box sticking out, as if Howard had been removing it when his horse bolted.

Cody frowned. That blue label looked familiar. Because he saw no reason not to, he reached into the saddlebag and took out the box.

"Jesus H. Christ!" exploded from his lips. "Rat poison!"

He stared at that box for a long time, calculating things in his brain. Then he looked up and squinted over to where Howard Wilmeth stood. He was a couple hundred yards away, but Cody could tell he had his feet planted apart, and that his manner remained belligerent.

What in the world did Wilmeth need poison for? He couldn't think of any reason at all to haul it this far out, unless . . . unless. "Was that bastard going to poison the river?" he asked the horse. This part of the Hondo fed directly into Cody's ranch. It was what his own cattle drank from. It was what *he* drank from and, as a consequence, what Melissa and Luis and even baby Katie would drink from. Fury welled up in him like bubbling lava.

Any man who'd poison another man's water supply was worse than a snake. He was worse than the lowest coyote or polecat. Cody searched through both saddlebags to determine if Wilmeth had been armed with anything besides rat poison. Not that rat poison wasn't more than enough. He didn't find anything.

Cody tried not to fluster the horses when he remounted, holding both the box of rat poison and Howard's horses reins. Howard's horse, calmed by Cody's gentle demeanor, followed along docilely at Cody's side as he led it back to Howard.

"It took you long enough," Howard growled, glaring up at Cody.

Cody lifted his eyebrows. "If you don't like the way I got your horse for you, I'll be happy to let go of the reins and leave it for you to catch." He smiled sweetly.

"Don't be an ass," Howard advised. He reached for his horse's reins, but Cody backed up and he missed.

"You know, Mr. Wilmeth, out here it don't do for a man to rip up at a fellow who's just helped him out of a fix. It isn't considered polite. Polite is saying *thank you* when a man fetches your horse for you. Now, I expect you didn't know that, bein' a newcomer and an easterner and all, so I figured I'd just let on about it, so's you'll know how to go on in the future."

Howard looked rebellious for another second or three, then grumbled a grudging, "Thank you."

Cody handed over the reins and tipped his hat. "Sure thing, Mr. Wilmeth." Then he held up the box of rat poison and had the satisfaction of watching Howard's face turn ashen under its recent layer of sunburn. "Looky here what I found, Mr. Wilmeth. In your saddlebag."

Howard regained his composure much too quickly by Cody's reckoning. He wondered how much practice he'd had in doing nefarious deeds, that he could snap back from discovery so fast.

"That's mine," said Howard. "What the hell do you mean, sneaking through a fellow's property like that?"

"It was stickin' out, Mr. Wilmeth," said Cody softly. "And I was mighty curious, as I'd told you to get the hell off my property a good hour or two ago. I thought it was kind of peculiar, you still hanging around here by this time. And bein' at the head of the river that feeds my cattle with a box of rat poison in your saddlebag is even more peculiar."

"I was taking that back to Blackworth's ranch."

"Got a rat problem, does he?" Cody hoped Howard caught his implication.

"Yeah." Howard sounded both mean and scared. Cody figured he'd caught it.

He leaned over and pointed his shotgun straight at Howard Wilmeth's heart—if he had one. Cody doubted it. "I want you off my property, Wilmeth. You were here to poison my water with this." He held up the box of rat poison. "And any man who even thinks about doin' something like that deserves the rope. I'll spare you bein' hung, though. Next time I see you anywhere near my property, I'll shoot a big hole in your gut and watch you die in a lot of pain instead."

He saw Howard's Adam's apple bob up and down as he swallowed.

Cody squinted hard and poked Howard's belly with his shotgun. "You understand that?"

Howard nodded.

"I'm a man of my word, Wilmeth. Ask anybody in these parts. They all know me."

Again Howard nodded. Cody got the impression he'd already heard about Cody O'Fannin's reputation as a man of his word. He hoped so. Hell, not even Hugh Blackworth, who had something against damned near everybody, had anything against Cody.

"I'll let you go this time," Cody continued. "For the sake of your wife and baby, even though you don't deserve either one of them."

Howard frowned and looked like he might argue the point if the odds were better. They weren't, and he kept his mouth shut.

Cody decided he'd said enough—hell, he'd spoken more to Howard Wilmeth in fifteen minutes than he'd spoken to his cousin Arnie in six months—and he liked Arnie. He wheeled his horse around and began to ride off. He didn't get very far before Howard regained his composure. Damn, the man was a bodacious son of a bitch.

"Hey!" Howard called as he scrambled to mount his skittish horse. "Hey, you still got my gun."

Cody sighed. After all that, the polecat was worried about his gun. Not his wife. Not his baby, but his gun. He'd heard about people like Howard Wilmeth; he'd never met one before, and considered himself fortunate for it.

"Oh, yeah." Cody let him have a sweet grin over his

shoulder and heaved the gun as far away from him as he could, into the Hondo River. By the time that louse waded into the river, fetched his gun, and got it loaded again, Cody'd be too far away to shoot at. If he gave the gun to him outright, old Howard might try to shoot him. Even if his aim was bad, he might be able to hit Cody's horse, and the poor animal didn't deserve that.

"Damn you, O'Fannin! Why'd you do that?"

Because I don't trust you not to shoot me in the back wasn't the sort of thing a man in these parts said to another man, not even one like Howard Wilmeth. Cody pretended he didn't hear and continued riding away.

All at once, he thought of the perfect way to get back into Melissa's good graces. First, before supper, he'd apologize abjectly for subjecting her to his base lust. If he was lucky, and if she was as large-minded a woman as Cody believed she was, she'd forgive him. He also expected a certain uneasiness would lie between them.

Then, tomorrow, he'd go up into the hills and chop her down a Christmas tree. It would, after all, be little Katie's first Christmas. While Cody knew the baby'd never remember it, he figured Melissa would, for the rest of her life. If he went out of his way only a little bit, he could make this Christmas a happy one for her. A Christmas tree would provide the right touch, he hoped, to make her forget how indiscreet he'd been. It might also brighten her life, the future of which must look pretty bleak from her perspective.

Cody would never forget that kiss; he knew it for a rock-solid certainty. He expected his nights would be plagued with remembering it, in fact. But if he played his cards right, he could at least get Melissa back to relaxing around him.

It would take all day to ride far enough to where the piñons grew and back again, but he could have Luis do chores around the cabin so Melissa wouldn't be left alone. He didn't expect Howard Wilmeth would come back to torment him so soon after today's foiled escapade, although he didn't imagine for a minute that Wilmeth would give up. He was too damned mean to do anything so rational. But Cody could make Christmas happy for Melissa, and he aimed to do it.

As his plans spun around in his mind, Cody forgot to be embarrassed about Melissa and furious about Howard. Instead, he pictured the look of happiness on Melissa's face when he brought her a Christmas tree tomorrow evening, and his heart warmed up until it fairly glowed.

What she would do was apologize as soon as Cody walked through the door.

No. What she would do was act as though nothing had happened. That's what she'd do.

No. She really wanted to clear the air between them. She would ask him to please sit down and talk to her for a few minutes after supper. Then she'd apologize and tell him how sorry she was.

No. Sitting down with him was what had caused the problem in the first place. What she'd do was pretend it had never happened.

Melissa set the cast-iron pot full of chicken and dumplings on the stove with a crack and wiped her forehead with her apron. The weather wasn't warm outside, and the kitchen's atmosphere was rather pleasant. It was her agitation, heating her from within, that made her perspire. "Heavens above, how can I ever forget that kiss?"

Katie, who was cooing in her cradle in the corner, offered no suggestions. She took the opportunity to blow a rude-sounding raspberry, however, and Melissa wondered if babies knew more than people gave them credit for.

Cody's kiss had been the single most amazing thing that had ever happened to her, barring Katie's birth. How she'd pretend it had never happened was a mystery. She was still pondering the matter when Cody came home and, ready or not, she had to greet him.

She did it with a smile she figured looked as full of trepidation as she felt. He strode into the house as if he didn't have a care in the world, and smiled his sunny smile back at her. She felt minimally better. He flipped his hat onto the rack he'd made out of a pine branch and several Texas longhorns when he was a boy in Georgetown. Melissa loved that hat rack. It seemed so appropriate for a ranch out here in the wild and woolly New Mexico Territory.

"Afternoon, Mrs. Wilmeth."

"Good afternoon, Mr. O'Fannin." His color, Melissa noticed, seemed high. Of course, that might only be the result of his having been riding outside all day—all day since their indiscretion, at any rate.

He shuffled his feet. "I—er—I'm sorry I didn't stick around to help you bottle the apple juice, ma'am."

"Oh, that's all right," she rushed to say. "I didn't have any trouble at all. There wasn't a whole lot of juice to bottle, unfortunately. It's so good, I was hoping to have lots of it to last through the winter. I was surprised, since we'd used so many apples. I used the pulp for applesauce. Of course, I had to take the seeds and skins out. And add some water, because we squeezed all the juice out."

She laughed nervously, decided she sounded like an idiot, and quit at once. "There's plenty of juice for supper tonight and breakfast tomorrow, though." There. That might make him happy.

It seemed to. He smiled again. "Good. That's good, ma'am. Applesauce sounds nice, too."

"I hope you'll like it. I used a little of the nutmeg Mac gave me. Mrs. Bowlus had the recipe."

"Sounds good."

"And molasses. Just a little bit, so it wouldn't overpower the nutmeg." Melissa wished she'd just shut up. She was chattering like a magpie and making a fool of herself.

He shuffled again. "Well, I reckon I'd better get cleaned up for supper."

"Yes. It's almost ready."

"Sure smells good in here."

"Thank you."

He nodded and kept smiling. "Good. I mean, thank *you*, ma'am."

"Of course, Mr. O'Fannin."

He wheeled around to head outside to the wash trough. Then he stopped suddenly and turned around again. "Ma'am—Mrs. Wilmeth, I'm awful sorry about what happened earlier. I reckon you don't need a big brute like me pawing at you, and I'm very sorry."

Shocked by his assessment of her wicked behavior, Melissa cried, "Oh, no, Mr. O'Fannin! The fault was all mine, and I'm very, very sorry."

His brows drew together. "No, ma'am. It was my fault, and I'm sorry."

Puzzled, Melissa said, "I don't see it that way, Mr.

O'Fannin. It was my fault, and I'm the one who should be sorry—and I am."

He seemed puzzled, too. He peered at her hard, as if trying to figure it all out. At last he shrugged. "Well, all I know is I'm sorry, ma'am, and it won't happen again."

"No," said Melissa. "It won't happen again."

The truth made her unhappy.

"Good chow," said Luis around a mouth full of dumpling.

Melissa was so glad to have Luis at the table with Cody and herself, she could have kissed him. She frowned and decided she couldn't either have kissed him, since kissing was what had caused all her problems in the first place. She certainly appreciated him being there, at any rate. "Thank you. This is another one of Mrs. Bowlus's recipes. Chicken and dumplings. She had me serve this every other Sunday."

Cody looked up at her and said curiously, "What did you serve the other Sundays, ma'am?"

"Oh, sometimes a roast beef, sometimes a roast of pork, sometimes leg of lamb. It depended on whether she had company or not."

"Lamb?" Cody's mouth worked uselessly for a second. "You ate *lamb?*"

Bewildered, wondering what could be wrong with eating lamb, Melissa said, "Yes."

Cody took another bite of chicken, chewed it, and swallowed. "I never heard of such a thing."

She got the feeling she'd somehow managed to shock him witless, and was curious as to why that should be. "What's wrong? Don't you care for lamb?"

"Couldn't say," he muttered, his head down.

Melissa peered at him closely. "What's wrong with lamb, Mr. O'Fannin?"

199

He looked up at her over his fork, which was full of dumpling and dripping chicken gravy. His spectacular brown eyes held real perplexity. "Well, ma'am, I don't reckon I've ever met anybody who's eaten a sheep before, is all."

"We eat sheep all the time in my family," said Luis.

Cody turned and stared at him for a moment. Then he shrugged. "Well, sure, Luis. But you're a Mexican."

Melissa wondered what being a Mexican had to do with eating sheep. Cody had made his pronouncement as if it needed no further explanation. She knew she had a lot still to learn about her new home, but she hadn't figured such intricate social variations as whether one did or did not eat lamb would comprise a part of her education. There were so few people out here; until now, she'd figured they were all pretty much the same—except for the Indians, of course, and everyone seemed to be united against them.

Luis laughed. "Texans don't hold with eatin' woolies, Mrs. Wilmeth. They think sheep are like some kind of sickness on the land."

"Oh." Hmmm. Melissa'd had no idea. She decided to say so. "I've never heard of that before."

"My people, we eat sheep and goats all the time. Roast 'em whole for parties." Luis took another bite of his supper and looked quite happy, which was pretty much the way he always looked.

Melissa said, "Oh. I've never eaten goat meat, although I rather like lamb. Mutton isn't my favorite, though. It has such a strong flavor."

"I wouldn't know." Cody looked at his plate.

Melissa's mouth worked. She tried not to smile but couldn't help it. After all those kind things he'd said to her this morning when she'd confessed to her miserable origins, it was difficult to believe she'd managed to appall him at last—by admitting she'd partaken of a forbidden meat. He hadn't seemed to believe she was a wicked woman after learning about her disgusting upbringing. Or that kiss. But lamb . . . "I do believe you think less of me now that you know I've eaten lamb, Mr. O'Fannin."

His head jerked up. "Lordy, no, ma'am. I don't think less of you at all. I—well, I just never thought of you as the kind of woman who'd eat a sheep is all."

Luis grinned and nodded at Melissa, as if to say *I told you so*. Melissa laughed until tears ran down her cheeks. She couldn't help it. Cody watched her for a minute, clearly feeling as though he'd missed the joke. After a while, though, he joined in, too. Melissa thought that was just like him, and loved him all the more for it.

Cody left early the next morning. Melissa wrapped up some food in a bandanna for him to take on his journey. He looked at the lumpy bundle doubtfully.

"Shoot, ma'am, that's an awful lot of food."

Melissa clasped her hands behind her back. "Well, you said you'd probably be gone all day. I only put in enough for dinner and supper. I packed you some chicken sandwiches and tucked in some apples and some molasses cookies. There's a little jar of applesauce in there, too, and a spoon. I'd appreciate it if you brought the jar and the spoon back, because you don't have many of them."

Cody looked from the bundle to her and back at the bundle. "Thank you, ma'am. I, er, reckon I can tie it onto my saddle. Somehow."

Oh, dear. Melissa wished she'd learn what was expected of a housewife—that is, a housekeeper—out here on the frontier. She'd thought Cody would be pleased that she'd packed him so sturdy a bundle. It didn't look awfully big to her. After all, he was a large man, and he ate a good deal at meals.

Later, when she asked Luis if she'd done something wrong, he laughed. "No, ma'am. Cody, he's just not used to havin' a female take care of him. Before, when he and Arnold went off somewheres, they'd pack up some jerky and some hard biscuits and head on out."

"Oh." Melissa frowned over her washtub. "That doesn't sound very nourishing."

"No, it don't."

"Do you think he minded?"

"No, ma'am," Luis said without hesitation. "He don't mind at all."

Melissa felt a little better after that.

Luis was working on the front porch and Melissa was still working on the wash later on that morning. She'd got her clothes all boiled and rinsed and was about to hang them up on the lines in the backyard near the kitchen garden when the sound of Perry's shrill barking made her jump. Then she heard hoofbeats and her heart leapt.

Wondering if Cody had finished his business more quickly than he'd anticipated, she ran over to pick up little Katie, who'd been cooing in her cradle. She dashed around to the front of the house.

She would have screamed if she could have got her throat to work. When it unclogged, she only managed to whisper the word, "Indians," and squeezed Katie until she protested.

Three Indians—Melissa could tell that's what they were even from this distance—had almost reached the windmill tank. Frantically, she debated the merits of running back inside and bolting the door, marching boldly out to greet these men, or sneaking around to the garden and trying to become invisible. Invisibility was a difficult prospect out here, where there weren't even any trees to hide behind.

Perry was running around in circles like a dog possessed and yapping fit to kill. Melissa wished he'd be quiet; she was quite distracted enough without his piercing barks to drive her even crazier.

"Don' worry, Miz Wilmeth."

Luis! She'd forgotten all about Luis. She turned and saw him standing amid a heap of lumber and sawdust. She'd never been so happy to see anyone in her life, and walked over to stand next to him. Her knees felt like rubber.

Perry sounded hysterical by this time. His shrill yaps pierced Melissa's worried heart like sharp little daggers. If she'd been an Indian, she might be inclined to shoot him with an arrow just to hush him up. On the other hand, he was obviously trying to protect them from those intruders, and she appreciated him for it. She wished he'd been so persistent about protecting them from Howard.

"Shut up!" Luis snapped. Perry shut up, put his tail between his legs, and crawled under the house.

Some protection *he* was, Melissa thought bitterly.

"It's only Running Standing. He probably come out here to meet you."

Luis's explanation jolted her. She cleared her throat. "Running Standing? To meet me?" Her voice squeaked at the end, and she frowned. This was no way for a frontier woman to behave. She had to be fearless; she had to be brave. Feeling decidedly cowardly, Melissa squared her shoulders and endeavored to look proud and unwavering. Her insides were wavering around like drunken sailors on the Boston docks.

The three horses trotted into the yard and came to

a halt in a cloud of dust. Melissa sneezed and felt stupid. She drew herself up straight again and looked with mingled curiosity and trepidation at the man who dismounted. She'd never seen a real Indian up close before.

A tall fellow, his features were sharp and his skin more brown than red. His hair was parted in the middle and braided. He didn't wear one of those headbands she'd always seen in illustrations of Indians, but had on a black felt hat, floppy and rusty-looking with old age and hard use. His clothes were a little out of the ordinary in that he wore a buckskin shirt and trousers. The shirt had some kind of quill-work down the front that Melissa would have liked to inspect if it weren't on an Indian. He was actually quite an imposing man, and rather handsome, although he did have a feral, unpleasant smell about him. Melissa tried not to wrinkle her nose in distaste.

Luis lifted his arm in a gesture of greeting. "Hey, Running Standing. How ya doin'? Don't gen'ly see you here this time of year."

Running Standing gestured with his head toward his mounted companions. "My brothers and me, we come to see Cody's woman."

Cody's woman. Melissa liked the sound of that. She'd have liked it better coming from the mouth of a white man. Still and all, this Running Standing fellow didn't seem particularly hostile. He didn't smile, but he wasn't aiming an arrow at her heart or anything either.

"Sure," said Luis with a friendly grin. "This here's Melissa Wilmeth. Miz Wilmeth, meet Running Standing."

Deciding that if she was ever to prove her worth as a territorial woman, now was the time to do it, Melissa took a firm step forward and held out her hand. "Pleased to meet you, Mister—er—Running Standing."

Running Standing looked down at her hand as if wondering what he was supposed to do with it. Ultimately he ignored it and said to Luis, "Got some medicine for Cody's woman."

Medicine. He'd brought some medicine for her. Melissa had heard about Indians and their medicine—good medicine, bad medicine. She'd always believed "medicine," in frontier context, was a word to be used in the metaphorical sense, not unlike good luck and bad luck. She took the small clay pot Running Standing held out to her.

"Thank you."

He nodded.

Melissa opened the pot. It contained some substance that looked like grease and smelled bad. She wasn't sure what she was supposed to do or say, so she glanced at Luis.

"What's it for?" Luis asked.

Melissa was surprised by his lack of subtlety. The direct approach seemed to work, however, because Running Standing said, "Burns, cuts. Good healing medicine."

Oh. Exactly like medicine, in fact. "How kind," she said.

"Good for babies." Running Standing patted his own buckskin-covered bottom.

Diaper rash? Was he talking about diaper rash? Good heavens. "Oh. Yes. Thank you." Taking what she considered to be a big chance—after all, she didn't know what etiquette prevailed in situations like this—she smiled at Running Standing. "Thank you very much. If you'll wait right there, I'll bring you something, too."

Running Standing nodded and Luis grinned. Melissa caught a hint of approval in Luis's expression, and she was very grateful. She thrust Katie into Luis's arms, hurried into the house, grabbed two jars of applesauce, and rushed outside again. She wasn't sure if two were too many or too few, but she had an intuitive feeling that two would be proper payment for a pot of stinky grease.

"Here." She held the jars out to Running Standing. "I just made this yesterday. It's applesauce. From apples." Figuring she'd already made enough of a dolt of herself, she clamped her lips together.

Running Standing nodded again as he took the jars. He handed them up to one of his companions. Melissa, who hadn't paid much attention to those other two men before, tried not to stare now. They looked much more like Indians—at least the kinds of Indians Melissa had seen depicted in the newspapers back home—than Running Standing did.

Running Standing turned back to Luis, ignoring Melissa. "See baby."

Melissa stood stock-still and held herself as stiff as a lamppost while Running Standing yanked the blanket away from Katie. Her fingers curled up until her nails were biting into her palms, and she told herself not to panic. It was too late for that, but she held her panic in check and didn't snatch Katie away from Luis. She had a strong feeling that would be the wrong thing to do.

She almost shrieked when Running Standing peeked under Katie's diaper. She didn't, and was proud of herself.

"Girl," said Running Standing. He didn't sound impressed.

"This isn't Cody's baby," Luis said, as though he was explaining away a defect. Melissa frowned.

Running Standing nodded, as if Luis's explanation made sense.

"When Cody and Melissa have babies, they'll be boys," Luis assured him.

Melissa gasped.

Katie's tiny white hand closed around Running Standing's long brown finger, and he smiled.

Chapter Twelve

Clutching her baby to her bosom, Melissa sank down onto an upended nail keg set next to the front door. Her knees shook, and she was pretty sure that if she tried to stand up, she'd fall flat on her face.

"He's a pretty good fellow, Miz Wilmeth," Luis said.

She looked up and found him watching her, a grin on his face. She turned back to watch the disappearing Indians again. She didn't feel comfortable not watching them.

"Good. I'm glad to hear it."

Luis peeked inside the pot of medicine Running Standing had brought. "This is probably real good stuff, ma'am. Them Indians, they know how to live out here, 'cause they been doin' it for so long. This'll probably be good if you get any burns or scrapes. He give Cody and me a liniment for the horses that works better'n anything else we ever tried."

"Really? How nice."

Luis chuckled. "Reckon you don't have no Indians in Boston, ma'am."

Melissa licked her lips. "No. No, we don't." Not anymore they didn't. She frowned slightly, wondering what had happened to them all.

"That was a good idea to think about givin' him the applesauce, ma'am. He'll like that. It shows your good faith."

Good faith. Melissa managed to tear her gaze away from the cloud of dust that signified the departing Indians and glanced at Luis. Good faith was an important thing to have established, she supposed. "I'm glad." She stared after that cloud of dust some more.

"He liked Katie, too."

"He did?" She peered at Luis out of the corner of her eye. "I thought he didn't like it that she was a girl." She felt her face heat up when she remembered Luis's assertion. "Why did you tell him that? About Mr. O'Fannin and me, I mean."

This time Luis gave a good, hearty laugh. Melissa didn't appreciate it. "Shoot, ma'am, these Indians, they don't set no store by girl babies. Any brave worth anything has boys."

"But—but, Luis, you talked about Mr. O'Fannin and me. We aren't even married!"

"I know that, ma'am, but it don't do to go tryin' to explain complicated things to people who can't understand 'em. You're livin' here on Cody's ranch. The Indians figure you and him are a pair and will be makin' babies together. It's what they understand."

Melissa had seldom felt so embarrassed. To have Luis say these things about her, even to an Indian, made her want to crawl into a hole somewhere and hide. Like Perry.

She scowled at the dog, who only then decided to

show himself. He looked scared yet, and his tail remained between his legs. Melissa guessed she didn't blame him much, but she still thought he'd shirked his duty as a dog. Nevertheless, she chirped softly and held out her hand. Perry wiggled his way to her on his belly and licked her hand.

"Useless dog," she muttered. Her voice held affection, Perry heard it, and his tail wagged, churning up dust which Melissa had to wave away from Katie's face.

Luis laughed again.

With a sigh, Melissa decided she'd better not waste any more of her time on leftover fear. Wondering if this was how most frontier women survived the perils of their lives in this godforsaken land—by simply picking themselves up after frights and shocks and getting on with the work they had to do—she shoved herself to her feet, walked around to the back of the house, deposited Katie in her cradle, and resumed hanging out the wash.

Perry frolicked at her feet for awhile before deciding he'd have more fun chasing lizards. She watched him charge off and shook her head. "Useless dog," she grumbled again.

What an astonishing place this New Mexico Territory was, to be sure. It frightened her, she loved it, and she wondered if she'd ever get used to it.

"Indians," she murmured. "For heaven's sake."

Supper long over, Melissa folded clothes and tried not to worry about Cody having been gone for so long. When she heard someone riding into the yard, she stopped still and wondered if this sound of horses' hooves betokened Cody's return or more Indians or something else entirely.

"It's only one horse," she mumbled, proud of herself for being able to distinguish the sound one horse makes from the sound several horses make. Perhaps she *was* learning something about her new home.

Quickly, she folded the shirt she'd been holding. She wondered if she'd ever get used to washing out here. The water was so hard that the clothes were as stiff as sticks by the time they dried. With a small sigh, she guessed that only meant she didn't need to use starch. Not that she'd have bothered with starch out here, where there were no other women to pass judgment on her housekeeping and laundering skills, but still . . .

"Stop being ridiculous, Melissa Wilmeth," she advised herself as she hurried to the front door.

Her heart executed a wild leap when she saw Cody dismounting. Generally he rode his horse straight to the stable when he got home from a day on the range. She stepped outside, prepared with a big smile and the offer of some soup and a sandwich for the returning traveler.

Then she spotted the tree and forgot all about soup. An involuntary "Oh!" leaked from her throat, and Cody turned and saw her standing there.

His grin was the most beautiful thing she'd ever seen.

"Howdy, Mrs. Wilmeth. Look what I brought home for Christmas." He held the little tree out in front of him in the pose a mighty hunter might have adopted to display his kill and impress his woman back in caveman days.

Melissa clapped her hands to her cheeks. She'd never had a Christmas tree. Not of her own, she hadn't. Of course, she used to decorate Mrs. Bowlus's tree, but that was different.

"Oh, Mr. O'Fannin, how wonderful!" She hurried over to him. "Oh, thank you!"

She felt foolish as soon as her thanks hit the air. After all, this tree was for his home; it wasn't intended for her any more than those trees of Mrs. Bowlus's had been. She couldn't help feeling that he'd somehow brought this one for her, however. Perhaps it was the proud way in which he'd displayed it that gave her the notion.

"Thought you and Katie might like a tree, ma'am. For her first Christmas."

"Yes. Oh, yes, we would! How thoughtful of you." He *had* done it for her. Melissa didn't think her heart could get much warmer. "Thank you so much, Mr. O'Fannin." She looked up into his eyes and discovered she was wrong.

They seemed to look at each other for a very long time. At last Cody cleared his throat and wrenched his gaze away. "I'll just take this inside and then put my horse away and clean up, ma'am."

Melissa jerked out of her trance. "Of course. Yes, certainly. And there's soup and sandwiches if you're hungry, too."

Cody lifted an eyebrow. "Ma'am, you packed so much food to take with me, I expect it'll be the day after tomorrow before I'm hungry again."

Melissa blushed.

It turned out that Cody had exaggerated his state of satiation. While Melissa sang Christmas carols to Katie, who seemed to have a touch of colic this evening and occasionally punctuated the serenade with a bellow of her own, Cody ate soup and sandwiches and watched with delight the goings-on in his parlor.

Luis joined them and helped Melissa paste paper rings together and string them into garlands. They sat on the floor on a sheet with a pot of Melissa's flour-and-water paste between them and a big pile of cut-up paper beside the pot. It was old butcher paper Cody had saved from various excursions into Rio Hondo, but neither Melissa nor Luis seemed to care about that. Melissa said she considered the dried bloodstains on the paper in light of decorations. They were having fun, and Cody was glad of it.

"I can make paper stars, too. See?" Melissa held up a lopsided star she'd folded into shape. She frowned at her handiwork. "Well, it takes practice, I guess. I used to be better at it."

Cody thought the star was beautiful. "That's right pretty, ma'am. It don't matter that it's not perfect. Shoot, nothing's perfect. Nobody'll even see that it's a little crooked."

He noticed the smile of gratitude Melissa bestowed upon him. In fact, his whole body noticed it, and he had to lecture it severely to get it to calm down again. Living in the same house with a woman for whom he harbored lustful thoughts was awfully hard on a man.

He cleared his throat and tried to do the same with his mind. Good intentions didn't have the effect he'd hoped for, so he decided to distract himself. He hadn't yet told Melissa about his encounter with her husband the day before. He'd warned Luis to be on the lookout for dastardly deeds, but he didn't want Melissa to know about them. Cody figured she already blamed herself for everything; telling her about Howard's having tried to poison Cody's water supply would only make her feel worse.

"So old Running Standing paid you a visit today, did he?"

Luis chuckled and held up his own version of Melissa's star. It was more crooked than hers had been. "Sure did."

"Indeed he did," confirmed Melissa. Cody saw her shudder, and recognized that she was making a valiant attempt not to show how her encounter with the Indian had affected her. With a grin, he said, "Running Standing's a good fellow, Mrs. Wilmeth. I don't expect any trouble from that quarter."

"No," she said. "He seemed merely curious."

"Said he wanted to meet Cody's woman," Luis offered happily. Melissa blushed. So did Cody.

"No. Did he?"

"Yes, he certainly did." It didn't sound as though Melissa found the Indian's purpose in visiting the ranch amusing. Cody didn't, either.

"He brought some kind of ointment, though, and Luis said it will probably be good for burns and cuts, so I set it out on a shelf in the shed to keep the grease from going bad if it ever gets hot."

"Oh, it'll get hot, ma'am," Cody assured her.

"Sure will." Luis nodded as he pasted.

The shed sat in the sparse shade of one of the trees Cody and Arnold had planted. Cody had told her before that it got hotter than blazes here in the summertime, and he hoped the shade would keep the shed cool. Melissa had told him that she hoped so, too, although if it got as hot as everyone said it would, she expected that tree would require several more years of growth before it performed its function to any effect. He'd agreed with her.

"Well, it's there in the shed, at any rate, if you ever need it."

"Good idea." Cody nodded, as if he'd given the matter a great deal of consideration. In truth, he was still trying to curb his lustful thoughts about Melissa. Damn it, every time she moved, her full breasts pulled across that bodice of hers, and Cody remembered almost being able to feel the shape of them.

His desire to explore them in detail was about to drive him crazy. He found himself almost envying little Katie because she got to nurse at those delicious breasts several times a day. Hell, he must be warped, if he was going around feeling jealous of a baby.

"I gave him two jars of applesauce. I hope that's all right. Luis said he thought it was a good thing to do. In exchange for the salve."

Melissa's big blue eyes searched Cody's face for any hint that he might disapprove. At the moment, Cody was as far from disapproving of anything Melissa Wilmeth cared to do as he was from the Atlantic Ocean. He managed to say, with a fair degree of composure, "Yeah, that was a real good idea."

Her smile nearly knocked him over backwards. "Good, I'm glad. I didn't feel right in giving away your food, but since Mac had just found the apples and all, I didn't think you'd mind. I thought they were—oh, sort of a bonus, if you know what I mean."

"Yeah," said Cody, his mouth dry and his body quivering. "I know what you mean."

When he heard the sound of a horse drawing into the yard, he greeted the arrival of whomever this was with profound relief. Even if it was Howard Wilmeth, come to demand his wife back or challenge Cody to a shoot-out at fifty paces—which was the sort of addlepated thing a tinhorn like Wilmeth, whose education about the territory evidently consisted of what he'd read in dime novels, might do— at least it would get Cody's mind off of what he wanted to do with Wilmeth's wife. These feelings of his were getting out of hand. He had to find a way to keep them in check, or he'd drive Melissa off, sure as the devil. He wasn't certain he could stand it if she left him.

That thought alone was enough to make him wish they'd never met. Why in the name of mercy was he thinking of *any* woman in that way? It wasn't Cody O'Fannin's way at all, to be dependent on a female's presence.

"I'll see who it is." As he rose and went to the door, he harbored the glum thought that whether it was his way or not, somehow or other Melissa's presence and the state of her happiness had come to mean the world to him. He considered it a grave weakness, not unlike the fever and ague that had plagued him as a boy, and hoped like thunder he'd get over it, as he'd gotten over the influenza.

He wasn't altogether surprised to find Alexander McMurdo standing at his front door, beaming at him like the summer sun.

"Mac," he said.

"Cody, m'lad!" Mac's greeting carried infinitely more enthusiasm than Cody's.

"Fancy seeing you here."

Mac winked at him. "Brought Katie a little something for Christmas, m'boy."

Cody stood aside and opened the door wider. "Come on in, Mac. Mrs. Wilmeth's just decorating the tree I brought down from the mountains today."

"You brought her a tree, did you?"

Misliking the tone of Mac's voice, Cody said rather sharply, "I brought a tree for the house, yeah. Hell, Mac, it's comin' on toward Christmas, and I never had a kid at the ranch before. I figured Mrs. Wilmeth would like to give her baby a nice first Christmas."

Mac winked at him again. Cody scowled. "Of course you did, m'boy. Very sound thinking."

Cody rolled his eyes. "I'm pretty sure there's soup and chicken enough left for another sandwich or two, if you're hungry."

"Why, thank you, Cody! That's the kindest offer I've had in quite awhile."

"I'll bet it is."

Mac laughed his way through the door and into the parlor.

Melissa jumped up, scattering paper strips. "Mac! It's so good to see you!"

She ran over and hugged the old man hard, and Cody experienced a pang of jealousy for the liberties assumed by the elderly. She'd never in a million years hug *him* like that.

So far, in the space of a single evening, he'd been jealous of a baby and an old man. Cody wondered if he had a fever. He'd never entertained such idiotic fancies in his life until now.

"Look what Mr. O'Fannin brought down from the mountains today, Mac!" Melissa stepped aside and swept an arm out dramatically. "A Christmas tree!"

Cody looked at the tree, which was a fairly small specimen—after all, he'd had to haul it back strapped to his horse—and at the woman. Melissa's enthusiasm seemed all out of proportion to the size of that stumpy tree. He wished he'd taken the mule along so he could have brought back a bigger tree, one that would soar to the ceiling, one that would more nearly deserve this much excitement on her part. Still, he couldn't help but feel a tiny lick of pride for having thought of a tree in the first place.

"It's a fine tree," Mac said approvingly. He walked around the tree, eyeing it from all sides. "A fine tree indeed." He lifted his hands, and for a second the tree seemed to be engulfed in those tiny little sparkly things. The effect was breathtaking, and it made Cody blink. Of course, as soon as he blinked, it all vanished, and his tree stood there in its bucket of sand, as plain and un-glittery as the simple, small piñon it was.

Unless . . .

Cody stared hard at that tree. Did it look bushier than it had a second earlier? Was its shape the tiniest bit more perfect? He gave his head a good, jarring shake to rid it of its visions.

Jehosephat, what was the matter with him? Thinking lustful thoughts about his housekeeper, being jealous of babies and old geezers, seeing sparkles in the air, thinking cut trees had changed their shapes. Maybe he should break out the whiskey he kept for medicinal purposes and take a good slug of it before he retired to bed. He obviously needed something. His aunt Luella used to dose him with castor oil when he got to feeling sickly, but Cody thought he'd prefer whiskey.

Mac took a judicious glance around Cody's parlor and nodded approvingly. "The place looks better than it ever has, Cody."

Cody squinted at him. "How would you know, Mac? You've only been here once before."

Mac laughed, as if Cody'd uttered a wildly funny joke. "Perhaps. But it's the truth, isn't it?" He watched Cody with those piercing blue eyes of his, and Cody shuffled and had to glance away.

"Yeah. Yeah, it's true all right."

"I knew it," Mac declared happily. "I knew you needed our Mellie's touch on your ranch. Why, she fits right into your life here, doesn't she? A diamond in the rough, our Mellie, and you've given her the chance to spread her wings and shape herself into a perfect specimen of frontier womanhood. She'd be an enhancement to any fellow's life. Don't you think so, Cody, m'boy?"

"Mac!" Melissa's cheeks turned a bright cherry red. Cody had to look away from *her*, too.

"Yeah," he mumbled. "Sure."

"Running Standing thinks so, too." Luis plopped his comment into the conversation like a big, fat trout. Cody wanted to tape his mouth shut.

"Smart man, Running Standing," Mac said. "I always said so."

"I don't remember you ever saying so to me," growled Cody.

Mac laughed again. "Ha! Well, it must have been to somebody else, then. But it's true."

"Humph." Cody took Mac's hat and heavy outer coat after the old man had shrugged himself out of it and carried them to the hat rack. He was almost afraid to turn his back on the old fellow, even though he knew the feeling was merely the product of his generally disordered senses. He had the eerie sensation that he might turn around again and discover that Mac had deposited an elephant or a coach-and-four in his parlor.

"I brought you some popcorn, Mellie, m'dear, and some corn syrup. Thought you might like to make popcorn balls for Christmas treats."

Cody peeked over his shoulder, relieved. Popcorn sounded benign.

Melissa's eyes shone like stars, and Cody forgave Mac for being old and too-knowing and faintly magical and the recipient of Melissa's hugs. He had to busy himself with Mac's overcoat or lose control, stomp over to Melissa, and hug her. "I love popcorn balls, Mac! I used to make them for the Bowlus children when they came home for Christmas."

Cody's head swiveled and he saw her smiling like an angel at Mac. She made popcorn balls for the Bowlus children? She didn't make them for her own family? He recalled her halting description of her childhood, and he wondered if even popcorn had been too expensive for her mother to provide. Of course, by the time Melissa was old enough to make popcorn balls, most of her family was run off or gone to the orphanage, he guessed. Or were dead. The thought made him sad.

"Good, good," Mac said, all jollity. "And here's something for little Katie, too, for her first Christmas."

Like a magician conjuring a flower out of thin air, Mac reached inside his jacket and whipped something out. His hand moved so fast it was a blur. When it stopped, Cody realized there was a bright red stocking, with a rabbit-fur edging, dangling from his fingers.

"A Christmas stocking," Melissa breathed as if a Christmas stocking was the one thing her life had been missing.

Mac nodded. "Katie's very own Christmas stocking!" He said it with the air of an auctioneer announcing a sale.

Melissa pressed a hand to her cheek. "How pretty it is!"

She took the stocking, and Cody saw tears standing in her eyes when she looked up at Mac again. Shoot, the woman was sentimental. Imagine crying because somebody gave your kid a Christmas stocking. He wished like hell he'd thought to do it.

"Thank you so much, Mac." She kissed his withered old cheek once more.

Cody, watching these goings-on with a frown, didn't appreciate it when Mac winked at him again over Melissa's pretty blond head.

"Ye can fill it with nuts and popcorn balls, Mellie. Little Katie's got no teeth for the nuts or the popcorn, but you and Cody lad here and Luis can eat 'em for her and tell her how good they were later." He reached into his pocket, hauled out a handful of walnuts and peppermint candies, and let go of of another hearty laugh. "And marzipan candy! All the way from Rome."

"My goodness!" Melissa, pink-cheeked and breathless, took everything from Mac, and she laughed along with him.

Luis, still industriously pasting paper garlands together on the floor, joined in. Cody, who felt unaccountably cranky for a second or two, ultimately gave up his grump and laughed, too.

Melissa fetched a bowl of soup and a sandwich for Mac, then plunked herself back down on the floor and resumed her decorating duties. "I think I'll make Katie a rag doll to put in the stocking, Mac," she said cheerfully. "And make hair out of yarn to put on it."

"What color yarn will you use?" Cody wondered if that was a stupid question, but he was unaccountably curious about this doll of Katie's.

Melissa pondered for a minute. When she did that, her face turned serious, and she clamped her tongue between her teeth. Cody almost groaned with frustrated desire. She looked so appealing sitting there with her own blond hair in disarray, concentrating on her silly Christmas garland.

Generally Melissa wore one of those big floppy sunbonnets when she was outdoors—a judicious thing to do out here, where the sun beat fiercely down on a body. When she was indoors, she took her bonnet off and knotted her hair at the back of her neck. Tonight, her knot had unwound a bit, and her hair gleamed in the firelight like burnt honey. Cody loved her hair. He wanted to bury his fingers in it and stroke through it.

He imagined it would feel like silk and wanted to know if he was right. Damn.

"You know, I'd like it to be the color of Katie's own hair, but since she's bald, it's hard to tell what that will be."

She laughed again, a tinkling laugh that Cody decided distilled the Christmas spirit into one beautiful musical sound. He wished he could snatch it out of the air and put it into a music box that he could wind up and play whenever he needed his spirits lifted.

"I'd use yellow yarn," Mac said after a judicious pause.

Cody got the impression the old man had deliberately waited to say anything until the effect of Melissa's laugh had dissipated. He sighed and decided he wasn't going crazy; he already was crazy.

Nodding thoughtfully, Melissa said, "Yes, you're probably right. After all, everyone in my family was blond, and Howard's hair is kind of light." Her smile faded into a frown at the thought of her husband. The mood in the room changed subtly; it wasn't happy any longer.

Almost imperceptibly, Mac moved his hand. If Cody hadn't been watching him, he'd have missed the gesture. He didn't miss it, though, and this time he *knew* he saw those damned sparkles fly from Mac's fingers and dribble over Melissa, who immediately cheered up.

Mac slanted Cody a grin. Cody didn't know what to make of that grin. Hell, he didn't know what to make of anything anymore.

"Don't fret yourself, Cody lad. Everything will be just fine."

Cody wasn't so sure about that. His indecorous feelings for Melissa Wilmeth were about to consume him from the inside, Howard Wilmeth was evidently determined to undermine Cody's ranching operation, Arnold might bring Loretta Pine back to blight his life any week now, he persisted in seeing things whenever Mac was around, and he had a sinking notion that he was out of his mind.

How could everything be all right with a man if he had to contend with all that?

Chapter Thirteen

As the days edged along toward Christmas, Cody discovered life wasn't too hard to bear after all.

Luis had talked his brother Carlos into coming to work on Cody's ranch. After the new year, as the weather warmed into spring, Cody would have to hire more cowboys to see him through the spring roundup and drive the herd through Rio Hondo to the huge lot where he'd be selling his beeves. Until then, the Morales brothers would work out just fine, and they were happy to do the range work while Cody finished his front porch.

He told them both to keep a weather eye out for signs of poisoning, rustling, water diversion, brand-altering, or anything else that might smack of subversion on Howard Wilmeth's part. He made sure both men understood that, if they found Wilmeth alone on Cody's property, they were to capture the bastard and bring him to Cody. If others were discovered perpetrating vicious acts with him, and if Luis and Carlos saw them at it, they were to split up. One of them was to ride directly to Cody's nearest friendly neighbor, Noah Partridge. Even if Noah himself hadn't returned from his trip to Chicago yet, his foreman, Gus Spalding, who used to work for Blackworth and knew his wicked ways, would help. The other Morales brother was to ride like the devil to fetch Cody.

With luck, the band of honorable ranchers and their hands would be able to round up Howard Wilmeth and his gang. A neighborhood necktie party would without doubt be suggested as appropriate in such a case, but Cody wasn't sure he wanted to hang Wilmeth. Not that Wilmeth didn't deserve to dangle at the end of a rope.

Cody got an uncomfortable feeling when he considered killing Melissa's husband, however, and he'd just as soon avoid such a permanent solution to the Howard Wilmeth problem if he could. Cody wished the bastard would simply return to Boston and spare the Seven Rivers community his unpleasant presence. Or maybe he'd be obliging, get bit by a rattler, and save everyone the bother of dealing with him. Such a simple solution would be too much luck, though, and Cody didn't anticipate it.

Besides, although Wilmeth had his own personal ax to grind with Cody, he was in the employ of Hugh Blackworth. Cody had a feeling Blackworth would be almost as eager to see Cody and Arnold's business fail as Wilmeth. It was difficult to determine whether Howard was acting on his own or at Blackworth's bidding. Whatever his motivation, Cody would bet money the scoundrel enjoyed his work.

He decided not to waste any more time worrying about what Howard Wilmeth might or might not do.

What Cody wanted was to get the front porch finished in time for spring, so that Melissa could sit on it in the rocking chair Cody planned to give her for Christmas. He'd already ordered it from McMurdo's; it would be delivered some few weeks after the new year began.

He'd thought about the rocking chair when he'd noticed Melissa knotting rags for a rug while seated on a stump next to the back door, where she'd gone one evening to watch the sun set. Hell, a woman shouldn't have to sit on a stump; she should have a rocking chair in which to do all those things women did with their hands. Cody's own mama used to do her knitting and mending in the rocking chair she'd inherited from her grandmother. Even Aunt Luella, a woman so formidable that Cody seldom looked to her when he contemplated what females might need to make their lives easier, had used a rocker for her sit-down chores. A female needed a rocking chair. No matter how much he didn't understand about women in general, Cody was certain of that one thing.

Of course, the weather would get mighty cold before spring hit. There'd be no sitting out of doors after the nights got to freezing, the snows fell, and icy winds started blowing across the plains. Still, Cody figured Melissa could use the rocker in the parlor by the fire until then.

Occasionally he wondered if she'd still be here by springtime. He invariably thrust the doubt aside. He'd deal with whatever happened when it happened. If Arnie brought Loretta Pine back to the ranch, well . . . Cody always ran out of thought when the unhappy prospect of Loretta Pine struck him.

He trusted his wits, however. They'd carried him out to the Territory, into a successful ranching business, and were continuing to sustain him. Cody was dead-bang certain *something* would occur to him in the event of Loretta.

He was almost certain that Loretta was exactly the sort of female Arnold needed, being of the managing and bossy variety. He was equally certain he wouldn't have been able to tolerate living in the same house with Loretta even if he'd never stumbled across Melissa Wilmeth.

Melissa had come into his life, however, and she was exactly the kind of woman Cody needed. As a housekeeper. Luis was right about the property being plenty big enough for two cabins. Maybe Arnie and Loretta could live in one house, and Cody and Melissa could live in another.

He frowned as he hammered nails into the framing of his front porch. That didn't sound right, somehow. It sounded permanent—like they were an old married couple or something. He wished like thunder matrimony would quit cluttering up his brain. He had enough to worry about without muddling his brain with thoughts of marriage.

For one thing, Cody was too damned young to be married. Hell, he was only twenty-six. He had lots of wild oats to sow before he contemplated settling down. Of course, the very idea of riding into Rio Hondo and sowing some of those oats with the women at the Pecos Saloon—the same women who consorted with Howard Wilmeth—filled him with disgust. He tried not to think about that almost as much as he tried not to think about marriage.

Mac was right about one thing, though: Cody's household had never run more smoothly than it did with Melissa Wilmeth at the helm. Cody didn't have to do any of the household stuff any longer—neither laundry nor cleaning nor cooking. Not, of course, that he'd done very much of any of those things before she came.

Cody supposed that was the whole point. The house sparkled. There was no way in glory a body could keep the dust out of a house out here on the plains. Hell, the wind blew across like a banshee most days come evening, and there wasn't a tree or a house or anything else in the way to stop it. A favorite saying in these parts was that there was nothing between the North Pole and Rio Hondo but a picket fence—and it was down.

Dust crept in under the doors and leaked through cracks in the windowsills, and even whooshed down the chimney. But at least Melissa was there with a damp rag, every day, to wipe it away again. She even put some kind of wax on the wood tables once a week so that they shone like anything. Spit and polish, that was Melissa.

And Cody always had clean shirts and trousers and underwear. Before Melissa came, he and Arnie used to wait until they were practically naked before either one of them would wash anything. Even then, they'd grumbled and moaned and hated washing their duds. Cody expected Melissa didn't much like doing the laundry, either, because it was damned hard work. Yet she did it without complaint, every Monday. Then, on Tuesday, she ironed all the clothes she'd washing on Monday. Like clockwork in her chores, she was.

And food? Cody grinned as he thought about the food she fixed for him and Luis every day. She was a damned good cook. He and Arnie had subsisted on beans and salt pork because beans and salt pork were easy to fix and required no thought. Now, he had food the likes of which he hadn't eaten since he lived in his mother and father's house in George-

town. Hell, if Melissa fixed it, he might even condescend to eat a blasted sheep.

In fact, his denim trousers, the ones he used to
have to hold up with a belt, fit quite well now without
the belt. He wondered if he'd better start watching
how much he ate. Melissa's life with old lady Bowlus
had evidently not been awfully happy, but she'd sure
learned her way around a kitchen.

She sang Christmas songs, too. At the moment
Cody could hear her as he worked on his front porch.
She was in her room, feeding Katie. He tried not to
think about *that*, as thinking about Melissa's breast
in any context at all led to voluptuous cravings, and
he was ashamed of them.

He couldn't help but smile, though. She had a
pretty voice. It wasn't full and rich like his aunt
Luella's, but it was pleasant, light, and tuneful, and
it fit her. Cody particularly liked it when she sang
"God Rest Ye Merry, Gentlemen," because she made
it sound jolly, and it put him in mind of his mother
reading "A Visit from St. Nicholas" to him when he
was a boy.

He got to wondering if he could maybe get his
hands on a couple of books. He and Arnie weren't in
the habit of reading much, but Melissa sometimes
sighed and mentioned books and periodicals, as if
they were something she missed. Next time he saw
Mac, he'd mention books to him. Knowing Mac, he'd
have "found" a whole library in his back room before
the question was out of Cody's mouth.

There was were other things about Melissa that
Cody appreciated too, although he wouldn't allow
himself to dwell on them. The way her smile brightened the day for him; the way her hair gleamed in
the sunshine; the way the house felt empty when she
wasn't in it; the way he loved to sit and talk with her

in the evenings—she'd always be doing something. He grinned. Females. They didn't believe in idle hands.

Then there was the way she pursed her lips when she was thinking; the way she looked at Katie. Sometimes Cody found himself just staring at her, like a moonstruck calf, and had to shake himself awake again; the way she told stories to Katie, even though Katie was too young to understand anything at all, much less a story. She'd love to be able to read to the kid. Yup. He'd have to talk to Mac about getting some books, all right.

Cody scowled at the iron nails in the can beside him for a full minute as he pondered the mysteries surrounding Alexander McMurdo and why his mind seemed determined to dwell on Melissa Wilmeth's finer qualities as a person, when all he wanted was to think of her as his housekeeper. Then, when Melissa struck up a cheerful chorus of "Deck the Halls," he stopped frowning, forgot Mac, and didn't even notice that he was hammering in time to the music.

Mac paid Cody and Melissa another visit on Christmas Eve. Luis and Carlos had gone home to celebrate the holiday with their family. Their relatives lived in Picacho, several miles to the southwest of Cody's ranch, up in the mountains, so Cody and Melissa had been alone together all day.

The weather had turned suddenly, as it had a habit of doing out here, and frost nipped the air. Melissa's Monday wash had frozen dry almost before she'd hung it out, and she'd taken refuge in Running Standing's greasy balm to rub on her chapped hands and Katie's bottom. Cody'd had to stop work early on Christmas Eve because he didn't fancy freezing his fingers or the tip of his nose. He also wanted to see what pleasures—besides the turkey—Melissa had planned for Christmas Eve dinner. She'd been humming all day.

Cody greeted Mac's arrival with distinct relief. He'd begun to feel too much like a domesticated animal, what with only him and Melissa there and all the Christmas coziness permeating his house. And the feeling felt too right. It made him nervous. He was a bachelor rancher, dammit. In a couple of years, after his ranching operation was securely established and Melissa Wilmeth's divorce had been finalized for a while, maybe then he would . . .

He couldn't make himself complete the thought. Anyway, things might be different then. But they weren't different now.

He was only marginally surprised when he opened his front door and saw the wizened wagon-yard owner standing there, holding a bundle of packages. Peering over the old man's shoulder while Perry danced and barked at his feet, Cody didn't spot a wagon or any other means by which Mac might have carried all those packages.

Mac's horse stood placidly in the yard, looking as though he'd been ridden six yards rather than the several miles from Rio Hondo. That didn't surprise Cody much either. In fact, nothing about Alexander McMurdo surprised Cody any longer. He considered asking how Mac had managed to carry that armload of parcels all the way from Rio Hondo on that one remarkably rested horse, and decided he really didn't want to know.

"Shut up, Perry."

The dog looked up at him and wagged his tail. Mac laughed. Cody sighed.

"Merry Christmas, Mac." He held out his arms to take some of the packages.

"And a happy Christmas to you too, Cody, m'boy."

"C'mon in, Mac. I think Mrs. Wilmeth's almost ready to put dinner on the table. I'm sure there's plenty if you'd like to join us."

Mac sniffed the air appreciatively. "Ah, smells delicious, Cody, m'lad. What's for dinner?"

"She found a turkey in among the chickens this morning, and I butchered it for her. That's what we're havin' for Christmas dinner." Cody shrugged, unable to explain a turkey's presence among his chickens.

"A turkey? Saints be praised! Where in the world do you expect a turkey came from?"

Cody would have sworn on a stack of Bibles Mac wasn't anywhere near as amazed about that turkey as he pretended to be. "I don't know, Mac. It just showed up."

"A miracle, that," said the old man, with one of his rich, fat chuckles.

All at once, Cody thought of Father Christmas. "Yeah."

"Where's our little Katie today?"

"I think she's eating her supper right about now."

"Ah, then let's us arrange these packages around this fine tree of yours, Cody, and surprise Katie's mama when she's done feedin' the wee lassie."

The suggestion found favor with Cody. It did the same with Perry, who decided he wanted to unwrap the presents himself. Cody dissuaded him sharply, and the two men arranged parcels beneath the tree while Perry hid himself under a chair. The tree, of which Cody felt secretly rather proud, was now densely decorated with paper garlands, popcorn strings, cut-out stars, and paper snowflakes. It was topped with a tin angel.

Mac eyed the angel thoughtfully. Several smaller

tin angels and some tin stars twinkled among the piñon's branches. They captured light from the fireplace and the kerosene lamps that had been set on the furniture and winked it back at him. He took care to inspect those little tin ornaments, too.

"Where'd you get those pretty things?"

Cody mumbled, "I made 'em," and dove in among the packages, pretending he had to rearrange them.

"Ahhhh."

When Cody looked up, frowning, he saw Mac smiling upon him like an angel about to bestow a blessing. "Well, hell, Mac, all's it took was to cut up a couple old sardine cans with the tin snips and bend 'em some this way and that."

Mac nodded wisely. "Of course. Of course. Now why didn't I think of that?"

"I wouldn't know." Cody felt crabby, and he didn't appreciate Mac's knowing smile. Hell, Cody was a good hand at tin work. A man had to be good at lots of things out here in the Territory, since there weren't craftsmen handy to do stuff for him. Hell, he and Arnie had made the windmill tank out of tin when they first set up out here. It was no big deal, his having made those ornaments. Why, they'd last for years and years. Katie could use them on her own trees when she grew up and had kids of her own.

Where that thought had come from, Cody had no idea, but he wished it hadn't.

As he'd greeted Mac's arrival at his front door with relief because it saved him from being alone with Melissa, he now greeted Melissa's entry into the parlor with relief because it saved him from being alone with Mac. She was, needless to say, ecstatic to see the old Scot. They embraced warmly. Cody tried not to be envious of the sly old devil.

"Oh, my goodness, Mac! Did you bring all those

packages from town?" Melissa fairly goggled at the packages now piled on the floor around the Christmas tree.

"I did indeed, my dear."

She gave him another kiss. Cody discovered himself scowling, and stopped. "I have something for you, too, Mac. It's under the tree somewhere. I thought I'd have to wait until we went into town again before I could give it to you."

"Well, now you can give it to me on Christmas Eve, m'dear, just like real folks." He laughed again. So did Melissa. Cody wondered why he should feel miffy because Melissa'd made something for Mac and not for him.

"Can you stay for dinner, Mac? It's almost ready, and it's extra-special today, because we found a *turkey*, of all things, in with the chickens this morning! Can you believe it? A turkey ! And not one of those scrawny prairie turkeys either, but a real, live, fat, back-East-type turkey." She laughed gaily.

Mac said, "Cody told me about it, Mellie. Amazing, the things you can find flappin' around out here, isn't it?"

"Indeed, it is. And the meat will keep, too, because it's gotten so cold these days and nights, we can freeze it."

"Good thing, that."

"Indeed, it is. Why don't the two of you sit in the parlor while I get dinner on the table? Mr. O'Fannin found a bottle of whiskey in the shed, and I stirred up some eggnog. Would you each like a glass of Christmas cheer?"

"Eggnog, is it? Sounds delicious, my love."

Melissa tripped off to fix her eggnog. Mac twinkled at Cody. "Aren't you two callin' each other by your first names yet, Cody lad? You're slower than I took you for."

"She's my housekeeper, Mac, not my sister." Cody realized he'd spoken more forcefully than necessary. He frowned to make up for it.

"No, indeed. Mellie isn't your sister, my boy. I was thinkin' of her bein' something a trifle dearer to you than a sister."

Cody got up and laid another log on the fire burning merrily away in the fireplace. He did that forcefully, too, and a shower of sparks danced up the chimney. "Well, she ain't," he said shortly.

"Mmmm."

Because he didn't like Mac forcing his hand in this unsubtle way, Cody added, "Anyway, my aunt Luella and her husband used to call each other 'Mr. O'Fannin' and 'Mrs. O'Fannin' even after they'd been hitched for thirty years. Names don't mean anything."

"Hmmm. I expect you look to your aunt Luella and her husband as models of matrimonial perfection."

"Aunt Luella and Uncle Jeremiah? Hell no! Those two hated each other until Uncle Jerry died to get away from the old bat."

Cody realized Mac had trapped him and didn't appreciate it. "Dammit, Mac, I don't need any models of matrimonial perfection! I don't aim to get married."

"Of course not."

"Anyhow, Mrs. Wilmeth's still married to Mr. Wilmeth, for cripes' sake."

"Of course."

Melissa came back into the room bearing two glasses of nutmeg-sprinkled eggnog. She looked pretty and happy, and Cody's heart tugged painfully. He heard a noise from Mac and glared at him. But

Mac had repositioned his angelic expression and was now smiling at Melissa. Cody felt beleaguered.

"Here you go." She handed one glass to Mac and the other to Cody so graciously, Cody had a sudden vision of her doing this sort of thing in his home for the rest of their lives. He tried to squelch the vision, but it was terribly appealing and didn't want to go away. It played in his imagination like a fiddle—himself and Melissa, old married folks with their children and grandchildren—and Mac, of course—come over for Christmas Eve. Cody and Melissa entertaining friends on a winter's evening, with Melissa serving up one of her fine dinners and everybody envying Cody his good luck in having married her.

Damn it all, what in hell was the matter with him?

"Thanks," he muttered as he took his drink.

"You're welcome," she said in much more friendly a tone than he'd used.

"Delicious, Mellie!"

"I'm glad you like it, Mac. It's another recipe I remembered from Mrs. Bowlus's house."

"That Mrs. Bowlus might have been a sorry old cow, but you sure learned plenty there," Cody offered. He smiled at her to make up for the tone of his prior thanks.

Melissa laughed again. "You're right, Mr. O'Fannin. I think of my tenure under Mrs. Bowlus as in the nature of an education, I guess."

"You were a good student, Mellie, m'dear," Mac said, his voice as warm as Cody's had been sharp earlier.

"Thank you, Mac."

Cody thought it was sweet the way she blushed when people praised her. He'd never known a female to take such pleasure in simple praise before. He reckoned it was because she'd been so shortchanged of appreciation until now.

She served up the most delicious Christmas dinner Cody'd ever eaten, even at his aunt Luella's house when he was a boy. Whatever else he thought of Aunt Luella, she was a damned fine cook. But Melissa outshone even Luella in the kitchen.

After dinner, she cleaned away the plates and set the dishes to soaking in a washtub, and the three of them retired to the parlor once more. Mac dug into his other coat pocket and produced a handful of chestnuts. Melissa's eyes went as round as the nuts themselves.

"Chestnuts! My goodness, I haven't eaten a roasted chestnut in years."

"Well, now's your chance, Mellie, m'love," he said with a wink.

"Where'd you come up with chestnuts?" Cody asked before he could stop himself. He anticipated Mac's answer and wasn't disappointed.

"Oh, they just turned up," he said with an airy wave. "Somebody coming through must've left them."

One of Melissa's laughs could last a man for a year or more, Cody decided.

"Alexander McMurdo, I do believe you're something of a rogue."

"You're right, Mellie. Don't tell anybody, as I'm trying to keep it a secret."

"I won't." She fetched a long-handled pan in which to roast the chestnuts.

The rest of Cody's Christmas Eve was spent in eating chestnuts, singing Christmas songs, dandling Katie and watching her being dandled on various knees, and listening to stories. Mac had a million of 'em. Cody wondered how many Christmases he'd

237

lived through to have collected so many stories. He didn't ask. Again, he wasn't sure he wanted to know.

Melissa didn't have many Christmas tales at all, although she listened with delight to the ones Mac told. Cody had a feeling it was because her own Christmas experiences weren't very happy, and his soft heart took to aching for her.

He had a few tales of his own that he shared. A couple of them had Melissa almost rolling with laughter, and he got the pleasant feeling that he'd bestowed a great gift by giving her laughter.

She hadn't only made Mac a present. She presented Cody with his with a shy smile and much self-deprecation.

"It's not much, of course, but I hope you can use it." Her cheeks were pink; Cody wasn't sure if the pink was due to heat from the fireplace or a blush, but he suspected the latter.

"Thank you, Mrs. Wilmeth. You shouldn't have gone to the bother of giving me anything."

"Oh, no, Mr. O'Fannin! You saved my life. And Katie's. I'll never be able to thank you adequately for that. This gift is nothing."

It wasn't nothing. It was a prettily knitted woolen scarf, and Cody thought it was one of the nicest presents he'd ever received. Not only had Melissa chosen yarn in colors that he liked—green and gold and brown—but she'd obviously been listening when he'd told her how cold it got out on the range in the winter months. Hell, this thing was long enough to wrap around his neck twice—and there'd still be plenty left to cover his nose and mouth and wind up over his ears. If he feared he might look like a damned tenderfoot while wearing such a dandified garment, he guessed his credit with the other ranchers hereabouts was solid enough that he could carry it off.

He got a little choked up when he considered the thought behind this scarf, in fact.

"Oh, dear, Mr. O'Fannin, I hope you don't dislike it."

When he heard the worry in Melissa's voice, Cody realized he'd been staring at the scarf for several moments. He glanced up to find her kneading her hands and watching him.

"Dislike it?" Cody swallowed. "Ma'am—Mrs. Wilmeth—this here's the prettiest thing anybody's ever give me. Thank you. Thank you kindly."

Her smile took his breath away. "Oh, I'm so glad! I got worried there for a minute."

"You don't have to worry about our Cody not liking anything you'd give him, Mellie dear," Mac assured her. Cody frowned at the way Mac had expressed himself, although he reckoned he'd spoken nothing but the truth.

"Yes, ma'am. I surely do like this scarf. It'll be great for keepin' the cold off."

"I'm so glad."

She settled into her hard-backed chair, and Cody wished he'd gotten her something, too. Oh, the rocking chair was a blamed nice present and all, but still, it would have been nice to have something to give her tonight, with everybody else opening up stuff.

He cleared his throat. "I don't reckon your present's got to to Rio Hondo yet, ma'am. I wish it had, so's you could have it tonight. I surely do."

"My present?" Her cheeks turned as red as roses.

"Yes, ma'am. I ordered it at Mac's, but I don't reckon it'll get here until after the first of the new year."

"My goodness, Mr. O'Fannin!"

Emma Craig

"Well, now, Cody, m'lad, don't be too sure about that."

Cody and Melissa both swiveled their heads in Mac's direction. Cody got a funny, fluttery feeling in his stomach when he realized the old geezer was grinning like an imp.

"What do you mean, I shouldn't be too sure about that, Mac? It had to come all the way from St. Louis. There's no way in hell—pardon me, ma'am—it could have got here so soon."

"Ah, but astonishing things happen sometimes, my boy, especially out here, where there's enchantment in the very air we breathe." McMurdo's voice was as smooth as molasses in July.

"Yeah?" Cody squinted at Mac. He'd never noticed any damned enchantment in the air.

Mac nodded solemnly. "And it just so happens that the exact same thing as you ordered was delivered by accident to me the day before yesterday. When the one you ordered arrives, I'll just ship it off to California, where this one was supposed to have been sent."

"Now wait just a blasted minute here, Mac." Cody knew as well as anyone that shipments to the Territory often went awry. But he also knew that too much coincidence was too much coincidence. That a rocking chair intended for California might have ended up in Rio Hondo by accident was too fortuitous a coincidence to swallow.

Mac's face went as innocent as baby Katie's. His cherubic blue eyes might have graced the face of St. Peter. Cody didn't buy it for a second. Not for half a second.

"I can't explain it myself, Cody lad, but I swear on my granny's grave that a rocking chair, exactly like the one you ordered for our Mellie here, showed up

240

in my mercantile establishment, as bold as brass, not two days since."

"Mac—"

"A rocking chair?"

Melissa's squeak shut Cody's mouth for him. He peered at her, feeling sheepish. "Thought you might like to have one, ma'am."

She stared at him as if he were a blessing sent from heaven. Cody wished she wouldn't do that. He might could get used to it, and then where would he be?

"You bought me a rocking chair?"

Oh, God, she was going to cry. Cody saw her fumbling in her apron pocket for a handkerchief and looked helplessly at Mac, who winked at him. Hell of a lot of good that did.

"You shouldn't have done such a thing, Mr. O'Fannin! It's too kind. Too good of you. I don't deserve such a lovely gift."

"Nonsense!"

Mac's sturdy tone seemed to dry up Melissa's tears. She sniffled a couple of times but didn't start bawling. Thank God. Cody nodded his thanks at Mac, who winked again. Cody wished he wouldn't do that.

"In fact," McMurdo continued, "if we were to step out through the kitchen and take a peek out the back door, we might just find this marvelous chair of yours sittin' beside that stump Cody stuck there. And maybe even something else, too."

"You brought a rocking chair—on your horse—and set it beside the back door? Along with all those other presents?"

Cody could feature Alexander McMurdo as a magician. He could even feature him as a good-hearted fraud. What he couldn't feature is how the devil he managed to get all those Christmas presents—and a full-sized rocking chair—from Rio Hondo to Cody's ranch without so much as a wagon to haul them all in.

Mac chuckled, as if this was the grandest joke of all. "I had me some help, m'boy. Don't fret yourself."

He'd had help. Cody frowned, wondering where Mac's help had disappeared to. He scratched his head. Try as he might, he couldn't figure out any way Mac could have brought everything here—unless he was telling the truth. Since he couldn't figure it out any other way, he guessed he had to accept Mac's story of having received help. From somebody who had hightailed it out of the yard as soon as Mac had arrived. Silently.

Cody gave up thinking about possible modes of transportation as too taxing. "Well, hell, let's go out and fetch it inside before it rains and the wood warps."

"What a splendid idea, to be sure. Good thinking, Cody." Mac jumped up from his own chair, as spry as a boy.

Melissa was still sniffling, but she was game as a pebble as she followed Mac and Cody through the kitchen and to the back door. As soon as Cody opened the door and she perceived what she claimed was the loveliest rocking chair she'd ever beheld in her entire life, though, she burst into tears. An identical rocker, made for a child, stood beside the adult-sized rocking chair.

Then she threw herself into Cody's arms. Mac smiled at the two of them like a representative sent from heaven by the Christmas Angel himself.

Since Cody's eyes fluttered shut as soon as his arms closed around Melissa, he didn't see the perfect flood of showery sprinkles that flew from Mac's fingertips to wash over them.

Chapter Fourteen

The weeks following Christmas passed in a happy blur for Melissa. The gaiety of the day itself had lasted, and she and Cody had seemed more at ease with each other ever since. Melissa didn't understand it, but she was glad of it. And if she still ached with longing occasionally, and if she still harbored improper urges for him, and if every now and then she forgot herself so far as to imagine herself as Cody's wife—still, she was happy.   •

They all drove into Rio Hondo on New Year's Eve, and spent a festive afternoon and evening at McMurdo's Wagon Yard. Lots of other ranchers and ranch hands in the area did the same thing. Melissa was astonished to find fifty men of various ages and stations in life gathered there for the celebration. Until now, she hadn't even known fifty people lived in these parts. They ate and sang and drank cider and laughed and had a big bonfire, and after the sun set on a perfectly delightful day, Mac set off some fireworks.

"Did you just happen to 'find' these in the back room?" Cody asked with a laugh as he helped Mac set up the display.

"How you talk, Cody m'lad!" Mac grinned like a devilish sprite. "I ordered these fireworks special, all the way from New York City."

"Last time my pa and Uncle Harold tried to set off fireworks, they'd gotten wet and didn't work," Cody mentioned.

"Don't worry about these. These here fireworks will work just fine."

Melissa saw Cody look slantwise at Mac. His eyes narrowed thoughtfully. "Yeah," he said. "I'm sure they will, Mac."

Mac chuckled jovially. Melissa didn't understand.

The fireworks worked just fine, as Mac had promised. The huge booms created as the rockets launched startled Katie and made her cry. Melissa rocked her in her arms and spoke soothingly to her, but her gaze was glued on the spectacular displays overhead. The fireworks were glorious.

Melissa had the wistful thought that if she and Katie were allowed to remain here in the Rio Hondo area, in a couple of years Katie would enjoy this as much as her mama did. Her heart spasmed painfully and she lost her smile for a moment, until a huge flowery starburst overhead made her forget her uncertain circumstances.

Everyone, including Cody and Melissa, camped in the wagon yard that night and drove home the next day. Cody and Luis and Carlos chatted the whole way about the news they'd had from other ranchers, and their enjoyment of the prior day's festivities. It was the first time she realized she hadn't seen Howard there. In fact, Luis mentioned that nobody from the Blackworth operation had shown up.

Cody shrugged. "Maybe Mac didn't invite 'em."

"Naw," Carlos said. "Mac invites everybody."

"Maybe Blackworth's just too unsociable to have a party with the likes of us," Luis said, laughing.

Cody laughed, too, but Melissa didn't think his laugh sounded genuine.

Life on Cody's ranch settled down to a steady routine after the holidays. It took on a routine that was so peaceful, in fact, that Melissa often didn't think about Howard or her divorce for hours at a time. She loved living here with Cody, and cooking for him and Luis and Carlos. They were all friendly, kindhearted men, and they all treated her with a respect she'd never received before in her life from anyone. She wasn't sure she'd ever get used to it, but she sure liked it.

Katie was growing like a weed, in Cody's honest, albeit artless words, and Melissa was glad of that, as well. Melissa had seen too many babies die in her life. Children were always taking sick in the Boston slum in which she used to live. Raw sewage spilled into the gutters in front of her mother's tenement. More rats and roaches lived in those crumbling buildings than humans. Sanitation—what there was of it—was abysmal. Cholera, diphtheria, consumption, typhus, influenza—she remembered all of those diseases taking babies, and she watched Katie like a hawk.

"Reckon we have those troubles out here, too, ma'am," Cody told her once when she voiced a concern. "But it's not like in a city, where you get exposed to a lot of stuff." She took heart from his sensible observation.

Now that she lived in the relative comfort of Cody's

ranch house in the middle of nowhere, Melissa realized how lucky she'd been to have been able to sleep in Mrs. Bowlus's home. She hadn't fully appreciated it at the time, since Mrs. Bowlus had been such a hard-hearted old shrew, but she did now. Mrs. Bowlus's house had even been equipped with indoor plumbing.

Children who lived in Mrs. Bowlus's Beacon Hill neighborhood seldom died from diseases rampant in Melissa's slum. Melissa would do her level best to make sure such diseases never sullied Cody's home, either. Melissa herself might have been born into poverty and squalor, but as she lived and breathed, she'd make sure her daughter never had to live like that.

The only problem with Katie's thriving so wonderfully was that she was outgrowing her newborn flannel gowns. Melissa didn't despair of finding a means of keeping her daughter clothed, however.

One of the packages Mac had brought with him on Christmas Eve had contained a variety of fabric pieces. They were all different sizes and all different materials, from heavy denim for work shirts to pretty patterned calicoes for dresses to soft flannel for baby nightgowns to cotton lace for trimming. Melissa had stared, goggle-eyed, at the mound of fabrics.

Mac, of course, had winked and laughed and said he'd "found" the pieces in his back room, and that they were bolt-end scraps and nothing to go on about. So she hadn't gone on about them. Instead, she'd taken them out later, in her and Katie's room, and marveled at the bounty in private. She'd already cut out several dresses and had begun sewing them for Katie to wear when she grew a little bigger.

Another one of Mac's presents had been a wicker basket he claimed was one of those things that had been delivered by accident to his mercantile establishment. The basket had a petit-point pattern embroidered on the padded lid cover. Inside the basket resided an abundance of threads, a pair of scissors, several thimbles, two darning eggs, papers of pins and needles, and a measuring tape. Melissa had never owned such a basket, although she'd coveted a few like it that she'd seen displayed in the windows of expensive stores in Boston.

Luis and Carlos had returned from their holiday in Picacho in time to go to Rio Hondo for Mac's New Year's Eve party. Luis had come into Cody's house on New Year's Eve morning to say hello and marvel at Melissa's new rocking chairs. In fact, he'd been quite goggle-eyed to see the chairs sitting before the fireplace in Cody's parlor.

"Them are two fine chairs, Mrs. Wilmeth." His voice held awe. Melissa didn't find Luis's surprise anything to wonder at.

She rubbed her hand over the finely carved maple. She'd been doing that ever since Christmas Eve, when Mac and Cody had revealed the beautiful chairs to her.

"Aren't they wonderful? Mac says that when you order the adult-sized chair, the company always sends the children's chair along for free. Isn't that something?"

She searched Luis's face, trying to determine whether Luis detected anything fishy about the scenario Mac had painted for her and Cody. Such generosity on the part of a furniture manufacturer didn't seem feasible to her. On the other hand, her knowledge of furniture purchasing—indeed, any kind of purchasing—had been severely limited. She didn't know beans about buying things because she'd never had any money.

Luis scratched his head. "I heard about drummers carryin' baby-sized furniture on their wagons, and then givin' the customer the kid's furniture if they buy the big pieces. Never heard of no back-East outfit doin' that. Reckon it makes sense."

"It does?" Melissa felt a great sense of relief, which lasted until Luis muttered, "I reckon." He didn't sound the least convinced.

On the last Thursday in January, her washing and ironing and baking done, Melissa sat in her chair and rocked. She cleared her mind of worries and frets and allowed a peaceful feeling to settle into her heart.

Katie was being obliging and had been napping in her cradle for an hour. Melissa was deep into daydreaming about how she'd like her life to be when the rumble of a wagon making its way into the ranch yard caught her attention. She lifted her head. At the same time, the back door opened, and she heard Luis call out, "*Hola*, Miz Wilmeth. Cody sent me in to get the ball of twine he left in the kitchen yesterday."

"All right, Luis." She sighed heavily

She had no business lazing around in her chair anyway, no matter how beautiful and comfortable and wonderful it was. She had sewing to do. After she got herself organized, *then* she could sit in her rocker again. She could get some work done at the same time, thereby mitigating the intense joy she felt every time she relaxed in her wonderful Christmas present. It didn't seem right to take joy in something when she wasn't gainfully occupied.

She got up and hurried to the front window. Luis evidently heard the wagon, too, because he came into the parlor, the twine in his hand.

"Who's that?"

"I don't know, Luis." She stepped to one side, so

that he could look out the window, too.

Visitors were a rare occurrence on Cody's ranch. Miles and miles of nothing separated neighbor from neighbor in this part of the territory, and decent roads had yet to be built. Melissa had a faint hope that this visitor would turn out to be Alexander Mc-Murdo, although she couldn't imagine why he'd come out here again so soon after his Christmas-Eve visit. After all, he had a wagon yard to run.

She hoped like thunder it wasn't Howard. Cody wasn't working on the porch today. Something had happened to some of his cattle, and he, Carlos, and Luis were attending to it. She didn't understand these things and had not questioned him about it.

She and Luis squinted out the small front window. The sun shone directly into their eyes and made identification of this visitor difficult. The wagon veered off to the left, and Melissa's eyes nearly started out of their sockets when she beheld a middle-aged woman, clad all in black, with a face like a hatchet, driving a wagon pulled by a team of oxen.

"Good heavens! Who can that be?"

"Shit—shoot, ma'am, that there's Mrs. Black-worth." The fact clearly astonished Luis.

Melissa glanced at him sharply. "Mrs. Black-worth? You mean, Mr. Blackworth's wife?"

Of course, Melissa, you gaping idiot. Who else would Mrs. Blackworth be?

Luis didn't seem to share Melissa's disdain for her question. "Yes, ma'am," he said in an awed-sounding voice. Then he said, "Um, I'd better get back to work, ma'am. Cody's gone out to the range already, and Carlos is saddling up the horses. Um, think I'll go back out the kitchen door, ma'am."

"All right, Luis."

Melissa allowed herself only a second or two to wonder why Luis seemed so nervous. Then she smoothed her apron, made sure Katie was still sleeping soundly, and opened the front door, armed with the biggest smile she had in her. She hadn't set eyes on another woman since Howard got them kicked out of the wagon train. The prospect of talking to this one, even if she did appear rather intimidating, was so exciting that Melissa couldn't wait for a knock at the door.

She walked over to the wagon. "Good morning!"

Mrs. Blackworth looked her up and down without smiling. To Melissa, it seemed as if the visitor was evaluating her. It was an unpleasant sensation.

Nevertheless, the prospect of having a chat with another female propelled her into saying, "Luis Morales told me you're Mrs. Hugh Blackworth. It's so nice of you to visit, Mrs. Blackworth."

The older woman said nothing, but concentrated on setting the brake on the wagon

Melissa was beginning to feel quite nervous in the face of Mrs. Blackworth's silence. She also had the irrelevant thought that Blackworth was a good name for her. "Of course, you've come to see Mr. O'Fannin, but I'm afraid he'd not here at the moment. I'm not sure when he'll be back. I hope you'll come inside and take a cup of tea and a piece of cake with me. There are so few women out here, I—I—" She took a deep breath and told herself to calm down. "I'm sorry. I'm babbling like an idiot."

"Humph."

Oh, dear. Melissa swallowed and clasped her hands under her apron, as she used to do when Mrs. Bowlus was ripping up at her. "Er, my name is Melissa Wilmeth."

"I know who you are."

A Gentle Magic

Mrs. Blackworth heaved herself out of the wagon and secured the oxen to the hitching rail Cody had built several yards away from the house. She narrowed her eyes and surveyed the house and the surrounding countryside. Then she nodded.

"Fair place O'Fannin's got here. Not a big spread like Mr. Blackworth's, but tidy. Very tidy."

Her gaze swiveled back to Melissa and sharpened. "I didn't come here to see Mr. O'Fannin, young lady. I came here to meet you."

Melissa felt her eyes open wide and her mouth get dry. She forced herself to smile. "Oh. How kind. Please come inside and have a cup of tea, Mrs. Blackworth."

For the first time, Mrs. Blackworth allowed her severe expression to relax. Melissa couldn't exactly find a smile in the woman's face, but she didn't look as mean as she had at first.

"Don't mind if I do. Name's Susan, by the way. My folks called me Sukey when I was a girl, but Sukey's a damn-fool name for a woman of my age and looks. You can call me Susan."

Melissa stopped gaping, and stammered, "Th-thank you, Missus—er—Susan. Please call me Melissa."

"Frilly name," Mrs. Blackworth growled.

Melissa didn't argue. She was of the same opinion herself.

"Suits you."

She didn't argue about that, either, although she wasn't sure she agreed. She also didn't know if Mrs. Blackworth had meant the comment as a compliment or the opposite.

She guided Mrs. Blackworth, who limped and used a cane, into the parlor of Cody's house, feeling dreadfully ill at ease. She'd lived in the Seven Rivers

251

country for long enough to understand that the Blackworths were rivaled only by John Chisum in wealth and power. She also knew Blackworth and Chisum were mortal enemies and that when people got between them, they often didn't survive. Cody had told her often enough that he preferred to stay out of local politics and rivalries. Melissa honored his good sense. She had no idea what this visit of Mrs. Blackworth's boded.

To have the wife of one of the two most powerful men in southeastern New Mexico Territory taking tea with her made her edgy, however, especially since she got the feeling she was being sized up and judged. She knew she'd be found lacking. She *was* lacking.

In spite of her fears and insecurities, Melissa served tea and leftover pound cake and showed off her baby, just like a normal woman. She felt somehow as though she belonged here in Cody's home, doing these things. The feeling was an illusion; she knew it and felt it anyway.

"Pretty little thing," Mrs. Blackworth said of Katie. The words came out sounding as if she didn't want to concede even that one small point. She did, however, condescend to hold the baby for a few minutes. Katie didn't object, for which Melissa silently blessed her.

"Thank you. Katie's a very good baby. Sleeps all night long, most nights."

"Humph."

Anxious as a cat, Melissa babbled on. "I'm glad of it, since I hate to have her cry and wake Mr. O'Fannin up. He works so hard all the time. I'm sure he needs his sleep."

"I'm sure he does."

Susan Blackworth leveled another appraising

glance at Melissa, and she felt herself grow warm. She tried to telegraph the message that there was *nothing* of an improper nature going on between herself and Cody O'Fannin—and that, no matter how unworthy a vessel Melissa herself was, Cody was a gentleman and incorruptible.

Not at all sure she'd conveyed her message, she cleared her throat and decided to change the subject. "It's such a pleasure to be able to talk with another woman, Susan. I haven't even set eyes on another female for months now." She elected not to mention how her husband's pugnacity had cut short several friendships Melissa had begun on the wagon train.

"No. Not many females out here yet. There's Mrs. Partridge, Mrs. Hornbeam, and me, and that's about it. That's why the place is so wild. Good cake." Susan took another bite of day-old pound cake and nodded her approval. Melissa felt like she'd passed some kind of test.

"Thank you. I got the recipe from a woman for whom I used to work in Boston."

Mrs. Blackworth thinned her gaze again. When her eyes squinted up that way, they put Melissa in mind of Mr. Pincher, the butcher in Boston who could never be made to understand that Melissa wasn't stealing from him. He used to watch her like a hawk every time she did the marketing for Mrs. Bowlus. His scrutiny used to make her very uneasy. Mrs. Blackworth's did the same now.

"So you're from Boston originally?"

"Yes." Melissa tried and failed to think of a reason being from Boston could be construed as a bad thing.

"And you worked for your keep back there, did you?" the older woman asked after several uncomfortable moments. They were uncomfortable for Melissa, at any rate.

"Yes. Yes, I did."

Mrs. Blackworth nodded. Melissa couldn't tell whether her admission raised or lowered her in Mrs. B.'s esteem.

"Doing what?"

Her guest barked her question out sharply, and Melissa had to take a deep breath to steady her jumping nerves. "I was a housekeeper, as I am here."

She got another nod for this piece of information.

"Good thing you're used to working. Females come out to these parts expecting their men to take care of them, they're in deep trouble before they start."

"Yes, I can imagine. I've never expected anybody to take care of me, though." Melissa gave a little laugh, and wished she hadn't admitted to such a thing. After all, her husband worked for this woman's husband. She wondered if Howard had been spreading tales about her, and her nervousness edged up. Such a thing would be just like him; he enjoyed malicious rumors, even when he had to make them up himself.

"Good thing you're accustomed to earning your keep, if what I hear's true."

Melissa's heart dropped like a boulder in an avalanche. "What—what have you heard?"

"That you're divorcing your husband, of course. It's common knowledge." Mrs. Blackworth waved her hand in the air in a dismissive manner.

"It is?"

Melissa got another shrewd look for her silly question. "Can't keep any secrets out here, dearie. Too few folks and too little news. Folks eat up gossip like candy."

"Oh."

"McMurdo says you're a sensible gal with a good head on your shoulders and the heart to work. He says the trouble's your man's fault. I expect he's right. Mac's got a keen mind, and he's a shrewd judge of character."

Melissa's heart started to lift again, albeit cautiously. "Yes. Yes, he does."

"And from what I've seen of your husband, he doesn't have much of a mind at all."

Melissa wasn't sure if she was expected to comment, so she didn't. An unanticipated chuckle from her guest sounded like the creak of a rusty hinge, and it startled her.

"Anyone who gets to know you and that husband of yours will have a pretty fair notion who's at fault." Mrs. Blackworth pinned another sharp look upon Melissa. "Anyone who marries a bad man like Howard Wilmeth might well be held at fault, however."

Melissa bowed her head. "Yes, I understand what you mean, and I agree with you."

She was startled to feel Mrs. Blackworth patting her knee, and glanced up into a pair of almost friendly eyes that were so dark they reminded her of black olives. "Oh, don't look so downhearted, dearie. Everybody makes mistakes. Some of 'em aren't as permanent as marriage and some of 'em are. Anyway, divorce isn't nearly the sin out here that it's held to be back East, where folks are civilized."

"It isn't?"

"No. In fact, I expect there's more than one man out here who's never bothered to get a divorce back home, but who wouldn't think twice about marrying up with another female if he could find one."

"Good heavens!" This was startling information indeed.

"No need to take on so, dearie. It's just the way things are." Mrs. Blackworth frowned at Melissa, who tried not to look as shocked as she felt.

"I, ah, suppose you're right about that."

"I know I am." Mrs. Blackworth heaved herself to her feet. "Reckon I'd best get back home again. I only came out here to look you over."

Melissa blinked at her and felt herself blush.

"I know, it's an officious thing to say to you, but a body hears things, and I wanted to find out for myself what was true and what wasn't."

"Oh." Melissa thought about taking exception to Mrs. Blackworth's assertion, but decided it would profit her nothing to antagonize the woman. Mrs. Blackworth was obviously a force to be reckoned with. If she approved of Melissa, she could probably do her a world of good with the rest of the ranchers and their wives. If any of the other ranchers had wives; Melissa didn't know. If she didn't approve of Melissa, then Cody might suffer. She would do anything to prevent that from happening.

"Thank you very much for coming all the way out here, Susan. I enjoyed your visit." That was true, sort of, and it earned Melissa another softening of Mrs. Blackworth's severe expression.

"Yes. Well, don't do anything else stupid, girl, if you can avoid it. Stupidity don't work in this territory, as you'll find to your sorrow."

Good heavens, what was a body supposed to say to that? Melissa opted for a bland, "I'm sure you're right."

"Certainly, I am."

With that, Mrs. Blackworth unwrapped the oxen's reins, hefted herself back up onto the seat of her wagon, and rumbled away without a backward glance in Melissa's direction. Melissa hoped that was because Mrs. Blackworth was keeping her eyes on the path before her and not because she'd decided Melissa wasn't worth the effort.

She wandered back into the house and picked up her sewing things, but it was a long time before her heart was easy again.

"Mrs. Blackworth?" Cody stopped in the act of putting up his hat and turned to stare at Melissa, flabbergasted.

She nodded and didn't seem inclined to look at him. "Yes. She visited for a half-hour or so this morning. I gave her a piece of cake and a cup of tea."

Cake and tea be damned. "What in Hades did she want?"

Cody didn't like this turn of events. Not one little bit. Blackworth was a bastard and a devious, conniving snake—the perfect employer, in fact, for a devious, conniving bastard like Howard Wilmeth. Cody had never met Susan Blackworth in his life, but he figured anyone who'd marry Hugh must be cut of the same cloth. He didn't like knowing such a specimen had come out here while he was gone and examined Melissa behind his back. Cody couldn't think of anything Melissa might have let slip that could have hurt him or his ranch, but that was only because he wasn't sneaky like Blackworth.

Still, he wished he hadn't asked his question so sharply. Melissa had taken to wringing her hands beneath her apron the way she did when she was worried.

"Actually," she said in a small voice, "she said she came out here to look me over."

"To look *you* over?"

Melissa nodded and murmured, "Yes."

"Oh." That put a different light on the matter, he

guessed. If Melissa was right, maybe the visit concerned merely female curiosity and that sort of thing. "That's good, then."

"It is?"

When he looked down into her pretty blue eyes, Cody got lost for a moment. He shook himself out of it. "Sure." Because he didn't trust himself around her, he walked into the parlor. "Smells good in here."

"Thank you," she said absently. "Why is it good that Susan Blackworth came out here to look me over, Mr. O'Fannin?"

Cody picked up one of the newspapers he occasionally got from San Antonio. Mail delivery was sporadic in the Rio Hondo vicinity, and he often didn't see a paper for months on end. Then he might get six at once, and often in so damaged a condition, they were scarcely readable. They kept him up with the news, after a fashion, so he didn't complain. On Christmas Eve, Mac had brought five of them, and Cody'd only had time to read three of them through so far.

When he'd sat in his chair and taken a firm grip on the newspaper to keep his hands busy, he dared to look up at Melissa. "Well, it stands to reason that she came out to meet you. There aren't many women in these parts. Reckon she wanted to make friends."

"Do you think so? She—she didn't seem awfully friendly."

He frowned and contemplated the matter from many sides, but he couldn't come up with another reason for Susan Blackworth's visit—unless it was to spy on him for some purpose beyond his ken. He didn't want Melissa to worry about that possibility, so he didn't mention it.

"I reckon she's just out of practice bein' sociable." His solution made sense to him since he'd lived out in the virtual wilderness of southeastern New Mexico Territory for a few years. Hell, unless one talked to oneself, one often didn't talk at all.

Melissa didn't seem to find it as comforting an explanation as he'd have liked. She looked doubtful, although she didn't pursue the subject. "I'll get supper on the table."

Cody wished he had more experience in dealing with females. The truth was, *he* was out of practice in being sociable, too. When he'd lived here with Arnie, sometimes they wouldn't talk to each other for days on end. Females expected conversation. He felt as though he'd failed in this one, and didn't know how to rectify his mistake. He decided he'd be extra friendly at supper. He even began wracking his brain to come up with suitable supper-table conversational subjects and couldn't think of a single one.

It turned out that he didn't have to work very hard at the supper table, after all. Luis and Carlos kept Cody and Melissa entertained with tales of doings in Picacho. Cody was pleased when Melissa seemed to relax. She even laughed a good deal.

He was less pleased when the brothers retired soon after the meal was over and he was left alone in his house with Melissa and the baby. After she'd finished the dishes, she settled into her new rocking chair with her sewing. Cody had picked up the newspaper he'd abandoned when she'd called him to supper. Katie gurgled in her cradle. She always did that for awhile before she went to sleep. Cody thought it was cute.

The weather had become colder and colder these past few days, but his house stayed relatively warm. He and Arnie had built it from adobe bricks and there weren't any chinks to speak of. The stove and the parlor fireplace did a good job of keeping the chilly outdoor weather outside where it belonged.

Melissa had a habit of wrapping hot flatirons in toweling and setting one at his feet in the evening, too, which kept his toes toasty. He considered it a right thoughtful gesture and told her so. She, of course, had blushed and said Mrs. Bowlus had demanded it of her. Cody still thought it was a considerate thing to do. After all, *he* didn't demand a blamed thing of her, and still she did these nice things.

She'd also fashioned what she called a door snake out of those rags she worked on all the time. She'd knotted up a whole bunch of them, sewn them into a long roll, and covered the roll with a strip of the calico Mac had given her at Christmas, and embroidered a cunning face on the thing. She set it against the crack under the door so the icy wind couldn't get in. Cody was, in fact, very comfortable as he read his newspaper in his parlor.

It occurred to him that this domestic conduct was awfully close to the way an old married couple might behave. The scene was warm and cozy, and it bothered him a good deal. Not that he had anything against warm and cozy; he enjoyed both, in fact. No, what he objected to was that it was against both his principles and his judgment to harbor home-oriented feelings about life with Melissa Wilmeth.

"I'd better go outside and check the horses," he said, slapping the newspaper down on the rough wooden table beside his rough wooden chair.

Melissa jumped and looked up at him, startled. "Oh. Is there something wrong with the horses?"

"Don't know." He hated it that her eyes seemed to draw him like a fly to honey. He wanted to go over to her rocking chair, lean over, and kiss her good-bye—and he was only going outside for a second or three. And he was only doing that to get away from her. Damn, he had to get a grip on his urges.

She didn't say any more, but only looked slightly disconcerted. Cody flung himself over to the long-horn rack, snatched his fur-lined coat, and shrugged it on. He grabbed his hat and had just crammed it on his head when he opened the front door and stopped dead in his tracks.

"What is it, Mr. O'Fannin?" he heard Melissa say uncertainly at his back.

In front of his eyes, a carpet of silent whiteness greeted him. Well, hell's bells.

"It's snowing."

"What?" Her voice held a world of wonder.

"It's snowing." And, indeed, it was. Flakes drifted gently to the ground like confetti. Sometimes they danced in the wind currents, but there was very little wind. The spectacle presented by the gods of weather was about as serene as one ever got to see out here, where the very air was hard and men hung on to their lives and hopes by wrestling the land into submission.

"My goodness."

He didn't understand why she sounded so blasted surprised. Hell, they had snow in Boston, didn't they?

She answered his crabby question even though he hadn't asked it aloud.

"It used to snow a lot in Massachusetts. I didn't know it snowed at all out here."

He was disconcerted to find her at his elbow, peeking over his shoulder.

"Oh!" she exclaimed, sounding both breathless and happy at once. "Isn't it beautiful?"

Cody stiffened when he felt her hand on his shoulder. Even through the thickness of his heavy jacket, her small hand felt like fire on his skin. "Yeah," he croaked. "It's real pretty."

It was, too. The moon grinned a pale crescent in the black sky, the stars were out, and the pristine white layer of snow seemed to stretch out in front of their eyes forever. Nothing had sullied it yet; no footprints marred the snow's surface. It lay like a blanket, hiding the plain brown desert and making it all appear immaculate and beautiful. As they watched, a jackrabbit shot out from behind the barn and loped across the yard, leaving a trail of dents in the snow.

They both laughed. Melissa's hand tightened on Cody's shoulder, and the self-control he'd been endeavoring with all his might to master for weeks now snapped like a melting icicle. He turned around—straight into Melissa's embrace. He could tell by the expression of shock on her face that she hadn't been prepared for this. But he felt as though something beyond his mere human nature was driving him tonight.

He might have been able to stop himself if he'd tried, but he didn't try.

A sudden hitch in the atmosphere caught Alexander McMurdo's attention. He looked up from his reading, cocked his head, determined what it was, and smiled. Then he went to his room, fetched his robe, and went back to the parlor. Things were changing for Melissa and Cody, and he was glad.

For a long time, he stood before his window in the parlor of his tiny house in the back of his wagon yard in Rio Hondo and peered out at the snow. He held his ancient briar pipe in his gnarled hands. His long black robe, adorned with shimmering silver stars and moons, fluttered around his feet, stirred by mystic breezes. He seldom wore this robe, even though it marked his exalted position in the ranks of the elect. He didn't approve of flaunting himself in such a showy manner.

The conical cap that went with the robe resided in the back room still. Even at his most mystical, Mac couldn't make himself wear *that* thing. A thousand years ago, maybe. But the world had been different then. *People* had been different then.

No one believed in the Magic any longer. Humans looked to science and industry to bale them out of the silly problems they got themselves into. Mac was so old, and he was so wise, and his sense of humor was so keen, that he found the situation more pitiable—and more amusing—than tragic.

At the moment, he was pleased as punch.

"It's about time, you silly younguns," he muttered to himself.

Smoke circled his old white head, and he laughed and laughed. He laughed so hard, in fact, that the stars and moons on his robe shifted places. He laughed so hard that the jackrabbits who lived near the wagon yard gathered in front of his window to stare up at him. He laughed so hard, he sent a perfect blizzard of sprinkly sparkles across the whitened plains to envelope Cody O'Fannin's little adobe house, situated close to the banks of the Hondo River, in a blanket of magic.

Chapter Fifteen

Melissa uttered a tiny squeak. Cody caught it in his mouth. He feared she might resist him, but after that one inarticulate cry of surprise, she gave up any hint of resistance.

"Oh, Cody," she murmured as she flung her arms around him.

"Melissa." Her name purred from his lips. If he'd been in possession of his wits, he'd have thought his voice pathetic. His wits had long deserted him, though, and he didn't even notice.

He kissed her with all the pent-up longing in his soul. He desired her as he'd never desired another woman. He lusted after her. He longed for her. He adored her.

He loved her. God save him, he was in love with another man's wife.

Well, to hell with it. To hell with Howard Wilmeth and society and Mrs. Hugh Blackworth and his own ambitions and every other thing standing in the way of their shared hunger. Tonight, Cody couldn't think about those things. He couldn't think at all.

His passion was so strong, it lifted Melissa right up off the floor. He only realized what he'd done when he felt her leg hook around the back of his thigh so she wouldn't fall.

As if he'd ever allow her do such a thing! Cody O'Fannin would never let this woman fall. Even if she was married to that damned rascal Wilmeth, even if she could never be legally free of him, Cody would protect her. He'd protect her with his life if he had to.

"I love you, Cody," drizzled into his ears. The words shocked him so much, he almost forgot his desire for a second.

He reared his head back. "You do?"

"Yes. Oh, yes. I love you very much."

Her eyes shone like stars and held such honesty, Cody couldn't help but believe her. She loved him. *She* loved *him!* Well, hallelujah.

Before he could lose his nerve, he whispered, "I love you, too, Melissa."

Then he kissed her again, before his confession had a chance to settle into his brain and scare him. She tasted like cinnamon. She felt like heaven. Her full breasts flattened against his thick jacket, but Cody could feel them even through the layers of fur and fabric. Her hands played on his neck. Her fingers crept into his hair and he felt them nudge his hat.

"I've got too many clothes on," he gasped, and let her go for only long enough for him to rip off his jacket and hat. He didn't bother to hang them up again, but let them fall. Hell, the floor was as clean as the coat rack. As he lifted Melissa into his arms, he was vaguely aware that Perry had sidled over from where he generally slept in front of the fireplace and was settling down on his jacket. Cody didn't care.

Bless Katie for a sainted child, she slept like a log. Cody paused beside the cradle to make sure there would be no interference from that quarter, before he carried Melissa into his room. He deposited her on his bed like something precious, which she was. Indeed, Cody had never held anything or anybody more precious than Melissa.

The look on her face stopped him for a minute. She was staring up at him as if he held the answer to all her problems, as if she knew he'd never hurt her. As if she trusted him. For a moment his scruples threatened to spoil everything. Then Melissa moved her hand to her bodice and began to unbutton it, and Cody's scruples flew right out the window and into the snowy night.

His hands shook when he unbuttoned his own shirt. Thank God he'd removed his boots earlier, because he didn't feel like struggling with them now. He also spared a moment to be grateful for the thorough washing he always gave himself before supper.

Melissa slipped her simple gown down to her waist, and then hesitated. She looked shy. Although he hardly blamed her—after all, what they were about to do was a shocking breach of the principles that had been drilled into him since infancy—he whispered, "Don't be scared, Melissa. I'll never hurt you."

He'd spoken the truth, and Melissa apparently understood it. What he wanted to tell her was that it didn't matter to him what she'd come from, who she'd been entangled with before she met him, or what conventional society might think of what they were about to do. He loved her and would care for her from now until the day he died, and if it was within his power, she'd never suffer again. He wanted to convey to her his deep respect and commitment to her, that his love and his honor were hers, that he'd never loved a woman before and didn't expect ever to love another.

He didn't have the words for all that, so he only repeated, "I'll never hurt you, Melissa. I swear it."

"I know you won't, Cody. I trust you."

Those were the finest words anyone could say to Cody O'Fannin, whose life had been spent in honorable pursuits. He sat on the bed next to her and drew her into his arms.

"You're the finest man I've ever met, Cody. You've been so kind to Katie and me. I'll always love you."

Those words settled happily in him, too. He kissed her deeply, exploring her mouth with his tongue, as his hands explored her body. He helped her slide her gown over her hips to her feet, and eased her back against his pillow.

"Let me help you get these things off." He lifted one of her small feet onto his lap and unlaced her boot. Frowning, he muttered, "You need new shoes, Melissa." The ones she wore looked like they were a million years old. The leather was cracked and scuffed, and there were holes in the soles. Why had he never noticed before?

"I—Mrs. Bowlus used to give me her old shoes." Her voice was very small.

"You mean these weren't even new when you got them?"

"Oh, no. I've never had new shoes."

He turned to find her clutching at the bedclothes, her fingers opening and closing convulsively. She looked as if she was ashamed of her footwear. He reached over and lifted her chin with his finger.

"You couldn't help being poor, Melissa. Hell, we were poor when I was a kid, too, I reckon, although we never knew it. My brothers and me, we never had shoes at all, except in the winter time, and then we kept handing down the same pair from kid to kid. Being poor don't mean you're bad. You get that notion out of your head right now."

She stared at him wide-eyed for a moment, before she nodded. "Thank you. Yes, you're right."

He got the impression she believed him—at least for the moment—and was glad. His mind's eye pictured those fancy new boots that Howard Wilmeth had worn, and he got mad. He suppressed his rage because he didn't want to frighten Melissa.

When the snow melted and the plains were fit to travel again, he was going to march Melissa Wilmeth straight into Rio Hondo and order some shoes for her from Mac. Damned if he wasn't. And some for Katie, too. So what if she couldn't walk yet?

She had skin like silk. It was cool beneath his callused, work-worn hands. He worried that his rough skin would hurt her. "You're so pretty, Melissa. You're the prettiest woman I've ever known. And the smallest."

Which scared him a little. The whores at the Pecos Saloon were big and solid. Fleshy. They weren't delicate and small like this.

"Will you help me with this thing, please, Cody?"

She referred to her corset, and Cody had to lick his lips. Her breasts pillowed over the top of the garment. He knew they were bigger than normal because she was still nursing Katie, and he hoped he'd be able to see them in their natural state one day. They were covered in a plain cotton chemise at the moment, but they were closer and more tantalizing than he'd ever expected them to be. His hands closed over them, and he groaned. So did Melissa. Her head fell back, and Cody pressed his lips against the smooth column of her throat. Damn, she was gorgeous.

"You're so pretty, Melissa," he gasped when he drew breath again. He wished he knew how to be more eloquent.

"Thank you. You're the most handsome man I've ever seen."

His hands shook even harder when he turned her around so he could unhook her corset. The skin on Melissa's back was satiny and smooth and warm. As soon as her corset fell away, he wrapped his arms about her and drew her back to his chest. Carefully, he slid his big horn-hard hands under the straps of her chemise and drew them down her arms. For the first time, his hands cupped her naked breasts, and he thought he might explode then and there.

"Lordy, you're beautiful." Her nipples had puckered into rigid peaks, and his thumbs rubbing over them made them harder. Watching over her shoulder, he saw his big brown hands against her white, white skin, and wondered if he'd last long enough to do his duty. His erection threatened to burst from his trousers. Her head rested against his shoulder, and he eased her back against his pillow again.

She lay before him, naked, and the most magnificent sight he'd ever beheld. Her cheeks flushed pink under his scrutiny, and she crossed her hands over her magnificent breasts.

"I've never shown myself before," she confessed in a tiny voice.

Cody thoughtfully blew out the candle burning on his bedside table. Fortunately, there was still light enough for him to see her by, because he couldn't seem to stop staring.

"You're so damned beautiful," he murmured.

In fact, since he couldn't think of anything else to say and he meant it, he repeated it several times. His gaze traveled from her face, which held an interesting combination of excitement and trepidation, to her creamy shoulders, to her quite gorgeous breasts, to her stomach, still rounded from having given birth.

He saw faint stretch marks, and reached out to follow them with his forefinger. "These are from the baby?" he asked, feeling foolish about the question, but needing to know everything about her.

She nodded. "Are they awfully ugly?"

"Ugly?" He wasn't sure he'd heard her right. "Ugly? Lordy, ma'am, there's nothing about you's ugly." To prove it to her, he leaned over and gently traced the path of those stretch marks with his tongue. "You're beautiful. Every inch of you is beautiful." When he looked at her face again, he was horrified to see tears staining her cheeks.

"Ma'am?" he said uncertainly. "Melissa?" Oh, Jesus, he hadn't meant to make her cry. What had he done?

"Nobody's ever said I was beautiful before," she whispered thickly.

He shook his head in disbelief. "That's hard to believe, ma'am, because you're the prettiest female I've ever seen in my life." Which, he guessed, wasn't saying much, since he'd lived out on the frontier for most of that life. Still, it was the truth, and he marveled at the shortsightedness of the men Melissa'd known before him. "Am I really the first one to tell you that?"

He got a partial answer when she suddenly sat up, flung her arms around him, and cried, "You're the most wonderful man in the world, Cody O'Fannin, and I love you so much I can hardly stand it!"

Good, he thought when his brain started working again. *That's good.*

With the utmost care, he laid her back on his bed once more. Then, loath to leave her side, he stood up and struggled his trousers off. They were a tight fit, what with his arousal aching to get out and all, but he managed.

A little worried, he watched Melissa while he disrobed. He really didn't want to scare her. Not now, for sweet heaven's sake. Her eyes popped wide open when he stood naked before her, but he didn't linger there. Quickly, he lay beside her and took her in his arms, smoothing his hands over her back and buttocks and down her thighs.

When his hand closed over the soft curls between her thighs, she stiffened. "Are you going to be all right, Melissa? I won't do anything to hurt you."

If he had to stop now, he'd die, is all. He didn't say so. He was an honorable man; he wouldn't continue if she told him to stop.

"I know you won't, Cody. It's just that I haven't done anything like this since a long time before Katie was born. I—don't know if it will hurt or not—you know—because of having the baby."

He licked his lips and prayed his next words would turn out to be the truth. "We'll go real slow, Melissa. We'll go real slow and take it easy, and I'm sure it won't hurt."

He hoped like thunder it wouldn't hurt, anyway. Shoot, to the best of his knowledge, he'd never made love with a woman who'd had a baby barely three months prior—although, he admitted to himself with a pang of guilt, he had no idea what the women at the Pecos Saloon did in their off hours. For all he knew, they all had kids. The thought made him sad until he banished it.

He did decide, however, then and there, that he'd never pay a woman for sex again. It was too demeaning to the prostitute, and to himself as well.

"Thank you, Cody. I know you'll never hurt me."

Under the circumstances, Cody considered her faith in him remarkable.

He took it very slowly and very gently. When he dared investigate between those silky curls with his finger, he was encouraged to find her wet and warm. Taking it as a good sign, he dipped one finger into her passage and found the nub of her pleasure with his thumb.

He reckoned those times with the ladies at the Pecos Saloon—he hadn't gone *that* many times—had been good for something, anyway. It had been one of those women who'd explained a female's anatomy to him. That lady—Janie was her name—had taken great pleasure in disclosing the differences between men and women to him.

At the time, Cody had enjoyed the education immensely. Janie had told him she was taking extra time with him because he was so young and good-looking.

Cody appreciated Janie more than he could say as he endeavored to give Melissa the pleasure she deserved. He appreciated her more than he *would* say, at any rate. If people did such things, he'd have written her a note of thanks, in fact.

Women were more complicated than men. Cody both deplored and was fascinated by the fact as he watched Melissa react to his touch. Janie had explained to him that all men needed was a place, while women needed a reason. For Janie, it was

272

money. For Melissa, Cody guessed it was love. He felt humbled.

Melissa grabbed his arm. Her fingers dug into him like clamps. "Oh, Cody, that feels so strange."

Her voice was breathy and wisped around him like feathers. "Does it feel good, sweetheart?"

"Yes." She licked her lips. "Yes, it feels very good." Then she moaned and shut her eyes. She seemed to abandon herself to the pleasure of his touch, and Cody bent to kiss her again.

Her climax caught him by surprise. It did her, too, from the looks of it. He was in the middle of a delicious kiss, when she suddenly turned her face away, uttered a ragged cry, and trembled under him. He watched, fascinated. Sweet glory, he'd had no idea he could move a woman to this much rapture. It was a heady feeling. It also made his own situation more desperate.

"You all right, honey?" Cody asked.

She nodded and didn't seem able to speak. She did grab him by his shoulders, however, and pull him down on top of her. Cody took this as a good sign.

"Thank you, Cody. That's never happened to me before."

Well, there was only so much nobility in even the best of men. His head reeling and his body straining, Cody propped himself over her. Then, taking a gulp of breath and praying this wasn't going to hurt her, he plunged into her.

"Sweet glory," leaked from his throat. He'd never felt anything as good as this.

Her arms clamped over his shoulders and she wrapped her legs around his back, lifting her hips. Then she moved, and it was all over for Cody. He'd done a masterful job of controlling himself until now. When he felt Melissa's body arch beneath him, he gave himself up as his release came in a shocking burst of pleasure.

Drained, he lowered himself onto her. It was an effort, but because he didn't want to smother her with his heavy man's body, he slid to one side. His hairy leg lay on top of her thighs, and he was surprised when he felt her put a hand on it. He pried his eyes open and blinked at her hand, which was stroking him as if he was something adored and special. His heart turned to slop.

Although it was almost too heavy to lift, he managed to raise his hand and cup Melissa's cheek. He felt her tears, shoved himself up, and propped himself with his elbow. He was too tired for this, but he wasn't about to let Melissa cry.

"Are you all right?" His voice, he noticed with a frown, sounded like it came from a hoarse bullfrog.

He felt her nod before he heard her trembly, "Yes. Oh, yes."

Because he did, and because he sensed she needed his reassurance on the matter, he murmured, "I love you, Melissa."

She turned her face so that her lips kissed his palm. "And I love you, Cody. You're the best man I've ever known."

She'd said that before, and it touched him now just as it had then. "Thank you," he said simply. Of course, if all the men she'd met until now had been like Howard Wilmeth, he didn't wonder at her assessment. Still, it was a fine thing to say. The good Lord knew, Cody tried his damnedest to be a good man. It was nice that Melissa had noticed.

He was too exhausted to stay propped up like that for very long. His muscles felt like water, and his brain had gone almost as sloppy as his heart. He lay down again, and pulled Melissa to his chest.

It felt right to fall asleep like that, with his arms around her, and her soft rump cushioned against him. He liked it. He didn't know if it was still snowing or not, but the silence that came with snow prevailed, and Cody fell asleep at once.

Melissa's feeling of wonder that Cody O'Fannin, a good man and a proper one, should actually have declared that he loved her was only rivaled by the mingled satisfaction and fear she felt.

Mercy sakes alive, she'd never, ever felt the things Cody had made her feel. She hadn't known women could feel those things. She'd always assumed that women did their duty by affording men pleasure, and that was that.

Her mother hadn't told her a single thing about the physical relations that occurred between men and women. She'd only scolded and fussed and made it plain that she considered Melissa a lost cause and doomed to moral failure—even before Melissa knew in what ways men and women could sin together. Mrs. Bowlus had been used to warning her to stay away from men because a female from Melissa's walk in life couldn't be trusted around them and was sure to fall for the first sweet-talking fellow who came her way.

In the still, silent darkness of Cody's bedroom, Melissa reflected that both old witches had been right about her. The knowledge gave her an acute pang.

Yet what she and Cody had done together didn't seem like a bad thing. She guessed it wouldn't be bad at all if Melissa was married to Cody instead of to Howard. It certainly hadn't felt like sin.

"Oh, dear," she murmured softly, wishing she

could wave a magic wand and change everything. She thought briefly of Mac.

She had no wand, however, and knew no magic. Nor did she have the ability to think of a solution to the problem she foresaw now that she'd succumbed to her wicked nature and lain with Cody O'Fannin in a carnal way. How would she ever be able to face him in the morning?

Nothing had occurred to her before she drifted off to sleep in the comfort of his arms. She wished they could stay like this forever—snowed in and thus separated from the ugly world and the judgments and censure that existed beyond Cody's ranch.

Katie squawked to be fed in the middle of the night, and Melissa slipped away from Cody's embrace. She donned her chemise, which she found crumpled up on the floor, and went into her own room to fetch her flannel robe, since the fire had burned down and the parlor had become chilly.

Singing softly to her baby, Melissa stirred up the fire. Soon the room was warm again. Melissa's heart was cold, though, and it ached.

"What have I done, Katie?" she whispered softly as her daughter suckled at her breast. "What in the name of heaven have I done?"

She hadn't found an answer by the time Katie had eaten her fill. After she put her back into her cradle, Melissa pondered whether to return to Cody's bed or retire to her own. Ultimately, she'd discovered her weak character was unable to contemplate climbing between her icy sheets alone, so she rejoined the warmth of Cody in his bed. As she slid into his arms once more, she decided to forego punishing herself with recriminations until the morning. She'd have plenty of time to revile herself later—she'd have the rest of her life, in fact.

It wasn't the cold gray dawn's arrival that awakened Melissa the next morning. Nor was it a bellow from her daughter, because Katie slept the sleep of the innocent. It was soft lips nuzzling her neck that stirred her. She turned over in Cody's arms.

"You awake?" drizzled into her ear.

She almost groaned when she realized that yes, she was awake. And now she'd have to face the consequences of her moral lapse.

"Yes," she murmured. She knew herself to be wicked beyond redemption when she couldn't stop herself from snuggling more closely into his warm embrace.

"I think we're snowed in."

She blinked and opened her eyes. She found him watching her, his own beautiful brown eyes brimming with merriment and something she couldn't identify. Was that love she saw reflected there? Affection? Whatever it was, it was too heady for her to take this early in the morning. She had to close her eyes against it, and hope that whatever it was, he meant it.

"Good heavens. Is that bad? I mean, do you have to get out and go anywhere?"

"Naw. The snow never lasts long around here. It'll melt pretty soon. In the meantime, reckon it's you and me and Katie, Melissa. Like a little family."

Like a little family. Those were the most beautiful words Melissa had ever heard. Since she knew they weren't a little family at all, but a man and a woman who had no moral right to be sharing the same bed, she murmured, "And Luis and Carlos."

Cody laughed and threw back the bedcovers. The room had become freezing cold by this time, and Melissa gasped and grabbed for the quilt. At least she was more or less decently clad in her night dress.

277

She'd had that much modesty, for all the good it did her.

"Shoot, it's cold!" Cody hopped around the room, picking up his clothes. Then he plumped down on the bed and drew on his trousers. "I have to check on the cattle, darlin', but I'll be in soon for breakfast. Have to make sure the cows haven't been hurt in the storm."

"Breakfast will be ready when you come back. Don't you want to eat first?"

"Better not. I'll be back in a half-hour or so."

"All right."

She waited until he'd left the room before she climbed out of his bed and made it up neatly. Her muscles were sore this morning. They weren't used to that sort of exercise.

It was over an hour later before Cody, Luis, and Carlos showed up in the kitchen for breakfast. Melissa felt nervous, waiting for them, although she had plenty to do to keep herself occupied.

"The mush is probably pretty leathery by now," she said, feeling apologetic even though it wasn't her fault they were late.

Cody said, "It's all right."

"Don't matter," muttered Luis.

Carlos didn't say anything. He only took his plate and sat down. Melissa realized they all looked glum, and her stomach turned over.

"Is something the matter?"

Cody shook his head. "It's nothing, ma'am."

It wasn't nothing; Melissa could tell. Her gaze played among the three men. There was something they didn't want her to know, and she couldn't understand it. Unless . . .

Oh, Lord. "Is it Howard?" Her voice was brittle.

"Has Howard done something to your property, Mr. O'Fannin?"

His head jerked up. For a moment, Melissa feared he was going to lie to her. Then he sighed. "I can't say for sure, ma'am."

"But you suspect him of doing something?"

"Two cows was dead, Miz Wilmeth," Carlos said around a mouthful of fried cornmeal mush he'd slathered with butter and syrup.

"Poisoned," Luis elucidated.

"Poisoned?" Her heart pitched crazily. "Do you think Howard is poisoning your cattle?"

Cody didn't speak for a minute. He chewed deliberately, as if he was trying to think of something diplomatic to say.

"He tried to poison the water supply a month or so ago, ma'am," said Luis into Cody's silence. Cody glared at him.

Melissa sat with a thump, her heart thudding, her insides shaking like jelly. "He did? You know that? You caught him at it?"

Although he looked like he wished the subject hadn't come up, Cody said, "Reckon I did, ma'am." He looked up at her, and Melissa knew he wished he could spare her. She loved him so much right then that she hurt with it.

"Oh, my God."

"He only got the two of 'em, ma'am. It's nothin' for you to be worrying about."

"But he killed your cattle!"

"Ain't the first time," Carlos muttered. Cody kicked him under the table; Melissa saw it.

She sucked in a sustaining breath. "What else has he done, Mr. O'Fannin?"

"Don't worry about it," Cody mumbled.

Luis said, "He busted the corral gate last week."

Melissa thought to ask if they were sure it was Howard, but stopped herself before she blurted it out. Of course it was Howard. Who else but Howard would do such hurtful, underhanded things?

She was surprised when Cody's hand covered hers. "We'll catch him one of these days, ma'am. Try not to worry about it."

"When did all this start?"

Cody shrugged.

Luis said, "Day you told him you was divorcin' him, ma'am."

"That long? He's been plaguing you for that long?" Her heart hurt so much, she wasn't sure it wouldn't break.

"It's not your fault, Melissa," Cody told her sharply. He sounded angry.

Melissa knew he was wrong. Howard was her punishment. He was her plague. He was her retribution. Howard was what she got for being born bad.

"He won't leave you alone as long as I'm here." She looked into Cody's eyes, searching for confirmation. She didn't find it.

"We'll catch him one of these days, Melissa. I know we will. Try not to worry about him, ma'am. You'll be rid of him soon enough." He squeezed her hand, and she turned it to lace her fingers with his before she remembered they weren't alone. When she did remember, she tried to draw her hand away, but Cody didn't seem inclined to let it go.

"Try not to worry, Melissa," he said again. "This will all get settled one of these days. Probably pretty soon."

She wished she believed him, but she couldn't. There was something wrong with her; some problem in her nature. That's why she'd been born in the slums instead of on Beacon Hill. Now whatever moral defect she'd been cursed with was infecting Cody O'Fannin, and Melissa wasn't sure she could stand it.

Chapter Sixteen

Cody was right about the snow. By the time four o'clock rolled around, there were mere patches of it left behind, and the ground had turned into a soggy bog. Melissa sighed as she looked out the kitchen window and saw Perry galloping through the garden, flinging mud out behind him. She ought to have Luis or Carlos put a higher fence up around the garden to keep the silly dog out. It would never do to have him chasing after jackrabbits, his big clumsy paws churning up the cabbages come spring. It wouldn't do to have the jackrabbits eat the cabbages, either.

On the other hand, if Melissa did what she knew she ought to do, she'd never know if the cabbages she aimed to plant would grow or not. She ought to have Cody take her back to Rio Hondo. Then she ought to look for work there—if there was any. Surely she could think of something to do to earn her and Katie's keep. It would be wicked of her to stay here and continue to contaminate Cody's life.

The prospect of leaving him was a melancholy one, and she tried hard not to allow it to depress her spirits. Her mother had allowed her circumstances to beat her down—not that Melissa blamed her, because her mother's circumstances had been terrible.

It wasn't Katie's fault that her mama was a fool, however—any more than it had been Melissa's fault that her mother's marriage hadn't prospered. Melissa owed it to Katie to remain superior to her situation. The good Lord knew, she wasn't superior to anything else in the world.

"Stop it," she commanded herself. That was exactly the sort of negative thinking that had dragged her mother down.

Cody had taken her aside after breakfast and talked very kindly to her. He'd begged her not to take Howard's viciousness as a reflection on her own actions or moral rectitude. He'd told her again that he loved her, and that he aimed to see that nothing bad ever happened to her or Katie. She thought how like Cody it was to say such things. Then he'd kissed her, and it was all she could do not to cling to him.

She sighed again and gave herself a hard mental shake. She had to stop mooning and finish supper preparations. After a last look outside, she turned to get back to her potatoes. Just as she picked up her paring knife, something caught her eye and she wheeled back around to stare out the window. Perry started barking like a hound possessed.

"Good heavens, what's going on out there?" She opened the back door. Cold air hit her like a fist and she shivered. Still, she stepped outside and looked around.

"Well, for glory's sake."

Perry, his tail held high, bounded over to her, a

283

large meaty bone in his mouth. "Where in heaven's name did you get that thing?" Melissa shaded her eyes with her hand and squinted into the distance.

Something was going on out there, by the barn. Cautiously, she took another step outside, being very careful because the ground was slippery. She jerked upright, and her hand fell from her eyes to cover her mouth. "No! It can't be."

Staring hard and leaning forward, Melissa shaded her eyes again and tried to focus on what she'd thought she'd seen. That couldn't be. . . . No, of course, it couldn't. Why, it was still daylight. He'd never attempt something sneaky and pernicious in broad—

It was!

"Oh, my land."

Melissa felt sick. Howard! It was Howard, and he was carrying what looked like a torch. It wasn't lit, thank goodness, but Howard's purpose could only be malignant. Why else would he have bribed the dog with a bone and now be sneaking toward Cody O'Fannin's barn with a torch in his hands?

Without even stopping to think about it, Melissa raced back to the parlor, dragged a chair to the fireplace, climbed on it, and plucked the shotgun down from the wall. Cody had told her he kept the thing loaded, in case of emergencies. If this wasn't an emergency, Melissa didn't know what was. She was only sorry Cody wasn't here. He at least knew how to aim and shoot the blasted thing.

"No." After she'd thought for no more than a second, she contradicted her earlier wish. "I'm glad he's not here to see what that creature's trying to do."

Melissa didn't check to see how her daughter was faring before she rushed outdoors and walked as fast as she could to the barn. The ground was wet, and the clay soil made for slippery footing, but her purpose was solid, and she didn't slip. She found Howard kneeling in the mud on the far side of the building, attempting to strike up a flame with a flint and a stone. Her heart turned to lead and contempt filled her.

"Didn't you even have brains enough to fetch a sulfur match with you, Howard? I thought you were more adept at criminal activities than this. You certainly were in Boston."

Her voice shocked him so much that he gasped and dropped his flint. He jumped to his feet, slipped in the mud, and almost fell down. He caught himself with a hand on the side of the barn.

"Damn you, Melissa!"

"What sweet words of greeting, to be sure." Melissa cocked the gun. She didn't know how to use it, but she suspected that drawing the hammer back was a good way to begin.

"What the hell are you doing with that thing?" Howard's voice dripped with scorn, but Melissa wasn't fooled. He'd always been a coward. She used to pretend he wasn't, but she'd left all her illusions about him behind her that day on the plains when he'd deserted her in her extremity. The only thing pretending had ever got her was Howard, and she was through with it. She knew he was afraid of her gun, even if he wasn't afraid of her.

He took a step in her direction, and she yelled, "Stop, or I'll shoot."

The words sounded melodramatic as they rang out in the frosty winter air, but they stopped Howard in his tracks. Since that had worked, she added, "Put your hands in the air, Howard." She wasn't sure why people always said that in novels, but she wasn't about to question tradition at this point.

"Put that thing away, damn it, Melissa. What the hell do you think you're going to do with it? Shoot me?"

Without hesitation, she said, "Yes." She had the satisfaction of watching a look of shock cross Howard's face before his natural deviousness could stop it.

"Get out of Mr. O'Fannin's yard, Howard. Get out of here now, and I won't shoot you."

"Hell, Melissa, you won't shoot me anyway, and you know it. I'm your husband, dammit."

"We've been through this before, Howard. I'm divorcing you. Remember?"

"You'll never get away with it! I'm the father of your baby!"

"And isn't this a fine time to remember *that*?"

"Yeah, well, you'll find out what the courts think of women who run away from their husbands and go take up with other men."

Although Melissa feared he was right, she remained undeterred. Whatever the courts thought of her, she knew she'd been right in leaving Howard. "Don't be stupid, Howard. Get out of here. Do it now, and I won't kill you."

"Kill me?" He laughed, and it almost sounded convincing.

Melissa, who'd known him for years, didn't believe his posturing. He was scared. Triumph soared like an eagle in her breast. Since she'd come to live on Cody O'Fannin's ranch she'd managed to take Howard aback twice—the only two times in her life, in fact.

"You're a low-down, stinking, no-good polecat, Howard Wilmeth. I was stupid enough to marry you before I knew better, but I know better now, and I'm rectifying my mistake."

"Bull," he said. "No judge in the world will grant you a divorce, you damned slut."

Melissa's finger tightened on the trigger. "Don't make me angry, Howard. I'm the one with the gun here."

"I've got a gun, too, in case you didn't notice."

She did notice—as soon as he mentioned it. His handgun resided in a pretty leather holster strapped to his hip.

"I can pull this trigger a whole lot faster than you can reach for that gun, Howard. Pull it out with two fingers and drop it on the ground."

"Damned if I will!"

Melissa, who'd always known him for a tricky devil, revised her opinion of him as a sly, dirty polecat slightly. For the first time, she realized he was also a damned fool. "Don't be any more stupid than you can manage to be, Howard." Until that minute, she hadn't known she could sound so sarcastic. She was proud of herself. "Do it. Drop your gun on the ground. Don't try any of your tricks, either."

"All right, all right."

He reached for his gun. Because she didn't trust him, Melissa watched him like a hawk. Sure enough, as soon as he had gripped the gun, he lifted it instead of dropping it. Fury burst inside her, and she squeezed the trigger without thinking.

The explosion from the shotgun knocked her backwards several paces and the recoil hurt her shoulder. Smoke and dust billowed up, and she heard Howard scream through the ringing in her ears.

Time seemed to stand still. Because she was so frightened, Melissa didn't dare shut her eyes against the sting of smoke and cordite. Her brain held everything in suspense for what seemed like hours but could only have been a split-second. When it jerked into gear again, Melissa was sure she was going to find Howard bleeding on the ground.

She was shocked to find him still standing before her. He no longer held his gun, and the expression on his face would have given her great satisfaction had she been in a condition to appreciate it. She wasn't. Even though she hadn't known she knew how to do it until that moment, she expelled the spent shell from the shotgun and kept the gun aimed at Howard's chest. Actually, she'd believed it had been aimed at his chest before. Since he wasn't dead, she guessed her aim was off. She wasn't about to tell him so.

"Get out of here, Howard. Now." Her voice was as steady as a rock. So was her gun. For the first time in her life, Melissa felt she'd found her calling. She was cut out for this frontier life. Damned if she wasn't.

"D-don't shoot again, dammit, Melissa. For God's sake, what's wrong with you?"

"You, Howard. You're wrong with me. But you won't be for very much longer. Get out now." When she pulled the hammer back this time, it sounded like thunder crackling in the still air. Since Howard had brought his gun and had tried to aim it at her, Melissa figured she'd get off with self-defense if she shot him, and she was glad of it. Glory be, she was really pretty good at this!

"Jesus, I'm going. Let me take my gun."

"Don't be ridiculous! You were going to shoot me, weren't you?"

"Shoot you?" Howard managed to sound offended.

The contempt Melissa felt for him trebled. She sneered, something she'd never done before in her entire life. "Get out, Howard."

He got out. She kept the shotgun trained on him

while he slipped and slid his way out of Cody's yard. He'd left his horse tied to a scrubby mesquite bush several yards outside the split-rail fence that demarcated Cody's yard from the range. No wonder she hadn't heard him ride up. If Perry hadn't started barking, Howard could have burned the barn down before Melissa had even known he was in the yard. She blessed Alexander McMurdo for giving her the dog in the second it took her to think about it.

Howard had come during the day because he knew she'd be alone in the house then, the filthy coward. He'd known Cody and his hands would be on the range repairing the damage he'd wrought out there. Howard had believed that he knew her, and had reckoned that she wouldn't oppose him. Well, Melissa guessed he'd had the Boston Melissa pegged pretty well. The New Mexico Territory Melissa was a whole 'nother animal, and she was so grateful, she could hardly stand it.

It wasn't until Howard and his horse had disappeared from her sight that Melissa sat down with a thump on the brand-new front porch steps and started shaking.

Cody's heart thundered like a stampede of rampaging longhorns as he raced back to the ranch house. Luis, who had been with him on the range when they heard the shotgun blast, couldn't keep up.

Oh, God. Oh, God. Please let her be all right. Cody'd known he shouldn't have left Melissa alone at the house. But, dammit, there were only the three of them running this place—Cody, Luis, and Carlos—and they couldn't keep repairing Howard Wilmeth's deviltry and have one of them stick around the house to watch her, too. *Oh, God. Oh, God.*

When he'd heard that shotgun blast, Cody's heart

had stopped. Then he hadn't even taken time to explain matters to Luis, but had wheeled his horse around and begun galloping home.

He saw Howard Wilmeth from a distance, racing the opposite direction from him, and his heart tripped up again. He shouted, "Go after him, Luis!" and spurred his horse even faster in the direction of his ranch.

If that bastard had hurt Melissa, Cody would kill him. He hoped Luis would understand that Cody wanted Wilmeth for himself, although he couldn't take time to explain matters to him. He blessed Luis's quick intelligence when he saw that he'd obeyed his brusque command and turned his horse to chase after Wilmeth.

Cody didn't wait for his horse to come to a halt. As soon as he galloped into the yard, he leaped down and charged over to the porch. Melissa sat there, her head in her hands. When she heard him, she lifted her head, and Cody saw she was as white as yesterday's snow and shaking like a willow branch in a wind.

"Melissa!"

She tried to stand up but thumped down again, as if she was injured or too shaken to maintain her balance. He grabbed her by the shoulders. "What's wrong? Are you hurt?"

She shook her head and opened her mouth, but nothing came out. Cody didn't repeat himself because his throat had suddenly closed up on him. He drew her into his arms and held her tight, rocking her back and forth. *Thank God*, ricocheted through is head. *Thank you, God.* Without thinking, he ripped the bonnet from her head and buried his face in her hair.

After a moment, he managed to whisper, "I was so

damned scared when I heard that shotgun blast. Oh, God, honey, I was so scared."

"So—so was I." Her voice was breathy and soft. Her hands clutched spasmodically at his shoulders.

Cody took a deep breath and managed to open his eyes. His heart still raced, there was a roaring in his ears, and leftover terror kept the blood humming through his veins. He would kill that bastard. He would. He saw the shotgun lying on the porch, next to where Melissa had been sitting. He nudged it aside with his boot and sat down, bringing Melissa with him.

Keeping an arm around her shoulders, he tucked a finger under her chin, lifted her face, and peered at her closely. "What happened, honey? Are you all right? Is Katie okay? What did that bastard do to you?"

"N-nothing. Not really." A shudder rattled her, and Cody's arm tightened.

"What happened, Melissa?" He sucked in a deep breath and told himself to calm down. He saw the shotgun again out of the corner of his eye and frowned. It looked like his, but it couldn't be. "Did he bring that shotgun with him, darlin'?"

She nodded. Then she shook her head. "No. He only had one of those small guns that go in a holster."

"A revolver?"

"I guess that's what it's called."

"Did he somehow get ahold of my shotgun?"

"No. I'm the one who fired it."

Cody's eyes popped open. "*You* fired my shotgun?"

"Yes."

By damn! Cody squeezed her again. She was something, all right, his little Melissa. When he'd first met her, he didn't think she had the spunk of a chipmunk, but by damn if she wasn't a tiger in disguise!

"Did you shoot it at him, darlin'?"

She nodded. "I missed," she explained, sounding sorry about it. "But I tried to shoot him."

Well, by gum. She'd pulled the trigger on her own husband. Cody was impressed as hell. He knew how guilty she felt about Howard Wilmeth—about divorcing him and all. About having married him in the first place.

He frowned again. Given her mixed emotions, she must have had a damned good reason for having tried to shoot him. It didn't take Cody long to think of one.

"Did he try to take Katie, Melissa? Did he try to take your baby away from you?"

"No. Oh, no. Howard doesn't want Katie. He only said that to scare me."

Cody grinned at the anger that trampled over Melissa's fear and made her voice strong again. "I know that, darlin'. I know."

"What he wants to do now is hurt you, because he knows that will hurt me."

Cody didn't know what to say. He nodded, though, because he thought she had expressed the matter pretty well.

"He's a sneaky, rotten, horrid person, Cody. He's a beast."

"I ain't arguing with you, Melissa."

"He tried to burn down your barn."

Her bald declaration shocked him. "He *what?*" He jumped up and stared down at her. He glanced wildly in the direction of the barn and saw it standing there in the winter sunlight, snug and compact, looking like a barn. A long stick—it looked like a torch, actually—lay on the earth beside the barn. Then he saw something else on the ground, next to the torch. Was that Wilmeth's gun there in the mud?

There was a hell of a hole in the ground beside it. A grin took him by surprise. That must be the hole the shotgun blast had made, and Cody'd bet anything that it had scared the living tar out of Howard Wilmeth.

"Looks like you caught him before he could do it, darlin'." He smiled down at her. Her eyes were as big as saucers and as blue as the sky, and Cody loved her in that moment more than he could say. More than he could think of words for, even if he couldn't say them.

"I saw him, Cody, and I got your gun and went out to stop him. I couldn't let him hurt you."

To Cody's horror, he saw those beautiful blue eyes fill with tears.

"I told him to drop his gun, but he didn't, and I'd have killed him, but my aim was off."

Her shoulders began to shake, and Cody sank down beside her and took her in his arms again. "It's all right, Melissa. It's all right, darlin'. Everything will be all right. Pretty soon, you'll be free of him, and then we can get married, and everything will be all right."

Those words, coming out of his own mouth as easily as if they meant nothing more than a howdy, astonished him. He'd been trying like the very devil to avoid even thinking about marriage, and all of a sudden, he'd just said the words. Just like that. And he didn't even feel bad about them now that they were out in the open and couldn't be recalled, either.

He was so amazed by his own audacity that he didn't realize at first that Melissa had started shaking her head in denial. When he did realize it, he gaped at her. What did this mean?

His hands tightened on her shoulders, and he gave her a little shake. "You will marry me, won't you, darlin'?" Hell, they'd slept together. No matter what Melissa thought of herself—and Cody had good reason to believe that she considered herself beneath him—she wouldn't refuse to marry him after they'd slept together. Would she?

She turned and buried her face on his shoulder. "Oh, Cody! I love you so much!"

Well, that was a definite start. Sounded promising, even.

"So what's the problem, honey? After you get divorced from Howard, we'll get married, and everything will be fine."

"No, it won't."

She sounded more sure of herself than she generally did. Cody didn't know what to make of her at all. He cleared his throat. "Um, why not?"

She shoved herself away from him, leaving him feeling cold and very surprised. Shooting to her feet, she took an agitated turn on the porch, leaving muddy prints in her wake. Cody knew she was upset, because Melissa was the tidiest person he'd ever met. She'd taken to sweeping the front porch three or four times a day to keep the dust and mud off it, ever since he'd finished whitewashing it.

"Because Howard will never leave me alone, that's why! He'll torment me and torment me and torment me until the day he dies. You don't know him, Cody! And since he knows I care for you, he'll take it out on you! He never cared about me when I was his wife, but his pride is hurt now that I'm divorcing him. He's ruthless, Cody! He's wicked, and he's mean, and he'll never give up as long as I'm living here with you!"

She looked down at him, hugging herself. Cody got the feeling she was trying in that way to hold herself together. Her voice sounded thick with tears and hurt when she added, "And, Cody, I love you too much to drag you into my world. It's an ugly world. Howard's only a small part of it. Your world is sunny and kind and peaceful. Mine is filthy and squalid and ugly."

"No!" His shock at her assessment of their respective worlds was profound. Hell, she was the brightest thing in his own personal world at the moment.

"Yes, it is. You can't imagine it, because you grew up out here in all this—this—splendor." She threw her arms out and turned in a circle. Cody, who had never thought of where he lived as splendid, got a hint of what she meant—but only a hint. He had a feeling she was talking about the relative effects their very different backgrounds had wrought on their respective characters rather than about the landscape.

"Your life doesn't have to stay that way, Melissa," he said gently.

She hung her head, and Cody felt awful.

"It will stay that way until Howard's no longer in it," she said. "And as long as Howard's in my life and I'm in your life, you aren't safe. And neither is your ranch. Or Luis or Carlos. I'm a jinx, Cody. An evil influence."

She shook her head, and Cody recognized both frustration and dogged determination in the gesture. He got a sick, sinking feeling in his gut.

"If you please, I believe I'd better go back to Mac's, Cody. At least until I figure out what to do with myself."

"Mellie!" He'd never called her Mellie before. He'd never even thought it. "You can't mean that. Melissa, for God's sake, I *love* you!"

"I love you, too, Cody. More than you can ever imagine. That's why I don't dare stay here any longer. I'll just bring sorrow and bad things down on you. Bad follows me around like a cloud. I was born bad."

"That's the stupidest damned thing I've ever heard! You don't bring me sorrow. You're not bad. You've brought me—you've brought me peace! And—and—and love." And the best cooking he'd ever eaten. Somehow that didn't seem to fit, so he didn't say it.

"Peace!" She sounded bitter. Cody'd never heard her sound like that. It worried him. "Peace? You call it peace when my husband tries to poison your water? When he kills your cattle? Cuts your fences? Does it give you a peaceful feeling to know he tried to burn down your barn?"

"Well, dammit, we'll catch him and make him stop."

She shook her head and began to wring her hands. "Oh, Cody! Please, take me back to Rio Hondo! Please, just do it! Howard's even right about one thing. We're living here in sin now! I've corrupted you, for heaven's sake!" Her determination seemed to crinkle up and her anguish showed through. Cody hurt to see it. "I can't rear my daughter like this, Cody. It's wrong. I've corrupted you."

"Dammit, you haven't either corrupted me!" He surged to his feet, her assessment of last night's events wounding him. "That's not true, Mellie. That's not true at all."

She sniffled and withdrew a handkerchief from her pocket. Shaking her head, she blew her nose and looked miserable. "Yes, it is," she whispered. "No matter how hard I try, the badness is still in me. No matter how hard I try to fight it, it won't go away. It's there. It's in me. It's part of me. I don't know how to get rid of it."

Cody didn't understand. He didn't even want to. The judgments Melissa had made about herself made no sense to him. She'd dragged herself up from what must have been a truly lamentable background. He caught himself on a shudder when he remembered her description—filth, corruption, drunkenness, rotting fish, walls, walls, walls. He couldn't quite imagine it.

He knew she was wrong about herself. Today she was a good person, even though he had a strong feeling that he wasn't going to be able to convince her. He also knew that one of the things she'd said was probably true. He didn't expect Howard Wilmeth would ever leave her alone—not until he found some other woman to torment. And since there were hardly any women living out here, that prospect was remote. He sighed heavily. Then he thought of something that cheered him up slightly.

"Luis and me, we saw your husband riding away. Luis turned to chase him, since we figured something bad must have happened here."

She brightened, too, and his heart felt lighter still. "Oh, do you think Luis can have caught him?"

"I don't know, honey, but if I know Luis, he'll try his damnedest—er, best."

"What will happen to him if Luis does catch him?"

Cody frowned. "I'm not sure. You saw him trying to burn down my barn. That's a real nasty thing to do in these parts. It's as much as a man's life is worth to hurt someone else's horses, you know."

Melissa clasped her hands in front of her. "Will the law take care of him? Will they lock him up somewhere? If he's locked up, he can't bother you or your property."

"Well, there isn't much law out here, you know, darlin'. If Luis can catch him and bring him here, we can ride him into Rio Hondo and take him to Mac's."

Melissa looked at him blankly. "Take him to Mac's?"

"There's nowhere else to take a fellow, honey. The sheriff's got an office in Carlsbad, I reckon, but there's nothing much here except Mac's." He shrugged apologetically. "Mac held another fellow for a couple of weeks once when he shot Billy Flynn."

"What happened to the other fellow?"

"Well, when the circuit judge got here, we had us a trial, and the fellow kinda proved he'd shot Billy in self-defense, so Judge Calloway fined him fifty dollars and let him go."

"Fifty dollars for a life?"

"Well, it was self-defense. Billy Flynn got real rowdy when he was drinkin', you see, and enough fellows saw the incident that Judge Calloway figured it'd be easier to fine him than haul him to Santa Fe." Cody shrugged again. "The fellow was a good hand. Better'n Billy Flynn."

From the way Melissa stared at him, Cody got the impression she didn't think much of frontier justice. In a way he didn't blame her, especially since Cody himself didn't know what to do about Howard Wilmeth. If he had his druthers, he and Luis would hang the bastard, although he wasn't sure where they'd carry out the execution, there being no trees handy.

Generally, such matters were taken care of by slinging a rope over the beam in somebody's barn, but Cody didn't expect Melissa would care to see the father of her baby hanged in Cody's barn, no matter how much she didn't like him anymore. He was pretty sure Hugh Blackworth wouldn't want it done on his ranch either, and Cody wasn't sure he wanted to involve Blackworth anyway. Hell, life could sure get complicated sometimes.

They stared at each other for what seemed the

longest minute of Cody's life. Then Melissa took in a shuddering breath and let it out on a sigh. "You'd better take me back to Mac's, Cody. Maybe he'll let me work for him for awhile until I figure out what else to do."

Cody stood up and settled his hands on her shoulders. Even through his thick leather gloves, she felt fragile. He wanted so much to protect her from the wickedness of life—the wickedness she believed was inside her, and Cody knew wasn't.

"I want you to stay here, Melissa. I love you." He didn't know what else to say. If she left him, he guessed he wouldn't die. He knew better than to believe folks actually died of broken hearts. He'd go on with his life, but it would feel bleak. And cold. Very cold.

"I have to go because I love you, Cody. I don't want to hurt you any longer."

"You aren't hurting me!" Damn, she had things so twisted up. Cody wished he could shake her and in that way get them untwisted. "It's your damned husband who's trying to hurt me, because he wants to hurt you, Melissa. Can't you understand that?"

"Yes! Of course! I *do* understand that! Can't you understand that's exactly the reason I can't stay here? Oh, Cody!" She threw her arms around him.

"You're not making any sense, darlin'. Not one little bit of sense." He shook his head and held her tight and wished he had the gift of gab. He was sure that if he could only say the right thing, she'd understand how silly she was being.

As things stood now, he supposed they could argue about it for the rest of their lives and never reach a satisfactory conclusion to their differences. He wasn't able to test his assumption, because Luis returned.

Cody heard him coming and lifted his head. He frowned when he saw that Luis was alone. That was a bad sign. Cody muttered softly, "Hell."

Melissa let go of him and stepped away. She looked as though she felt guilty about having hugged him, and the injustice of their situation hit Cody like a fist to the gut. They loved each other, dammit, and they weren't doing anything wrong. He didn't care what popular morality held, or what Melissa thought of herself. She was a good woman and he was a good man, and Cody hoped to God he'd be able to prove it to her. Until he figured out how to do that, he had to deal with matters the way they stood. Unfortunately.

"All right," he muttered. "All right, let's see what Luis has to say." If Cody's luck was real good, maybe Luis would report that Wilmeth had fallen off his horse again—and broken his neck this time. He had a sinking feeling his luck wasn't going to be good today.

Luis's horse limped slightly. That was the second bad sign. Cody walked over to him and eyed his horse.

"I think he's got a bruise," Luis said, swinging down from the saddle. "It's the rear left."

Cody lifted the horse's leg. "Yeah, I see it. Damned rock stuck in the shoe." Blast and hell. He peered at Luis over the horse's hoof. "Didn't get him, huh?"

"Naw." Luis took off his hat and wiped his sleeve across his forehead, which dripped with sweat even though the winter air was cold. "Damn horse picked up that rock and came up lame, and I had to come back. Didn't figure you'd want me to cripple him."

"Crap. No, you did all right, Luis. Wilmeth's not worth a horse."

Luis grinned, and Cody realized his assessment,

while true, had been less than diplomatic. "Take care of the horse. Wilmeth tried to burn down the barn."

"Madre de Diós!" Luis signed a cross, as if to ward off an evil spell. His face registered his horror. Anyone who burned a barn meant more than mere mischief. "What you gonna do about it?"

"Damned if I know." And that was the problem. Right there, in a nutshell. "If I go onto Blackworth's property callin' one of his hands a barn-burning bastard, what do you expect Blackworth will do?"

Luis thought for a moment. "Shoot you?"

"I expect that's about it."

The two men stood staring at each other for a few seconds. Cody could feel Melissa watching them.

He wished he had a solution. What with the absence of law or any witnesses to Howard Wilmeth's villainous intentions other than the wife who was trying to divorce him, Cody didn't know what to do. He felt helpless. It was a lousy feeling.

Chapter Seventeen

Alexander McMurdo stood at the gate of his wagon yard, smoking his old black briar pipe and looking like an ancient and contented gnome when Cody drove the wagon into Rio Hondo. Melissa sat beside him. She hadn't said three words during the entire trip, but only held Katie in her arms and looked sadder than Cody'd ever seen a woman look without a damned good reason.

She didn't have any reason at all, as far as he could see. This wasn't right. No way. Yet he hadn't been able to talk her out of it. None of his arguments had worked. She'd only insisted that she'd corrupted him. Then she'd said he was in danger as long as she stayed with him. Nothing he said would shake her of either opinion.

"If you're so worried about him hurting folks you stay with, what about Mac?" He'd hoped to stump her with that one.

He hadn't. "Don't be silly, Cody. Howard knows I'm not in love with Mac."

She had him there. He'd hitched up the team while Melissa packed her few belongings, and now they were back in Rio Hondo, where Melissa aimed to remain. He felt lower than he'd ever felt in his life.

He knew this arrangement wouldn't last forever. After all, surely her divorce would come through, and then she'd agree to come back to him. Wouldn't she? Of course, she would.

So how come his heart felt like it was busting in half?

Probably because he hadn't been able to wrest any promises from her. When he'd pressured her, she'd only shaken her head and looked sad. Damnation!

Because Cody was so frustrated, the fact that Mac looked like he'd been expecting them pecked away at his already frayed composure. He resented Mac for appearing nonchalant in the face of this catastrophe; he resented the smile on the old man's face; and he resented the twinkle he detected in those blue, blue eyes. Mac's eyes were brighter than an old man's eyes had any right to be.

"Not surprised to find us here, I see," Cody growled when he jumped down from the wagon. He scowled at Mac for good measure—and earned a chuckle for his effort, blast it. Cody's hostility only succeeded in making his twinkle more pronounced.

Mac ambled over to the wagon and held up his arms for Katie. "Not surprised, no, Cody m'boy. A little disappointed in the two of ye, truth to tell, but not surprised."

Disappointed? Cody almost snorted. Hell of a note *that* was. Disappointed, crap. Cody was so disappointed that if he'd been alone this morning, he'd have cried—and he hadn't cried since he was Katie's age. "Yeah, I'm a little disappointed myself."

"Cody . . ."

Cody turned and gave his scowl to Melissa, who turned pink and shook her head. "Nothing."

"I don't suppose it would do any good to tell you both that everything will turn out all right, would it?"

And how the hell would you know that? Cody wouldn't ask Mac the question. It would only give the old fraud a chance to be mysterious, and Cody was sick to death of mysteries. What Cody wanted were some solid, no-nonsense answers. And Melissa.

She'd come to his bed again last night. Making love had been even more wonderful the second time. She'd caught fire in his arms and damned near burned them both up. And then she'd felt guilty and tried not to cry. He'd held her and told her that what they were doing wasn't wrong. He couldn't make her believe that, either. It had been galling. Excessively galling.

What made everything all the more frustrating was that, deep down in his heart, Cody agreed with her. Hell, he had no business making love to a woman who wasn't his wife. Especially when she was somebody else's wife. The whole situation was about to drive him over the brink, and he didn't like it one little bit.

Cody O'Fannin liked things he could understand; concrete things; simple things; things like cattle and ranching and Arnold. Conundrums like Alexander McMurdo and Melissa Wilmeth gave him twitches.

Of course, his own feelings hadn't been sitting too well with him recently, either. His feelings for Melissa, for example, were about to unman him totally. The mere thought of leaving her at Mac's and driving home without her ate into his insides like acid. He couldn't figure out why people were so in love with love. Seemed to him that love hurt like the very devil. It complicated a body's life beyond bearing, too. As if life wasn't tough enough on its own.

What he couldn't figure out—and what Melissa hadn't been able to explain to him—was, if they loved each other, why should things be so blasted complicated?

"Dammit, Melissa, this don't make any sense, you going back to Mac's. It's not as if it'll solve anything."

She'd been as unmovable as any mountain. "It will solve the problem of my succumbing to my base nature and dragging you down with me!"

She'd actually hollered it at him, and he'd been shocked. "Your base nature?"

"Yes!"

Cody could tell how mad she was, because her eyes began to leak. He wondered why that happened to females. Hell, when he was mad, he didn't want to cry, he wanted to break things. He was relatively sure, however, that her tendency to cry when angry wasn't what she considered her base nature.

"I don't know what the hell you're talking about."

"*Don't curse at me!* Howard can't say two words together without one of them being a swear word, and it's one of the things I hate most about him."

"Don't you go comparing me to that husband of yours, Melissa. That ain't right." And that was another thing about females—they never fought fair.

At least she'd had the grace to realize it. She'd even looked ashamed of herself. "No, of course you're not like Howard. Not at all, and I didn't mean it. I just don't like to be sworn at, is all. And I don't want my daughter exposed to cursing. I want her to have a better life than I have any right to expect for her, I guess."

Cody refrained from telling her that if she didn't

want Katie to hear cussing, she'd come to the wrong part of the country. He took a deep breath, in fact, and apologized, something he considered mighty big of him under the circumstances. She'd looked suitably grateful, so he guessed she did, too.

But she didn't change her mind. She was as stubborn as a mule in the mud when she set her mind on something. Cody wasn't sure that was a good thing. "I used to think you were soft, Mellie," he grumbled as he set the cradle into the wagon. His heart gave a painful spasm when he did it. Damn, he'd miss that baby, for all that she set up her squawks at the most awkward moments and kept him awake at night.

Melissa had sharpened her claws on that one. "What do you mean by that? What do you mean, I'm soft?"

Surprised by the ferocity of her question, Cody'd said, "Well, I never knew you could be so blasted obstinate, I reckon."

"I'm not being obstinate! I'm trying to do the right thing, Cody O'Fannin."

"Damn-fool way—pardon me, ma'am. It 'pears to me this is a pretty stupid way to go about it."

Her lips had pinched together like Aunt Luella's used to do when she was riled at Uncle Harold and didn't want to holler in front of the children. "I'm trying to behave in a morally upright manner. Obviously"—she'd placed special emphasis on that *obviously*—"I'm starting a little late."

Her reference to their two incredible nights of lovemaking had hit Cody like a low blow, even though he knew society's opinion was on her side. He'd growled, "Well, if you think two people lovin' each other is morally wrong, I reckon we'll never come to an agreement."

"Oh, Cody!"

Then she'd started bawling again, and Cody'd wanted to throttle something.

Now she climbed down from the wagon, took Katie from Mac's hands, linked her arm with his, and started walking toward Mac's house as if Cody no longer existed. He took care of the mules, grabbed the cradle out of the wagon bed, and stormed after her. He'd be damned if he'd be dismissed, as if he was nothing more than that damned dog of hers. Hell, she'd cried and made a fuss when she'd realized she had to leave Perry behind—and she was walking away from Cody without a backward glance.

Mac ushered her inside and stood aside to grin at Cody. Cody didn't grin back. He was hurting and he was mad and he didn't understand any of this.

"It'll be all right, Cody lad. Give her awhile. She's got some things to sort out in herself."

"Yeah," Cody said. "Right."

He wanted to ask Mac what the hell he thought *Cody* was going through. What about *him?* Didn't *he* get to sort anything out? First he took this woman into his life—at Mac's urging. Hell, Mac had all but forced her on him. So Cody, being the relatively nice fellow he was, had complied—against his better judgment, if he remembered aright.

Everything had been hunky-dory, too, and it had surprised him. Melissa had fit right into his life, as if she was merely slipping into a space that had gone empty until she showed up. Everything had gone so well, in fact, that Cody had lost his heart to her.

She claimed she'd lost her heart to him, too.

And now she was leaving him! *Now.* After he'd confessed his deep and abiding feelings for her— asked her to marry him, for the love of God! And what reason did she have for doing such a downright mean thing?

What they were doing wasn't *right*. It wasn't *moral*. Oh, she could go on and on forever about how she was worried that her husband would do bad things to Cody if she stayed, but Cody knew that wasn't the real reason she was leaving him. She was leaving him because she thought their relationship was somehow dirty. Immoral. Bad.

Hogwash. What they'd done together had been the rightest, most moral, most upright and splendid thing Cody had ever done in his life. His feelings were hurt more than he'd ever admit by Melissa's assessment of their relationship.

He'd learned to love her. Passionately. Abidingly. Forever. And she was leaving him. And Mac said everything would be all right once she sorted some things out. Balderdash!

So how was it that *Melissa* was the one who had to sort things out? How was it nobody bothered to think about *Cody* in this situation? For the first time in his life, Cody wished men had the freedom women chose to exercise with regard to emotional outbursts. He'd love to have a foot-kicking, heel-drumming, hair-raising tantrum right there on Alexander Mc-Murdo's parlor floor.

His breath hitched in his chest when he walked through Mac's door. Melissa stood in a beam of light flooding in from the window, holding Katie. Her honey-colored hair caught the sunbeams and looked like a halo, and light bathed her unhappy face. She looked like some pictures Cody'd seen in the old Baptist church in Georgetown.

Well, she couldn't have it both ways, dammit. She couldn't claim to be a sinner and look like a saint. It wasn't fair.

He put the cradle down rather roughly in front of her. "Here. Reckon you'll need this for the baby." He stood back, stuffed his hands into the back pockets of his trousers, and glared at the cradle. He didn't want to look at her for fear his heart would soften toward her. He didn't want it to. He was mad, dammit.

He'd never given his heart to a female; he'd always considered romantic love vaguely unmanly and softheaded. That he'd succumbed to so foolish an emotion—and then had it flung back in his face—was almost more than his pride could stand.

When she put her hand on his arm, he winced. She withdrew it again in a hurry. "I wish I could make you understand, Cody."

Lifting his head, he searched her face. There was no denying that she was as miserable as he, which confounded him. He shook his head. "I don't think I want to understand, Melissa. I don't think I want to know how you can do this kind of thing to a man you claim to love."

"Oh, Lord." Her eyes filled with tears, and Cody hardened his heart against this further evidence of her feminine wiles.

Melissa saw and understood. Cody could tell.

"I wish you could understand it's *because* I love you that I had to leave."

"Yeah. You've said that before. It doesn't make any more sense this time than it did the last hundred and fifty."

She grabbed his arm again, and this time shook it. "*Why* won't you understand? If I stayed there, Howard would just keep trying to hurt you."

"I'm a big boy, Melissa. I can take care of myself and my own. I've been doin' it for years now."

"But I don't want you to *have* to—just because of

me! If we're ever free of Howard—if they let me divorce him—and if you still want me—"

"*If?*" Cody stared at her indignantly. "*If?* What kind of a man do you take me for, Melissa? Just what kind of a man do you think I am?"

"I don't have to think about it, Cody. I know you're a good man. An honorable man. The kindest man I've ever known."

"Yeah? Well, it doesn't sound like it to me. *If?* Dammit, Melissa, there's not a man in the territory who'd doubt my word. *They* know me. *They* know I'm a man of my word. I said I want to marry you. I take it mighty unkind in you to think I'd go back on my word to you! I'm not like that jackass you're married to, dammit."

She swallowed heavily. "I know."

Cody was too frustrated to argue any longer. He spat out a growl and turned around to stomp back to the wagon. There was still stuff in it—*her* stuff—and he had to fetch it for her. God knew, he wasn't about to hold her against her will.

When she stamped her foot and uttered a growl of her own, he was surprised and turned around again.

"What about me?" she asked him. "What about *me?* Don't you think I want to be honorable, too? Don't you think I should be as good as *my* word?"

Having never considered the possibility that females might have any truck with the concept of honor, Cody didn't know what to say. He only watched her warily.

"Well? What would you think of a man who left his wife and before they were even divorced took up with another woman? Most people think divorce, all by itself, is sinful, Cody O'Fannin. You certainly had no qualms in vilifying Howard for consorting with women of low moral fiber at the saloon. Why is it different for me?"

"Dammit, Melissa, my moral fiber isn't low!"

"I know that!" She sounded exasperated. "For heaven's sake, Cody, I *love* you! Don't you think I know what kind of man you are?"

Because he was mad, he said, "Blamed if I know. You married your precious Howard, didn't you?"

She gasped, and he was ashamed of himself for fighting dirty. On the other hand, she was driving him distracted.

"You told me you love me," he continued, feeling almost possessed. "Well, what did you tell old Howard, huh? Did you used to tell *him* you loved him? Is that what you do? Go around telling men you love 'em so they'll take care of you for awhile, and then mosey on to greener pastures when you feel like it?"

Her face, which had gone pink with indignation, now drained of color until her eyes stood out like blue puddles on white paper. Her bosom heaved with the deep breaths she was taking. Cody wanted to go over there and take her and Katie into his arms and hug them tightly to his chest and never let either one of them go again as long as he lived.

He didn't take back what he said. He only looked at her, defying her to make sense of this muddle for him, because he sure as the devil couldn't do it on his own.

"I married Howard for reasons that made sense to me at the time, Cody," she said, her voice almost a whisper. "I told him I loved him because I wanted to believe it when he said he'd take me away from that hell we lived in. You don't know what it was like."

"No," he said, offering no quarter. "I don't."

"It was wrong of me to marry him; it was stupid of me to believe him." She shut her eyes and shook her head hard. "No! That's not true! I *didn't* believe him! I was so desperate back then that I lied to myself. I knew what he was like. I knew he was a low, immoral, deceitful, corrupt man. Do you know what it's like to put your entire life into the keeping of someone whom you know doesn't value it? Do you know what it's like to throw your lot in with a man whom you *know* is unprincipled? A man whom you despise?"

"No, I'd never do such a thing."

"Of course you wouldn't. I expect that's because you were raised by people who instilled some kind of standards in you. Besides," she added with more than a hint of resentment in her voice, "you're a *man*. You have more choices than I've ever had or ever will have. Did you know that until I joined that wagon train with Howard, I'd never met a man worth spitting on? Did you know that you and Mac are the first two honorable men I've ever had more to do with than to say hello and good-bye to?"

Cody didn't answer. He searched her face and concluded that she believed what she'd just said. Such a circumstance didn't feel right to him. The men he'd known in his life were just like him, for the most part. Some were more sober than others. Some had more brains than others. One or two of them had an eye out for a good deal and didn't much care if it was shady or not. But they were all decent, fairly honest individuals.

Since he didn't say anything, she answered for him. "Of course you don't! You grew up with your family in Texas. Your father wasn't a drunkard who ran out on you. Your mother didn't have to give up two of her children because she couldn't feed them. You didn't have to go to work when you were nine and move away from home when you were twelve because you had to earn your keep! I had to do that, Cody. That's all I know. The people I grew up with were all like Howard or my mother. They were either criminals with money or dirt poor and honest. People like Mrs. Bowlus were like—like different kinds of animals. Like they came from another universe. They didn't have anything to do with me or people like me, except that we could serve them—at their whim—and do the things they didn't want to do. I didn't know anything else! I'm trying to better myself. Why can't you understand that?"

Her voice rose during her impassioned speech, until she was fairly shouting at the end. Cody listened to all of it. When she finally stopped, panting, he did her the courtesy of thinking over what she'd said.

After giving it a good mull, he said consideringly, "I don't think that's true, Melissa."

She gasped and glared at him.

"I don't think you're tryin' to better yourself. I think you're convinced you're bad and are using every excuse you can come up with to prove it to yourself."

"How dare you?" Her voice throbbed with rage.

" 'Cause that's the way I see it. You come to my ranch, and you did a blamed good job of running it. You sure did better than Arnie and me ever did— and there's nobody would call Arnie and me bad men. Hell, Melissa, you're already a good person. You don't have to prove anything. All's you have to do is keep livin' and breathin' to be good. But you're scared. 'Pears to me you're all set up to keep yourself down by not takin' advantages when folks drop 'em in your lap."

Her lips had gone pinchy again. Cody hoped she was thinking about what he'd said, because it was the truth as he saw it.

"Now, you've told me all about the dirty slums you lived in back in Boston, and I believe you. I'm sure it was real awful. You're not there any longer, though—and you sure as the devil proved you could take care of yourself out here. I don't see why you want to give it all up because, at the moment, circumstances are a little uncomfortable—"

"Uncomfortable?" Melissa shrieked.

Cody ignored her. "—*uncomfortable* right now. Hell, this ain't Boston. It ain't even Texas. Out here a body's got to make his own life with what he has. You and I have each other. It seems downright foolish to me that you're willing to split us up because some folks back East—that Mrs. Bowlus lady or whoever—might not approve. When are they going to point any fingers? Do you expect them to take a trip out here just so's they can scold you or something? You plannin' to write and tell her?"

"Of course not!"

"Life's different out here. Out here there's no rules and regulations about things. A fellow's got to make his own rules. If something from Boston fits, fine. If it don't, then for God's sake, chuck it out and do what works. It's foolish to cling to rules made for people who've been livin' in the same place for two hundred years and more.

"My daddy used to tell me that a man can't miss if he's shootin' at the ground. I never knew what he meant until now."

"I don't know what he meant, either." She was mad; Cody could tell.

"What he meant was that if you aim low enough, you can't hardly fail to hit your target. It seems to me that's exactly what you're doing. You took some old notion about propriety folks dreamed up in Boston and brought it out here with you, where life just ain't like it is back there, and you're holding yourself to it."

She gasped.

Relentless, he went on. "Of *course* you aren't living like a proper Boston lady would live. You can't. This isn't Boston. But you're still holding on to your Boston rules and judging yourself by them. What you're doin' is aimin' at the ground—and you're hitting it.

"I think it's because you're worried that if you aimed any higher than that, you'd fail. Well, hell, maybe you're right. Maybe we have no future together, but at least I'm willing to try for one. Damn it, I love you. You love me. That's a hell of a lot better start than lots of folks ever get."

He eyed her keenly. "Anybody you met out here been tellin' you you're a bad person? Besides you, I mean."

She took a deep breath and held it; for a second or two, he expected she'd use it to holler at him. At last, she said merely, "No."

He shrugged. "Didn't think so. I haven't noticed anybody pointin' any fingers at either one of us. Except that husband of yours, and I don't give two hoots about him."

He saw her swallow. "I have to give a hoot about Howard, Cody. He still has power over me. And he's still going to try to hurt you if I remain at your ranch."

Cody threw his head back and stared at the ceiling. Here they were, back to the beginning again. "We're like a snake biting its own tail, Melissa, talkin' around in circles. You keep sayin' he's tryin' to hurt me, and I keep sayin' I don't give a care. If we leap over that one, you'll get to sayin' you're trying to pull yourself up out of the muck by your bootstraps. Then I'll say you already have, and you'll say no you haven't. Then I'll say you can't live by Boston rules here in the New Mexico Territory. If we haul ourselves over that one, eventually you'll get yourself back to sayin' your husband's trying to hurt me."

He leveled his gaze at her once more, and his heart pained him. She looked so alone there, holding her baby and staring at him as if her heart was breaking. Well, dammit, his heart was breaking, too, and he didn't see any reason for it; not one single reason in the whole damned world, except that Melissa Wilmeth was refusing to take a chance. On him. On them. She didn't say anything.

At last he shook his head. "Just think about what you're doing, Melissa. To all of us." He swept out a gesture that included Katie. "I don't think you're bein' fair, is all."

She took a step toward him. His heart soared and he held his breath. She didn't come any closer, and he guessed her scruples had won out over common sense—and him.

He shook his head. "I'll be out there, talkin' to Mac, Mellie. If you change your mind or anything."

"Thank you, Cody. Thank you for understanding."

"Hell, I don't understand a blessed thing, Melissa."

"Thank you for trying to understand, then."

"Yeah." He wanted to kiss her but didn't dare.

Mac sat at his small kitchen table, a pot of tea on a tray in front of him, with a cup and saucer set beside it. The cup and saucer were pretty and delicate, made of painted porcelain. They matched the teapot, and reminded Cody of his granny O'Fannin's kitchen in Georgetown. She'd brought that tea set of hers over on the boat from England and out to Texas in a covered wagon, and none of her male grandchildren were ever allowed to touch it. She allowed the girls to take tea from it beginning at their sixteenth birthdays. It was kind of like a family coming-of-age ritual for the O'Fannin females.

Which was all well and good, but Cody didn't fancy tea at the moment. He arched his eyebrows when he lifted his gaze from the tea set and aimed it at Mac.

He received one of Mac's maddening winks in return. "For Mellie," the old man said. "I've got something a wee bit stronger for us."

"Thank God." Cody slapped his hat on the table and sat with a heavy groan. "I'll just have me a sip then before I go out and finish emptying the wagon."

"Hold on for awhile, Cody, m'lad. You never know what might happen out here. You might not have to unload it at all."

"What the hell do you mean by that? Do you know something I don't?" Cody eyed Mac, frowning heavily.

"Och, laddie, just you relax yourself for awhile. Anything's liable to happen. It's an unpredictable place, this great, grand territory of ours." Mac wiggled his fingers in the air and lifted his head as if he felt something strange in the air. "It's got a touch of enchantment in it, this territory."

What in the name of glory was Mac talking about now? Maybe the old man had been into the hard stuff already. Cody squinted as Mac picked up the tray and carried it to the back room, where Melissa and Katie—in other words, where all the meaning in Cody's life—resided. How the hell had *that* happened? he wondered, despairing.

Until three or four months ago—until he and Arnie had heard that scream in the desert—Cody had been a happy man.

"Shoot." He propped his elbows on the table and sank his head in his hands. "Women."

He'd known Melissa Wilmeth for not quite four months and she'd already made his world go topsy-turvy. Everything was all muddled up now. He didn't used to be muddled. He used to have everything all figured out. He'd had all his ducks in a row. All his aims arranged. He'd even had Loretta Pine figured out—hell, Cody had just planned to ignore her. He couldn't ignore Melissa or his feelings for her.

"Don't look so down-pin, Cody, m'boy."

Cody hadn't heard Mac come back, and his voice and the hand he put on Cody's shoulder surprised him. Lifting his head, he was distressed to see sparkles in the air.

"Dammit, what *are* those things?"

"And what things are those that you don't know the name of, my boy?" Mac strolled to the cupboard and fetched down two small glasses and a bottle of his prized Scotch whiskey.

"Every damned time I come here, I see a bunch of damned sparkly things in the air. They're like to drive me crazy."

Mac's grin seemed apt to split his face when he turned to bring the whiskey and glasses to the table.

"Pfft, lad, folks'll call ye daft if ye persist in seein' things that aren't there."

Too miserable to argue, Cody mumbled, "Yeah. I s'pose so." He tossed the first shot back and welcomed the burn as it traveled down his gullet and spread through his stomach.

"There's the ticket, lad. Just you sit there, and I'll sit here, and you tell old Mac all about it."

Mac winked again, but this time Cody didn't resent it. Unhappiness spread through him along with the whiskey and seemed to loosen everything that had tightened in him. He felt abused and misunderstood and woeful, and he hated it. Since he was a man—

and a Texan—he'd never bent anyone's ear about his problems before. He stared at the whiskey glass, wondering if it was Mac's special whiskey that made him want to unburden himself now.

He was shocked when Mac's wrinkled old hand covered his. Cody was unused to being touched by other men. Oddly, he didn't mind Mac touching him. In fact, the gesture gave him a funny, mushy feeling in his chest. Mac cared about him. That's what Mac's hand on his made Cody feel, and he appreciated it. He needed to know somebody cared about him right then.

"So tell me all about it, Cody. I might not be able to help, but it'll ease your soul to talk about it. A man gets stomach trouble when he holds everything inside him, you know."

"I didn't know that."

Mac nodded wisely. "It's true, though."

Cody heaved a big sigh. "I expect you're right."

Mac filled his glass again—to encourage him to spill his guts, Cody figured. He wasn't a big drinker, but he appreciated Mac's hospitality. He fiddled with his glass. Then he lifted it almost to his lips and put it down. He glanced up at Mac, found him watching him benignly, and glanced away again. He opened his mouth and shut it. He lifted his glass and took a sip and set the glass down with a clunk. A little of the whiskey splashed onto his finger and he licked it off.

"Aw, hell, Mac, I l-l-love her."

Shoot, he'd never said anything like that out loud before in his whole entire life. And he'd just said it to another man. He'd only mentioned the state of his emotions to Melissa reluctantly and in private.

Because it was such an outlandish thing to have said aloud, Cody hunched his shoulders and squeezed his eyes shut, as if in that way he could ward off repercussions from his astounding confession.

"Of course you do. Sensible thing to do, loving Mellie."

The old Scot's soft confirmation dribbled over Cody like a gentle dew; he slitted his eyes open and was surprised there weren't any sparkly sprinkles floating around in front of his eyeballs to torment him. He slid a glance at Mac. "It is?"

The old man's chuckle, which often annoyed Cody because it came at extremely inconvenient times, today made him feel slightly less wretched.

"Of course, it is. Why do you think you found her in the first place? Destiny knows what it's doing, m'boy. For the most part, anyway." He tipped his head to one side. "Sometimes it needs a little help."

"Destiny?" Cody's squint got thinner. "You think it was destiny got us together?" He kind of liked the sound of that. Took some of the burden off his own overburdened shoulders somehow.

Mac winked again. "I know it was." He sipped his whiskey delicately. "Mind you, you were a tough nut to crack, laddie, and perhaps destiny needed more than a little help in your case, but yes. For the most part, it was destiny, all right and tight."

"What do you mean, destiny needed help in my case?" Cody was getting a funny feeling about this, and he was pretty sure it wasn't the whiskey giving it to him.

He didn't get an answer. Instead, Mac lifted a finger and cocked his head. "Why, I do believe I hear someone coming into the wagon yard, lad. P'raps I'd best see who it is and what they want."

Mac didn't sound at all surprised that he should be having another visitor today. Cody glared after him as he walked to the door and out into the yard. He looked at his whiskey and contemplated finishing it, then decided he didn't need to be miserable and drunk both. Either one of those conditions was enough for any man. He left his glass on the table and followed Mac out the door.

Chapter Eighteen

"You can't miss if you're shooting at the ground." Melissa spoke the words aloud, puzzling over their meaning. "Aim low, and you can't fail to hit your target."

She wasn't sure she appreciated Cody's father in that moment, although she acknowledged he'd come up with a catchy little axiom.

"Do you suppose he's right, Katie?" She spread Running Standing's greasy balm over her baby's bottom—it was the best thing Melissa'd used yet for diaper rash—and thought hard. "Do you suppose I've already overcome my background and am holding myself back by not believing it? By not believing in myself? By not giving Cody and me a chance?"

Katie returned no answer, but gurgled and grinned and drew her chubby legs up, making Melissa think of a little pink frog. She couldn't help smiling at her daughter, even though her heart ached.

"I didn't mean to hurt him, you know, Katie."

The fact that she had hurt him astonished her. Melissa hadn't given herself credit for holding that much power over Cody O'Fannin. He was so competent, independent, respectable, and solid. And good. He was a good man; a genuinely, deep-down good man, unlike any other man Melissa had ever known. And he loved her.

Even though Melissa thought little of her own charms—after all, the only man she'd ever attracted before Cody was Howard, and Howard was a snake—she couldn't feature Cody lying about his feelings for her.

"If a good man like Cody O'Fannin can love me," she murmured, muddling things over in her head, "perhaps I'm not completely lost to goodness after all."

Striving to be dispassionate about herself, Melissa tried to analyze her life. For the nonce, she attempted to put judgments aside and look at herself without old, time-worn assessments coloring her understanding.

There was no denying, certainly, that her origins were humble. People like Mrs. Bowlus would never look upon Melissa's mother, who had been deserted by her husband and forced to give up two of her children, as anything but undeserving. Evidently, things like being deserted by a husband didn't happen to "good" women.

Trash was the word Melissa had most often heard used to describe herself and the people who lived in her neighborhood. Detritus. Refuse. As if they had no intrinsic worth as human beings and ought to be swept up and discarded, making Boston a better place by their absence. Melissa, who had believed it, too, now wondered if she'd been unkind to her mother—and, by extension, to herself.

Certainly, Melissa's mother was an unhappy woman. Given the circumstances of her life, Melissa guessed any woman would be unhappy.

"She chose to marry my father." Melissa often thought she hated her father more than she hated anyone else in the world. After having come to know Howard, she wasn't sure her opinion still held, but she certainly disliked her father a good deal.

"I chose to marry Howard."

Although the reasons for her having done such a foolish thing were almost clear in her mind, this was the first time Melissa had bothered to wonder if her mother had been motivated by the same reasons when she'd married Melissa's father. Neither man was what Melissa considered *good*. Neither possessed the kind of natural goodness of heart that Cody O'Fannin had. Or Mac. Or, Melissa imagined, Cody's cousin Arnold. From everything she'd heard about Arnold, he wasn't bright and he didn't necessarily have perfect judgment—but he was good. Honorable. Respectable. Upstanding. All the things Melissa had always wanted to be and had believed herself incapable of.

"There's different kinds of strength. There's strength of morals and strength of character," she decided. After giving the matter some thought, Melissa decided her morals were good. At least she strove to be honest and trustworthy. She would never cheat another person, nor would she steal or hurt another except in defense of herself or her baby. She'd certainly been willing to shoot Howard for the sake of Cody and his ranch.

Her character, she decided, was not so good. If she'd had more strength of character, she'd have looked for other avenues than Howard for escape from her life.

Perhaps Melissa's mother had married her father for the same reason—to escape. Perhaps she'd been hoping against hope that, even though he appeared to be a weak person, he could get her out of the hell in which she lived. That's why Melissa had married Howard. It seemed almost clear to her now—and it also seemed ludicrous. How could she have even dreamed that Howard would turn into a good man just because he married her? Foolish, foolish Melissa!

Her heart gave a spasm of pain. "Oh, Mother," she whispered. "I'm so sorry."

She looked at her baby and wondered how she'd feel if she was faced with the choice of giving Katie up or watching her die of some horrible disease spawned by poverty—or die of starvation. "I'd do it," she decided, her heart wrenching with the knowledge. "I'd do it, just like Mother did."

It seemed pitiful that a woman should have to give up what she loved most in the world for the sake of that love, but Melissa guessed that's what her mother had done. She'd given up her boys because she felt they were better able to deal with life in the orphanage than the always-sickly Katherine or the baby Melissa.

"What a choice to have to make." Her throat felt tight.

She wished, now that she couldn't do it, that she'd taken time to talk to her mother more often. She wished she'd tried to understand her. She hadn't.

Instead, Melissa had been ashamed of her mother and tried with every breath she took not to be like her. She'd even studied Mrs. Bowlus's Beacon Hill accent and adopted it so people wouldn't know by listening to her that she'd come from Boston's dock-side slums. She'd taken the rudiments of reading and writing Katherine had taught her and studied every book and magazine she could get her hands on so that she wouldn't appear uneducated.

She'd abandoned her mother as surely as her father had.

"Oh, my goodness." She picked Katie up and rocked her at her breast, wishing she could give her mother a hug.

"The least I can do is write to her," she said softly. "So that she'll know I'm all right, and you're all right." Melissa didn't know what she'd say about Howard. Divorce was such an ugly word, and it carried such a taint with it. Yet she supposed her mother deserved to know the truth.

Of course, none of these meandering thoughts were helping her decide what to do about Cody. She needed to talk to Mac. Mac would guide her. Mac had been her friend from the beginning. He could tell her if she was being merely silly in worrying about bringing grief to Cody. Mac could tell her if what she and Cody were doing—living in sin, is the way Melissa had always heard it described—was actually bad, or if Cody was right and they were merely behaving rationally, and in a territorially accepted manner.

"It's all so different from what I'm used to, Katie."

Which was a good thing, Melissa realized as soon as the words were out of her mouth. She'd longed to get away. Well, she was away now. With a vengeance. A rueful chuckle caught her off guard.

"I wonder if Cody and Mac are still talking out there." If they were, Melissa didn't want to disturb them. She knew Cody was angry and hurt. He probably needed to talk to Mac as much as she did.

"Maybe I'll just take a peek into the next room."

Carefully, making sure the door didn't squeak, Melissa glanced through the crack and peered into the parlor. The room was empty. Her head jerked up when she heard voices coming from outside, in the yard. "Now who do you suppose that could be?"

Cody had told her that the ranchers in the area were getting ready for the spring round-up, and that Rio Hondo was liable to be thin of company until the drives started, what with the rounding up and branding and sorting of cattle. He'd explained that he himself was about to hire on some more hands to get the work done, and Melissa had been prepared to start cooking for them. He'd said that Mac generally had no visitors this time of year, except for the occasional westward-bound settler who'd stop by on his way elsewhere, to repair equipment and restock supplies.

If that was a band of settlers in Mac's yard, it was evidently a large one. Melissa hadn't heard so many voices from people gathered in one place since New Year's Eve, when everyone had been here for Mac's party.

She pondered for several moments, unwilling to interrupt something that was none of her business. She also didn't want to intrude on anything Cody was doing. She'd given him enough grief for one day.

At last she shrugged, bundled her daughter up in blankets, gathered her woolen shawl more tightly around her shoulders, and headed for the door. If this congregation turned out to be none of her business, she'd just go back indoors again.

Cody blinked and put a hand up to shade his eyes when he stepped out of the much darker parlor into the crisp, sunny morning. When he managed to adjust to the light, he was surprised to find Wilson

Hornbeam, his closest neighbor, riding into Mac's yard with several of his hands. Hornbeam's operation was larger than Cody and Arnold's, but it was small compared to Blackworth or Chisum.

Mac had already walked over to greet the arriving men. Cody raised his hand and called out a greeting of his own. "Howdy, Hornbeam. What're you doin' here?"

Hornbeam's bushy eyebrows looked like two gray caterpillars crawling down his forehead to his nose. He was definitely not a happy man. "Same thing you're doin', I expect."

Cody doubted that. With a grin he knew was wry, he said, "I come to bring Mrs. Wilmeth back to Mac's."

The caterpillars arched up until they looked like they were dancing over Hornbeam's eyes. "You don't say! Why, I thought she was settled in at your place right fine."

Cody shrugged and wished to Jupiter his chest didn't hurt so much. Then he decided *to hell with it*, and told the truth. "She's afraid of what the neighbors will think."

"Huh?" The caterpillars shot down again.

Cody gave another shrug. He didn't know what else to say.

Hornbeam slung himself off of his horse. A middle-aged man, he had ranched in Texas before heading to the Territory hoping to better himself. His legs were bowed from a lifetime spent on horseback, and his skin was as leathery and brown as the tobacco pouch he now yanked out of his breast pocket.

"That's the damned-foolishest thing I ever did hear," Hornbeam said in the direct manner he had. Cody couldn't argue.

"Susan Blackworth even likes her."

"Yeah?"

"Come around to my place a couple weeks ago and told my wife that Mrs. Wilmeth might have a frilly name, but she was full of pluck and a credit to the neighborhood." He snorted. "Wish she could say the same for her old man."

Cody almost forgot his own problems for a second. "You having trouble with Blackworth, too?"

"Ain't everybody?" He held out his tobacco. "Smoke?"

"No, thanks. Never acquired the habit."

"Good thing. Ain't good fer ya."

The habit's unhealthiness evidently didn't weigh heavily on Hornbeam's mind. He frowned and rolled himself one. "Thing is, Blackworth and Miz Wilmeth's husband're causin' me all sorts of problems."

"What kinds of problems?" Cody perked up, interested.

"Bastard's run off a bunch of my cattle and tried to poison one of my wells."

Cody shook his head. "Damn." And here he'd thought he was the only one. Melissa should hear this. At least she'd know that Howard wasn't singling Cody out for special treatment.

"I expect several of the ranchers with property abutting that of Mr. Blackworth are having similar problems," Mac interjected.

Cody shot him a sideways glance. The old man looked solemn and serious, and not at all mysterious at the moment. "You know something about it, Mac?"

"No more than folks have told me. But I've heard similar stories from almost everyone."

The group of men shuffling around in back of Wilson Hornbeam muttered agreement.

"Hell," Hornbeam muttered. He struck a sulfur match on his boot heel and lit his lopsided cigarette. "I'm sick of it, myself. I don't aim to take it any more, neither. That's why I come here. I want to get the ranchers together and figure out how to put a stop to it."

"You suppose Chisum would be any help?"

As soon as he offered the suggestion, Cody shook his head. Chisum was a law unto himself. He didn't need anybody else, and he didn't help anybody else.

"Well, look'ee there."

Cody and Hornbeam and all of Hornbeam's men turned to see what Mac was talking about. Cody was astonished to see a contingent from Noah Partridge's ranch churning up dust as they rode into McMurdo's Wagon Yard. Mac went over to greet these newcomers. Cody and Hornbeam remained where they were, but they exchanged a significant glance.

"You s'pose he's here for the same reason?" Cody ventured.

"I expect," muttered Hornbeam, and puffed on his smoke.

"You tell anyone you were coming here today?"

"Nope."

Cody peered closely at Mac as he waved a friendly greeting to Partridge and his men. Naw. If Mac had decided to host a gathering of disgruntled ranchers in his wagon yard, wouldn't Cody have known about it beforehand? And Hornbeam? He shook his head and decided some things were best left unexamined.

Partridge, a taciturn, standoffish man at the best of times, looked every bit as aggravated as Hornbeam when he limped over to talk to them. Mac followed serenely. He reminded Cody of an elf again.

"Mr. Noah Partridge here also claims to have had

trouble with Blackworth and his men," Mac said by way of introduction.

"I swear to God, if it isn't Grant Davis riding off my cows, it's that damned Howard Wilmeth killing antelopes and heaving the carcasses in with the horses to attract cougars."

"He did that?" Cody stared at Partridge, appalled.

"He did." Partridge didn't appreciate it one little bit, either, it was plain to see. "I swear. I moved out here to get away from cockleburs like that, and one moves here right after I do." The unfairness of Partridge's situation hit a sympathetic chord with Cody and Hornbeam, who exchanged a glance.

"He tried to burn Cody's barn," Mac offered.

All of the men turned to stare at Cody. "Yeah," he said. "He tried all right. Mrs. Wilmeth run him off with a shotgun."

For the first time since he'd arrived, Partridge grinned. "Did she, by God?"

"She did."

"Mrs. Blackworth said she was a game gal," said Hornbeam. "Come by and told my Fanny so."

"I do believe she dropped by and said the same thing to my Grace." Partridge said his wife's name softly and with respect, and Cody admired him for it. He thought a man should honor his wife. By God, he did.

But, shoot. Cody wondered if Mrs. Blackworth had visited all the nearby ranchers' wives and spread favorable reports about Melissa. His heart warmed toward the starchy old woman. She was obviously worth two of her husband. Maybe three.

"Too bad Mrs. Wilmeth's husband's giving her such a bad time."

The men shifted their collective gaze to Mac. He'd managed to light his pipe, Cody noticed, and smoke encircled his head like a halo. In spite of himself he grinned. If there was one thing Mac wasn't, it was any kind of angel.

Mac nodded at the questioning glances aimed at him. "Yep. He's got it in his head there's something sinful going on between Mrs. W and Cody here, and he's been tryin' to poison his water, and run off his cattle, and burn his barn, and cut his fences, and practicing all sorts of tricks."

"Damn," muttered Partridge.

"Bastard," agreed Hornbeam.

"The man's a coward and a vandal," said a new voice.

Cody twisted around and discovered their ranks had swollen again, this time by Septimus Poe, another rancher, and several of his hired hands.

Poe added, "Bastard killed one of my prime bulls."

"Shoot, somebody's got to stop Wilmeth. I don't care if his wife is a saint. Her husband and Blackworth are a menace to everybody in the territory."

"I hear he's been spreadin' lies about her, too, 'cause she aims to divorce him."

This was another new voice. It belonged to Gerald Evans, whose ranch abutted Cody's to the southeast. Cody looked around and was astonished to discover there were at least fifty men now gathered in McMurdo's Wagon Yard—and they all seemed to have similar problems.

"Aw, hell, divorcin' him's probably the best thing she's ever done in her life. I can't even feature a feller leavin' his wife alone in a wagon havin' his child." Evans shook his head.

"Soon's the divorce is final, you oughta marry up with her, O'Fannin," Poe said. "Mrs. Blackworth says she'd make some rancher a fine wife."

"If'n you don't want her, I'll take her," Evans said, winking at Cody.

Cody opened his mouth, then shut it again. He didn't want to say the wrong thing, and couldn't figure out for the life of him what the right one was.

Mac, who didn't suffer from these problems, said, "I think our Cody has Melissa all sewn up, gentlemen." He twinkled, and all the men laughed. Cody looked at the ground and muttered something unintelligible as his face heated up.

"Yeah, we all figured as much," said Hornbeam. Cody realized Hornbeam's eyes could twinkle almost as much as Mac's, and his embarrassment deepened.

"We all think you're a lucky feller, too," said Poe.

Cody didn't argue. He agreed. If Melissa'd have him, of course. He wished to heaven she was here to listen to these men's opinions of her. When he turned and saw her standing at the door of McMurdo's house, looking as though she couldn't believe her ears, he grinned to himself.

Good. This should teach her a lesson. Out here, men judged people by their actions; they'd judged Melissa the same way, and found her to be everything she claimed she'd always wanted to be. She hadn't believed him when he'd told her; if she didn't believe all these fellows, there was something wrong with her.

Men continued to arrive. All afternoon they poured into Mac's wagon yard. If any of them besides Cody wondered what had drawn them all here today, nobody asked. Cody wondered, though, and he kept shooting glances at Mac.

Melissa came away from the door after awhile and nodded to the men she hadn't seen since New Year's Eve. Then she set about preparing food and coffee. By that time there were at least seventy-five men in the yard, but she didn't cavil at the numbers. Mac had a huge pot of beans soaking in an iron kettle over the fire, and she added beef and onions and spices until the savory smell permeated the atmosphere. Nobody thought to ask Mac why he'd been prepared to feed such a crowd.

Melissa dispensed with more fashionable accompaniments like corn bread or biscuits, and Mac retrieved what looked like a thousand tortillas he had stored in his kitchen. He said he'd bought them from a local Mexican gentleman. Melissa couldn't help but wonder why he'd done such a convenient thing, but she didn't question him. He was busy as a bee himself, helping her set everything up.

There wasn't a cowboy alive who didn't travel with his own tin plate, cup, and spoon, so as soon as Mac rang the dinner gong—and where he'd had *that* piece of equipment stored, Melissa couldn't fathom—they all headed for their saddlebags and hauled out the required gear.

She saw more than one man slap Cody on the back and congratulate him on snaring such a fine cook, and wondered if she'd ever truly adjust to life out here.

"Cody was right," she murmured to Mac as they sat back, exhausted after feeding the throng.

"What was he right about?" Mac dipped a tortilla into his stew, took a big bite, and smiled as if he were dining on the nectar of the gods.

"About people out here accepting people for what they are and not what their background is."

"Aye. I expect he was. Smart lad, Cody."

She shot him a glance, but he was absorbed in his meal.

"Yes, he is, isn't he?"

Melissa decided the men were right about her

cooking, too; this meat-and-bean concoction was really quite tasty. As she ate, she rocked Katie's cradle with her foot. Cody had brought the cradle outside so she could keep an eye on her baby while she worked.

Actually, it had been he who'd picked Katie up and rocked her in his arms when she began to fuss. And she'd giggled and cooed and enjoyed his funny faces and tickles as much as any child enjoyed the attentions of her father. Melissa's heart, which she already knew belonged to Cody, became more firmly attached to him as he played daddy with her baby.

She'd learned a lot today. She hoped she wouldn't ever forget these lessons.

After supper, as the sky began to take on the deeper tones of evening and the clouds reddened with sunset, the social aspect of the gathering slowed, and the men began discussing their problems again.

"It appears to me," said Poe, "that the main problem here is Blackworth. He's hired Wilmeth, and who knows who else, to ruin our businesses. We've got to get him to leave us alone."

Partridge agreed. "Blackworth's costing us all money."

"And that damned Wilmeth oughta be hung."

A sea of heads swiveled around to see if Melissa Wilmeth had heard Wilson Hornbeam's sensible suggestion. If she had, she didn't indicate it by so much as a blink. She looked up from the kettle she was scrubbing out and smiled at them.

Cody went weak in the knees. The rest of the assembly took her smile as an endorsement.

"Well, then, what do we do? Anybody got any suggestions?" Recovering his composure, Cody peered around at the men.

"How's about a necktie party," one man suggested. There were mutters of approval from several people.

"I don't know as I like that idea," Cody demurred. "I don't care to break the law if I don't have to."

"What law?" one of them scoffed. Cody had no answer.

Mac, who was sitting back and not adding much to the conversation, laughed. Cody appreciated the humor of the scoffer's comment, but wished Mac, who could wax so eloquent when nobody wanted him to, would think of something to say now that might turn these men's minds away from violence.

"Ain't no more breakin' the law than that damned Wilmeth's been doin' alterin' brands so's they're all the runnin' B, for Blackworth," Evans grumbled. Cody couldn't think of an argument for that one, either.

"If'n you don't want to see him dancin' on air, mebbe we could still give him a little somethin' to think about."

"Like what?"

Cody hoped Hornbeam wouldn't come up with anything too grisly; he truly didn't care for brutality and didn't want Melissa exposed to it.

"Back in Tennessee, when folks exercised bad manners that the law couldn't touch, we touched 'em ourselves, usin' tar and feathers."

Approving noises swelled up from the crowd of ranching men. Tar and feathers was a time-honored remedy, all right. Cody nodded slowly, pondering. It wasn't fun to have hot tar poured over your body and was the very devil to clean off afterwards, but except for a few burns most folks didn't suffer too much. It wasn't anywhere near as permanent a punishment as being lynched. He honestly couldn't think of very many objections to tar and feathers. Since he figured

Mac could probably think of several, he turned and lifted his eyebrow in question. Mac only winked at him. Hell of a lot of help *that* was.

The assembly mulled over the various merits of tarring and feathering Howard Wilmeth, Hugh Blackworth, and/or Grant Davis. Wilmeth and Blackworth were the two men most hated by these hard-working ranchers. They were the ones who'd caused the most trouble for their neighbors.

"Davis is a scoundrel, but he doesn't do much harm," Partridge explained when asked why he wanted to leave him untarred.

"He works for Blackworth," Hornbeam pointed out.

"Yeah, but he doesn't do anything. It's Wilmeth and Blackworth who're the ones doing all the damage. Besides, it's more trouble to tar and feather three men than two."

"Good point," murmured Cody.

"I feel sorry for Mrs. Blackworth," Partridge muttered. It was well known in the area that Mrs. Partridge and Mrs. Blackworth were good friends, and that Noah Partridge, who had a musical disposition, had repaired several of Mrs. Blackworth's instruments.

"Don't we all?"

"Women marry up with the damnedest fellers sometimes," Gerald Evans said, scratching his head as if the fact boggled his mind.

"Isn't that the truth," affirmed Partridge, whose own wife had been married before. "Look at my Grace—or that nice Mrs. Wilmeth. Not that Grace's first husband was a bad man, but Howard Wilmeth—well . . ."

They all understood, and no one contradicted his well-taken point.

"What say we fetch us up a barrel of tar, fellers?" Hornbeam looked out over the assembled men.

"I'll run inside and fetch a pillow," Mac offered, startling Cody, who still didn't know if he fancied the idea of tarring and feathering people—even two such uninspiring examples of the human race as Blackworth and Wilmeth.

A chorus of agreement lifted at Mac's suggestion. Cody decided *what the hell* again. He was about to follow Mac into the house and try to explain things to Melissa when he heard another horse nearing the wagon yard.

"Now who in blazes ain't already here?" he wondered aloud.

Mac smiled. "Well, lad, why don't we just go to the gate and see?"

The idea found favor with Cody, so he walked over to the gate with Mac. The gate creaked like seventy-five rusty hinges as it opened. The effect was eerie in the deepening twilight; Cody hadn't noticed the gate squeaking like that before, and he wondered if Mac had done something to it. It would be just like the old charmer to make the damned wagon-yard gate sound like a castle drawbridge for the effect it had on a man, although how he could have done such a thing mystified Cody. Which wasn't unusual.

A lone rider stood outside the gate, straddling his horse as if he had all the time in the universe and didn't have a single other thing to do for the rest of his life but sit there and wait for the gate to open. Cody stared at him, stunned, until he found the wit to shout with joy. *"Arnie!"*

Arnold grinned at his cousin. " 'Lo, Cody."

"Howdy, Arnold," said Mac.

Arnold smiled vacantly at him. " 'Lo, Mac."

"Well, for God's sake, come in!" Cody shook himself out of his astonishment and lunged for his cousin's hand. Then he shook it until Arnold's whole body bobbed up and down in his saddle.

"I come back," Arnold pointed out.

Cody laughed. "So I see. Come in and get down, Arnold. Everybody's here tonight."

"Yeah. I see." Arnold took his time dismounting. Arnold took his time about everything. "How come?"

"How come everybody's here?"

"Yeah."

"C'mon over here, Arnold," Hornbeam called out to him. "We're all a-settin' here tryin' to figger out what to do about Hugh Blackworth."

"Blackworth?" Arnold took the tin coffee cup one of the men offered him. His eyes looked blank, as if he'd never heard of Hugh Blackworth before in his life.

Nobody seemed surprised. "He's been causin' trouble," said Hornbeam helpfully.

Arnold nodded. "Yeah. I know."

"So," said Cody in a kindly voice, knowing he'd have to explain things slowly and carefully if he expected Arnold to understand, "we're gathered here tonight to try and decide what to do about it."

Arnold scanned the big group of men, looking even more befuddled than was usual for him. Cody tried not to be impatient. It surprised him, however, to realize how quickly he'd become used to Melissa's quick intelligence. Having to slow down his own wits for Arnold was a wrench in the opposite direction, and it threw him.

"We want him to stop pesterin' us," he said by way of explanation.

Arnold's gaze came to rest on Cody's face. "Don't have to do nothin', Cody."

Grumbles of disagreement came from the throng.

Arnold looked at them and appeared mildly troubled. "Honest," he said. "You fellers don't have to do nothin'."

Cody frowned at Arnold. Arnold wasn't quick, and he wasn't talkative, but he'd never, in all his life, been disputatious. Therefore, Cody couldn't figure out why he was bothering to disagree now, when he was newly come from Georgetown and couldn't possibly know what had been going on in Rio Hondo since November. This was most unlike him. Instead of arguing, which seldom got a body far with Arnold, he decided to take a different approach.

"How come, Arnie? Tell us how come we don't have to do nothing about Blackworth."

Arnold shrugged helplessly. "Why, 'cause it's true, is how come." He held out his empty hand in a gesture of bewilderment. "Hell, why do nothin' if the law's gonna take care of it for ya, is all I'm wonderin'?"

Almost a hundred mouths dropped open, and nearly two hundred eyes goggled. Arnold tucked in his chin, embarrassed. He'd never enjoyed the limelight.

Chapter Nineteen

"What do you mean, the law's going to take care of Blackworth for us?" Cody demanded. He wished he'd used a milder tone when Arnold looked at him as if he were a dog Cody'd just kicked. "I mean, this is the first any of us have heard about any kind of law taking a hand in Blackworth's affairs." He smiled his friendliest smile to show Arnold that he wasn't mad at him.

Scratching his head and obviously uncomfortable about being questioned by Cody and stared at by so many people who weren't even related to him, Arnold mumbled, "I only know what I been told."

"And what's that, Arnie?" Cody patted him on the back for encouragement. He knew having to explain things was hard on Arnold, especially when his listening audience comprised more than one cousin.

"Well, I only know what the marshal told me."

"The marshal? What marshal, Arnie? You can tell

us." Cody spoke in the most soothing voice he could muster under the circumstances. He wanted to shout at Arnold to spit his information out, but knew such a tactic would only shut poor Arnold up like a scared clam.

"Why, the marshal I rode from Georgetown with," Arnold announced, as if Cody should have known that.

"You rode to Rio Hondo with a United States Marshal?"

"Sure." Arnold gave Cody a judicious nod. "Safer with two folk ridin' together, don'tcha know."

"It surely is, Arnold. That was real smart of you both."

Arnold grinned.

"What did the marshal tell you?" Cody asked gently.

His cousin shrugged. "Jist that Blackworth's been sellin' bad beef to the Indian Agent over to Fort Stanton, and he ain't paid his loans to the territorial gov'ment. The Indian Affairs people canceled his contract, he said. Reckon Miz Wilmeth's husband's in fer it, too, 'cause he's been doin' bad things."

This last piece of information caused such a swell of commentary from his audience that Arnold blinked and took a step closer to Cody, who patted him on the back again. "Er, do you know what the law plans to do to Blackworth and Wilmeth?"

"I don't rightly know, Cody. The marshal, he said he was holdin' two warrants—one fer Blackworth and one fer Mr. Wilmeth. Reckon he aims to take 'em back to Texas with him."

"To Texas?"

"Yep. 'Cause of his cheatin' the Texas gov'ment and the Fed'ral gov'ment, too."

Such a buzz arose from the crowd of men at this

announcement that Cody had to grab Arnold's arm to keep him from running away. "It's all right, Arnie. Everybody's just surprised, is all."

"Don't know why anybody's surprised," grumbled Arnold. "The marshal says Mr. Wilmeth's been braggin' to anybody who'll listen about how he's been poisonin' wells and killin' cows and changin' brands. He done it to gov'ment stock, too. Changed the brands. The gov'ment don't take kind to that sort of thing."

All chatter stopped. Arnold looked scared.

At last Cody said, "He changed government brands?"

"Well, that's just what the marshal told me." Arnold sounded apologetic, as though he didn't want anyone to think he'd made up his shocking news, and that he was willing to change his opinion should anyone ask him to.

Cody knew better than that. Arnold wasn't capable of making up stories of this magnitude. "And your marshal had the warrants with him?"

"He ain't my marshal," Arnold explained patiently. "We jist rode together."

"Yes, yes, Arnie. I understand. But the marshal who rode to Rio Hondo with you told you that he had warrants for Mr. Blackworth and Mr. Wilmeth?"

Arnold scratched his chin. "Well, he didn't rightly ride all the way to Rio Hondo with me, you know."

Cody glanced up at the sky and tried to quell the impulse to grab his cousin and shake him until his head rattled. "Right, Arnie. But the marshal told you about the warrants?"

Arnold frowned at Cody. "I didn't make nothin' up, Cody. He showed 'em to me. I seen them warrants."

"I believe you, Arnie. You bet I do."

343

"The names was Blackworth and Wilmeth. I seen 'em."

"Right. That's good, Arnie."

"I felt bad about that one for Mr. Wilmeth, on account of Miz Wilmeth."

"I'm sure you did, Arnie. We all feel bad for her because of her husband."

Arnold appeared satisfied. "And the marshal, he said Blackworth's bank ruptured, too."

"His bank did what?" Cody tried to deduce from those words what the marshal might have told Arnold, but Arnold's expression was as dense as his brain, and Cody was unsuccessful.

Mac cleared his throat discreetly. "I believe he means that Mr. Blackworth has gone bankrupt."

"That's right!" Arnold beamed at Mac, who nodded amiably.

"Hellfire!" Cody's imagination fairly exploded with the implications.

"No, Cody, Mac's right. That's what the marshal told me, all right," said Arnold, who had misunderstood Cody's exclamation.

"I believe it, Arnold. I'm just surprised, is all." His head had already begun to fill with expansion plans for their ranch.

Arnold shrugged.

"Good Lord," mumbled Partridge.

"I'll be damned," muttered Poe.

"Son of a gun," agreed Hornbeam.

Cody looked at Mac, who winked, so he rolled his eyes and turned to Hornbeam. "Don't reckon we'll need that bucket of tar any longer."

"Don't reckon we will."

"Don't reckon you'll need to sacrifice your pillow either, Mac."

"Don't expect so, laddie." Mac cleared his throat.

"You know, Cody lad, if Mellie was worried about Mr. Wilmeth trying to get custody of their daughter, I should think this will ease her mind considerably. I don't expect any judge in the entire United States or any of its territories would award custody of a wee baby girl to a convicted felon."

Cody had been attending to Arnold, trying to soothe his cousin's tattered sensibilities while holding his own burgeoning excitement at bay. At Mac's words, he whipped his head around and stared at the old Scot.

"By damn," he whispered, awed. All thought of buying part of Blackworth's spread at a price reduced by the government for quick liquidation vanished instantly. "By damn, you're right, Mac." He shot a glance at the house. Melissa stood at the door holding Katie, and she appeared worried. "By God. She can't use losing Katie as an excuse any longer. Or her old man's tricks."

He took a step toward the house, but Arnold clamped a hand on his arm. "Wait a minute, Cody."

"What is it, Arnie?" Cody was impatient to break the news to Melissa. This would be a test. If she really loved him, she'd have to admit she had no excuses left. If she really loved him, she'd agree to marry him as soon as her divorce was final. If she really, *really* loved him, she'd come back to his ranch now, before the final divorce papers came in. Cody wasn't sure how long these things took, but he didn't want to wait, whatever the time period. He couldn't see one single reason to wait, in fact.

He had to wait at least a few moments longer, however, because Arnold showed no inclination to let go of his arm. "Got somethin' else to tell you, Cody."

"What is it, Arnie?" He tried not to sound as impatient as he felt. He'd build another cabin, is what he'd do. After having lived with Melissa for four months, Cody didn't think he could go back to dealing with Arnold, and he already knew he couldn't tolerate Loretta.

Arnold hung his head. Cody thrust his impatience aside in favor of worry. Lordy, he hoped everything was all right back in Georgetown. Mail was so hit-or-miss out here that if somebody'd died, the message might have gone astray. "What is it, Arnie?" he asked more gently. "You can go ahead and tell me now. Whatever it is, I won't get mad."

His eyes as limpid and sad as those of an orphaned calf, Arnold said, "It's Loretta, Cody."

It's Loretta. Still in the dark, and now anxious as well, Cody tried to contain his urge to yell at his cousin and frighten the words out of him. "What about Loretta, Arnie? Is Loretta sick?"

"Lordy, no! Last I seen her, Loretta was just fine, Cody. You ain't got a telegraph wire or nothin' sayin' any different, have you?"

Now Arnold looked scared. Cody sighed. "No, Arnold. I haven't heard a single word about Loretta—or you, either—since the day you left. Not until right this minute. You tell me, Arnold. What's wrong with Loretta?"

"Ain't nothin' wrong with her."

Unable to think of a way to explain himself that wouldn't entangle him more securely in Arnold's web of incomprehension, Cody opted for silence. Evidently, everyone else in the wagon yard was eager to hear about this latest wrinkle, too. They all leaned toward Arnold, quiet as a herd of mute mice, their faces vivid with suspense.

After a moment, Arnold took a deep breath and blurted out, "She ain't comin'."

346

Cody wasn't sad to hear it, although he was surprised that Arnold didn't seem more miserable. He knew with what devotion his cousin viewed Loretta. "I'm real sorry, Arnie. I know you were looking forward to marrying up with her."

"Oh, I'm still marryin' up with her."

"You are?" Cody tilted his head to one side and concentrated hard on Arnold's face, trying to divine the thought processes going on behind his expression of stolid calm. He used to be pretty good at reading Arnie's mind, but he'd gotten out of practice lately.

"Yeah. But Loretta, she says she don't want to come out here to the Territory. Says it's too rough for her. Says she wants me to go back to Georgetown and work in her daddy's store. Says she could keep an eye on me better there."

"Oh." Although his cousin's words surprised him, Cody discovered they didn't grieve him. Not at all, in fact. "What about your share in the ranch, Arnie? You want I should keep runnin' it for the both of us?"

Arnold shook his head. "No. That ain't fair, Cody."

"You want me to buy you out?" The idea held little appeal. While the ranch was no longer running in the red, there wasn't much profit yet since Cody sank virtually every penny back into the operation. He had been hoping to use some of his hard-earned cash to buy out what he could of Blackworth's spread. Blackworth's herd was prime—which only made sense, since he stole most of his neighbors' best beeves.

Again, Arnold's head shook back and forth. Cody wondered if he'd be able to hear Arnold's pea-sized brain rattle if he listened hard enough, then decided the thought had been unkind.

"No. I told Loretta that it weren't fair, and she

347

agreed with me. What I aim to do is deed my share of the ranch over to you. You put up the money for the place anyhow, and all I done was work. I know it'll be hard for you, runnin' the place on your own. Loretta and me, we both figured that if I give you my share, you wouldn't be out anything. You might even could afford to hire some more hands to help you out."

Cody stared at his cousin, feeling curiously emotional. "You thought of that all by yourself, Arnie?"

Arnold nodded. "Yup."

"I—I'm touched, Arnie. That was very nice of you."

Blushing, Arnold traced the toe of his boot in the dirt. " 'Twasn't nothin', Cody. I told Loretta it was only fair. I'm leavin' you in the lurch."

"And she agreed with you?" Cody would never tell Arnold how astonishing he found Loretta's compliance in this matter.

"Well, she didn't like it at first, but I told her it was fair. And I told her if she wanted me to marry up with her, she'd either have to come out here or let me give you my share of the ranch."

"You told her *that?*" Cody, who would not have given his cousin credit for making such an intrepid decision—much less for daring to declare it to Loretta Pine—before this minute, wondered if he'd been unjust to Arnold all these years. There were evidently depths to his cousin he'd never dreamed of.

"Yup. 'Cause I couldn't take no money from you, Cody, when it was me left you. 'Sides, we're family."

"Thank you very much, Arnie. That's—that's right square of you."

A big grin took possession of Arnold's face. "I knew you'd like it, Cody. I told Loretta so."

Cody was still rather surprised that Loretta had offered Arnold so little pressure. From what Cody recalled of her, she wasn't one to give up on a position lightly. On the other hand, she probably knew no other man in Georgetown would have her, and if she wanted to get married—and have a compliant husband—Arnold was her best, if not her only, bet.

Arnold went on, surprising Cody no less than the other men, who'd turned to chat among themselves. Like a pile of steel shavings being drawn to a powerful magnet, at the sound of Arnold's voice their heads swiveled, and they leaned toward Cody's usually taciturn cousin.

"I told her 'bout Miz Wilmeth, too, Cody. Hope you don't mind, but I figgered you and her'd probably get hitched once she got divorced."

"You told Loretta that?" Cody discovered himself once more astounded by his cousin's perspicacity.

"I seen the way you looked at each other, Cody. Couldn't hardly help it." Arnold shrugged.

"Oh." Cody didn't argue. Arnold might not be articulate, but he was a man. Surely he'd notice something that obvious.

"I told Loretta if she come out here, she'd have to share the cabin with you and Miz Wilmeth—only Miz Wilmeth'd be Mrs. O'Fannin by then, I reckon."

Vastly impressed, Cody declared, "By God, Arnie, you did real good!"

Arnold's grin shone out like the sun breaking through a bank of thunderheads.

"Thought you'd like it. I know you never took to Loretta like I done."

"Oh, I like Loretta fine, Arnie. Just fine." He did now, anyway.

Before Arnold could question him about how much he admired Loretta Pine, Cody broke away. He fairly tore up to Melissa, who had begun slowly walking toward the group of men.

"Mellie! Did you hear what Arnie said?"

"Yes." She sounded as bewildered as she looked.

Joy had the running of Cody now. He plucked her right up off the ground and whirled her around. Katie, startled, uttered a protest, but it changed to a babyish giggle when Cody set Melissa down and blew a raspberry on Katie's cheek. "I'm gonna be your pa now, Katie. You better not fuss at me."

I'm gonna be your pa. The words he'd spoken with such glee struck him and Melissa at the same time. He sobered immediately. Melissa's beautiful blue eyes opened up as round as platters.

Some of Cody's exuberance gave way to fear. He licked his lips. "That is, if your mama will have me," he amended softly.

"If—if—" Melissa's words choked to a halt.

Cody took one of her hands away from the baby's blanketed bottom. "When your divorce is final, will you marry me, Melissa? Can we be a family together? I'll adopt Katie all legal and proper. She'll never even have to know her name was Wilmeth if you don't want her to. Although," he added conscientiously, "I think it's right to tell kids the truth."

She nodded, although Cody wasn't sure she'd taken in what he'd said. He hoped they'd have ample time to discuss the matter soon.

"You still want to marry me?"

She sounded incredulous. Cody shook his head. "Shoot, Melissa, don't you trust me yet?"

Her lips pinched together. This time the gesture didn't look like anger. It looked like she was having to contain tears of some other emotion. Cody hoped it was happiness. He saw her swallow hard.

"Of course I trust you, Cody. I love you."

Cody expected his grin was as big as the sky. "And I love you. So, since we both love each other, and we already know we can live together pretty well, what do you say? Will you marry me?"

"Of course, I'll marry you, Cody. Of course, I will!"

This time when he picked her up, he kissed her. She threw her free arm around his shoulder and kissed him back. Cody forgot all about Arnie and Mac. He forgot about Hornbeam and Partridge and Poe and Evans and all the other ranchers for whom he was putting on a show. He forgot baby Katie was squashed between him and Melissa. He forgot about everything except that Melissa had agreed to marry him. He'd never been so happy in his life.

Until Katie bellowed in his ear and the masses started cheering. Then he set Melissa down and blinked at her. She blinked back. Then they both blushed. Knowing that he was the man and, therefore, obliged to take the lead in such matters, he put a protective arm around her waist and turned to face their audience.

He had to clear his throat before he could speak. "Gentlemen, I'd like to be the first to introduce you to the lady who has agreed to become Mrs. Cody Patrick O'Fannin. As soon as her divorce from Howard Wilmeth is final."

Another cheer erupted. Hats flew into the air and boots stomped up a cloud of dust. The noise was so intense, horses whickered in their stalls, upset by the commotion. Katie stopped bellowing and watched, big-eyed and intense.

Mac was the first to come forward, his hands outstretched. "I knew you two couldn't be so thickheaded for much longer."

Cody leveled a jaundiced gaze upon him. "You knew that, did you?"

"Sure." Laughing, Mac clapped Cody on the back and gave Melissa a smacking kiss on the cheek. Then

Emma Craig

he did the same with Katie, who cooed happily.

Cody shut his eyes against the sparkles flying like gnats in the air around them. This had been a long, trying day. He didn't even want to begin to think about what those sparkles meant. He'd wasted enough of his life worrying about them already.

Mac's voice brought his eyes open again with a flash.

"So, I got some papers today that I think you'll be very interested in, Mellie, m'dear."

"Papers?" said Melissa.

"Papers?" said Cody.

"Divorce papers. Judge Calloway brought 'em. He had the authorities speed things along for you. Your divorce is final!"

Cody stared at Mac, flabbergasted. So did Melissa.

"You—you mean, her divorce is actually *final?*" Cody had always believed these things took months, if not years.

He got another wink for his trouble and tried not to resent it. "Cody, m'lad, I do believe that when Judge Calloway understood the magnitude of the crimes Hugh Blackworth and Howard Wilmeth have been perpetrating in the Seven Rivers country—as evidenced by the warrants sworn out against the two varmints—he realized it would be to Mrs. Wilmeth's and Katie's advantage to hurry things up a bit."

"I see." Cody didn't understand.

"He knew about the warrants?" Neither, evidently, did Melissa.

"Well," Mac said judiciously, "Judge Calloway, being the circuit judge and the only law in this neck of the woods that we can rely on for anything, was probably informed about the warrants before anyone else."

Cody scratched his head, almost dislodging his

hat. "But I thought they were taking Blackworth and Wilmeth to Texas."

"I wouldn't know about that, m'boy."

And that was that.

Or not quite.

Henry Calloway, according to Mac, had arrived at his wagon yard the previous day and was putting up there, in the absence of more civilized quarters. One day, Mac always said to whoever would listen, civilization would hit Rio Hondo, and someone would build a hotel. Until that day came, his establishment served the purpose.

The portly judge took that moment to walk through the still-open gates of Alexander McMurdo's Wagon Yard, cleaning his teeth with a toothpick. He stopped when he saw all the men gathered, and looked around, clearly interested and perhaps a little wary.

"How-do," he said by way of greeting.

Everyone offered greetings in return.

"Er, what's up?"

"A friendly little gathering of the local ranching men," said Alexander McMurdo noncommittally.

Cody blessed him for not mentioning the afternoon's discussions. As those discussions had circled around the comparative value of lynching versus tarring and feathering several individuals, he wasn't sure the judge was the proper person to tell.

"Neighborly," Judge Calloway said with a benevolent smile. "I've been over to the Pecos Saloon. Had me a little supper there."

Judging from the complacent look he wore and the number of hours he'd been away, Cody would have bet he'd had a little something else there, as well, but he'd never mention it. Hell, judges were men, too, he guessed, and subject to the same weaknesses of the flesh as the rest of their mortal brethren. To gauge by the look of him, Calloway might have more fleshly weaknesses than most. The good Lord knew, he had more flesh than most. He probably had more money, too, and the girls at the Pecos Saloon would certainly go out of their way to show him a good time.

Nobody commented on Calloway's reported meal.

Mac finally took up the conversational bones and ran with them. "I told Mrs. Wilmeth here that you'd brought her final divorce papers with you, Judge Calloway."

Calloway bestowed a benevolently judicial look upon Melissa. "Good, good. It's wise to get these things cleared up, my dear, especially when the object of the suit is evidently not a man of good moral fiber."

"You can say that again."

Cody was surprised by the wry tone coming from Melissa's lips. She'd always seemed so serious before. He grinned at her, and hoped this new tone of voice sprang from a newfound confidence and relaxation. She grinned back, and his hope spurted higher.

"And I do believe that Mrs. Wilmeth and Mr. O'Fannin here would be interested in tying the knot themselves, if you have time to perform the ceremony," Mac continued.

Cody considered it extremely diplomatic of Mac to ask about the judge's time constraints. Anyone who could spend an entire morning and afternoon in taking supper at the Pecos Saloon didn't look to him as if he was pressed for time.

Calloway smiled at Cody and Melissa. Cody's arm tightened around Melissa's waist. This looked promising.

"Why, I do believe I can perform such a ceremony. You'll need a license, of course."

Cody's mood drooped. "Where do we get a license."

"Oh, I have them," Calloway said. "Mr. McMurdo here suggested I bring a license with me on my next visit, the last time I was in Rio Hondo."

"He did, huh?" For some reason, Cody wasn't surprised to hear it.

"I certainly did, Cody, m'boy. It pays to be prepared, I always say."

"I bet you do."

"Indeed, preparation is essential to the judicial life," Calloway said pretentiously. "One never knows what one will be called upon to do as one travels the circuit, you know."

Cody didn't, and he wasn't about to ask. "So how much does the license cost?" He hadn't figured on buying anything when he set out for town and hoped he had the ready cash.

"Only cost you ten dollars." Calloway smiled at him, as if he understood Cody's urgency. If he'd been doing what Cody suspected he'd been doing that afternoon, Cody expected he did understand.

"It's a bargain," declared Cody, for whom ten dollars might mean a month's supplies. Melissa giggled.

"Let me buy the license for you, my dears," McMurdo said, twinkling as brightly as the sparkles Cody saw shimmering around his head. He refused to close his eyes this time. Maybe if he stared at them hard enough, they'd disappear. They didn't. He decided to ignore them instead.

"Thank you kindly, Mac. That's right nice of you."

"My pleasure, Cody, m'boy. My distinct pleasure."

Cody believed him.

* * *

Thus it was that Mrs. Melissa Irene Smythe Wilmeth became the bride of Mr. Cody Patrick O'Fannin in the village of Rio Hondo, in the Seven Rivers country of the New Mexico Territory, on the fifth day of March, 1871. There were about a hundred witnesses to the ceremony, but only Alexander Socrates McMurdo and Arnold George Carver signed the marriage certificate.

Mac broke out his fiddle after the marriage was affirmed, and dancing ensued. Since Melissa was the only female present, she'd nearly been danced off her feet by the time everyone left, but she didn't mind.

Neither did Cody, when at last the party broke up and he led her into a small back room in Mac's house. Katie had chosen to be extra polite this evening. She'd slept through the festivities, and only woke up for dinner right before Cody and Melissa were about to disrobe for bed.

Cody watched his wife feed their child with a tenderness he hadn't even known lived in him until he'd met Melissa.

His wife. He could hardly believe it. "I love you, Mellie," he said more than once, testing the words and finding them delicious.

"I love you, too, Cody," she said, with a smile that wrapped around him like cotton fluff.

"Calloway says he can send us adoption papers."

"I heard him."

Cody saw her getting misty-eyed and hoped she wouldn't cry.

They made beautiful love that night in Mac's back room. It seemed especially good to Cody, and he wondered if that was because he knew Melissa was really and truly his now. Forever and ever, until death did them part.

His tongue skimmed her nipple, and he massaged

356

her breast tenderly. "They're smaller now, Mellie."

"That's because Katie's just had supper."

"Interesting," he said around a mouthful of flesh. She arched beneath his tender assault, and he decided life was pretty grand.

"I never met anyone like you before, Cody," she whispered as her hands tested the muscles of his arms. "I never met anyone strong and good and kind like you." Her hand traveled over his back, to his buttocks, and then made a bold move to his stiff sex. Cody groaned.

"I used to think men were all alike, that they only wanted what they could get and didn't care about family or babies or anything."

Cody didn't care about families or babies at the moment, himself, but he decided it would be imprudent to say so. He moaned softly and continued to taste his way over Melissa's body.

"I think you're the most wonderful man in the world, Cody, and I'll love you forever."

A man of few words at the most relaxed of times, Cody couldn't think of anything at all to say now. Because he felt the same way about her, and wanted her to know it, he kissed her, deeply, passionately, showing her all the love he couldn't express any other way.

Melissa understood.

Chapter Twenty

Before Cody, Melissa, and Katie left for their ranch the day after Cody and Melissa's wedding, some interesting information reached them. The U.S. Marshal who had ridden from Georgetown to Rio Hondo with Arnold Carver had not been able to serve his warrants without incident.

Howard Wilmeth, a coward at heart and with nothing to lose, had surrendered peacefully enough. In fact, he met the marshal on the road to Blackworth's ranch. He'd ridden out on purpose, hoping to avoid the trouble at the ranch. He shook like a leaf when he approach the marshal, holding his arms in the air and pleading for his life before they were even in hearing range of each other. The marshal had been happy to comply since it saved him trouble.

Hugh Blackworth, faced with the collapse of his ranching empire and unwilling to give it up even against insurmountable odds, refused to surrender.

A desultory gun battle ensued, and Blackworth was killed. The circumstances were uncertain, since people both inside and outside the ranch house had exchanged bullets.

After the dust cleared, the authorities offered Grant Davis immunity in return for his testimony in the courthouse in Amarillo. During the month or two before Howard Wilmeth's trial and the investigation into Hugh Blackworth's death, several people offered Davis free drinks at the Pecos Saloon in exchange for his account of the gunfight.

"It wasn't no battle," he said the first time he was asked to explain what had happened that day. "Blackworth tried to shoot the marshal, and the marshal tried to shoot Blackworth. When it was all over, it looked like somebody inside the house done shot Blackworth. Ain't no other way he could've got shot in the back, I reckon."

When asked, Davis couldn't say who that somebody had been. Speculation ran wild, but Melissa whispered to her husband that she believed Mrs. Blackworth might be able to enlighten folks if she ever cared to do so.

She never did. Her reticence on the matter provided ample scope for Davis, whose accounts became more elaborate as time and distance separated him from the battle itself. After a year or so, anyone listening to him talk about the warrant-service at the Blackworth ranch might have thought another Gettysburg had been engaged there. He drank for free on his story for years until one day, drunk, he fell from his saddle and perished on the desert.

Katie O'Fannin grew much faster than the Lombardy poplars her daddy, Cody, had planted as a break against the prevailing southwesterly winds. By the time Katie's baby brother, Arnold, was born in

Emma Craig

May of 1873, she was, according to her fond papa, the biggest little girl in Rio Hondo. As she was one of only two little girls in Rio Hondo, no one contested his assessment of Katie's relative size. Besides, since the O'Fannins were universally liked in the area, it was probable no one would have argued even if he'd stretched the point.

Shortly after Cody and Melissa's wedding, Running Standing visited the ranch and brought Katie a beaded and quilled bag he said contained protective medicine. The gesture touched Melissa, who offered him another two jars of applesauce. She also bargained for some more of his healing, albeit smelly, baby-bottom balm.

Alexander McMurdo stood godfather to the several O'Fannin children as they came along. Cody and Melissa sometimes worried about overburdening their kindhearted benefactor, but McMurdo claimed not to mind. He only winked and continued to find interesting and useful items for the children and their parents in his back room.

Melissa never saw Howard Wilmeth again, but it was rumored that he returned to Boston after his prison term ended. When Melissa's mother moved to the territory in 1880, in fact, she told her daughter that it had been Howard who convinced her to take such a bold step. Howard, she said, had told her that he didn't understand the Territory, that it was like nothing he'd ever seen before, and that there wasn't a man in it who was anything at all like the fellows he'd grown up with in Boston. That was enough to convince Melissa's mother that her daughter hadn't exaggerated the enchanted properties of the place.

Cody, who never quite understood, was nevertheless pleased to welcome Katie's grandmother into his home.

Enchanted Christmas

Emma Craig

Noah Partridge has a cold, cold heart. Honey-haired Grace Richardson has heart to spare. Despite her husband's death, she and her young daughter have hung on to life in the Southwestern desert, as well as to a piece of land just outside the settlement of Rio Hondo. Although she does not live on it, Grace clings to that land like a memory, unwilling to give it up even to Noah Partridge, who is determined to buy it out from under her. But something like magic is at work in this desert land: a magic that makes Noah wonder if it is Grace's land he lusts after, or the sweetness of her body and soul. For he longs to believe that her touch holds the warmth that will melt his icy heart.

___52287-X $5.99 US/$6.99 CAN

The Magician's Lover — Flora Speer

Determined to locate his friend who disappeared during a spell gone awry, Warrick petitions a dying stargazer to help find him. But the astronomer will only assist Warrick if he promises to escort his daughter Sophia and a priceless crystal ball safely to Byzantium. Sharp-tongued and argumentative, Sophia meets her match in the powerful and intelligent Warrick. Try as she will to deny it, he holds her spellbound, longing to be the magician's lover.

____52263-2 $5.99 US/$6.99 CAN

More Than Magic

Kathleen Nance

Darius is as beautiful, as mesmerizing, as dangerous as a man can be. His dark, star-kissed eyes promise exquisite joys, yet it is common knowledge he has no intention of taking a wife. Ever. Sex and sensuality will never ensnare Darius, for he is their master. But magic can. Knowledge of his true name will give a mortal woman power over the arrogant djinni, and an age-old enemy has carefully baited the trap. Alluring yet innocent, Isis Montgomery will snare his attention, and the spell she's been given will bind him to her. But who can control a force that is even more than magic?

___52299-3 $5.99 US/$6.99 CAN

SONYA BIRMINGHAM

Song of the Lark

When the beautiful wisp of a mountain girl walks through his front door, Stephen Wentworth knows there is some kind of mistake. The flame-haired beauty in trousers is not the nanny he envisions for his mute son Tad. But one glance from Jubilee Jones's emerald eyes, and the widower's icy heart melts and his blood warms. Can her mountain magic soften Stephen's hardened heart, or will their love be lost in the breeze, like the song of the lark?

___4393-9 $5.50 US/$6.50 CAN

Dorchester Publishing Co., Inc.
P.O. Box 6640
Wayne, PA 19087-8640

Please add $1.75 for shipping and handling for the first book and $.50 for each book thereafter. NY, NYC, and PA residents, please add appropriate sales tax. No cash, stamps, or C.O.D.s. All orders shipped within 6 weeks via postal service book rate. Canadian orders require $2.00 extra postage and must be paid in U.S. dollars through a U.S. banking facility.

Name_____
Address_____
City_____ State_____ Zip_____
I have enclosed $_____ in payment for the checked book(s).
Payment <u>must</u> accompany all orders. ❑ Please send a free catalog.
CHECK OUT OUR WEBSITE! www.dorchesterpub.com

BAD COMPANY

CAROL CARSON

Trixianna Lawless is furious when the ruggedly handsome sheriff arrests her for bank robbery. But when she finds herself in Chance's house instead of jail, she begins to wish that he would look at her with his piercing blue eyes . . . and take her into his well-muscled arms.

___4448-X $4.99 US/$5.99 CAN

MIDNIGHT SUN

AMANDA HARTE

Amelia Sheldon has traveled from Philadelphia to Gold Landing, Alaska, to practice medicine, not defend herself and her gender to an arrogant man like William Gunning. While her position as doctor's assistant provides her ample opportunity to prove the stubborn mine owner wrong, the sparks between them aren't due to anger. William Gunning knows that women are too weak to stand up to the turmoil of disease. But when he meets the beautiful, willful Amelia Sheldon, she proves anything but weak; in fact, she gives him the tongue lashing of his life. When the barbs escalate to kisses, William knows he has found his true love in the land of the midnight sun.

___4503-6 $5.50 US/$6.50 CAN